Top Dog

Top Dog

JERRY JAY CARROLL

ACE BOOKS, NEW YORK

This book is an Ace original edition,
and has never been previously published.

TOP DOG

An Ace Book / published by arrangement with
the author

PRINTING HISTORY
Ace edition / September 1996

Cover art by Joseph Daniel Fiedler.
Book design by Fritz Metsch.

For information address: The Berkley Publishing Group,
200 Madison Avenue, New York, NY 10016.

The Putnam Berkley World Wide Web site address is
http://www.berkley.com

ISBN: 0-441-00368-0

ACE®
Ace Books are published by The Berkley Publishing Group,
200 Madison Avenue, New York, NY 10016.
ACE and the "A" design are trademarks
belonging to Charter Communications, Inc.

PRINTED IN THE UNITED STATES OF AMERICA

10 9 8 7 6 5 4 3 2 1

To my wonderful family:
Judy, Jessica, and Justin

[1]

Just running at first. Nothing before that. No memories of childhood and family. No early struggles. No career. No friends. No opinions. No country, city, neighborhood, no home where I laid my head at day's end. No idea how I spent those days.

Running. One minute oblivion and the next I'm in a forest, shafts of the dying day falling through the trees and dappling the ground with patterns of light and dark. Quail scurry, small animals freeze as I pass. I have no questions about my place in the scheme of things. The wind is in my face and nothing seems more natural than running. It's the beginning and the end and everything in between.

But there's something wrong. I detest exercise. If it didn't send the wrong message, I'd step from the Rolls and ride a sedan chair across Wall Street to the lobby elevators. The times what they are, my bearers would be a multicultural lot, a rainbow of muscular young men raising me above the mob. So some fragments of memory flash like strobe lights in a vast and dark chamber.

The flicker of feet beneath catches my eye. But they aren't feet. They are paws. Something soft and wet bangs the side of my face. My tongue. The realization slowly dawns as I run. I'm a dog, a huge dog.

A running dog has a brain on sensory overload. It can't handle all that the nose gathers. Smells flood in, an ecstatic rush of them. Each has its own mental picture. I'm aware of a rotting deer carcass (I master an urge to stop and roll).

Trees, each with its own particular sappy smell. Pale fungus growing in damp shadowed leaf mold. Birds in beshitted nests. Berries and nuts, the one full of juice and the other bitter oil. Worms working with sightless stealth. Clear running water and stagnant ponds that teem with odorous life. Bare dirt, still warm from the mote-filled pillars of daylight that are disappearing one by one as night comes on. Countless insects chewing, sawing, boring, proliferating. Two squirrels, a badger, three rabbits paralyzed with fear, a fox tracking a lizard, a skunk asleep in a hole, all sorts of other animals I'm not going to mention.

Hundreds of smells. They crowd in like Japanese on a bullet train. The brain works like crazy to sort them out. That's just part of it. My ears are pricked, scooping in a cacophony worthy of a modern composer. My eyes scan the ground ahead, picking a path past boulders, between trees, over exposed roots, down tunnels of fern. The world is full of menace. Quick reactions are rewarded with life, slow ones punished by death. There's no time for cognitive thought, to use a term that pops into my head. Words or phrases step forward like that to remind me I was different once. Sometimes they are like puzzle pieces with no meaning on their own. Other times they fit the subject at hand. Subject at hand—there's an example.

I come to a dinky village toward sundown and don't even slow. I lope down the middle of a narrow road. Cottages of weathered stone and thatched roofs face each other miserably. Their shuttered windows are like eyes shut tight to trouble. Toothless old crones in bare feet and raggedy dresses shrink back as if the Devil passes among them. Starving curs with rib cages and vertebrae sticking out rush toward me, yapping abuse. They skid to stops with comic clouds of dust when they get a better look. Then they streak back, nearly bowling over the old hags.

Out of the village and back into the shadow of the trees, the yammering of the dogs fading behind. I stop to lap water from a cold creek pouring over smooth rocks and lie down to rest, panting. What did I have for dinner to bring on a dream so vivid? I gave up Mexican food for this very reason. A pretty spooky forest, now that I notice. Big, dark trees with moss that hangs like spiderwebs. Plenty of spiders, too. Big ugly brutes with hairy legs. At the outer limit of my hearing, the trees seem to talk to each other. They grumble slow dark words in a language as gnarly and thick as bark.

I must have been running a long time. I put nose to paws and it's good-bye, lights out. Your average canine lies down for ten seconds and it's slumber time. We're overpowered by sleep. *Zzzzzzz.* Yet we're light sleepers. As I said, the world's full of menace.

I wake up refreshed and yawn so hard a whine is squeezed out. It would be dark if it weren't for a fat yellow moon. Something about the moon, I don't know what. It just hangs there making you feel sad. I begin to howl. Others far off take it up after a while, short yips followed by a long *Oooooo.* I reply more mournfully. Time passes and I notice their howls are closer. Then I understand. Rather than existential comment, their howls are signals. A hunting pack of wolves.

I make tracks. Not rushing off blindly, because you can't keep that up forever. When a pack is on your tail, it's marathon time. Start out burning rubber like a rabbit and pretty soon you're flopped down out of gas, squealing as they rip your windpipe out.

How do I know this?

Your guess is as good as mine. Dog wisdom, maybe. So a steady ground-eating lope is indicated. Hunting packs are hard to keep together. The group is important, but each individual looks out for No. 1. A wolf comes across something better than what's being chased, and it drops out every time.

It seems like the muttering forest is on their side. I keep tripping over exposed roots. Branches slash my face as if challenging me to a duel. Once or twice it seems like the boles of trees sway toward one another, nutcrackers closing. But the pack falls behind.

I see a clearing ahead and make for it, suddenly coming out onto a vast moonlit plain. One minute the forest and the next the wide open. It's as if somebody drew a line with a ruler. The moon is so bright you could read a newspaper if they had them here, which I doubt. Those crones had a real third-world look. Not enough teeth among them to skin a cob of corn.

I can see for miles. The plain is covered with tall grass. With its long swells, it looks like an ocean frozen in a photograph. I pick up the spoor of small rodents living in a large colony. Their twittering makes me realize I'm hungry. Whatever it was that upset my stomach and gave me this dream didn't stick to the ribs. Maybe it was bad Chinese.

Whatever these little creatures are, they're nosy. It makes them easy pickings. Pick a hole and lie down beside it, and you can bank on one popping up to see what's going on. I nail a fat citizen after five minutes of stakeout. One shake and he's off to rodent heaven as the other busybodies whistle warnings. What's it feel like? Warm blood fills the mouth, like au jus. Eat as little hide and hair as possible and be careful with the bones. As for taste, I wouldn't recommend it. Too gamey.

It isn't enough, but it will keep me going. I'm licking my chops when something busts out of the woods heading straight at me. A wolf, most likely the leader of the pack. I take off running, heading in the direction the moon sinks in the star-filled sky. I hightail it for a mile, more like two, before taking a look back. Still only him. His pals must have crapped out on him.

Damned if I'm going to run off every one of those calories I just ate, so I slow to a lope. I guess he thinks I'm played out and comes roaring up to make short work of me.

Instead, I turn and give him a shoulder. He grunts and reels back in surprise.

"You want trouble, pal? I'll give you all you want," I say. Snarl is more like it.

He says something in wolf I don't get. Even if he hadn't been chasing me, I'd hate him for his sheer wildness. Check out the difference between the eyes of a dog and a wolf sometime and you'll see what I mean. Wolves were too stupid to cut a deal with humans. They've hated us ever since for having the brains to do it. Their story is they had too many principles to sell out. *Right.* Winters they freeze their asses off nosing through snowdrifts in hopes of scaring up dinner and picture us full-bellied and farting by some human's fire.

We circle each other. Big as he is, I tower over him.

"Why chase me?" I ask. Imagine talking to a wolf.

Even crazier, he answers, sounding like he's talking in some Visigoth dialect. "You're a stranger. I'm going to rip your guts out. Your bones will be scattered from here to the dark mountains."

We keep circling.

"Where am I?" I ask. It would be nice to get that clarified, even if this is just a dream. Felicity would be interested.

"Where you'll die."

No give at all. He has sunk-in malignant eyes and fierce teeth. His face is scarred, I guess from fighting to stay on top.

"I'm a lover, not a fighter," I joke. Scary as he looks, I feel loose and confident. Why not? Nobody dies in his own dreams.

He sneers. "I wouldn't lift a leg on any bitch'd let a coward mount her." He stops circling. "Lay on your back. Maybe I won't kill you."

"Take your best shot, shithead," I say.

He drives at me snapping and we rise on hind legs to spar. He's fast and sneaky, feinting one way and coming another. I can see why he bosses the pack. I'm stronger, but it takes a while to figure out his style. When I do, it's time for the fat lady to sing.

"Want to quit?" I ask. He's finished, panting and spurting blood in three places. These teeth I've got are as sharp as the knives they sell on TV.

"Never!"

He flies at me again. I have to kill him. Get my jaws on his throat and squeeze until I feel the life leave. Live by the sword, die by it. An autopsy would say crushed windpipe. I look down at his body. I feel nothing.

Hungry as I am, I resist the temptation to feed on his remains, although I bet he wouldn't hesitate. I pad toward the setting moon. Part of my mind monitors the environment—owls hoot, coyotes bark, the wind makes a lonely sighing sound through the tall grass. The rest tries to figure out this dream. Then it dawns on me that it isn't a dream. The detail is too sharp and there aren't any time shifts and sudden scene changes.

I'm human, a pretty important one at that. So what am I doing here, a dog? And where am I? How did I get here? A spell? Nobody believes in that crap. This isn't the fucking Middle Ages. Questions crowd in. Did I die and somehow wasn't aware of it at the time?

Clouds of memories from the life I came from hover at the edge of crystalizing. But I try to call them up, and they fade like mist in the sun. Speaking of mist, a fog forms in the hollows of the plain and spreads over the grass. Moisture beads the blades and I lick them. The long run and fight left me thirsty.

Pretty soon, the moon is just a milky disc through the fog. A loon flies overhead making sad cries. I become aware of—well, not figures, call them shadows. It's as if the fog thickens in spots. I can't smell them, not even with my dog nose. Dozens move slowly through the fog in all directions. Despite their numbers, each seems terribly alone.

They don't notice me, but when I spot one of them I veer

off to be on the safe side. Every now and then one cuts loose with a moan that makes that loon sound like the Bluebird of Happiness.

I can't tell if they are wandering without purpose or looking for something lost. If it's that, it doesn't seem from those moans that they have much hope of finding it. After a while, the ground begins to rise and the fog thins. As it does, I see fewer and fewer. Then they're gone. I'd say they were lost souls wandering in purgatory—if I believed in souls and purgatory. But I'm a brass-bound atheist. Peddle that mumbo-jumbo someplace else.

The moon goes down and the sky is sprinkled with bright stars. I wish I'd paid more attention to astronomy so I could tell if it's the same sky I'm used to. Dawn is near, I know from some instinct. I trot, headed I don't know where. I don't see any point in changing directions. When there's a gray edge to the eastern sky, I stumble across a covey of quail scratching in the dirt. I nab a fat one before he can even squawk, and that's breakfast. Spitting out the last of the feathers, I look for a place to rest. There is a leafless tree a few hundred yards away that looks as if the earth raises a bony hand against an expected blow. When I get there, I take a careful look around and test the wind. It's free of menace. I turn in a circle three times to drive off serpents, cover my nose with my tail, and sink into dreamless sleep.

I sleep a couple hours. After a good shake to get the dust off, I press on. I have gone so far I don't see the tree line behind me anymore. Belly-deep in grass, the plain looks endless, broken by only the occasional tree. Not another soul in sight. An empty lonely place. A blue sky overhead like a bowl. Overpowering silence. It gets hotter as the day wears on. Mountains gradually become visible far off. The ones the wolf said my bones would be scattered to, I guess. I top a rise and see laid out before me an immense battlefield. Skeletons lay as they had fallen.

They stretch to the horizon, picked clean and polished by

the wind. Vultures and maggots must have fed to bursting. Some were horses, some men. Most, horse and man alike, wore armor that is rusted and brittle from exposure to the elements. Spears, swords, and shields lay everywhere. Maybe this is the Middle Ages after all.

I see an animal near one of the skeletons and move toward it. It's a mangy-looking fox. He cringes in terror, belly to the ground.

"You don't want me," he whines. "There's no more to me than this." He withdraws from the bone he'd been gnawing on.

"What happened here?" I ask.

He seems surprised. "Happened? The Two Legs fought. What else? That's all they do, isn't it? When they're not trying to kill us?" A country twang.

"When did this happen?"

The fox shrugs. "Before my mother was born and her mother too." His eyes slide side to side.

"Don't worry, I'm not going to hurt you."

He looks at me with hope. It fades fast. "You're a dog, aren't you? Dogs kill my kind when you catch us."

"I'm not a dog."

"All right, wolf," he says tiredly. "My eyes aren't what they were. You talk different, though."

"I'm not a wolf either."

"What are you, then?"

"What you call a Two Legs."

He's disgusted. "Only cats play with what they catch." He rolls over on his back and offers his throat.

"I said I wasn't going to hurt you."

There's silence between us. Then it seems as if he decides he'll play along and gets on his feet.

"Where am I?" I ask.

"Where?" He gazes around. "Here."

"I mean, what's this place called?"

"It's called here. What else'd it be called?"

"Does it have a name?"

''Here. It's called here.'' He's patient, as if he thinks he might be dealing with a moron.

I study him. Scrawny, coat dull, nose dry. Definitely down on his luck.

''You hungry?''

''I can't remember the last time I ate.'' A sad shake of his head. ''I'm too slow anymore. One day I can keep my belly full, the next day I can't. I've been waiting for The Call.''

''Stay here,'' I say.

He lies down and wraps his tail around his feet. ''Don't have the strength to do anything else.''

It takes me half an hour to find a jackrabbit. He sits still too long, maybe thinking I don't spot him. I get him before he can get up to warp speed and leave me in the dust. I take him back to the fox.

''This is yours.'' I drop the jack in front of him.

He's suspicious.

''You're giving me that rabbit?''

''Yes. It's yours.''

''Anything wrong with it?''

''No.''

He sniffs it doubtfully, trying to figure out the catch. Then his hunger gets the best of him. He makes fast work of it.

''Name's Quick,'' he says, licking his chops. ''What's yours?''

''Don't have one.''

''That's unusual for a dog. You're great ones for names. Where you from?''

I jerk my muzzle in the direction I'd come. ''That way.''

''That way? Nothing that way except the Terrible Woods. Nobody goes there.''

''Why not?''

''Stories they tell.''

''What kind of stories?''

A meal in his belly perks him up. He begins grooming himself, pulling with teeth at snarls in his coat. ''Never paid much attention. Animals go there and don't come back is what I hear."

"There are wolves there."

He gives a short bark of laughter. "Something more than wolves is what I hear. They say trees talk."

"They do. I heard them."

He pauses in his grooming. "What'd they say?"

"I couldn't make it out. It didn't sound nice, though."

"What were you doing there? You crazy?"

"I haven't figured that out yet. What's in those mountains ahead?"

He looks toward the far-off peaks. "Trouble. Trouble's everywhere these days."

"I'm headed that way. Want to go?"

Quick thinks a minute. "Nothing much around here for me anymore," he says at last. "You wouldn't think it to look at me now, but I was once pretty big in these parts. Had any female I wanted. Eight, nine litters. I can't remember them all. Then I started losing fights in spring. Young punks I would have beat easy before. Well, you know how that goes. The ladies like the winners. I've been alone for a couple years now. Empty burrows and lately empty belly."

He gives a long look around. "Sure, why not? I'll go with you."

[2]

We trotted panting under the hot sun toward the faint mountains, heat waves making far-off objects dance and squirm. Quick explained points of interest. "Caught me two cooing birds near that rock once. One on top of the other. Making babies, I guess."

"That's where I found a deer with a broken leg. Lucky nothin' bigger came round, 'cept some cleanup birds. Fed me a whole week."

"There's water under that tree. Tastes funny, though. There's better yonder a ways."

I didn't say much. I was back to thinking it was a dream. I hoped I could remember the details. Felicity would find all kinds of meaning in this. Guilt, suppressed longings, all that crap. I wondered who Felicity was.

"See those rocks? Hid under them once when a Uulebeet flew overhead. He didn't see me, otherwise I wouldn't be here today."

"What's a Uulebeet?"

He looked at me as if I was playing more mind games. "Everybody knows that."

"Not me."

"Never seen one flying? Big and ugly, skin like a snake? Claws long as your face and teeth even bigger. Smells like something a cleanup bird puked out. Scouting for Mogwert, as usual."

"Who's Mogwert?"

"Don't fool with me." He trotted growlingly. "I thank you for not killing me," he burst out. "But it don't give you the right to treat me like I got nothing in my head for your fun."

We pressed on in silence. Quick was a talker, though, and couldn't shut up for long. He reminisced about mates. They had names like White Paw and Half Ear.

"Sunrise was the nicest. She was the first. I had to fight a lot before I won her."

Don't foxes mate for life? It was one of those things I seemed to know before. Knowledge lay dormant in my head, waiting for something to turn the light on. Sometimes it was a word, other times a smell or sight. I asked him.

"I would've with Sunrise. Was everything you'd want in a bitch. Caught mice like nobody's business. She found more quail's eggs than anyone. Never fell for that broken-wing trick that fools so many. Real nice to be around. I don't just mean her sex hole, either. We'd sit and look at things get dark at the end of day and not say nothin'. Just enjoy bein' together. Smarter than me even, it comes to that. Braver too. Six pups in her first litter. Kept us both busy feeding them. Until . . ." Quick fell silent.

"Until what?"

"Until Mogwert got her and the pups. I came back one day and they were all gone."

I wanted to ask who Mogwert was again, but didn't. I asked how he knew.

"Mogwert smell was all over. Burns your nose, it does. Worst smell in the world. Like the hot springs where the earth farts. Worse than Uulebeets even."

"Why did they take Sunrise and the pups?"

"They were takin' a lot of little ones at that time. Lions, bears, deer, cats, rabbits—didn't make no difference, they just took 'em. Sunrise put up a fight. I smelled her death. Don't know why they took her along dead. To feed on, probably." He was quiet for a while. "She was the best. I barked at the moon I don't know how many nights."

We stopped to drink at a spring. The water gurgled in his guts. The plains looked scalded in the glare. Insects droned. We lay in the shadow of rocks until the day started to cool.

I sleep and dream I'm in a room with a big window that overlooks a floor where men shout. Even the jerk-offs on telephones are yelling. Numbers flash on the walls. It's a trading floor. I feel smug. I know something they don't, something that makes their frenzy a waste of time. As I turn to say something, a noise wakes me.

Quick was still snoozing. He was dreaming and his lips were pulled back in a noiseless snarl. His teeth were yellow and broken and the gums shrunken. He smelled bad, as if that jackrabbit had blocked up the works. If I hadn't come along, he would have died for sure. That was probably what waiting for The Call means. Weaken here and it's curtains.

What did that dream mean? What was I doing and why am I not still there, lording it over those sweating nobodies? That was where I belonged, not on these hot plains with only a fox to talk to. *A fox.*

What did I know that they didn't as I stared down at the antlike scurrying of the traders? I scratched behind one ear with a hind paw. Fleas. Quick opened a bleary eye.

"Let's get going," I said.

He shook himself. His hind legs were so weak he nearly fell. "What's so important in those mountains?"

"I don't know."

"Then why go?"

"Just because."

Afternoon was fading when I heard a sound like wind beginning to rise. But it was dead calm. "Did you hear that?"

Quick pricked his ears. One was notched from an old fight. "I hear it."

A couple of miles ahead it looked like a dark cloud was

moving across the plain. Now the sound was like the hum of a power plant.

Quick's eyes seemed to bulge, he was that scared.

He hightailed it and I followed. "An old den's not far," he yelled. "Nobody there for a long time."

"What are we running from?" I yelled back.

"Eaters."

The hum got louder and the cloud was closer. I shot looks behind. It rose two hundred feet above the ground and was a mile wide. Everyone was hauling ass. Hares, antelope, and other creatures flashed past. We overtook a tortoise lumbering as fast as it could.

"Not far now," Quick gasped. The ground dropped and he disappeared. Then I saw his tail go down a hole at the foot of a tree. We wiggled down past hairy roots. The tunnel took a turn and when I bumped against Quick it was as dark as the grave.

"What now?" I asked.

Before he could answer, the hum grew deafening. Dozens of insects came swarming down the tunnel, then hundreds. They burrowed into my fur and bit. I snapped at them, crushing the little bastards right and left. Quick was doing the same, yelping.

"I'm getting out of here!" I shouted.

"No!" he cried. "They'll get in your eyes and your nose and mouth and crawl right into your guts."

What seemed like hours passed, but probably was only minutes. The roar outside dropped as if a switch had been thrown. I pushed up the tunnel, nearly crazy from the bugs. Outside, laggards were trying to catch up with the main body. They smacked into me and crawled buzzing underfoot, but the black cloud was a quarter-mile away already. It looked like the twister in *The Wizard of Oz*.

Quick panted at my side. "Lucky I remembered that den."

We scratched and shook until all the bugs were off. They had round faces and needle-sharp little teeth. "Trees that talk, ghosts, eaters,'' I said. ''What else has this fucking place got?''

Quick crunched one of them. ''They're not too bad. They'll fill your belly, anyway.''

He was right. They weren't too bad.

I've learned you can't be a picky eater. You have to keep the furnace stoked. It had to be really gross before I would turn my nose up. You eat even when gorged in case a couple days pass before the next meal turns up.

The Wizard of Oz. How did I remember that, even know how the story went? Little girl runs away from home with dog, gets conked on head and wakes up in weird place. Scarecrow, tin man, cowardly lion, wicked witch, etc. All she wants is to get home again, like me. I saw it maybe ten times when I was a kid. The point was it was just a dream.

Maybe I got conked on the head like Dorothy in the movie. Came out of a building and slipped on ice or something and now I was in a hospital with tubes stuck in me having this dream. Some say the only reality is the creation of neurons and synapses doing their thing. When you die, the universe does too. If you point out that millions die every day but the world goes on, the eggheads say that's just part of the dream. I had a hunch I hadn't wasted a lot of thought on that before, and sure I didn't have time for it now.

But say I was lying in a hospital bed, just needing a good pinch to wake up. I would get my clothes on and head for the nearest bar for a couple belts and then get on with life.

''What're you doin'?'' Quick asked. ''Only time I saw anybody bite themselves like that was when they went crazy eating pink weed.''

''I'm trying to wake up from this dream.''

''What do you mean?'' he asked suspiciously.

''I'm having a dream and you're part of it.''

''Me part of a dog's dream? You're crazy, all right.'' He trotted toward the mountains with a sarcastic look.

The pinch-me-and-I'll-wake-up theory didn't hold water,

unless I was just dreaming I was biting myself on the ass. So a dream within a dream? You could kick this around until the cows come home.

Another idea. I wasn't superstitious, but what if I had crossed somebody who had strange powers? Let's say a witch, for the sake of argument. This witch casts a spell that puts me here. Maybe she's mad because she's lost her shirt in the scam I had going—some insider trading dodge is my guess—and wants revenge. Strange I could remember *The Wizard of Oz* but not what I was up to beyond that feeling that I pulled the wool over the eyes of some pretty sharp operators, hence the pardonable pride. On the other hand, maybe this witch was a broad I was banging and she got steamed when I said take a hike. Hell hath no fury and all that. No. There had to be a reason why looking down on the floor of the exchange stuck in my head. There had to be a connection.

If this was punishment, wouldn't it be better if I knew what I did? The aim is to get the wrongdoer to think about what he did and repent, unless I'm mistaken.

We passed through the devastation left by the eaters. They had chewed up everything in their path. The long prairie grass looked like it had been mowed. Animals that couldn't get away were covered with the bastards still chewing away. Their jaws sounded like tiny castanets.

''When they're full,'' Quick said, ''they dig into the ground and you don't see them no more until the next time.''

At the end of the day the mountains didn't look any closer. ''How much farther?'' I asked Quick.

''Tomorrow we'll be as far as I've ever been.'' He looked uneasy. ''It's not right to go where you never been.''

''Where would we be if Christopher Columbus believed that?''

He shot me a look. ''Who?''

''He discovered America.'' They don't think that in PC places like Berkeley, but who gives a shit?

"What's America?"

"Forget it."

I'd already figured out you couldn't have a conversation with Quick that went much beyond how long ago rabbit shit was dropped and where's the possible meal now.

We went in different directions looking for dinner, but we both struck out. I picked up the scent of a rat, but it was hours old. He was probably back in the hole fornicating with Mrs. Rat. I checked out Quick's breath when he came back to make sure he wasn't holding out.

"This country's never been much good for the belly." He lay down, covered his tail with his nose, and started snoring.

I was so goddamned sad that when the moon came up I climbed a knoll and howled. A minute later Quick was by my side yipping.

Later that night toward morning, a thought came to me. What was my fucking name?

I jumped to my feet. "Uulebeets?" Quick asked wildly.

"I forgot my name!"

Quick lay back down, grumbling that there had been enough crazy talk to suit him.

I paced back and forth, whining. I would have held my head if I'd had hands. Why did it take this long to realize I didn't know my own name? If you can't remember your goddamned name, you might as well throw in the towel.

Sidney, Fred, John, Phillip, Morton, Norton, Horton—I could be any one of them. There are hundreds of first names. And that's the easy part. Get into last names, and the sky's the limit. What did I look like? Another good question. Tall, short, thin, fat? Blond, dark? Bald, curly-headed? Young, middle-aged, old?

Who is Felicity?

Maybe my name was floating around in my brain looking for the right association for the light to come on, like knowing that foxes mate for life. I concentrated, commanding my mind to deliver. No soap.

Whoever put me in this pickle was more evil than I had thought. Bad enough being a stranger (and a dog!) in a strange land, but a stranger who doesn't even know who he is—that's diabolical.

Maybe I had made a pact with the Devil the way what's-his-name did and welched on the deal. I got dragged to an opera in Italian on that very subject. I fell asleep, so any tips I might have picked up for dealing with Satan were lost. I wouldn't think you'd want to screw around with him if you had a deal, but maybe I was desperate. Short on a margin call or something. Get into that squeeze and anything goes.

I picked up the sound of something scratching upwind. My nose told me jackrabbit. This country was lousy with them. I flattened my belly to the ground and crawled. At the end of my creep, I was ten yards away. His ears were scissoring back and forth, so I knew he suspected something. It was just light enough so you could begin to pick things out.

I lunged and nailed him two yards before he would have been gone for good. A feeble struggle, then it was breakfast time.

I was hungry enough to finish it off myself, but Quick showed up to panhandle. When the edge was off my hunger, I said, "The rest is yours." He grinned.

We set out toward the mountains again, lavender in the morning light. I mulled over names. David, Eric, James, Arnold, Peter?

One thing about being a dog is when you get up in the morning you don't have to worry about brushing teeth, shaving, wardrobe choices, or the rest of it. One shake and you're set, ready to go.

The land softened from staring plains to looking as if it had been farmland long ago. We followed the faint traces of roads until they petered out and passed through overgrown orchards and the ruins of small villages. It looked like war had blasted them to rubble. We took a detour when

Quick or I spotted a big cat or a bear ambling along. There were plenty of wolverines, stringy coyotes, and grazers like elk and antelope who watched us from a distance. At noon we came to a small, rotting bridge over a stream. We started to cross when my nose picked up a swampy, hairy smell, old and obsolete.

''What's that?''

''What's what?'' Quick said.

''That smell.''

He tested the air. ''Nasty, ain't it?''

By then we were mid-span.

''Hold up,'' I said. ''It's under the bridge.'' Quick spun and ran back with me following.

Just as we made it to the end of the bridge, I saw a blur out of the corner of my eye, something trying to head us off. We stopped a safe distance off and looked back. On either side of the bridge were two of the ugliest things I'd ever seen. They were wet-looking and kind of purplish with warty lumps all over. Greasy, lank hair hung down over their faces. They motioned with thick arms. They had squashed-in mugs with yellow fangs and red eyes. Jesus, what a sight.

''Trolls,'' Quick said, shivering. ''They nearly got us.''

I looked at him in amazement. ''Trolls?''

''Once they were gone from the world; then Mogwert brought them back.''

Trolls. I was in a goddamned fairy tale.

Quick and I swam the river a long way upstream and pressed on toward the mountains, now close enough so I could begin to pick out detail. I didn't like their looks. Dark and gloomy, as if they hid secrets. They could keep them as far as I was concerned.

What more could happen? I was a dog in a fairy tale, unless I was lucky enough to be comatose in a hospital dreaming all this.

''Have you ever seen Mogwert?'' I asked Quick.

"Once."

"What'd they look like?"

"Dark."

"What else?"

"Just dark, like they sucked in the light. Everything around them looked gray, like at the end of day. Cold. Dark and cold, that's all I can say. I was comin' out of a burrow when I saw them. I went right back down and stayed there tail over my face. Didn't come up until the next day. Where Mogwert'd been it was like winter passed through. Flowers looked touched by frost. Trees lost their leaves."

"Is Mogwert big or little?"

"Dark. Cold and dark."

Bill Ingersol. It suddenly popped into my head. That was my name, I was sure of it.

"Bill Ingersol." I said it aloud.

Quick ignored me. "See them cleanup birds flyin' over there? Might be there's something for us." A dozen or more circled in the cloudless sky, spiraling lower.

We topped a rise and spotted what was drawing them. It was a man lying on his back on the ground. The vultures landing and waddling toward him said he was near the end. They don't hurry if they see any fight is left. The boldest and biggest were already elbowing for the eyeballs. They scattered with indignant squawks when we came closer. Quick hung back.

"It's bad luck foolin' with Two Legs," he warned.

He was a big strapping man, handsome if a broken nose doesn't bother you. Red hair, freckles. He was wearing a kind of leather skirt and helmet and body armor. Roman-looking, if you know what I mean. It looked as if he'd been in a hell of a fight. The armor was dented and had a great tear in the chest plate. Dried blood was in the rip, which looked like it had been made by a can opener. One sandal was missing. He was muttering.

"Apian Bollard of the Border Rangers reporting." Dark eyes fixed on something far away didn't take us in. "Early patrol—signs of nervousness by the animals, as though they were . . ." His tongue licked cracked lips. "If I could just have a small drink of water, sir." His Adam's apple bobbed as if he was drinking. "Thank you, sir. Real dry out there."

He coughed wetly. "When the moon changed, we headed back as ordered. We saw evil portents—owls and bats flying in broad daylight. Wolves howling at noon. Strange monsters—hairy things with glaring eyes. They followed but kept their distance. Something bad is starting."

I had never seen anybody dying before. You read about it or even see it happen on TV on those programs where a camera follows the cops. But it's different when you're watching it in person. This guy was a total stranger, but I couldn't help feeling bad.

"Let's go," Quick whined, looking around edgily. "Let them have him."

Bollard looked like he'd been in a lot of wars. His hands were big and calloused and his arms were covered with old scars. His sword was a few feet away, the blade scored and nicked. His breath started sounding rough and ragged.

"It's all in my report." His hand moved toward a leather bag stuffed with something. He made a slight motion as if handing it to somebody.

"No, I don't need thanks. Just doing my duty as a Cor of the Third Dirk of the Border Rangers."

"C'mon," Quick said. "Let's go. He's trouble, like 'em all. Always been, always will. They'd be trouble even if they didn't stir up Mogwert."

I ignored him.

"Stronger this time," Bollard said. "All these years . . . stronger. We thought we could . . ." His cracked lips moved but no sound came out. Then he spoke again and the words sounded like they were being pulled up from a well of despair. "Thought we could withdraw to the Fair Lands and they wouldn't follow. Wrong. Wrong. We were wrong."

A vulture, bigger than the rest, hopped closer. Quick rushed at it snarling and it flapped off. The rest retreated with spread wings. They looked like fat ladies running with raised skirts.

Quick returned. "We're askin' for it. Stayin' around here is just askin' for it."

"What are we supposed to do, leave him for the birds?"

Quick looked surprised. "Unless you want to eat him yourself."

"Jesus," I said. "What kind of animal do you take me for?"

"A dog."

"Never mind. And shut up. He's trying to talk."

I bent low, my muzzle nearly in his face. "Came at us just before dawn. Sentries sleeping, I think. In on us before we knew it. Pigs. But they could stand." His right hand closed and waved back and forth as if he was swinging his sword.

He did that for a while. "Think I'm the only one who got away. Horse killed when a Uulebeet found us in the open. I cut him up pretty good but he got me too. Flew off dripping yellow blood. I kept going until I got back." His speech was getting slow and faint.

"Now, sir, if I could just rest for an hour." He stopped breathing and that was it. Fini. He had a peaceful look on his face.

Quick stared toward the west. "I hope it's not what I think it is."

He was watching a dot in the sky. The vultures lifted off in a body and flapped off in the opposite direction.

"Uulebeet," Quick said. He was so scared a little trickle of urine dribbled down from his belly and made a dark mark on the dirt.

Nearby there was a broken-down wall made of stones piled on each other that looked like it had been a corral a long time ago. Quick headed for it as fast as his name.

I snatched up the leather bag with my teeth and followed. Hidden there, we heard the slow, steady approach of big wings. All the other sounds of nature—the *whirr* of insects, chirp of birds, everything—fell silent.

I watched through a small hole between the rocks. The Uulebeet was as big as a Volvo. Think of a cross between a snake and a bird and you get it. It was a dirty yellow with black beak and talons. Pale reptile's eyes as big as dinner plates. Its muscles moved with repulsive smoothness under taut skin. It landed heavily, kicking up dust, and looked around. Its head revolved at the end of a long neck corded with tendons. Teeth as well as that beak. If I was dreaming, I had to hand it to myself. Lucas or Spielberg didn't come close. After its suspicious look around, the Uulebeet waddled slowly toward the man. It nosed his body over and seemed to be looking for something.

The leather bag.

When it didn't find it, it looked around suspiciously. Took a step toward the wall.

Wake up. Wake up. Wake up. The voice screamed in my brain. I hadn't been this scared when they unsealed the indictment. Twenty-seven counts of fraud and SEC violations. "A million dollars if you get me out of this mess," I told my lawyer, Bill Clancy.

"A million and a half," he answered when he saw the look on my face. The scene popped into my head as the Uulebeet decided whether it was worth the trouble to look behind the wall. Terror must have broken down some barrier in my mind and freed the memory.

Luck went my way and it turned back to the dead man. It put one talon on his chest, reached down and plucked off his helmeted head as neatly as you would take a grape from the stem. Then it raised its wings, ran clumsily but swiftly and was airborne, headed east. When the Uulebeet was far off, birds sang again and insect drone resumed.

"It didn't eat the head," Quick said. "Must be takin' it back to the nest."

We watched the Uulebeet until it was a tiny dot in the sky in the direction of the mountains. By that time, the vultures were wheeling overhead again, waiting to see what we would do.

"Wonder why it didn't take the whole thing," Quick said, sniffing at the decapitated body. "What a stink. Not even those cleanup birds will touch it now." He was right. The Uulebeet's smell burned the nose.

"That something to eat?" Quick asked. He meant the bag.

"No."

"What're you gonna do with it?"

"I don't know." We left.

"The Uulebeet headed toward those mountains you're so interested in," Quick pointed out after we'd gone a mile.

"I noticed."

I was thinking hard. Ever since I dropped into this nightmare I had traveled toward those scary mountains. It was as if I was being drawn there. The question was, why? The closer we got, the worse the vibes. The Uulebeet flying back there settled it.

"I bet that's where Mogwert are," I said.

Quick stopped dead in his tracks. "Mogwert?" he cried. He looked around wildly. "Where?"

"I was just thinking those mountains are probably where they live."

"Nobody knows where Mogwert live," he said fearfully.

"Uulebeets—are they connected with Mogwert?"

Quick considered this for what looked like the first time. "I believe they must be," he decided finally. "You see Mogwert and pretty soon you'll see Uulebeet. Or if you see Uulebeet, you'll see Mogwert."

[3]

We traveled four hours and Quick tired, so we lay in the shade of a huge oak tree. I yawned. You don't stay awake for long when you're a dog. I've said how quickly it's lights out when you put head to paws. You would think I'd dream about the hideous Uulebeet or the trolls, those nightmares being so fresh. Instead, I'm in the Silver Cloud returning to Long Island. A beautiful woman is giving me head as I tell the driver to speed up.

"I'm late," I say.

In the rearview mirror the driver gives me a lewd wink.

Home is a big place built at the turn of the century. The headlights pick out sweeping lawns as smooth as billiard tables, a horse barn partly hidden by trees, a gazebo where Felicity likes to give gala luncheons for charity in summer, Felicity being my wife, as I now remember. She married me for my money. That's all right. I married her for her social connections. They are useful in a business way. The third marriage for both.

I zip up and give my traveling companion five one-hundred-dollar bills and slip the driver another C note to keep his lip buttoned and step from the car. It returns at six o'clock in the morning, seven days a week, for the ride to Manhattan, where I have offices in one of those glass buildings that look like an ice cube tray. The doorman wears a Beefeater uniform and uses his stave to keep the bums moving.

''You're late,'' Felicity says when I hurry in. ''Dinner's about to be served.''

''Sorry, darling,'' I say, pecking at the marble cheek turned to me. Tall, bony as a greyhound, cheekbones so high they say the steppes are in the pedigree—you know the type if you read *Town and Country.*

Felicity wants to recreate the 19th-century salon where big shots and poets traded witticisms. ''The art of conversation has nearly expired,'' she says. Bored rich ladies adopt a charity or a cause. Felicity's is reviving ''intelligent'' conversation. She got a grant to conduct symposia at Harvard on ways to foster conditions to revive the bon mot. ''People think they're spontaneous,'' she explains, ''but they're not and never were. They require as much thought as poetry.'' The money came from the same federal agency that paid a woman who paints pictures with her menses. You tell me the bigger waste of taxpayer's money. I sent a letter to my congressman in complaint but didn't sign it. Felicity has red hair and a temper to match.

A smattering of wealthy grandees is always invited to her levees, meaty gentlemen with red faces and names like Vanderbilt and Mellon, and their rail-thin wives. Studying the guest lists, the newspapers had the impression a major cultural event was occurring. You read about it in the gossip columns for days afterward. Guests faxed aphorisms they wished they had uttered to columnists. Others hired writers beforehand to compose witty banter.

I don't enjoy these dinners. Diplomats talking with International Monetary Fund bankers about something nobody but them gives a shit about is not my idea of a good time. Restructuring third-world debt, to give one example. Playwrights and poets, a seedy-looking bunch who gorge themselves and drink prodigious amounts of my liquor, are always there. You can see them mentally composing savage paragraphs that will appear in the next book or play where everyone looks stupid. Felicity doesn't like it if I hustle her rich friends for one of the deals I always have on the burner, so I usually make small talk about sports or the weather.

The brass plaque on the door of my company reads Ingersol, Drake and Burns. Drake and Burns aren't active anymore. We formed the company in the late Seventies, just in time for the boom. We each had seats on the New York Stock Exchange, but I saw early on that stock trading was peanuts compared to the money made buying companies and spinning off assets. We rode the boom the way a glider rides thermals.

''He's so boring,'' I heard Felicity tell somebody one night when I finished up a story about a great takeover I had masterminded. I admit I had told it a few times. Her voice rang out into a silence that fell when everyone was trying at exactly the same time to think up something witty to say.

I could have made points with her by coming up with some reply that would be quoted in the columns. But I was steamed. The best I could do was, ''Fuck you, bitch.''

The silence that fell was broken by one of the writers Felicity had taken up. He drunkenly yelled, ''Attaboy.'' I think she was more upset by his betrayal than what I said.

I woke when Quick farted. It was early afternoon and the smell of cat was in the air. I got up and Quick jerked awake. He saw me testing the air and put his own nose to work.

''Spotted cat,'' he said.

''What's that?''

''Trouble.''

''Is there anything here that isn't?''

''It must have seen the birds.''

He jumped up on the wall. ''There she is.''

I looked. It was a huge cat, with eye teeth like tusks, ambling slowly toward the headless body. It had the heavy, unhurried manner of a creature who fears nothing. Her tan hide had dark blotches like a leopard's spots, only bigger.

''It looks like something from one of those Lost Island movies,'' I said.

Quick gave me a look but I didn't bother to explain.

''What do we do?'' I asked.

''Do?'' Quick said. ''Go.''

He trotted off. I caught up, carrying the leather bag in my teeth. ''Where are we going?''

He gave me a sardonic look. ''Not in such a hurry to get to them mountains now?''

He had that right. Scary as they were, I still felt pulled. It was as if they called to me, weird as that sounded. Not an actual voice, but something that reached me at a deeper level.

''One part of me feels like I belong there but another says I don't,'' I said.

''Listen to the one that says don't.''

If not to the mountains, where I had been heading from the start, where should I be going?

After thinking about this I asked, ''Where do the Two Legs live?''

''Long ways from here,'' Quick answered. ''Never been there, but I've seen them coming and going.''

''What direction?''

Quick nodded toward the west.

''I guess that's where I better go.'' As I said that, I felt a stab of anxiety. I looked back toward the mountains. They didn't want me to go.

We headed west through more countryside laid waste a long time ago. Orchards gone wild, roofless stone farmhouses and the bones of abandoned wagons. Now and then a little crossroads village lay in ruins. They had been in that state for a long time by their look.

''Lots of chicken and geese here at one time, or so the stories go,'' Quick said. ''No belly hurt from hunger then.''

A cold wind began to blow from the direction of the mountains, and dark storm clouds rushed overhead in a hurry to get somewhere. Birds dropped from the turbulent sky and roosted in tossing trees.

Quick and I padded along. He kept looking over his

shoulder. "Don't usually get a wind like that until later," he said. "It belongs to the time of cold."

We kept moving until sundown. We passed nervous deer peering from thickets and beavers on their log dams uneasily facing the wind. "They don't know what to make of it neither," said Quick.

We felt drops of rain. "That'll turn into snow," Quick said.

"What do we do then?"

"Look for a place to hole up."

The rain turned to sleet and then snow began falling, lightly at first, then heavier. Quick's head turned side to side as he looked for shelter.

We found a small cave beneath a big tree. A squirrel too stupid to go inside chattered insults from high up. "Smells like badger in there," Quick said. "But it's old smell." There were a few bones here and there and clumps of rabbit fur. Quick touched the bones with his nose. "Not worth bothering with."

The storm rose and the tree groaned. But it was cozy enough in the darkness. Quick recalled past meals, his favorite conversation, then curled up for sleep.

It was long past midnight when I heard a sound outside.

"Badger," Quick warned. "Don't let him get in."

I moved up to the entrance just in time to bump noses with something. He was as surprised as I was.

"Who's that?" he snarled. "This hole's mine."

He tried to force his way in and we fought, our teeth clashing.

"Don't let him get under you," Quick shouted. "You're finished if he does."

That was his style of fighting, for sure. He twisted to get beneath. I stayed low and after a minute he backed off.

"How'd you like that?" Quick barked from behind me. "There's plenty more waiting."

"Is that a fox yapping down there?" the badger growled.

"Come and find out."

"Pretty brave with your wolf friend in front, aren't you?"

"He's not a wolf."

"What're you doing in my hole?"

"We'll go soon as the storm's over," I replied.

"What am I supposed to do, freeze?"

Quick held his tongue for a change and I couldn't think of an answer, so the three of us listened to the wind.

"Can't see your nose in front of your face," the badger complained. "I've never seen such a storm so early."

The cold was seeping into the ground and the cave was getting on the cool side despite our body heat. I could imagine what it was like out where he was.

"You can come in if you promise no trouble," I said.

Quick yapped hysterically. "You can't trust a badger."

There was a suspicious silence outside. Finally, he said, "All right."

I backed up and he shuffled in, covered with snow. He shook himself, sending ice crystals flying. "Brrrrrr. Be a lot of critters die in this storm. Nobody's ready," he grumbled. "Bears look ahead more'n most and they just started fattenin' up."

Now that he was inside, butter wouldn't melt in Quick's mouth. "They're not good times," he whined.

"And getting worse," the badger said. "You hear things."

He didn't look like he was going to add to that so I asked, "What things?"

"Bad things. Mogwert're ready to move again."

"What do you mean?"

"They're stronger than before. I wouldn't want to be the Two Legs." He muttered for a while. Badgers are solitary and mostly talk to themselves.

"Problem is," he said to Quick and me, "the Two Legs are the only ones that'll stand up to 'em. They're cleverer than Mogwert in some ways. They've got magic and weapons. But it won't do any good this time, if you believe what you hear."

"From who?" I asked.

"Cleanup birds. Snakes. That sort."

"You can't trust them," Quick said. "They're liars."

"Not to each other they're not. Not about Mogwert. I get around. I hear them talking. Cleanup birds see a big feast coming. Snakes—well, snakes has always been friendly with Mogwert and do what they're told."

"What do they want?" I asked.

"Want?" The badger snorted. "What they've always wanted. Everyone to be slaves. Because of Two Legs they haven't had their way. But now the talk is they're real cocky. They're waiting for one last thing to happen."

"What is that?" I asked.

"Someone sly to guide them." He grumbled to himself for a bit and then commenced to snore. Quick whimpered and yipped in his sleep. I listened to the blizzard outside.

Sly is a loaded word. But maybe the badger meant smart. I wondered if Mogwert have been waiting for me.

[4]

We dug ourselves out of the badger hole the next morning. Three feet of powder, great for skiing. The sun on it was so dazzling I wished I had shades to put on. My unplugged memory reminded me I was fond of winterscapes, but not this kind. I like them on the other side of a double-glazed window with a blaze crackling on my side, a hot drink by my elbow. Something with a good lacing of brandy. We spend a couple weeks every January in Gstaad, where I keep a suite in the best hotel. Nobody runs hotels better than the Swiss. The best of everything, including tiptoeing servants. Swiss hotels, English suits, Italian cars and Japanese consumer electronics, that's my style.

We entertain various strains of Eurotrash, lesser royalty and members of decayed aristocracies who look for new fortunes to marry into. Or at least Felicity does.

''Why do you bother coming at all? All you do is stare at people or smile sarcastically,'' she asked one night as she removed her jewelry. We had returned from a party for a Polish count. His claim to fame was he could trace hemophilia in his family five generations back to a king I never heard of.

''Do you ever listen to these people?'' I answered. ''They don't talk about anything that matters.''

''Nothing matters to you unless it has a dollar sign in front of it.''

''That's not true,'' I said. ''The German mark is a quite

acceptable currency.'' When she was silent, I explained I had made a joke.

''Even your jokes are about money.'' She applied cold cream, meaning I wouldn't be getting any that night.

Looking now at snow that stretched to the horizon brought all that back. What a comedown, Gstaad to a badger's hole. A saint would be bitter. Quick crunched a bird that had fallen frozen from a tree during the night. The snow was dotted with feathered corpses. The badger and I followed his lead and ate our fill. As they are mostly bone and feather, you have to put away quite a few to make a dent on hunger. As we ate, the sun started to melt the snow. The badger didn't like that either.

''When winter comes it should stay,'' he grumbled.

Quick and I looked at him.

''That storm was Mogwert's, done for their own evil purposes.''

In the animal world you don't say good-bye, so Quick and I departed when our bellies were full. Quick was worried.

''You think he's right?'' he asked.

''About what?''

''Mogwert and the storm.''

''How would I know?''

He whined. ''Too many strange things, beginning with you. I want them simple again.''

Amen to that, I thought. I remembered the Chinese curse, ''May you live in interesting times.'' This line of thought made me think how much I missed Chinese takeout. Which made me realize how much I missed Italian food. And all the other cuisines, except English. The image formed in my mind of a simple hamburger on a kaiser roll with lettuce, tomato and onions, one side of the roll smeared with Dijon and the other with mayo. A beaded bottle of beer. I felt like howling.

I would be well into the work day at this hour in the real world. Two of the four cigars I allow myself would already be ash. I would have made maybe forty calls and got as many. When you are in the takeover game, information is all-important. A lot of what you get is worthless, but you expect that. Even gossip can be valuable. Is it true that Atrim Corp., the fast-rising software firm, is going public because its founder and CEO is HIV-positive? Sure, people can live for years with that. But the poor bastard won't be giving the company 100 percent anymore. He's got other things on his mind. So you don't touch Atrim if you're smart, no matter how good the earnings statement. That's the value of gossip. Pity is unknown on Wall Street and it should be. If the lion lies down with the sheep, he should get up only when the bones have been picked clean. You want pity, move someplace where there's socialism. See how you like it.

By noon the creeks were high from snowmelt and the ground was muddy. Quick and I traveled in silence. The animals we passed looked confused and worried, as if they wondered what came next. The woods steamed in the sunlight.

I was trying to remember what I might have known about physics. It wasn't much, which wasn't surprising. You don't make money knowing physics. But I must have read something somewhere about parallel universes, maybe in an airline magazine. Sometimes, when the weather is bad and planes are stacked up, that is all there is to read. The phrase sticks in my mind. It's some kind of theory, which means it stands a pretty good chance of being a crock. But maybe something like that happened to me. A time warp or some *Star Trek* kind of deal and here I am pitched into this other universe. But why as a dog?

And why me? I'm not the victim type, not W. B. (for Bogart) Ingersol. I had a gun permit, a state-of-the-art security system at home and bodyguards as needed, such as when I was working a corporate takeover that would put thousands on the street. I got a lot of death threats then. Some compared me with Carl Icahn and T. Boone Pickens.

I considered this a compliment, as they are both fine gentlemen and good Americans. I had a skull and crossbones on my private stationery and flew the pirate's flag on my yacht. Some didn't see the humor, I admit. Fuck them. The media gave me heat, not that it bothered me. You didn't screw with me if you were smart. So a victim I most definitely wasn't.

Yet one way of looking at this situation is I've lost way more than if I'd been some poor schmuck who gets mugged on the street and is buggered into the bargain. At least he would still have the world he grew up in. TV would still be turning minds to mush and politicians telling lies as usual. There would still be the verities, is my point. The poor schmuck could still buy himself a good cigar, a Kansas City beefsteak and a shot of good whiskey to make himself feel better. Insurance might cover part of his loss, maybe all of it. He could start fresh. I can't even find anybody to report the crime to.

Toward the middle of the afternoon I saw something far ahead that looked like a finger. Fate giving me the middle one, I thought. When we got closer I saw it was a snake, coiled and swaying in a way that would be hypnotic if I were a rabbit or a white rat.

"Let's go around," Quick said. "I hate those thangs."

That was all right with me. We started to detour when the snake spoke.

"What's your hurry?" He had kind of a fruity Oxbridge accent you hear on "Masterpiece Theater." His forked tongue flickered in and out. Jet-black eyes like currants. "Can't we talk?"

"No thanks," I said.

"You might learn something."

I slowed. "Like what?"

"Come closer."

"Don't trust him," Quick whispered.

"I've been looking for answers. Maybe he's got some."

I lay belly down opposite the snake, not so close that he

could suddenly lunge and sink fangs into me, if that was what he had in mind. Quick sat suspiciously behind me. He always liked me positioned between him and danger.

"You want to talk? So start," I said.

"You have friends here." He had the kind of voice that insinuated things. Not only friends, it implied, but friends who could provide valuable services.

"I haven't seen any so far."

"Maybe you haven't looked in the right place."

"Where might that be?"

"The mountains."

"He's one of them," Quick barked. "Let's get out of here."

"Mogwert are in the mountains," I said.

"Yes," he hissed.

"Mogwert are my friends?" Something cold clutched my heart.

"Your only friends."

"Mogwert are evil," Quick yapped. "Their friends are evil, like you."

It was as if Quick was too minor for notice. "It would be better if you went to them on your own," he said to me.

"What does that mean?" I asked.

"They have many helpers."

"Like those flying lizards?"

"And others."

"What do they want from me?"

"Your help."

"What's in it for me?"

"Wealth and power. All you've ever dreamed of."

That sounded all right but I needed details. "What kind of help?"

"Just your . . . advice."

"Advice about what?"

"They'll explain."

"Why me?"

The snake swayed for a moment, considering his answer. ''Why not you?''

''I'm a financial guy. I buy companies and sell them. I don't see much use for that around here. This place is pre-industrial.''

''You have cunning. That's useful always.''

Cunning is a loaded word, like sly. I wasn't sure I liked a snake calling me cunning. ''I look for the edge, if that's what you mean.''

''That's a much better way to put it,'' he was soothing.

''How did I get here?'' Maybe the snake had some answers.

''Magic. What else?''

I scoffed. ''Nobody believes in that shit anymore.''

''They don't?'' The snake was surprised.

''Maybe where people are ignorant they still do. Not where I'm from.''

''Where's that?''

''The United States of America.''

He was silent.

''You probably never heard of it.''

''I am told only what I need to know. I'm a simple servant.''

Fake humility. Why use a snake to give a pitch, anyhow? Mogwert could use work on their image. You have to pay attention to that. I had the same agency that handled Donald Trump—incidentally, a nice guy who is basically misunderstood because of faulty PR strategizing.

''If there's no magic,'' the snake said slyly, ''what are you doing here?''

''Lately I've been wondering if somebody slipped LSD or something like that into my drink. Maybe this is a bad trip.''

''LSD?''

''It's a drug that makes you hallucinate.''

''Hallucinate?''

''It's like you're having a dream or something.''

He was amused. "You think this is a dream?"

"I don't know. How come I'm a dog, anyhow?"

"Ask Mogwert."

"Who are those guys, anyhow?"

"The winners. You care about winning, don't you?"

"It's the only thing, like Vince Lombardi said."

"A sorcerer?"

"A coach. One of the best."

He wasn't interested in Coach Lombardi. "Mogwert will be victorious in the battle to come."

"Over who?"

"The Two Legs, of course. The only opposition that remains. Mogwert will rule the world and all will bow down."

Quick whined.

"Why should I throw in with you guys? The Two Legs are people like me."

"Look at yourself. You're a dog."

"This is just temporary."

The snake hissed. I wondered if it was his way of laughing. "Why do you think that?"

"You mean it's not?" I fought the howl that rose in my chest.

"I'm only a servant. It's for Mogwert to explain."

"So what now?"

"Wait. When night falls, someone will come. You'll be taken to the mountains for the Final Council."

"What's that?"

"The last meeting before the war commences and the Final Victory is won."

What good does being rich and powerful do me if I am still a dog? I get all the bones and squeeze toys I want?

"Can Mogwert change me back?"

"Everything will be explained. That bag you're carrying belongs to Mogwert."

"I got it from a Two Legs."

"Mogwert want it."

I didn't say anything.

"The Two Legs don't know their end is near. If they had warning, it might delay the Final Victory."

"When those border guards don't show up, they'll know something is wrong."

"They'll wonder at the delay, no more. In the long peace they've become careless in the Fair Lands."

"If Mogwert are so strong and Final Victory is a lock, how come you need me?"

"You'd give us—what was your word?—the edge. You were human. You know how they think. In the past, our failure to anticipate Two Legs' thinking was costly. Victories in our grasp were . . . nullified."

So it wasn't as cut and dried as the snake said. Maybe the Two Legs had a chance. Before I decided who to throw in with, it would be smart to get a better handle on the odds.

As if reading my thoughts, the snake said, "It's hopeless for them. We—Mogwert—have assembled an invincible army, terrible to behold. None can stand before it. Your cleverness will enable us to achieve the Final Victory sooner. But, as I said, the outcome's not in doubt."

"I got to have time to think about it,"

"There is nothing to think about."

"He could decide not to join Mogwert," Quick burst in.

The snake looked at him, for the first time. "As your kind did long ago. Your historic error will soon become even more plain."

"Come on," Quick moaned to me. "Let's get out of here."

"I'm going to think about what you said," I promised. "Sit in the shade someplace and give it some deep thought. It might take a day or two."

The snake swelled. "It would be better if you came to us freely. The world is to be divided between masters and slaves. Conquerers or conquered. Up or down. Your choice."

"I'm going to think about it, honest."

"Leave the bag."

Quick and I trotted past him.

"LEAVE THE BAG!"

His shout was like a rifle shot. Quick and I both jumped.

"Maybe you should do as he says," Quick whimpered.

"Fuck him," I said. That bag had value. I learned a long time ago that if you part with something, make sure you get something back worth more. That's Business 101.

"Adios, pal," I said to the snake. He dropped to the ground and slithered after us with surprising speed. Quick and I broke into a lope to leave him behind.

Quick shuddered. "Snakes—somethin' about them."

We traveled in silence for a while. Repulsive as the snake was, I've seen its equal in the business world. You have to learn to get beyond appearance. Locke Hughes, who is chairman of one of the big merchant banks I use, is so monstrous-looking that little kids burst into tears on the streets. It is ugliness that is not just skin deep, either. It goes down to the bone. But you can't find anybody who can crunch numbers in his head better than Hughes. A mind like a mainframe.

"I hope he's wrong about the Two Legs bein' defeated," Quick said, as we trotted along.

"Thought you didn't like Two Legs."

"I don't. No use for them. They kill critters. But seems like they always have a purpose when they do, like us. Except when fightin' among themselves. Great bunches get together and fight like no animal you ever heard of. Just leave bodies lyin' where they fall and jig around like they're happy or crazy. Or dig holes and put the dead in so nobody gets the use of 'em. Mogwert're different. They don't fight amongst themselves, anyway nobody's ever seen 'em, but they kill other critters for the fun of it. Torture, too. And that's not the worst of it. They want to make you slaves. They'd be even worse if they weren't always wonderin' whether Two Legs'll come back from the Fair Lands one day.''

''Men,'' I said. ''Two Legs are called men and women.''

''Men. Women. That what they call themselves?''

''Yes.''

It didn't interest him much. ''Mogwert're all-powerful,'' he said. ''Or anyhow think they are, as you saw from Mr. Snake back there. They're as proud as the Dark One himself. But Two Legs—men and women as you call 'em—never bowed down to Mogwert, like just about everyone else. Fought 'em from time to time, according to legend. Then there was a big war a long time ago not won by either. Both crawled off in different directions. Then men, as you call 'em, fought among themselves back at that place where I met you, may the day be cursed. There's been peace ever since. I guess Mogwert went up into those mountains to lick their wounds and the Two Legs that survived their war went to the Fair Lands.''

He trotted along worriedly. ''Now it sounds like Mogwert're comin' down from the mountains.''

''Who's the Dark One?''

Quick looked scared. ''You don't talk about him.''

''You just did.''

''He makes bad things happen.''

''Is there somebody who makes good things happen?''

Quick looked at me like I was stupid. ''The Bright Giver.''

''Is it okay to talk about him?''

''He puts us here and takes us away when our time is done and The Call comes. He makes the rain that turns the land green and the sun that warms it so we can all eat. There are many stories about the Bright Giver. We'd be happy if it wasn't for the other.''

''The Dark One?''

''Yes.''

It looked like we were talking about the Devil. I never thought much about him—he's a guy, right? I figured the Devil for one of those fables or myths, whatever, that priests thought up way back when to keep people in line. Meanwhile, the popes fornicated away merrily, ate like pigs, and otherwise enjoyed themselves in ways not allowed the peons.

Where I came from we believe evil is the result of bad environment, inadequate nutrition, poor schools and that sort of stuff. This is why we have welfare and Head Start. You can go your whole life and not give a second thought to good and evil. The clergy is paid to deal with this so the rest of us can attend to practical matters. You can't be worrying about good and evil and get ahead in the business world, where you know who takes the hindmost. When I have a problem, there's only one question I ask—How do I solve it? Goodness doesn't enter into it, unless there's some PR angle you need to watch.

"What's the connection between Mogwert and the Dark One?" I asked Quick.

He said he didn't know. "But there must be one, the misery Mogwert cause."

We left behind the land that used to be settled and moved into woodlands dotted with meadows. It sort of reminded me of the Appalachians, where I went once to look at some coal mines for sale. I got a good deal and they returned a nice profit once we got some environmental laws repealed. Not all politicians are bad.

Every now and then I caught Quick looking behind. I finally asked him what the trouble was.

"We're being followed."

I looked around and worked my nose until it was flooded with smells—salamander in wet leaves, toadstools, a weasel that passed by a half hour or so ago, etc.—but I couldn't detect any menace.

"That bird's been watchin' us a long time," Quick said. He was looking at a big black bird staring down from a tree. "That ain't a bird's way. They mind their business and don't care about nobody else's."

When it saw us looking, the bird rose from the branch and flapped off. Big and black. Of course it would be a raven. I suppose Poe himself will step from behind a tree any minute now.

"That was what was watchin' us. Something else is followin' us," Quick said.

"I don't see anything."

"Nothing you can see. You have to be a fox to feel it."

A breeze picked up from the direction we were heading. It gathered strength by the minute.

"First a storm and now this wind," Quick groused. "Ain't normal."

"Nothing here's normal to me."

Pretty soon the wind was a gale and getting stronger. Trees whipped back and forth and flying grit filled the air. Quick's ears laid back flat on his head. "Any other time I'd say take shelter. But that'd give whatever it is back of us time to catch up."

Darkness started to fall and the wind continued to shriek. Small limbs joined the grit in the air.

"Let's keep going," I said.

We pressed on into the teeth of the wind. Every now and then you'd hear a crack and then a crash as a tree fell.

"We still being followed?" I asked after a couple of hours.

Quick stopped and turned in the direction we'd come. "Yup," he said after a pause. "Gettin' closer, too."

Whoever it was had to be pretty strong to remain upright in this wind, let alone make up ground. There was an outcropping of pale rock suddenly before us. It broke the terrible wind, and Quick and I huddled before it. "We can't stay here," Quick yelled. "It's getting closer." The rest of what he said was snatched away by the wind.

I stared back in the direction we had come. Something big and black moved toward us in the darkness. It had tiny points of cold blue light for eyes. When Quick saw it, he gave out a low moan and tried to squeeze behind me.

He couldn't because I was flattened against the rock. Whatever it was looked ten feet tall. Quick would be useless in a fight, so it was me against it. Christ! It would chew me up and spit me out like a cherry pit.

Then, suddenly, I was inside the rock, looking through a milky film at whatever it was barreling up. It was so ugly it made the Uulebeet look like a beauty contest winner. More like twelve feet tall, now that I had a closer look. People can't dream up something like this, so when I say it was worse than your worst nightmare it doesn't mean much. Take your worst nightmare and double it. Double it again and you still wouldn't get the picture. The creature was more a huge insect than an animal. A thick bony bridge stuck out over those glowing eyes. It had three fingers on each hand like pincers. Nostril holes rather than a nose and a mouth like a snapping turtle's.

Quick was cowering flat on the ground. The thing picked him up and ripped him apart quicker than it takes to say it. Quick's legs flew in one direction, his head in another and his torso in a third. Jesus, it was sickening. No sooner was he finished with Quick than he was looking around for me. Those cold blue eyes blazed.

They couldn't see me, though. As soon as I realized that, I started looking around. How had I passed through solid rock? It is a question I would have spent a lifetime puzzling over back home. But I've seen so many unbelievable things since I awoke running through the woods in this dog's body that I dismissed it. There was a faint light in the rock, just enough to show a narrow tunnel.

The thing outside was furious at not finding me. It attacked the rock with its beak and pincers, sending chips flying. In case it knocked a hole in the rock, I moved quickly through the shaft. It led downward at a steep pitch and after a few yards I was in total blackness. Dogs can't see in the dark any more than people can, so I would have been in trouble if it wasn't for a faint scent to lead the way. It was an outdoors smell; sun on grass describes it best.

Faint as it was, it stuck out in that sterile rock. I followed my nose, as the saying goes.

I felt bad about Quick, strange to say. I mean, what's one fox, more or less? Felicity has three or four coats made from fox in a large closet devoted just to furs, none of which she dares wear because of the animal-rights nuts.

I'm a lone wolf kind of guy. I don't mean now, but back before. Friends I don't need. Self-sufficiency is my credo. You make a friend, and you're creating a situation where sooner or later he touches you up, asks for a "favor." This usually means you have to reach for your pocket. But Quick wasn't a bad egg, plus he was company. At least he went without too much suffering. One second alive and the next scattered in pieces in that wind.

I don't know how long I was in that tunnel. I moved through it until I was tired and then curled up and slept. Then I woke not knowing how long I slept. This happened many times. If I was just taking catnaps, I could've been in there a couple of days. If I was sleeping regular, it had to be a week. After a long time the tunnel began to climb. Just when I was beginning to get scared it might not have an end, I saw a dim light ahead. I picked up the pace and the light got brighter. I passed through something that seemed as thin as the skin of a soap bubble and then I was outside, blinking in bright sun.

I looked back and saw I had exited a boulder the size of a house. I touched my nose to it and scratched with my paws but it was unyielding from this side. I was in a wood on a slope that ran down to a stone farmhouse with smoke coming out of the chimney. Brown cows grazed in a fenced field (they're as stupid as you've heard) and the sound of wind rustling through dry stalks came from a big field of corn. Not a bad layout, if rural is your thing.

When I got close I saw the fences were split logs stuck on notched tree trunks. They were the kind Honest Abe built.

The cows tossed their heads and stared with tails switching.

"Duh," one of them said. Horses? A little smarter, but not all that much.

The farmhouse had stone walls with lichen on them and a thatched roof that looked like a blonde on a bad hair day. Shutters hung from loops of hide. The wind came in one window and out the other. You could have light or stay warm on a cold day, take your choice. Hens squawked and ran and geese lowered their heads and hissed. A woman came outside to see what the fuss was about.

"Father," she called to someone behind her. "C'mere and look at this big old dog." She was barefoot and wore a long gray shapeless dress so worn you could almost see through it. Her face was deeply tanned and lined from the sun. Felicity avoids the sun like a vampire for this reason. She wears big hats and must have a hundred creams and lotions. Have I said she's got red hair? I can always pick her out in a crowd because she's the one who looks like her head caught fire.

Father came to the door. A thin, stringy guy in leather pants and vest that made him look like a Hell's Angel down on his luck. His clothes had a made-on-the-premises look. He was barefoot, too.

"Look at that bag in his mouth," the woman said.

"Ugly thing, ain't he? And big."

I laid the bag down and spoke in a civil manner. "I've come a long way. Could I get something to eat?" Maybe we could work a deal about payment. I could herd animals for a day or guard the chickens.

"What's that sound he's makin'?" the woman asked.

"Excuse me," I apologized. "It's been awhile since I used my voice."

"Never heard a noise like that from a dog. Sounds like he's tryin' to talk, don't he?" he said. They looked at each other and laughed. Most of their teeth was missing. The blackened stumps they showed as they cackled didn't look like they had much mileage left.

I made a couple more tries before it was clear they didn't understand anything. I could talk to wolves, foxes and snakes but not to humans. It made me feel as bad as anything so far.

The man made kissing sounds and snapped his fingers, meaning I should come closer.

"Biggest dog I ever saw," the woman said. "Bigger'n the Fodd's."

"Lots bigger," he replied. "Look at them eyes. I bet he's real smart. Wonder where's he from."

"He's comin' right up to you. Can't be that wild."

"Maybe his master's somewhere close by."

"Pa," she said, "wouldn't it be nice to see a strange face?"

"Don't start on that."

He scratched behind my ear. As much as I was in the dumps, I had to admit it felt good.

"He's waggin' his tail," the woman said.

I looked back. Goddamned if she wasn't right.

"Think he'll let you have that there bag?" the woman asked. "Maybe there's somethin' in it."

I smelled uncertainty. "I don't know about that. Looks like he's real attached to it." He yanked up on his pants and looked at me.

I growled.

"I ain't gonna chance it," Father said. "Not until the boys come down from the high parts with the sheep."

"He's gonna stay that long? He could be carryin' that someplace special."

"If he does, he does," Father said irritably, "If he don't, he don't. I'm not gonna chance losing a finger over somethin' might be worthless, us so far from a healer."

"Tell me how far we're from things," she said bitterly. It sounded like an old argument.

"Two more springs," he said tiredly.

"I'd never said I'd come if I knowed it'd be so lonely. I'd almost look forward to Mogwert just for somethin' different.'' She shivered. ''I don't mean that, but you see what I'm sayin'.''

His face was stubborn. ''They're payin' us well enough.''

''No place to spend the money,'' she flung back. ''Can't even hold it in your hand. Might as well not have it.''

''It'll be worth it when we go back. All that money saved up. Three hundred faloons.''

She swooped on the point. ''If we live to collect it. You've talked yourself about how strange the animals are actin'.'' They didn't look at each other and a bad-marriage stillness fell. She gave me a sharp look. ''And now this.''

Faloons—they have money, the first encouraging thing I've heard. A society with money is one I can figure out.

Father stared out toward the corn, looking for a way to change the subject. ''Sun's ripenin' it good. Be nice and sweet, worth a lot at market.''

''I think we should just walk away,'' she said with sudden spite. ''Take what we can and go. Let the crows get the corn. Or Mogwert, more likely.''

He shook his head. ''We'd lose everything. Not one faloon would we get. All this time out here for nothing. That's the agreement. We made our marks.''

A reference to literacy, or in this case its absence? The last time I saw marks mentioned was in ''Long John Silver,'' or whatever that kids' book is.

''Mogwert haven't been seen for years,'' he said. ''Might've died off even. The Border Rangers haven't seen them since long before I was at my mother's paps.''

''Died off,'' she said in an acid way that reminded me of Felicity. ''Sure they did.''

''No point in arguin' on it. We're here and that's that. Don't know how many times I've said that.'' He walked inside.

She started to cry. She looked nearly used up. It reminded me of a John Wayne movie where he said ''injun'' country was hard on womenfolk. Felicity and I watched a lot of videos, she in her study and me in mine. She watched women's stuff about feelings but I liked the Rambo and Terminator stuff.

"You want somethin' to eat?" the woman asked me, wiping her tears with swipes of her hands. "I'll get you somethin'."

She went inside and came back with a joint of beef. She tossed it on the ground. "Work on that awhile." She went back inside.

I gnawed on it. These jaws I have are real crushers. Dogs get dreamy chewing on a bone, I don't know why. It's mesmerizing, like a hypnotist who puts you under with a swinging watch. I forgot my problems for awhile. But when I finished they came right back, bringing a new one.

What happens if I get hurt? The man mentioned a healer, but it's probably some guy who paints his body blue and dances around in a mask. And even that would be for humans. A dog is on his own, I bet. Dying like a dog—there's a reason for that saying.

There are more ways to get hurt in the wilds than I like to think about. Step in a hole and break a leg and it's a death sentence for sure. But even a sprain would be doom because you couldn't catch anything to eat. Other risks—a snake bite, a big cat dropping from a tree and severing your spine with one bite. Or make a tiny mistake in timing when you pounce and get an antler or horn in your gut. No way you recover from that. Infection sets in and you're history. Lap up bad water and get parasites that weaken you and make you a mark. What about rabies and distemper, not to mention Mogwert and all those monsters?

It was getting on toward darkness when the man came to the door. "You want in?" He didn't have to ask twice.

I trotted in, pouch in mouth. I lay on the dirt floor near the fireplace. A pot hung from a hook over a nice blaze. I couldn't believe how great it was to have a roof overhead and not fear something out of the Brothers Grimm was sneaking up on me. I dozed, aware that the woman who slapped around in bare feet as flat as pancakes made supper. The man sharpened a spear.

Primitive living, bad as it is, is a giant step up from life as an animal. But maybe it wouldn't be smart to hang around. No telling how far behind me Mogwert's stooges were. Plus, the sooner I checked out how strong the Two Legs were, the sooner I'd know who to cut a deal with.

"Real quiet tonight," the man said, coming in with a pail of milk so full it slopped on the dirt floor.

"Is that speckled hen laid yet?"

"Nope."

"She goes into the pot tomorrow." The woman stood tiredly at the fireplace, stirring with a spoon. "Sit down. It's no good cold."

Stew of some sort, meat and root vegetables. She plopped it onto wooden plates with a hand carved spoon. Milk, still warm from the udder, was splashed from the bucket into wooden cups. They sat down, not bothering to wash their hands. Did they know about soap? Tallow candles sputtered on the rough table, making shadows jump. Outside the light faded.

The woman had a point. Living out here in the boondocks, you were a kind of distant early warning system. Three hundred faloons must be a lot of money, at least from Father's point of view. As much as he could hope to make in a lifetime? You'd have to raise the ante pretty high to get takers. Typical of women, she was willing to walk away. A lot of women have strange ideas about money. Not Felicity. I exaggerate only a little when I say she spends money as fast as I make it. I'll give you an example. A couple years ago, the place next door came up for sale and she wouldn't shut up until I bought it. I had to go to Europe for a few weeks and when I came back the big house that used to be next door was gone and a lake framed by transplanted trees where it used to be.

"What happened?" I asked the morning after I got back.

"I never could stand it. Too big and gloomy."

"You had it moved?"

"Nobody would've wanted that old thing."

"You had it knocked down?" I had trouble taking it in. "That place was worth five point two million." I think there was a quiver in my voice.

"That included the property." She was doing her nails. She held her hand out and squinted at them.

"There was a house there—a goddamned mansion—and now it's fucking gone. What about the Historical Register?"

"What about it?"

"That place was on the Historical Register!" I was yelling now. "You have to tell the goddamned federal government if you're going to change the paint on the front door, much less tear the fucking place down." I felt veins pound in my forehead. This was massive coronary territory.

"Oh, pooh. It looks much better from the library with the lake there. The swans are from England."

There was no point in arguing. Felicity tuned you out. The federal government fined me one hundred thousand dollars for tearing the house down. Architectural Digest said I was worse than a barbarian.

"Oh, pooh," Felicity answered when I told her about the fine. "I spent that much on an antique French boiserie yesterday." I didn't know what the hell that was, so it started another argument.

Father leaned back in the chair and belched, showing he had finished eating.

"That mean you liked it?" Mother asked in that sweet voice women use when they're sticking the knife in.

"Would've said so if I didn't." He looked at me. "Shall we let him stay in tonight?"

"I don't care." She was scraping food from the plates back into the pot. Breakfast tomorrow, I guessed. Lunch after that and dinner again. I thought about the splendid meals I've had at some of the world's great restaurants—rack of lamb at Entrecôte de Paris came to mind—and I whimpered.

The man was looking at me, sucking what teeth he still had. ''No. He might shit.'' He opened the door. ''Git.''

I trotted outside with the pouch. The first thing I saw against the moon was the silhouette of that big black bird in a tree. I yelled a few choice words. Asshole, shithead, cocksucker. It looked down, cool as a cucumber.

''Why's he barkin' at that bird?'' the woman asked.

''Maybe he don't like birds.''

The bird sat silently, not moving. Its feathers were so glossy they reflected the moonlight.

It would fly back to its masters and report where I was. My guess was it had been looking for me ever since I disappeared into in the rock. Or maybe it was a different one; they all look the same to me. The man and women were silent.

''We have to leave,'' she suddenly burst out. ''I have a feelin'. Somethin' bad's waitin' to happen.''

''That's just women's fears,'' he said, but he didn't sound so sure. ''Let's get inside. I'll put the second bar on the door and windows.'' The door slammed shut and I was alone.

The moon and stars were so bright you could've read the Racing Form. I had a Thoroughbred once that finished fourth in the Preakness. Horse racing was one of Felicity's enthusiasms for a time. She said we met a better class of people. She meant the owners, most of them members of the idle rich. Not that I have any prejudice that way. Damned nice people, most of them. You meet the occasional bad egg, just as in any other group. It's the same as saying not all the poor are lazy. Some work hard but have bad luck. A small minority, I admit, but you find them if you look hard enough.

The pouch swinging from my jaws, I headed into the corn field. The raven would lose sight of me in the rows, which stood six feet high. They cut off the light from the night sky and I moved in darkness through the stalks. They rustled as if restless. The rustle was from gnawing rats and other vermin. The couple and their boys up in the mountains would be lucky to split the crop fifty-fifty with the pests.

It took fifteen minutes to get to the other side, where the long grass began. I trotted, alert for game. Bones are a good chew, but like Chinese food they don't stay with you. It was warm and the sound of hunting owls came to me. With those around, the raven might stay put rather than follow me. I saw an owl in the moonlight crouched over a long-tailed mouse. He looked big as a cat and willing to mix it up to defend his meal. "Keep away," it hissed.

I pushed on rather than maybe lose an eye over that mouthful. Toward midnight I caught a weasel. Tough little buggers, all muscle. Look out for the scent glands near the anus. While I was licking my chops, I saw faint points of light moving in a grove of oak trees. I pricked my ears and stood still, trying to make out what it was. There was the hint of something nice in the air, like lavender or rose. I don't know much about perfume other than the more it costs the better women like it. But this wasn't perfume—more a natural smell, very light.

I did my predator's belly crawl through the grass to get closer. Now my ears picked up singing by tiny voices, real silvery. It sounded nice but I had learned to be suspicious. I watched the lights whirl as if they were dancing with one another. Then one separated from the group and headed straight for me.

"What are you looking at, dog? There's nothing here for you." It hovered a few feet away. It was a tiny female no bigger than a firefly wearing what looked like a gossamer gown. Her wings beat so fast you couldn't see them.

"I'm not a dog. I'm a Two Legs."

Instead of scoffing or laughing, she was sympathetic. "A spell?"

''One minute I'm in my world and the next thing I know I'm running through the woods looking like this.''

Her tiny face looked thoughtful. ''Poor thing. We've heard Mogwert have grown strong again.''

''They wiped out some Border Rangers. I'm carrying this bag from one of them to the Two Legs. People, I mean.''

''To Gowyith.''

''What's that?''

''The city of the Two Legs.''

''Is it far?''

''Far enough.''

''Are you fairies?''

She laughed. ''It's not what we call ourselves, but it's as good a name as any. Come and greet the others.''

I followed her to where the fairies or whatever they called themselves danced. They broke off to swarm around me, calling out welcomes in tiny tinkly voices. There were forty or fifty of them, the males in tunics with daggers the size of bee stingers at their belts.

''We come out every night at this time to sing and dance,'' said the one who had come out to meet me. She told me her name but it was as long as ten regular names and sounded like a brook running over stones. I'll call her Fairy A.

''What do you do the rest of the time?'' I asked.

''We play or sleep.''

''Nice work if you can get it.''

''Work?''

''It's something we do where I came from so they can tax us.''

''Tax?''

''That's when somebody takes what they figure is their share of what you've earned by the sweat of your brow.''

''Without permission?''

''Don't make me laugh. They throw you into jail if you don't pay.'' I've spent a fortune on accountants and lawyers fighting the I.R.S. You can't win against those bastards.

''They sound like Mogwert.''

''You've got the right idea.''

''Tell us more about your world.'' One by one they dropped down with folded wings on grass stems that bent beneath their weight. If you've ever seen dragonfly wings, that's what theirs looked like.

''It's got big cities, cars, freeways, television, movies, consumer goods—anything you'd want.''

''What's a city?'' asked a guy fairy who I'll call Fairy B.

''A place with tall buildings and lots of people.'' I thought I'd keep it simple.

Fairy B made a face. He was so small I almost missed it. ''Sounds noisy and dirty.''

''That's cities for you. But if you've got money, they're not bad. Get a nice place with security, a car and driver, and they're livable. A car's something with a motor that carries you places, like a wagon without the horses. A freeway's a road you can go real fast on.''

We had what Felicity calls a pied-a-terre but I call an apartment near Central Park. We stay there when she wants to go to the opera or has tickets to another goddamned charity ball. She'd drag me to one a week if I didn't put my foot down. If it isn't Jerry's Kids, it's AIDS or some tropical rain forest being bulldozed. I've given to every bleeding heart cause in the world, including funds to protect endangered species so ugly they deserve to die. Don't get me wrong about Jerry Lewis, though. I know the guy personally. The funniest man in the world, take my word for it. When he does his spastic number, you're on the floor. Our apartment on the eleventh floor has fourteen rooms, about twelve more than we need. It has a saluting doorman and valet parking.

I gave the fairies the low down on television and the rest of it and life in general in the Big Apple. A pretty good presentation, if I do say so, but after awhile they seemed more polite than interested.

''So if you ever get there, be sure and look me up,'' I finished up.

There was a doubtful silence. ''How will you get back?'' Fairy A asked.

''You know any wizards or anything like that? If somebody or something did this to me in the first place, it can be undone.''

''There are many wizards,'' said Fairy A. ''Some are real, some false. Some are great, some are not. Some are good, some evil.''

''I don't want to waste time on phonies, but good or evil don't matter so long as the job gets done.''

They were suddenly still and watchful and I realized I'd made a goof.

''Did I say *doesn't* matter? I meant does. It makes a big difference. I don't want anything to do with bad wizards even if it means I have to spend the rest of my life here.'' The thought of that brought up a whine I couldn't keep a lid on. Luckily, the fairies thought this showed I was sincere and relaxed again.

They went back to singing and dancing, whirling just above the ground. Fairy B and I watched from the sidelines. It got a little boring after awhile.

''You guys seem real happy,'' I said, making an effort at conversation.

''We are. We celebrate each day the Bright Giver grants us.''

''Yeah? That's great. We could learn a thing or two from that.'' I yawned.

Felicity could learn from them for sure. ''Another day,'' she says with this flat, unhappy voice. Her problem is she could have damn near anything but doesn't know what she wants. It's odd that with the problems I've got right now I spend so much time thinking about Felicity. She wouldn't think so, though. She'd see it as natural.

Normally, I would have found out more about these little guys. I've got a talent that way. I arrive at a strange place, pick somebody who looks like he's got time to kill and pump him. You learn a lot not in the guidebooks that way.

But I couldn't afford to waste any more time with fairies.

"Well, I have to run."

"You'll get there faster," Fairy A said. Full size, she'd be a knockout if she could lose the wings.

"That's an expression where I come from. It means I gotta go."

"You want to see Helither. We've known him a long time. He is good, not like Zalzathar."

"Who's he?"

"He counsels Mogwert."

"Where do I find Helither?"

"In Gowyith."

I said see you later and left. Dancing fairies—another one for the book. I looked back once at them, little points of light spinning in the darkness.

The ground started rising again and I moved through pine trees that gave way from time to time to meadows of ferns and croaking frogs in mossy ponds. I caught a couple before they could plop into the water. Not bad, though they would have been better in a sauce.

At dawn I reached the top of a knoll and looked back. There was a big column of black smoke rising in the distance. It was right about where the farmhouse would be.

[5]

The pines and meadows gave way toward afternoon to a lonely high plain. It looked like hard winds blew through here. Everything was stunted and leaned in one direction. Which reminds me of a problem. Back home the media tells you what the weather's going to be. Here you don't know until it happens. Trot along dry as toast and an hour later thunder booms and rain pounds down.

To human ears the plain would seem silent, but mine picked up all sorts of sounds. Most of all, the insects: boring, chewing, digging, fighting, copulating. That is one of Felicity's words. I come to her bedroom at night and she looks at me with her amazing green eyes, sighs tiredly and says, "Does this mean it's time to copulate?" She knows it's part of the deal but lets me know she doesn't have to pretend to like it. Makes a person feel exactly one inch tall.

Insects are never at rest, especially ants. Always running around like those traders on the exchange. You would think they would have accomplished more in the time they have been on Earth. I had plenty of time for deep thoughts like that.

Other sounds: snakes slithering over hard ground, birds chittering to each other, rodents scampering and squeaking, pods blowing open and scattering seed. With these pricked ears, I can even hear the tiny blue and violet flowers toss in the wind. There were a few clouds high up that looked like the garlic potato puffs at Maxim's. I am tormented by memories of food.

Traveling close to the ground, you see things you'd be too high to notice on two legs. Horned toads blend in so well you wouldn't spot them nine out of ten times. Not that it does me any good. Foul-tasting things.

You see rocks with sparkly bits of mineral in them and other stuff that is sort of interesting when all you are doing is putting one paw in front of another, pacing yourself because you don't know how long the journey will be.

I was dozing under a thorn tree in mid-afternoon waiting for things to cool off as I digested a fat grouse when I heard something heavy shuffling my way. It was a huge bear, shaking his head as if he was puzzling over epistemology, a word I learned at one of Felicity's salons. A bunch of professors enjoyed a grand feed at my expense as they gassed about this and that. An argument about epistemology broke out. I couldn't make out what they were talking about, so I excused myself and looked it up. It means how people know what they know, a topic maybe one hundredth of one percent of the population is interested in, and that's being generous. I went upstairs before dessert and watched *Mondo Love*, a video from the adult movie club I belong to. Epistemology. Funny how memory comes back bit by bit, no pattern to it that I can see.

Anyhow, the bear spotted me and stopped in his tracks. "*Hoof*," he wheezed. "Where'd you come from?"

"A long way from here." Why get into it?

He looked at the feathers around me. "Ate a bird, did you? I can't catch 'em. Too fast." He had a deep voice, like Uncle Remus in a movie I saw when I was a kid.

He sat down as if he was tired. "Real hot today. I'm headed for the high country. Where you bound?"

"The city of the Two Legs."

He looked at me closer. "Oh, you're a dog. Thought you were wolf. Dogs be frien's with Two Legs, wolves don't. I throw in with 'em on that, though them and me ain't what you'd call close. Put a few together and they think they somethin'."

He looked at the pouch. "That somethin' to eat?"

"No."

He lifted his muzzle and worked his nose anyway. It told him I was telling the truth and he grunted with disappointment. "Been tryin' to get across the hot place fast as I can beat my feet."

I guessed he meant the plain. "What's your rush?"

"What I been hearin' and seein', thas what."

"Tell me more."

"Mogwert're comin' back after all these years. The other night I saw a Gutter, which I done thought was daid. My momma tol' me 'bout them and her momma told her. Scared me half to death. I tol' myself better shag ass up to the high country. I ain't stopped since, 'cept to do some fishin' in Wide River to comfort my belly. Salmon's runnin' good. Wisht I coulda stayed longer."

It must have been something to have scared this guy. I bet he was eight hundred pounds. Big teeth and claws like yellow steak knives.

"What's a Gutter?"

He stood to describe it. "And a mouth like a snappin' turtle." He was talking about the fiend who tore Quick to pieces.

"Seen two more of 'em since. Don't come out till dark. My momma said her momma told her they don't like the light none."

He dropped down on all fours and had a look on his face. As soon as I dropped my head to pick up the pouch, he charged. I just did manage to dodge clear. He came so close I got a blast of his rotten breath. He lumbered off without looking back. No matter how friendly they act, you can't trust anything here. Except the fairies, who are so small they can't do you any harm. Or good, for that matter.

I figured the Gutters—the name must come from what they do to you—are looking for me everywhere. So travel by day is best, even though it means those black birds can spot me better. When the shadows got long in the afternoon, I looked for someplace to hole up for the night. I took a long look around to make sure nothing was watching, then plunged down into a narrow canyon filled with trees and fanlike ferns. There was a stream on the floor of the canyon and I walked in it so the water would carry away my smell. An old Indian trick I learned from the movies. A quarter-mile into it I came to a little waterfall that rushed over a big boulder. Beyond the curtain of water there was a deep shadow that made me wonder if a cave was there. There was. It had the smell of big cat inside, but it was old. I circled three times in case snakes were in the neighborhood and lay down. As usual, it was lights out within seconds.

I woke up to a sound that pierced the noise of the waterfall. Something screaming in terror. I crept to the opening in time to see a big cat dash into a clearing below chased by something huge and dark. Don't let it be coming here, I thought.

If that was the cat's intent, it wasn't fast enough. It whirled and crouched, ready to attack. It was one of those big spotted bastards with tusks. Anything normal would not dream of tangling with something as mean-looking as that, but the Gutter waded in with utter silence. The cat raked it with its claws but they didn't even leave a mark. The Gutter pinched off a leg and the cat screamed and spun like a top. Then multicolored guts were flying in all directions. The whole canyon was stunned to silence. After the cat was ripped apart, the creature looked around with those eyes like laser beams and then up at the pale moon. It seemed to shrink from the light. I squeezed my eyes shut. If it was coming for me, I didn't want to know. The seconds and minutes dragged. When I finally opened my eyes it was gone. For a long time there was only the sound of the waterfall. Then the normal noise of the canyon started up, frogs croaking, owls hooting and the rest of it. I was shaking with fear.

I wondered as I cowered what Felicity was doing. Does she visit me in the hospital, if that's where I am? I doubted it. But she'd want to know if I was going to be a vegetable for the rest of my life so she could get control of my money. She would listen to the doctors explain my condition and nod, but she'd give me a pinch when no one was looking to see if I was faking. Why did I marry such a cold bitch, you ask. For a lot of reasons. I first saw her in a photograph in *Architectural Digest.* She was in a big castle in Italy, the home of her first husband. He was an elderly count, a member of an ancient family. The photograph showed her leaning on a balcony in a gown the same green as her eyes. There was a fantastic view of the Mediterranean behind her, and its blue light washed the walls. The grand room that led onto the balcony was filled with carved furniture and paintings by Flemish masters. A gleaming suit of armor stood in a corner holding a battle axe. Although it looked like a warm day, a fire burned in a fireplace big enough to walk into. You couldn't begin to calculate how many thousands of peasants were sweated into early graves to pay for that opulence. Old money doesn't have to worry. It has forgotten the crimes the ancestors committed. With new money, the memories are all too clear, especially if you're under indictment.

Felicity's first husband died two years after they married. It was rumored he was worn out, spent by her sexual demands. That talk was encouraged by the string of lovers she took after the count was laid in his grave. I have wondered from time to time if she cheats on me. The detectives I hire never turn up anything.

Like a lot of those Italian families with titles, there was land and grand houses and servants knuckling their foreheads, but not much ready cash. This soon was a problem, Felicity's tastes being very expensive. She's originally from Maryland, where her father raised race horses with Wall Street money. He was one of the wise men who came out of the woodwork to give advice when Republicans got the

White House. His payoff was appointment as ambassador to second-rate countries where Felicity picked up her royal airs. You were expected to call him Mr. Ambassador, even after he retired to his horse farm. He was opposed to her marriage to the count and her second one to the heir of an Irish brewing fortune. He died of a broken neck in a fall from a horse in a fox hunt when some animal-rights crackpot jumped out from the trees and scared the beast. They found Felicity making out with a baronet when they went to break the news. By the time she got to me, her father was confined to a wheelchair from a stroke and didn't know what day it was.

"Dad wouldn't like you," she told me. Felicity didn't hold things back.

"He could join the club."

Was it too late to go back to the mountains and turn myself in? I could claim I misunderstood the snake. His word against mine. Jesus, if they want me this bad, why not bow to the inevitable? But the situation hadn't changed. You go with who does you the most good, and I still hadn't checked out Gowyith in the Fair Lands. It would be stupid to throw in the towel now. Besides, these Gutters just might have orders to wipe me out wherever they found me, never mind if I was coming back to give myself up. My guess was more were behind me than ahead.

I crept out of the cave when the sky lightened. I had to go some distance before I got beyond the bits and pieces of the cat the Gutter had flung around. Farther on I came across what was left of a skunk, after that a moose and a rhinoceros. Those aren't supposed to share the same continent, let alone the same canyon. But as I say, nothing surprises me. The rhino's horn had been wrenched from his head and thrown a hundred yards.

I traveled through the day into country that grew increasingly beautiful. Meadows filled with blowing flowers, rushing streams, tall trees. It would have been pleasant if I wasn't always looking over my shoulder. I caught a chipmunk at the edge of a pond and made a meal of him. As I crunched the meager bones, I thought of the roast lamb at the Four Seasons. They treat you like a king if you come in regularly. Raw chipmunk gulped down still hot with life isn't the same thing.

Out of the corner of my eye I saw something glide through the pond, making a V in the water. I waited on the chance it was a beaver or something else edible. A huge mouth full of teeth came boiling out of the water. I moved even faster than when the bear chased me. It was an alligator a good thirty feet long. It gave up the chase almost immediately and slid back into the pond, water pouring from it. It looked as big as a submarine and was so heavy it left grooves in the mud. My heart pounded so hard I was afraid it would burst.

Later, I passed through cultivated fields. Hay and barley and other crops I didn't recognize. I saw a pretty little village, smoke rising from chimneys. Maybe two hundred brick homes, small with steep roofs and each surrounded by its own garden. White picket fences in front, cobblestone streets. What a glad sight. My heart rose. When I got closer, the steps in front of each house looked as if they were scrubbed daily. The doors were stout and had polished knockers. The homes had windows with small panes. Most had vines climbing on them. Wander in the wilderness dodging ugly monsters and you'll know how relieved I felt. I bet there were big beds inside with goosedown pillows. But I supposed dogs wouldn't be allowed on them.

People strolled the streets, looking astonished and apprehensive as I padded past. They were plump and kindly-looking, the way people look when they're not getting a pounding on the urban anvil every day. The women had sensible bonnets above long dresses and the bearded men wore homemade trousers and shirts, boots and caps. Many smoked small pipes. It must have been a holiday, judging from how nobody was working. From what I guessed was a pub came good smells. Not much happened here, that was plain. Everything ordered, each day like the one before. Did they have a surprise coming.

I crossed a narrow street to cut off a yellow dog. He saw me coming but pretended to smell a bush in hopes I'd pass by. He cringed when I loomed over him.

"Excuse me," I said. "What's the name of this place?"

"Belyrie," he said faintly.

We smelled each other's anus. For dogs, it's like shaking hands.

"Where're you from?" he asked.

I gave my stock answer. "A long way from here." We touched noses. "You live here?"

"My masters are the Styries." He said this in a way that told me I should be impressed. "They have the biggest house in the village. The handsomest horses and nicest wagon. You have to watch out for Bas, who pulls on the side the driver sits. He kicks. What's that you're carrying?"

"Something for . . . my master."

He turned his head so I could admire the white ribbon around his neck. "I know lots of tricks. I can roll over, walk on my hind legs and bark for bones."

"That's swell," I said. "Where's Gowyith from here?"

"I've never been there. The wagon goes and comes in four suns when my master has business there."

His ears pricked and I turned to see what he was looking at. It was a cat strolling with insolent slowness. He was off like a shot and the cat ran for it. They disappeared around a corner.

I looked around the village until I saw there was no police headquarters or military outpost where I could drop the pouch and its dispatches for whatever credit I'd get. I found a place to dig a hole and pushed the pouch in, nosing dirt over it. No sense to risk losing it. I was pondering what to do next when a door opened and a stout, bald gentleman well into middle age came out to look at the sky. He was wearing rolled-up sleeves and suspenders that held up pants that looked like they began life carrying potatoes. He saw me after he nodded approval of the weather.

"Well, you're a big one."

He reached his knuckles toward me. His hand smelled like cornbread and jam and his morning pipe. He had twinkly eyes and a rosy face. His baldness made me remember my hair was thinning in real life. I had been wondering whether to go the transplant route. When I asked her opinion, Felicity was watching an Oprah program about men who wanted to be women. I remember when people kept that sort of thing to themselves. Bald as an egg or hairy as an ape, she answered, it was all the same to her.

"How'd you get your nose so dirty?" the man asked. "Digging where you're not supposed to, I bet. Hungry?" My tail wagged on its own. I was used to it by then.

"Come in then. I've got something from last night's dinner that might interest you." He didn't have the hillbilly manner of the farmhouse people. I wondered how long it would take before it was discovered they were dead.

I followed him inside. The rooms were small and fussy, full of handmade furniture with big pillows for cushions. He led the way to the kitchen, where wood snapped and crackled in a fireplace. He opened a door and disappeared down a cellar that smelled of spices and apples. When he came back, it was with a big bone. "I was saving it for soup." He stooped stiffly and put it on the plank floor in front of me. I set to hungrily.

He relit his pipe, sat down in a chair and was watching me lick my chops when the front door opened. He got up with a guilty look as a bony old woman with a face as sour as a pickle bustled in.

"The Bright Giver above," she cried, taking off her bonnet. "You're feeding a dog off the floor?"

"I was going to clean up after."

"Clean up! You've never cleaned up in all the years I've

known you, and I bet all the time you were married to your poor suffering wife on top of that.''

She picked up a broom and gave me a wallop.

''Here now,'' the man said. She wheeled on him, and I thought he was going to get it next.

''No need to get yourself excited, Famzel.''

''Excited? I've been cleaning your house eight full turns of the seasons now. Hard enough at my age to keep a bachelor's house clean, him not too careful where he drops his boots; and them most likely carried in something nasty from outside. I come back after a week and it looks like you've been cooking for all of Belyrie. Pots and pans all crusted over and nothing where it belongs. I took this job when Idi died because I felt sorry for you. But I've been thinking it was time you got somebody younger. And then I come to find you feeding a dog on a floor I've spent more hours on my hands and knees making shine—I thought . . .'' She gulped and burst into tears.

He was thunderstruck. ''Why, Famzel, I didn't know I was such a burden.''

She pulled out a bandanna and sobbed into it. ''I was happy to do it when I was able.''

He looked relieved. ''Why, if you're not able any longer you mustn't do it.''

She stopped crying. ''You're sure?''

It was clear they'd both be happy to end the arrangement. It's funny how people get stuck in ruts.

''I'm sure,'' he said, beaming. ''I'll get someone else. Better yet, I'll do it myself.''

''You?'' She couldn't have been more doubtful.

''You're not to worry any longer,'' he said briskly. He dug in a pocket. ''Here's your full wage.''

''No, I really couldn't,'' she said. But she took the six-sided coin he offered. After a lot more asking if he was sure, she was gone. The door was no sooner shut than he broke into a dance. He laughed like someone who had just walked through the prison gates to freedom.

''Hee hee, that woman'll never be in my hair again!'' He patted my head. ''And I owe it all to you, my friend. I've been wanting to get rid of her for years. I couldn't bring myself to do it. She thought she was doing me a kindness with her damned fussing.''

He looked around. ''Look at this place. You're afraid to even sit down for fear of putting something out of place. I always heard about it if it was.''

None of the men I've seen here are big, averaging maybe five foot eight. He was a trifle shorter than that and had a pot belly. His pants were blue, his shirt a faded yellow with a wide collar. Boots sturdy, handmade. The general look in the village is like where people yodel to each other across alpine valleys.

''Time for work,'' he said, putting on an apron and heading to the back of the house. ''Come on.'' Toenails clicking on the polished floors, I followed him through the back door toward a large shed.

''My workshop,'' he said, unlocking the door and waving me in. His name was Helmish, as I was to learn. He talked to himself—not like the crazies you see on the streets, but like people who live alone and get into the habit.

He looked around proudly. ''This is what they call the crackpot's roost. You might want to keep moving when you find out what the rest of Belyrie thinks of me. Crazy's one of the nicer things they say. They think I'm wasting time. Fooling around with silly stuff when I ought to be working the land.''

He looked at me. ''You never get anyplace worrying what others think. People's herd animals, most of 'em, just like cows.'' The workshop was full of junk, hand tools and stuff. There were thick pieces of glass lying on benches and tables and leaning against walls.

''They focus light. You could take the light from one candle and send it far as the farthest house in this village. Each one I finish is better than the one before. You wonder where I get the glass? I find a new square waiting outside my door whenever I finish one. I've tried catching whoever leaves them, but never had any luck. He's too smart for me. So now I don't bother watching or wondering. I just accept what I'm given, as the Bright Giver wants us to.''

He spent most of the morning polishing glass with a gritty powder, humming as he worked. I lay under a table, fagged out.

Afterward, he fooled around in his garden until lunchtime, pulling weeds and telling the vegetables they were doing mighty fine. I half expected them to answer back.

When I followed him inside at lunch, Helmish forgot to scrape the dirt from the garden off his boots and tracked it across the floor. The old woman would have a heart attack.

He cut thick slabs of bread and stuffed meat between them and ate standing, a contented look on his face. He looked at me. ''Folks say don't feed a dog more'n once a day. But you look like you've been doing hard traveling.'' He cut a chop and tossed it on the floor.

After lunch we napped. He lay down on a sofa after pulling his boots off and put a handkerchief over his face. I dropped off myself. I saw a Gutter coming in a dream and must have yelped because he tossed a cushion at me. ''Quiet, will you?''

He got up, pumped water into a sink and washed. ''Time to go down to the square,'' he said as he ran a wooden comb through his fringe of gray hair. ''Once a week a rider from Gowyith brings tidings.''

Helmish rattled on about this and that. I wondered if his wife was talked into an early grave. ''Most weeks it isn't worth the walk. The rider doesn't have anything more interesting than some farmer out towards the Dales put up eight dozen jars of apples from one tree, or some lie like that. Never known a farmer yet who told the full truth, though I suppose anything's possible. Births, marriages and people dying you never heard of. Or proclamations by the Curiam upping the levies, which now take one faloon in thirteen." He put on his coat and walked out the front door, snapping fingers for me to follow.

We walked through the village, Helmish lifting his hat to the bonneted ladies we passed, and arrived at a grassy square. Pipe-smoking men stood around shooting the bull.

I heard funny cracks about Helmish, which either he didn't hear or pretended not to as we moved through the crowd. "What're you inventing today, Helmish, a machine that will fly like a bird?" Yuks and backslapping.

There were a lot of comments about me, too, mostly about how big and ugly I was.

"He's big enough to saddle and ride. Famzel know you got a dog?" More laughs, Helmish oblivious to it all. He sat on a rude bench that creaked under his weight and looked around benevolently.

"A fine day," he said to me. "Say, you don't have a name yet."

W. B. (for Bogart) Ingersol, I said. It came out *woo-woo*, whine.

"I'd almost think you were trying to talk. Big. I think I'll call you Big, on account of that's what you are." He looked as proud of this inspiration as one of Felicity's writer friends. Their thin books are full of sour characters who talk about the pointlessness of everything. No action or plot that I can see when I riffle through them. They look at you with exaggerated surprise if you mention greats like Dickens. Not that I've read anything other than *A Christmas Carol*, and that for a school play when I was a kid. But mention his name to these schmucks and they smile with pity, as if you said you watch professional wrestling for its truths. As for their "great" conversation—the reason Felicity takes them up—it's mostly snide gossip and putdowns of other writers.

After a while, a dusty man on horseback cantered into the square on a lathered horse. He had a helmet with wings and wore pantaloons and a mesh tunic. There was a sword at his belt and a shield behind the saddle. A pewter mug of something foaming was handed up to him and he drained it like he was in a chug-a-lug contest.

He wiped his mouth and began to drone through the news with a deep voice like Walter Cronkite, if you remember him. I saw what Helmish meant. Sheds that burned down. Minor plagues of insects. Livestock that had strayed and rewards offered. Litters of puppies, no reasonable offer refused. A new bridge across the creek at Hornley, barley in bales for winter feed now being sold in Fletchly.

''They always get their crop in first,'' Helmish remarked loudly. ''They're not lazy, like some I could name.'' Dark looks were thrown his way. I was half dozing, head on paws, when the courier said, ''And lastly, the Border Rangers still haven't returned.''

''Sitting on their butts in some nice spot where the hunting's good,'' said the wit who had made the comment about the flying machine.

Laughter.

''We shouldn't pay them half what they ask,'' another man said, glowering.

''They're dead, you fools,'' I shouted. It came out a series of yaps and yodels.

''You tell 'em,'' the wit cried. When vaudeville comes in, this guy will be a headliner. Helmish looked embarrassed for me and heaved himself up off the bench. ''Come along, Big.'' We threaded our way through the crowd and walked to what looked like an alehouse off the square. It had beam ceilings, was dark and smelled of onions, pickled pig's feet and tobacco smoke.

''Best mulled queeg this side of Gowyith, and I'll bet the other side, too,'' he told me as he settled into a chair.

The aproned owner brought a tankard. ''None of your arguments and calling others stupid just because they don't agree with your line of thinking,'' he said to Helmish. He had a long jaw and a squint.

''Now, Balrothye, I'm the most easygoing man a

week's ride of here. I don't argue, I merely correct ignorance."

"Others might not be as clever as you—not saying you're any smarter than anybody else, mind you—but that don't give you the right to throw your head back and laugh at what people say. Makes them mad. Mad people find other places to drink queeg."

He walked away, making swipes at tables with his cloth. But from where I lay on the floor, it didn't look like sanitation was a major concern there. Bones, hard crusts of bread and other stuff fallen from plates or spewed from mouths—people here chew and talk full throttle—lay everywhere. The place filled as men pressed in from the square to discuss the news. Helmish sat by himself, smoking his pipe and taking everything in.

As a topic, the Border Rangers were down the list after the insect plagues and the new bridge. "About time they put that up," said a party with a toothbrush moustache nearly hidden by a big nose. "Most rainy times it's worth your life to ford the crossing. I lost a team and wagon three years ago and I wouldn't be here today if the river hadn't took pity and throwed me on the shore."

Helmish finished his queeg—nasty stuff, from the smell of it—and got up. He left, paying no mind to the jokes about hitching me to a wagon and saving himself a walk home.

He walked in silence for a while. "A worrisome business, Big, that patrol still out. These people think because Mogwert have not been heard of for so long there's nothing to worry about. Mogwert'll fix that some day." He stopped. "The way you're looking makes me think you understand."

Then he laughed. "They'd really think I was queer if they could hear me talking to you." On the way back to his house, I had a scuffle with a cur that came out of his yard stiff-legged and baring teeth. I sent him *ki-yiing* off. When we got back to Helmish's house, he put on his apron and went out to the workshop. He muttered to himself as he rubbed glass with the polishing powder. "Can't get that

patrol out of my head. Could be the lazy fellows are sitting next to a lake piling up field pay, like Falrod said. They wouldn't be the first nor the last, rangers being no better or worse than they ought to. By the Red Star in the sky, I'm nearly out of grit. I'll have to go into Gowyith for more."
I dozed off.

I had been on the run ever since I came to in the woods near that village of old hags. No telling how many miles I had gone. Hundreds, maybe. Everything had gone so fast I hadn't had time to think. So I decided it was a good idea to kick back and regroup until I got my bearings.

[6]

I fell into Helmish's routine as the days passed and tried to discover what I could about these people. As I said, order and routine were big. Early to bed and early to rise. At the crack of dawn, a reeking wagon creaked down the streets and women came out of the houses with buckets and chamber pots and dumped them in the back. Fires were started and the smell of cooking spread. Men rode off to work in the fields after breakfast along with the boys old enough to help. Women and girls cleaned the houses. Felicity would call this sexist. She and her feminist pals are big on that subject. The women shook rugs and swept with handmade brooms. They washed sheets in big pots heated over fires behind the houses. They baked twice a week, using niches in the fire-places as ovens. When the work was done, the women made calls on one another. They sewed while they gossiped.

The men and boys came home around sunset riding the big horses that pulled the plows in the fields. They washed up and sat down to tables. Dinner was ready by the time they arrived. After it was eaten, the wooden dishes and spoons were washed and not long afterward everyone tumbled into bed and the village was dark. When people say they'd like to go back to simpler times, they don't know what they're talking about. You do one of three things in simpler times. Work, eat or sleep. I'll take New York.

Once a week, people dressed up and went to what I guessed was a church. It had a crude carved sunburst on the sloping roof. As I lay outside in the shade, they sang or listened to somebody talk to them in a bullying way. But others in the village followed a man who wore a mask and dressed all in green out into the fields. He spoke under a canopy of cornstalks. I gathered each crowd thought the other followed a false god.

Every two or three days, a hunter pulling a two-wheeled cart stained dark from dried blood came to the door to sell game he had killed. Helmish was a big eater, so he was always a customer. He'd point out what part of the deer or elk or whatever he wanted, and the hunter hacked it off in the front yard as flies buzzed. Helmish took the meat down into his cellar where it was cool. He put away groceries in such quantities food didn't have time to go bad. Peddlers also came by with eggs and fresh vegetables. Helmish bought the vegetables if they weren't ready to be pulled up in his own garden.

One day a couple weeks later, I opened my eyes after a snooze and he was looking out the window at the twilight.

"That's the third time I've seen that bird flying overhead. He's circling like he's looking for something," Helmish said. I padded to the window and looked out. "Never saw one like it before. Black as the inside of a cellar with the door shut."

It was the raven that had been following me, or his twin brother. It slowly flapped over the west end of town. I ducked back from the window.

"What's spooking you, Big? Not afraid of a bird, are you? Ha ha ha!" His eyes returned to the raven. "Interesting things, birds. Nobody pays 'em much mind, but they'd be a fit subject for study. I don't have time and nobody else here has the brains. Cows, pigs and crops—that's their speed. It's different in Gowyith. People think big there."

It seemed from his tone that he had a pretty good opinion of Gowyith, same as we do of Paris or London, to name two of my favorite cities. Rome's not far behind. They may not have the sizzle of the Big Apple, the capital of the world in the humble opinion of yours truly, but they've got history going for them. No way those old buildings could be put up today, costs what they are and the unions. I pointed that out to Felicity once when I went with her to Paris for the spring collections and her annual fleecing by the fags. Spoken like a bean-counter, she said.

"If you earned the beans, you'd count them too," is what I should have answered, but it didn't come to me until a couple hours later. "Staircase wit," the French call it.

That night, Helmish was snoring away, sounding like he was clear-cutting timber under the quilts. I was lying against the wall under the window of the upstairs bedroom worrying over what was happening with some deals I had in the hopper back home. When my ears picked up a small noise outside. I would not have heard it if I wasn't a dog. A tree branch rubbing against a smooth surface in a light wind—that's what it sounded like. When I didn't hear it again, I silently got up on my hind legs and hung my head out the small window.

Across the cobblestone street, just visible in the faint light from the stars, a Gutter was peeking into a second-story bedroom window. From that angle, I saw it had a segmented tail that snaked out behind for balance.

My hackles rose—you can't control that any more than keeping your tail from wagging—and I felt a rumbling rising up from my doggy depths. I was just able to stifle it as the Gutter bent over as if bowing and peered into a downstairs window. My nose and ears told me there were others out there prowling around. Cats were aware of them, of course. Not much goes on at night they don't know. But they watch silently, looking out for themselves. Wait for a cat to raise the alarm and you'll wake up to find your throat slit and the silverware gone. The Gutter straightened and turned toward Helmish's home, pale blue eyes glowing. I cowered beneath the sill.

A house-by-house search of the whole town? There had to be too many houses for them to peer into on the off chance of spotting me, unless there are a host of them. If that's so, the game is over. The Two Legs wouldn't have a chance. But maybe the circling bird Helmish saw spotted something. Maybe the two of us have been together so much somebody put two and two together and guessed I'd be with him and so they had a rough idea where he lived.

As these thoughts flashed through my mind, I heard the Gutter move across the street, its horny feet nearly as silent as a cat's. It stopped just outside the window and I knew it was looking in. If it had the slightest suspicion I was there, it would tear down the wall to get at me. Acrid gusts of breath from its nose holes moved the curtains above my head. It tried to raise the window higher to stick its head in for a better look, but it wouldn't go any farther. When Helmish gave off an even louder strangled snore, the Gutter stood silent and watchful. When it was sure Helmish still slept, it silently stole away to check out the house next door.

[7]

I doubt I closed my eyes even to blink for the rest of the night. I strained to hear from my spot under the window, and my ears picked up stealthy sounds now and then. A couple times a faint breeze brought the scent of a Gutter hunting a few streets away.

A faint dawn came, and when roosters began to crow I figured I was safe for now. But that wasn't much comfort. Mogwert were upping the ante. It was as if they didn't care anymore if people knew they were on the move. I was kicking myself again for not agreeing to the deal the snake offered when Helmish gave one last gulping snort and awoke.

He stared at the ceiling for a minute and then threw the quilt back. "Good day to you, Big," he said cheerily. "What do you suppose the day holds?"

Death and dismemberment are good possibilities, I thought. He struggled into a robe like a pelt and slid his feet into rawhide slippers. He came rosy-faced to the window and looked out. "A fine morning."

I followed him down the steep staircase. "I suppose you'll be needing to do your business." He unbolted the front door and opened it. I stood in the doorway and looked around. I didn't see any black birds, but that didn't mean one wasn't spying from a tree somewhere.

"What are you waiting for?" He put a foot to my rear and pushed. "You act like you're afraid of something."

That made him laugh. Such a jolly man. He shut the door.

I lifted my leg against his picket fence. When I was finished I decided it was time to show Helmish the leather pouch with the dispatches. These yokels needed to know what hell was on the way. I padded down the dew-damp cobblestone street toward where I had buried it. There was only the faintest trace of Gutter in the air and then it was gone, overpowered by the rising smells of early morning. Blue smoke rose from chimneys, and a breeze brought the thick smells of paddock and stable. As I trotted, dogs whirled in frenzies in windows and yapped from behind the safety of gates. Their owners yelled at them.

When I came to the spot where I'd left it, the ground was dug up and the pouch gone. A gray cat watched from under a bush.

''Who did this?'' I asked.

''Did what?'' she asked lazily.

''Dug this hole.''

''Rats, I expect.''

''Did you see them?''

''I suppose I did.''

''What happened to the pouch?''

''What do you mean, pouch?''

Her slow drawl irritated me. ''It was animal hide and had papers in it.''

She stretched. ''I suppose the rats took it.''

''Where to?''

''Not far.''

''Show me.'' Maybe they hadn't chewed up everything.

''I can't.'' She nestled down with her tail curled around her feet.

''What do you mean, you can't?''

''I can tell but I can't show.''

She was playing with me the way she would a mouse.

''Tell me, then.''

''They gave it to someone.''

''Someone?''

"Someone very scary."

My heart sank. "What did this someone look like?"

"Very big. Very dark. Its eyes looked like there was light in them."

I trotted back to Helmish's house. The last time I felt this low was when my lawyers said even before the trial was over that they had a shot at getting my conviction reversed. Funny I could remember that but not what I got nailed for. The lawyers had even started mentioning how nice the federal minimum security prisons were.

"Rape isn't all that common," one said to buck me up.

Helmish was making breakfast. I scratched at the door and he let me in. "I heard dogs barking," he said. "Guess you stirred them up pretty good." He chuckled and went back to churning something in a pot on the wood-burning stove. When he was done he glopped it into a bowl and put honey and sugar on his. My portion went into another bowl as is. It tasted lousy. I thought about Spago's in Beverly Hills and Stars in San Francisco. They know me and I get good tables.

Felicity likes to be on the move. London, Paris, Rome, Barcelona. The Coast twice a year, where she hangs out with the Hollywood crowd. People beg her to stay with them and sometimes she does. But mostly she takes a suite at the Beverly Hills Hotel, where porters struggle with her vast baggage. I travel with her when I can, but she doesn't let me interfere with her routine. She goes to ladies' luncheons where they fall into each other's arms with little screams. They make plans there for dinner after the cocktail party. She goes to gallery openings and has coffee with a pet writer or a professor to get her deep conversation fix. I generally cool my heels at the hotel with the baskets of fruit and flowers she receives. Women love her because they know Felicity will stay married to my money, meaning they don't have to worry about their husbands or boyfriends. Men flock to her for the obvious reasons—beauty and fame.

Everybody loves Felicity. People were always telling me how lucky I was.

"So's she," I pointed out.

I keep in touch with business by telephone, fax and computer. Otherwise, it would be pretty dull. I wonder why I bothered tagging along. We do have breakfast together.

I had no sooner lifted my nose from the bowl when there came a knock at Helmish's door. A skeletal man with a body amazingly bent and twisted stood there. He leaned on a crooked walking stick and had a face that was all angles, as if drawn by a cubist. The thick hair that lay lankly on his long narrow head may have been washed at some point in the last couple of months, but I doubted it. He was the real-life crooked man who lived in the crooked house on the crooked street. I had been wondering if another storybook character would show up.

"Yes?" Helmish said. He turned to me. "Big, stop that growling. What's wrong with you?"

"Excuse this intrusion at such an early hour," the crooked man said. "May I come in?"

"Step right in, stranger," said Helmish, the genial host. "We've just finished breakfast. You're welcome to some if you're hungry."

"Thank you, no." He stepped in, leaned on his stick and took a slow look around, as if memorizing the place. He had one of those faces so full of cunning nobody could possibly believe anything he said. Nobody but Helmish.

"Don't mind the dog," Helmish said. "He won't hurt you."

"Yes, well, it's about the dog that I come. My name is Sterngeld. Heffernan Sterngeld."

"Pleased to meet you, Mr. Sterngeld. Helmish is my name. Faborten Helmish. The dog is yours? He showed up a while back. I fed him and he decided to move right in."

"My dog?" Sterngeld seemed surprised this would go so easily. His bony hands with their strange knobs washed one another. "Yes, he's mine. The rogue broke loose from my wagon."

"He's a big one. What breed?"

"He's . . ." Sterngeld hesitated over his witticism, then surrendered to it with a snicker. "He's one of a kind." He shot me a gloating look. It said you could run but you couldn't hide.

Helmish sat down in a chair, crossed his legs and loaded his pipe. "Where're you from and where're you headed?"

Sterngeld looked evasive. "East headed west." There was something about him, I realized. Shame. It hung on him like a smell. But that figured. He was a renegade Two Legs who had thrown in with Mogwert. I felt a contempt rising; then I remembered I was thinking of doing the same thing. But there was a difference. I was an innocent victim, torn from my world and thrown into this one as a dog. All I wanted was to get back where I belonged. He was part of this freak show. A big difference.

"Where in the east?" Helmish asked comfortably. It was clear he had no objection to a long gossip. "And where in the west?"

"Out Bournwye way," Sterngeld said vaguely. "Got sheep there."

"That's a long way you've come."

"And a long way to go. I wonder if I could trouble you for the animal now."

Helmish seemed not to hear him. "Bournwye. I used to know people there. The Cloggs. Yes, that's the name. He's a grain trader. Steal you blind if you let him, but a nice fellow for all that. You'd know him sure."

Sterngeld shifted uneasily. One eye was higher than the other and both looked in different directions. "Met him once or twice. Nice fellow, like you say. I best be on my way."

"I'm not stopping you," Helmish laughed. "Be on your way and the Bright Giver bless you."

Sterngeld took a step toward me and I rose with my teeth

showing. "Doesn't appear to care for you very much, Mr. Sterngeld," Helmish marveled.

"Headstrong," the crooked man said uneasily, "that's his trouble."

He didn't come any closer. "Is there a place you could keep him 'til the sun is straight overhead? I've got friends coming."

"Clogg," said Helmish. "He still got that red hair? Or I bet he's gone bald by now."

Sterngeld was looking at me with fear. He turned to Helmish. "Red hair—yes, he still has it. A little gray, but not much."

Helmish's face darkened. "I think you'd better leave, Mr. Sterngeld."

"Leave?" His mouth dropped open.

"Leave before I set the dog on you."

"Wait a minute, that's my dog. You can't . . ."

The crooked man half turned as I lunged. I sank teeth into stringy buttock and he shrieked.

"Big!" Helmish roared. "Turn him loose!"

I gave the crooked man a couple shakes, then let him go. He took a swipe at me with his crooked stick but missed.

"There's the door," Helmish said. "Use it."

"All right, I'll go," Sterngeld said at the threshold. "But I'll be back and you'll be sorry." He shook his crooked stick and limped away holding his butt with one hand.

"The man's a liar, Big," Helmish said as he lighted his pipe. "Clogg had blond hair when he was alive. He's been dead these five turns of the seasons."

I was impressed. It might seem you could pull the wool over his eyes, but apparently he was shrewder than he looked. He watched the crooked man limp down the street until he was gone.

"Wonder what that's all about," Helmish spoke in the voice he used for talking to himself. He looked at me. "It's a pity you can't talk, Big. You could tell me." He bent and scratched me behind the ears.

"He's a cruel master, I suppose. No wonder you ran away."

He touched a match to his pipe and looked like he was about to forget the whole thing. But I remembered what the crooked man said about friends coming when the sun was overhead. I whined to get his attention and looked him right in the eye. When I had his attention, I scratched at the door.

"You want out, Big?"

He opened the door and I took a few steps out into his front garden. I paused, looking over my shoulder.

Helmish laughed. "Well, the Bright Giver bless me if it doesn't look like you want me to follow you."

"That's exactly what I want, you idiot."

"Barking at me now." Another laugh. "Have it your way. Lead on, I'll follow."

I trotted across the street to the house opposite and stopped at the gate. When Helmish reached me, I cleared the gate with a bound, ran to the house and looked back at him. Helmish let himself in and walked to my side.

"What is it, Big? A wounded critter . . ." He fell silent when he looked at the flowers crushed by the Gutter when it peered in the window. The flattened blooms outlined the Gutter's claw print clearly.

"Look at that. Looks like an animal's footprint, doesn't it? But no animal's that big."

I barked at him, jumped the fence and ran back across the street to his house. Helmish followed. I stood alongside the footprint the Gutter had left in the clover beneath his bedroom window.

"Another one," Helmish said slowly. "This is strange."

I barked again and led him down the cobblestones. At every house I was able to point out a footprint.

"Stranger and stranger," Helmish said. "It must be some sort of prank, though I can't think who'd do it or why."

On our way back we passed homeowners in their yards puzzling over the footprints. Little kids jigged and yelled in excitement. "You want to see somethin'?" a man in a leather jerkin and a hat called to Helmish.

"That's not the only one," Helmish replied.

A long pause as the man digested this. "What do you make of it?"

"I don't know."

"It was mighty heavy to leave a footprint that deep."

They drew on their pipes and stood in halos of smoke as they studied the ground. After much head-shaking, they agreed it was a puzzlement and knocked out their pipes. Helmish walked thoughtfully back.

He climbed the stairs at home and I followed. "I don't like it, Big. Months go by—years!—and nothing out of the ordinary happens. And now you show up, we hear the Border Rangers are still overdue, a stranger comes to town looking for you, and something leaves big footprints all over town."

He packed a battered old cowhide valise as he talked. He shook out what appeared to be his best clothes from a little closet and carefully put them in. He stuck in two pipes, a bag of tobacco, a thick blanket, and various other items. He went downstairs and tossed a loaf of bread and cheese wrapped in a cloth on top of the clothes and filled a jug from the pump and stoppered it. Then he reached up on a rafter and took down a bag that tinkled. He tied it around his neck.

"Ready for Gowyith," he announced. He looked at me. "You want to come, Big?"

He locked the door and we left. We walked across town to a stable where chickens scratched in the dirt and horses stamped. Helmish went inside and came out after a minute, followed by a man stuffing his shirt into his trousers.

"No wonder nothing gets done," Helmish grumbled to himself. "People lying in bed until the morning is half gone."

The sleepy groom harnessed a brown horse to a two-wheeled cart with a hood and handed the reins to Helmish.

"Don't push her too hard, hear?" he said.

Helmish ignored him and climbed onto the cart. "Giddap," he said, touching the horse with a whip. The cart lumbered off slowly. We left town and entered the woods, following a sandy path rutted by use. The woods smelled nutty and green. Helmish got his pipe going and leaned back in his seat, the reins loose in his lap. I looked for ravens but didn't see any.

At noon we stopped for lunch. Or Helmish did. When he showed no signs of sharing his, I went hunting. After twenty minutes I managed to catch a squirrel dashing on the ground from one tree trunk to another. His mate screamed from a limb.

"Killer! Murderer! Meat-eater!"

I slunk away guiltily. She was right, of course. But it's a jungle. Eat or be eaten. Vegetarianism isn't an option for me just now. That made me think of the great vegetarian restaurants in New York, especially around the village. Maybe I'll swear off meat when I get back as a kind of penance. Only eat chicken, fish and pasta, like Felicity.

"Red meat is so disgusting," she says. Even when she makes a face, she's beautiful. *Life* magazine is planning a spread on the twenty-five most beautiful women in the world and wants her to pose. Felicity is thinking about it. She likes the idea because she is a publicity hound if she can control the spin. But she doesn't want her English period dug up again. I know what she means. The media never gave me a break.

Helmish had left by the time I got back, but my ears picked up the cart's creaking and I followed the path. When I rounded a curve and saw it through a screen of trees, I froze. Sitting on the hood of the cart where Helmish couldn't see it was a big raven. I sank to my belly, then followed the cart after a moment. The bird stuck its wings out from time to time for balance. It shit and a line of white dribbled down the hood. Its head moved watchfully side to side. Was it waiting to see if I'd show up?

Afternoon came and light slanting through the trees turned gold from motes in the still air. Helmish stopped the cart to give the horse a breather and stepped down. The raven didn't move from the hood, maybe thinking Helmish wouldn't see it. But when he walked around the cart to look at the axle, he spotted it.

"Would you look at that?" Helmish said aloud. "That's something you don't see every day." They stared at each other for a long moment. When Helmish stooped, the raven knew what that meant. It flapped into the air, easily dodging the stone.

The two of us watched it fly east. When it was gone, I trotted to the cart. "There you are, Big," Helmish cried. "I thought you'd deserted me. The oddest thing just now. There was a bird riding on top the cart. I don't know how long it'd been there . . ."

He stopped suddenly and gave me a keen look. "That's the same bird that had you ducking and hiding." We looked at each other.

"What is it, Big? I know you want to say something. Your eyes tell me."

"All hell is about to bust loose," I said. The words rushed out. "Monsters and fiends and Mogwert are on the way. I'm not a dog. I'm a human being like you. I have to find somebody who can change me and get me back where I belong before it happens."

Helmish shook his head. "Listen to him bark. The poor dumb thing wants to talk in the worst way."

He touched the horse with his whip. "Giddap." The nag sauntered forward, taking his time. Helmish looked up at the afternoon sky. "We'll reach the Inn of the Hare about sundown. I hope they've got a bed for me. I'm too old to lay on straw in the barn."

I moved into the woods and kept pace with Helmish, quietly threading my way through the undergrowth. If the raven came back, it would see only Helmish and the cart.

They moved so slowly I lay down now and then for forty winks.

Once when I woke up, a huge stag stared at me from a dozen feet away. He was too big for a deer. Maybe he was an elk. He shook his rack.

''Wolf or dog?'' he asked. For all his size, he spoke in a high tenor.

''Dog,'' I said, getting up. If he charged, I wanted the chance of ducking out of the way.

''You killed the squirrel?''

''It wasn't me.'' Never admit anything.

''The tree creatures are upset. It happened a few hours ago.''

Maybe he was some kind of animal sheriff. I thought of being tossed on those antlers.

I had an inspiration. ''Lots of strange and bad things go on these days.''

He seemed to relax a little. ''It's true. Many strange things. I'm moving deeper into the forest. Things are not safe anymore. Strange creatures are seen.''

''You mean Gutters?''

''I don't know them.''

''Huge things with claws and beaks. Eyes that shine in the dark.''

He shivered. ''Thanks be to the Bright Giver, I haven't seen anything that horrible. What I've seen is bad enough.''

''Mogwert? You seen them?''

He stepped back, shocked. ''You mustn't say that name. Nobody speaks of them.''

''Why's that?''

''Saying their name might bring them.''

They're on the way, pal, I thought. You better get really deep into the forest.

''What I've seen are bad enough,'' he said again. ''Dark creatures with small horns and pig faces. They run on four legs but can stand like the Two Legs. Their front feet are like hands. They have a terrible stink. They run in packs.''

"When did you see them?"

"Last night and then again this morning. They moved through the forest alongside the Two Legs road just like you."

"Headed in what direction?"

"Same as you."

"Are they big?"

"About your size. A little smaller perhaps."

I didn't say anything.

"You notice how quiet it is?"

I did now.

"Creatures are staying in their holes. Some are digging them deeper. My kind are staying clear of the meadows. Everyone is waiting."

"For what?"

"For something bad to happen."

I left him to catch up with Helmish. The forest was watchful, as the stag said. At the same time my ears picked up the sound of the cart, I caught the scent of something nasty. I slowed and moved more carefully. I passed through some fanlike ferns and saw it.

It was one of the things the stag had described. It peered through leaves at Helmish and the cart. What a stink it gave off, like maggot-infested garbage mixed with rotten eggs.

It had billy-goat horns and the pig face the stag described. It stood on its hind legs for a better look. Then it dropped down to all fours. A swollen purple ass like a baboon's stuck out beneath a stub of a tail. It moved silently through the trees, keeping pace with Helmish.

He was looking around as if he felt uneasy. He touched the horse with the whip from time to time and it broke into a shambling trot for a few yards.

Pig Face was so intent on Helmish it didn't hear me stalking. My mind went on automatic pilot the way it always did when I was hunting. Everything disappeared from my peripheral vision as I focused on the creature. The closer I got, the more nauseating its odor. Even Helmish must have smelled it through his pipe smoke. It may have heard me just before I leaped because its head half turned. I saw one malevolent eye under a thick outcrop of bone. It had a tough hide, but my teeth found the spinal column beneath thick neck muscle. A quick shake and it was finished.

I looked around for others. But the forest was empty and the creak of the cart was the only sound. I trotted down to the road and stopped in front of the cart so that Helmish had to rein in the horse.

"Big. What're you doing there?"

"Get down off there and follow me. I want to show you something."

"More of your barking. Well, I've learned to pay attention." He climbed down from the cart and tied the reins to the hand brake.

I moved toward the body of Pig Face and looked back over my shoulder.

"You want me to follow you. All right, here I come."

He plowed through the undergrowth after me. "Whew. What's that rotten smell?"

I stood by the body until he reached us.

"Bright Giver above!" Helmish said when he saw it. "What vile thing is this?"

He held his nose as he studied it, walking around the body to look at it from all sides. "Never was such a creature seen." He looked at me. "Did you kill it, Big?"

"It didn't commit suicide," I said. "And there might be more around."

He looked at me, trying to figure out what I was saying. "No. Bad as it smells, it's been dead some time. You came across it and thought I'd be interested. I wish there was a way to bring it along to show folks, but I couldn't bear the smell."

He looked at it some more and then snapped his fingers. "C'mon, Big. Let's go."

He crashed through the undergrowth back down to where

the horse stood with tail switching in front of the cart. He snorted and rolled its eyes at the smell that wafted from us. "Bad stink," he muttered.

"Tell me about it," I said.

Helmish climbed back up to the seat and said, "Giddap."

"More strangeness," he mused. "What an awful-looking thing." He looked around. "Never known the forest to be so quiet. I'll be glad to get to the inn."

I left him talking to himself and moved back into the trees on a parallel course. I worried about running up against more Pig Faces. If they showed up en masse, I'd duck out. Helmish was a nice guy, but I looked out for No. 1. Don't tell me you wouldn't do the same in my shoes.

The Pig Face obviously was left behind to keep watch. For what, though? Mogwert had the raven tailing Helmish. It would report that he was moseying along this forest track. There were no intersecting roads that I had seen, so they knew where he was going to wind up. The Pig Face I killed probably was backup insurance.

I didn't like the looks of that. It said Pig Faces could plot strategy and had a social discipline superior to that of wolves. There was no telling how they'd measure up in a fair fight. The one I killed didn't have a chance, which is the kind of fight I like. It was clear, though, that those horns and ugly tusks weren't just decorations. The stag was right; the front paws were like hands. Monkey hands.

The afternoon passed with no more unpleasant surprises. The moon was rising when the cart came out of the trees into a meadow. Set in the middle of it by a pretty little stream lined with cottonwoods was an inn built of stone and timber. "Got here later than I thought," Helmish grumbled. "This horse might be good for something, but I can't think what."

Smoke rose from chimneys and yellow lamplight showed from the inn windows. As we drew near, a gang of yapping dogs rushed out. One look at me and they kept their distance, woofing insults and warnings under their breath as they circled stiff-legged.

''Better not fool with me or you'll learn a lesson you won't forget.''

''You may be big but I've licked bigger.''

I ignored them. Helmish drove the cart past the entrance and around to the back where a stablehand gaped at me until Helmish spoke sharply. ''Stop staring and see this horse gets a rubdown and a good feed. We've got to get to Spyngle tomorrow.''

The inn was hazy with blue pipe smoke and noisy with traveler talk. No one paid any attention to Helmish and me. He settled with a heavy sigh into a chair near the fire and I took up a place under the table. I put my face on my paws and went into a semidoze.

I had a lot of deals cooking before I was snatched. No earth-shakers, but big enough to hold my interest. Finding an undervalued company and taking it over is a little like being a detective and a little like being the general of an invading army. You plow through stock listings and annual reports looking for the kind of conservatively run company that has lots of cash tucked away. Its shares don't trade very much because dividends are low and performance is on the dull side. What this is is a company pretty much run for the benefit of management. They pay themselves very handsomely, thanks to a board of directors drawn from the executive ranks of other companies, meaning people just like them. If I can't get a board to pay me to go away, and many are just stupid enough not to go that route, I file a notice with the SEC saying I'm interested in a hostile takeover. Stockholders see an immediate jump in their shares as the Wall Street sharks climb on for the ride and pretty soon they're pulling for me. They call and send faxes. You feel like a conquering hero.

Heavy footsteps approached. ''Yes sir, and what can I do for you tonight?'' a hearty voice asked. He was a thick man in an apron and rolled-up sleeves.

"A tumbler of queeg now and a meal and a room later if you have it," Helmish said.

"I can do all that. You almost always have to sleep in the barn arriving at this hour. But as it happens, we have plenty of room tonight. Kind of odd."

My ears shot up at this and Helmish straightened in his seat.

"Strange? How do you mean?"

"I've got five rooms vacant and two for ladies. They should all be full at this hour. Traffic on the road's fallen off today for some reason."

"The forest was real quiet."

"That so? A queeg was it? Coming right up."

"More strangeness, Big," Helmish muttered.

The innkeeper returned with a foaming can of queeg and plonked it on the table. "Possum stew tonight. The best you ever tasted."

"I've got an appetite that will do it justice." Helmish hesitated over his question. "Have you heard of any reports of strange things?"

"What is that under the table?" the innkeeper said in amazement. "Strange. That's the strangest thing I've seen."

"It's a dog," Helmish said with irritation. "What does it look like?"

"You could slap a saddle on it and ride it like a pony."

"I can't tell you how many times I've heard that," Helmish rasped. He stuck his nose into the queeg. The innkeeper moved off, still goggling. He told the others and pretty soon everyone was pointing and marveling.

"You'd think they had never seen a dog before," Helmish complained. Then, standing, he said in a loud voice: "As far as strange goes, this here dog is nothing compared to what I saw today."

There was a silence before someone said, "What'd you see?"

"A thing in the woods five or six miles east. It had a

face like a boar and horns like a goat. Hands like mine, only longer.''

A few beats passed before the laughter began. Pretty soon the room rocked with it. Red-faced, Helmish sat down and stared wrathfully into his queeg.

The mirth trailed off at last and the men returned to their talk. Now and then one looked at Helmish and laughed again.

''I thought the people of Belyrie were ignorant,'' Helmish said to himself. ''They're book scholars from Gowyith compared to this lot.''

He looked up sharply as a stranger stood by the table. ''What do you want?''

''Can I sit down?'' He was small and fair and looked nervous. He twisted a cap in his hands.

''Suit yourself,'' Helmish said grudgingly.

The fair man eased into a chair and looked around as if afraid he'd be overheard. ''You know what you said about a creature lookin' like you said it did?''

''What about it?''

''I saw somethin' like that today.''

Helmish said, ''Why didn't you speak up when all these strawheads were laughing?''

The stranger was embarrassed. ''I didn't want them laughin' at me, too.''

Helmish took a long, slow drink and when he put his queeg down it looked like he had recovered his good nature.

''Well, can't say that I blame you. Nobody likes to be laughed at.''

''It's the truth.''

''Where'd you see it?''

''It wasn't one. It was five or six. They were hidin' in the trees three miles west of here.''

''Five or six?'' Helmish whistled. ''What do you think of that, Big?''

''That your dog's name?''

"He's not really mine. He just showed up at my doorstep."

"You gave 'im the right name for sure."

Helmish waved that aside. "Tell me more."

"They was hidin', like I said. I saw 'em out of the corner of my eyes. I didn't turn my head to let on I'd seen 'em. I was scared so bad I nearly dirtied my pants, if you know what I mean."

Helmish ignored this. "You are a wagoneer?"

"Yes. There were three of us. The other two haven't showed up yet. I'm kinda worried." He looked around nervously again. "My team's the fastest but not that much. They shoulda been here an hour ago."

"You ought to tell somebody."

The fair man shrugged. "Who? There's nobody here'd care they're late." Another look around. "And I wouldn't want to say what I saw after what happened to you."

"The innkeeper says he's got five vacant rooms that normally would be filled."

The fair man didn't see the connection. He scratched an unshaven jaw. "I don't know about that. We take our meals here when we come through. It's a break from travel rations. But we sleep in the wagons."

The innkeeper announced that dinner was served and everybody tramped with a maximum of noise to a room with a long table. Dishes lined sideboards. Plates were passed and when the innkeeper ladled stew onto them they were hauled back down the table. If there were women at the inn, they took the meal into their rooms. Felicity would never stand for that. She would dominate the room, seeing to it conversation kept a high tone. She'd be tested by this lot, however. They were as common as dirt; rough sorts who swore and blew their noses with their fingers. Helmish sat among them like a martyr, eating silently and ignoring their digs.

After he ate, he came out of the dining room and snapped fingers at me. We walked to the kitchen where he exchanged a coin for a mutton leg about to go into the soup pot.

"Here, Big," he said. He walked outside to smoke a pipe and I followed with the leg in my mouth. He sat on a tree stump and watched as I crunched bone. The moon didn't have much effect against the night that pressed in. As I shook dust off, I caught the faint scent of Pig Face.

"What is it, Big?" Helmish said as I growled. He knocked out his pipe and stood up. "Is something out there?"

"If you're smart, you'll get inside, pal," I said.

Helmish looked around. The smell got stronger. I trotted toward the door of the inn and looked back at him.

"I know what that means." Helmish followed me. The travelers were back in the tavern part of the inn, drinking and talking loudly. I headed for the stairs and looked back. Smarter to be in an upstairs room, I thought. Helmish spoke to the innkeeper, got a key and mounted the stairs after me.

"It's outrageous what they charge here," he muttered. "Two faloons. The man should be out on the road with a mask on his face." He closed the door and locked it but didn't put the bar down until I stood and looked at it.

"What a nag you are, Big," he said with a sigh. "I've got nothing worth taking the trouble to steal."

"What about your life, stupid?"

Helmish looked at me thoughtfully. "What I wouldn't give to know what you're saying."

The room was a little bigger than a closet. Helmish complained to himself. "Two faloons and barely enough room to turn around. The bed nearly fills this wretched space." He opened the small window.

"That's not a smart idea," I said.

"Stop that barking. The innkeeper will throw us out." He looked at me. "If you think I'm going to try to sleep in this close room with the window shut, you can think again."

He sat on the bed, which sank under his weight. "I'll

have a backache tomorrow.'' He groaned. ''Two faloons!''

He undressed, blew out the lamp and lay down. His noisy snores began almost immediately. The smell of Pig Face glided in through the window and the yard dogs began woofing. Then they broke into wild barking. Then they were fighting for their lives.

Ears pricked, I heard the travelers below fall silent. Then they were outside and the Pig Faces were at them. Boozed up and unready for fight, they screamed and yelled curses, Helmish snoozed on.

He was snoring so loudly it was hard to make out what was happening below. When I die, I hope I go like that. One minute sawing logs so loudly the china rattles and the next a blood vessel in the brain blows out. You would never know what hit you. Sound sleepers don't know how lucky they are. Felicity uses a mask, ear plugs and a pill if Leno and Letterman strike out. I don't need much sleep myself. Five hours and I'm ready for the day. That's in the real world. As a dog, as I say, I'm always napping.

Two possibilities, I thought. The Pig Faces slaughter everyone or the Two Legs beat them back. In the first scenario, they'd come looking for me when everyone was dead. In the second, I'd climb down the stairs with Helmish in the morning and watch him stare around in dumb amazement.

Furniture was being smashed and thrown around below. I could wake Helmish by dragging him from bed by his nightshirt. But why bother? He might blunder into the hallway to see what was going on. I didn't want to have to fight my way through reeking hordes of Pig Faces just to get to a place where where I could make a run for it. They weren't much, but the lock and the bar on the door were better than nothing.

After a long time, the yelling and furniture-smashing stopped and an expectant silence fell. I didn't have to wonder who won for long. Snuffling sounds came upstairs. Rooms were entered and torn apart. The Pig Faces communicated with grunts and snorts.

"*Snooort, uh-uh, squeeeeee.*"

"*Snuffle, wheeee, squa-squa.*"

The doorknob turned and then the door was shaken. "*Snortle-qua*?" said a voice.

The pounding at the door woke Helmish. "Wha?" His hair stuck up as he sat up. "Who's there?"

The Pig Faces began a high-pitched squealing so bloodthirsty my hackles shot up.

"Get away from that door, damn you to the Dark Place. I'll have the innkeeper on you."

There was wild scratching and clawing at the door. It dawned on Helmish that something was wrong.

"What's going on? Who's there?" he asked me with a scared look. There wasn't any point in answering, even if he could understand me. There were sounds outside the window. Monkey hands appeared on the window sill, followed by a hideous leering Pig Face. It squealed in triumph and started to crawl in.

"Bright Giver above!" Helmish cried. He jumped out of bed in his nightshirt.

I bit the Face and it fell backward with a scream. There were angry grunts and squeals below. Another appeared in the window and I got another biteful of snout and shook it back and forth. Talk about squealing like a stuck pig. I let go and it fell backward. They kept coming and I kept driving them back. I suppose what I did was brave, and that later was Helmish's opinion. But I was fighting for my own life. What greater incentive is there?

After I sent the sixth or seventh Pig Face flying backward, I was panting. Helmish had pushed the bed against the door and wedged it against the opposite wall. There were no more attempts to storm the window. It finally occurred to the Pig Faces that this wasn't working. They grunted among themselves.

The porkers in the hallway meanwhile still scratched and clawed at the door. But at a whistle-squeal from below, they left off. A silence fell that worried me more than their hellish noise. I wondered if a Gutter was on the way. It would be nothing for one to buzzsaw through the side of the inn.

"What is it, Big? What are they up to?" Helmish whispered. I ignored him. There were sounds far off in the woods. My ears told me it was the Two Legs gathering for a counterattack.

They launched it just as the Pig Faces began to pound at the wall of the room with what sounded like an axe. The Two Legs rode up like the Seventh Cavalry. The pounding stopped and the Pig Faces clattered downstairs squealing. Helmish looked out the window. Torches flared below, making his silhouette jump.

"Get 'em. Drive 'em back to whatever foul place they come from," he yelled.

He yanked the bed away from the door, lifted the bar and turned the lock. When he flung the door open, I saw that they had clawed nearly all the way through. Only a few splinters kept them from getting in. Helmish felt his way down the stairs in the darkness with me behind. Downstairs bodies were all over, Two Legs and Pig Faces alike. We saw by the light from the fireplace that there wasn't a single piece of furniture that wasn't smashed. The smell of blood was everywhere and wet coils of intestines lay around.

Helmish picked up a table leg as a weapon and hurried outside, his nightshirt flapping around his bare calves. In the torchlight I saw Two Legs on horseback hack away with sabers at fleeing Pig Faces. Helmish looked for one to club but all were running for it except those who wouldn't take another step. He stooped over fallen Two Legs to look for signs of life, but all were done for. They were gutted like those inside.

Helmish sat on a stump shaking his head. "It's hard to believe. I was dreaming of my vegetable garden while this was going on.'' He looked around. ''Who are these monsters? Whence do they come?''

There's plenty more of them and worse, I thought. That got me going. ''We gotta get out of here,'' I barked. I trotted toward the paddock where horses milled with pricked ears and flaring nostrils. I stopped to look back at Helmish.

''I have to get my bag,'' he said.

I sat down to wait. ''Look!'' one of the horses cried. ''A wolf!'' They whinnied and raced around the paddock, first in one direction and then the opposite. As I said, horses are stupid.

Helmish was taking forever. Two more minutes and you're on your own, pal, I thought. Then he appeared with his valise and a sword picked up from the ground. He had a hard time capturing the nag that pulled his cart. The horse trembled as Helmish harnessed him to the cart.

''Blood!'' he said to me, the whites of his eyes showing. ''Killing!''

Helmish whipped him up and the cart creaked into motion. I began to have second thoughts. Maybe it would be better to stay at the inn until dawn. It was dark and scary in the forest. We hadn't gone a quarter-mile in the darkness before Helmish was saying the same thing aloud. But what if the Pig Faces came back to the inn or Gutters showed up? The Two Legs would delay them while we kept putting distance between us. That settled it for me. I trotted ahead and the horse clipped along to keep up.

As we hurried through the darkness, I wondered how much time had passed in the real world since I was catapulted into this one. Maybe time was different in this place. A minute or an hour as I lay in my hospital bed (if that's where I am) could be a day or week here. I pictured nurses in white nylon uniforms and rubber-soled shoes whisking in and out of the room, checking my pulse, taking my temperature. They'd report no change to the doctors when they came on their rounds. Did someone sit by the side of my bed now and then?

I doubted it. It wasn't a sacrifice I would expect from Felicity. It depressed her to be around someone who just had a bad cold. Illness reminded her she was going to die one day. She took a dozen pills and capsules a day to put this off as long as possible. Nobody from my company would come to see me. My employees hate and fear me. For good reason, I admit. I expect a high level of performance. When I don't get it, it's sayonara. Security escorts underachievers from the building with their personal possessions in a box. Everybody sees them go. One woman who was a vice president sued, claiming the walk out the door caused her extreme mental suffering. She lost. So my employees would be hoping I didn't come out of the coma. If that's what I'm in.

The shareholders would be upset. Not that they harbor any love for me either. But I give them a better return on equity than anyone else on Wall Street. They'd wait awhile to see if I was going to snap out of it with all my marbles. If not, they would dump me. No problemo. I'd do the same in their shoes, only faster. I wouldn't trust what the doctors said. They might sugarcoat the news for reasons of their own. I'd hire my own experts to cut through any unrealistic optimism and get the straight dope. I'd want to know the odds of recovery and how long it would take. Time is money, and you don't fool around when either one is an issue.

Stanford has been after me to build a wing at the business school. They decided a few years ago to overlook the inconvenient fact that they threw me out in my junior year. The dean of students called it cheating. I called it looking for the edge, the same principle that put me in the position to pay for a new wing. My name would go on it, they said. I've thought about it. There are tax advantages.

But suppose I'm under some sort of spell, a possibility I'm no longer able to arbitrarily reject. Shakespeare said there is more something-or-other than dreamed of in somebody's philosophy. I forget exactly what. The point is not everything is what it seems to be. You have to keep an open mind. If I'm under a spell, am I still going about my business? Being driven to the city mornings and home at night, taking meetings, making decisions, etc.? Maybe my conscious mind takes care of business while my unconscious mind goes through this nightmare.

"You notice anything different about Bogey Ingersol?"

"I know what you mean. Seems like part of him's not here."

The light wind that blew toward us brought the faint smell of Pig Face ahead. I stopped, and Helmish reined in the horse. "What is it, Big?" he whispered.

I gave him a look that said stay put and moved silently into the trees. The forest seemed normal—owls glided silently, rodents gnawed, predators tracked meals. Little scuffles and small screams marked their successes. I realized the Pig Face scent was old.

A hundred yards up the road I came across the dark mass of an overturned freight wagon. The horses were dead in their traces and the bodies of two Two Legs lay near the wagon. Guts torn out, of course. A short distance behind was another wagon and the same scene. I went back to Helmish and wagged my tail to give the all clear.

He climbed down from the cart when we reached the wagons and looked sadly at the bodies. "These must be the companions of the wagoneer I talked to at the inn." The smell of big cat came to me. It was drawn by the bodies.

"We'd better go," I barked.

Helmish obediently climbed back onto the cart. An hour later we came to a small figure in the road. At first I thought it was standing still, but as we got closer I saw it was inching along. Helmish lit a lantern, climbed down from the cart and shined it on a strange little man. He had a long mossy beard and wore a brown robe. He was bareheaded, and both hair and beard were snarled with small twigs. His face had deep lines and his eyes were hidden in deep hollows. The feet were strangest of all. I guess you'd call them bare. They looked like solid bark with tendrils of root sticking out.

"I've heard about them, but the Bright Giver bless me if I ever thought I'd see one," Helmish said. "It's a Woodman."

Helmish held the lantern out and examined the Woodman up and down, front and back. "They live their early lives as dwarfs in the forest. Very friendly with the woodland creatures. Then as some point—they're said to live very long lives—they begin to turn into trees. They put down roots in a place they like and grow out of their dwarfdom into treedom. It lets them slow the pace of life and think longer thoughts."

Helmish stooped to stare. "I wonder if he's lost the power of speech. They fall silent at some point in the changing and never say another word."

"Halloo," he yelled. "Do you hear me?"

After a long pause there came a deep, dry voice that sounded like the heavy creak of a tree trunk in a high wind. "Danger." Another long pause. "Flee."

That sounded like good advice to me. Helmish wanted to see if he had any more to say, but I barked until he climbed back on the cart. The Woodman was swallowed by the darkness behind us.

We traveled until dawn broke, waking the birds. Helmish dozed in the cart and the horse plodded along, taking no notice of anything but the road beneath his hooves. I was tired, but somebody had to stay alert. The forest was beautiful and fragrant in the early morning. Each smell is fresh and clear then.

Felicity isn't a morning person. It was unusual to see her much before noon, unless she was hosting a goddess weekend. Tents dotted the lawn then, women shared, chanted, sang and visited the sweat lodge down by the new lake at dawn. I was expected to make myself scarce so as not to put a damper on things. It was my place, yet I had to sneak around like a thief.

My father was a stockbroker. "That's a kind of salesman, isn't it?" Felicity asked me once. The education she got in her formative years in Switzerland made her believe work was something people did when they couldn't think of a more amusing way to pass time. She would have fit in perfectly in the 18th century. Maybe that was why she felt she had a mission to revive the salon. I haven't thought of my father for a long time. I wondered what he'd think of his son, the dog? Son of a bitch was a term he used often enough. We weren't close, as you might imagine.

My mother was his second wife. He had five before a heart attack carried him off in his middle fifties. He drank a bottle of whiskey every day and never took a step of exercise, unless you count heaving himself off the golf cart to address a ball. He was popular and seemed to count that as an accomplishment. He was one of those sorts who lead the laughter at their own jokes.

Ha ha. Hee hee. His face would redden and contort with a hilarity that never reached his suspicious eyes. He raised me after my mother died in a plane crash when I was three. By that, I mean he paid for nannies until I was old enough to be packed off to boarding school. His third, fourth and last wives didn't like me and I returned the favor. I came "home" on school breaks unless they could find a camp to send me to. I was in the way and the wives made sure I knew that. They had their own lives to live and they didn't have time for the little boy who grew into the wiseass adolescent.

But don't get me wrong. I'm not begging for pity. I wasn't some wretched little kid holding up a bowl for more gruel. My father sent me to the very best boarding schools, probably from a guilty conscience. That conscience is why he wasn't as successful as I have been. Or maybe it was because he lacked the jugular instinct.

Before he died, he would read about me in the *Wall*

Street Journal (where most of the time "controversial" shows up in front of my name) and telephone me. "Jesus, you're going to close another company and throw more poor bastards out of work just before Christmas?" He had a wheeze from smoking six Havanas a day.

"No point putting it off," I'd reply. Time is money. People forget that. For the record, it wasn't always just before Christmas.

"You're a heartless son of a bitch," he'd say. He never showed much heart himself when younger. But he seemed to think this was somehow more important the older he got.

"Your interest is appreciated," I'd answer.

He slammed down the phone until the next time he saw something in the paper. "Controversial," I might add, is what somebody is called who has the guts to do what others would like to but don't dare. Controversial means two sides to a question, strong and weak. On one side is the entrepreneur and on the other is the regulator. The creator and the waster of wealth.

Don't get me started.

The horse moved more and more slowly until it stopped. I was hungry, as usual. I began to scout around for something to eat. I caught a couple lizards torpid from the night's cold, but all they did was whet my appetite.

I scared a weasel off a rabbit he'd killed, no easy thing. Those little bastards are fearless. He snarled and snapped, but at last saw the light of reason and abandoned his kill. Afterward, I lapped at a spring where the water was cold and delicious. A full belly seemed to put last night's scare at a distance. It's not hard to make a dog happy.

Helmish was gnawing on cheese when I got back. He was relieved to see me. "I worried that one of those fell creatures got you."

"They don't run fast enough to catch me," I said.

He did his darned-if-he-isn't-trying-to-talk routine again. Then he touched the horse with the whip, and the cart creaked into motion. "Normally," Helmish said to himself,

"I'd bypass Spyngle. It's a no-account place. Nobody worth speaking of ever came from there. But Gowyith is too far. If we don't stay in Spyngle, we have to sleep alongside the road. He shivered. "I don't think we want that."

A shadow passed over the cart and we both looked up. "One of those big black birds," Helmish said. It banked in flight and looked back down at us with a glittering eye. I thought: shit.

If it flew off, I would strike off across country and take my chances. Whatever horrible fiends the raven brought back would go after Helmish, thinking I'd be with him.

But instead it landed in a tree and watched, turning its head side to side. As we crawled down the road, the raven lazily flapped from tree to tree to keep us in sight.

I didn't want to dump Helmish unless it was necessary. The old codger might have some use in Gowyith. At a bare minimum, he'd know his way around. Maybe I could find some way of communicating once I got there. Paw the ground like Trigger or something.

As the morning wore on, we passed travelers in wagons or on horseback headed in the opposite direction. They would nod, as would Helmish. A few asked how the road ahead was.

"You want to watch for a new creature that looks like a pig but has horns and can stand on its hind legs," Helmish told them. "Killers. They attacked the Inn of the Hare last night. Quite a few people died before they were driven off."

The travelers gave him funny looks or had half-smiles, waiting for the punch line. When Helmish didn't say more, I saw from their expressions they thought he was nuts.

Morning turned into afternoon and the shadows were starting to grow long when we sighted Spyngle. Where Belyrie had been neat and tidy, Spyngle looked like one step up from mud huts and cows in the living room. The streets were dirty and the people looked suspicious and unfriendly.

"Bone lazy," Helmish said. "They live to drink queeg,

rut whenever and wherever the mood takes them and generally carry on as if there's no tomorrow. Every day's a feast day for them, no matter if they don't have a crust to gnaw."

The cart rolled through narrow streets toward the center of town. Naked runny-nosed children shrieked and darted in front of the horse. A more spirited animal would have reared. He just plodded along taking no notice.

"No one tending them," Helmish groused. "Typical." His look was disapproving.

A yawning idler noticed it. "Look at him," he said to a friend who looked like he didn't have much to do either. "Bet you a faloon he's from Belyrie."

"They never see anything good enough for them," the other answered.

Helmish stopped the cart at a shabby-looking inn where the sign hung lopsided. I looked around and spotted the raven just settling on a rooftop. The inn was dark and smelled bad.

"Extra for the dog," a voice said when we went inside.

"How much extra?" Helmish asked, peering around for the source.

"A drago. Give me eight total."

"That's robbery."

"Suit yourself. I've got the last room in Spyngle. It's harvest week, as maybe you don't know. Field hands from all over."

"All right," Helmish grumbled. "I'll pay it."

"You're sharing the room."

The owner of the voice came into the light of a candle guttering on a table. Where I came from, you'd look at that face and assume a rap sheet as long as his arm. Big chest and the kind of neck that goes with heavy labor. His hair hung down into his brutal face.

"If he makes a mess," he said, indicating me, "you clean it up or I charge you."

"When's supper?" Helmish asked, counting out change from the bag he carried inside his shirt.

"Sunset. Supper's extra."

"On second thought, I'll make my own arrangements."

The innkeeper took the candle and led us to the room. It was long and narrow and had bunks on either side. Helmish counted them.

"There's eight beds. Seven dragos for a room with seven others?" How many dragos in a faloon, I wondered.

"I told you, it's harvest week."

Helmish dropped his valise on a bunk.

"Extra for this candle," the innkeeper said.

"I have my own. But I'll trouble you for a light."

There was no charge for that. Helmish stuck his candle on the bedpost and the innkeeper shuffled out.

The room had a small window at the end that looked too small to let in anything dangerous. The walls were stone, and there were heavy beams overhead. Cobwebs in the corners. The smell said bathing wasn't a big item for harvesters.

Helmish snapped his fingers and we walked outside. The raven was still looking down from the roof. We went to an outdoor market where peddlers had goods spread on blankets. Helmish bought meat grilled over coals by an old man with one leg and tossed a chunk to me.

"You might be able to eat the food at the inn, but I doubt I could." I growled at a couple of mongrels who showed interest in sharing my meal, and they tucked tails between legs and departed.

We were sitting under a tree in a trash-filled lot that looked like it might grow up to be a dump in time when a young man headed toward us. Most people in Spyngle walked like they had nowhere to go and plenty of time to get there. This man had a quick step and an alert manner. He was clean, too, another thing that set him apart.

He stopped. "Good day to you."

"It's about over," Helmish said suspiciously.

"I understand you've just come from Belyrie."

"That we have."

"What a big animal."

''That he is. Fact is, that's his name, Big.''

Helmish was looking the stranger over. ''I take you to be from Gowyith.''

''Yes.''

Helmish's manner warmed. ''That's where we're headed.''

The young man squatted on his heels. He had brown hair and intelligent dark eyes that were friendly. His clothes were far better quality than Helmish's and years newer. His boots even shined.

''Business or pleasure?'' he asked.

''Business. I'm going for grit.''

''Grit?''

''A powder to polish glass.''

''What kind of glass?''

''Lenses.''

The young man's expression was interested. I hire a lot of people and I've got good instincts. I'd hire him, provided his resume was in order. He had a presence, the kind of man who has steel behind the pleasant smile. I always have resumes checked out, by the way. Few resist the temptation to improve on the past. Any exaggeration I discover means thumbs down. If you can't trust somebody to tell the truth about themselves, they'll lie about other things and this can cost you money. It's one of Ingersol's Laws. If I build that wing at Stanford, I'll have the understanding that I teach a class as the mood takes me. I've got a lot of hard-won knowledge you can't learn from professors. Those panty-waists wouldn't know hardball if they got hit in the ass by one.

''Tell me what a lens is,'' the young man said.

''It makes light stronger.''

''You're from Belyrie, you say?''

Helmish laughed. ''I know what you're thinking. Belyrie—cows and dumb farmers, right?''

''No,'' he said diplomatically, ''hardworking people, salt of the earth.''

"Dumb," Helmish insisted. "You're thinking they're dumb and you're right. A considerable step up from this lot, but still dumb. Except for me, there's not much to choose between the typical man from Belyrie and the cow he milks."

"I'm going in that direction."

"There's not much there for anyone who comes from Gowyith," Helmish said, giving him a shrewd look.

The young man looked around to see if anyone could hear. The people of Spyngle continued to slowly go about what small business they had. Someone led a cow out of a house.

"If I could speak privately," he said.

Helmish looked flattered.

"My name is Angorstino Flaneer-Hayesendom."

"Helmish is mine."

"I'm a courier for the Curiam."

Helmish's mouth flew open. "The Curiam?"

"Keep your voice down. I'm going to Belyrie and beyond to investigate rumors that have reached Gowyith."

"About pig-faced marauders?"

Angorstino looked puzzled. "No."

"Well, add that to your list, for there are such things. Last night at the Inn of the Hare they tore the place apart. Killed I don't know how many before they were driven away."

"We know nothing of such creatures or such an incident."

"If it wasn't for Big, I wouldn't be sitting here talking to you."

Angorstino looked at me. "He's a very unusual animal."

"You can add him to your list as well. He just showed up one day with dirt on his nose, like he'd been digging. I opened my front door and there he was, big as life."

"Bigger than life, I'd say."

"The most intelligent animal I've ever seen. Sometimes I think he's trying to talk. I could almost say things started being queer when he showed up. There's another example." He pointed at the raven flying east, gaining altitude. "I never saw a bird like that before and now it follows us every day."

"It's all connected," I said. "You people better get ready because every monster in your worst nightmare is headed this way." The usual yodeling yaps came out.

Helmish was as triumphant as an Indy 500 winner. "See what I mean? It's like he's trying to say something."

My barking drew gawks, worrying Angorstino. "Do you have a place to stay?" he asked.

"I'm paying eight dragos for a room with seven others," Helmish said indignantly. "That includes one for the animal."

"Stay at the Curiam house. There's plenty of room."

Helmish didn't have to be asked twice. Angorstino accompanied him to the inn, where he collected his bag and got his money back.

The Curiam house belonged in a nicer place. It was a little outside Spyngle on a rise of ground with a view of the town. It had a sort of Moorish look to it, white walls with arches and a tile roof. It had an eight-foot wall around it and a gate where powerful-looking men decked out like the Border Rangers stood guard. They leaned against spears but straightened as we approached. They swung the gate open and bowed us in. Helmish was flustered and pleased but tried to act as if he was used to being kowtowed to.

Inside, the rooms were airy with high ceilings. Twilight entered from the open windows and servants were lighting candles and lanterns.

"The Censurom of the district is away," Angorstino said, motioning to large colored pillows. "Maybe it would be best to keep the dog off. His wife is a difficult woman. She's very proud of those pillows from Onxyered."

"Stay off, Big," Helmish said sternly.

Kiss my ass, I thought. I save your life and you tell me to stay off the pillows.

[8]

Head on paws, I watched an elderly servant bring scented towels and a tray of refreshments. Helmish smacked his lips over the oranges and melons. Something hot was poured from a silver decanter into cups with an official seal I saw duplicated elsewhere in the house. Nothing for me.

I guessed the Curiam is what the government is called. The Censurom is probably mayor or governor. Whatever it was, I bet he traveled in style. Ever notice how well government treats itself? The house on the hill, soldiers, servants. It's only taxpayers' money, after all. Faloons or bucks, here or there, makes no difference. When I make this point in tax court, where lawyers have taken my cases a couple times, the judges drum their fingers. Roll over and take it like a man, they think.

"Aren't you young to be a courier for the Curiam?" Helmish asked. He had recovered from his awe and lounged like a pasha on the pillows, looking as if he came every day. He peeled an orange after looking around to see if there was a flunky who would do it for him. "Are these Pordorian oranges?"

"Yes. Carried in ice from the glacier at Umuke. The Curiam like us young. In another two years, I'll be too old and they'll find another spot for me."

He didn't look a day older than twenty-five. I like youth in my organization. A man who works for me is pretty much used up by the time he's forty. That or he begins to want to spend more time with his family. Women are worse in this regard. Male or female, I get rid of them before they become deadwood. If Angorstino was too old in a couple years, it must have to do with physical demands. He looked in good shape, nearly as good as Thor, Felicity's personal trainer. He's a Scandinavian with muscles everywhere, especially between his ears.

I once joked that if Thor and Ingrid, her aerobics instructor, got married their kids would be Olympic champions. Felicity was painting at the time and didn't answer. She has no sense of humor, not that that's important. People say the same about me. It keeps coming up in media "profiles" of me. If she did, she'd see how laughable her paintings are. Blobs of raw color troweled on canvas without pattern. A kid could do better. But her pet writers praise them as genius. The queer ones give little cries and act as if they're going to faint. One of them, Petre Rymer—a made-up name, I think—dresses in black and claims to have occult powers. If I'm under a spell, I bet that little fairy has a hand in it.

I dozed, and when I woke Helmish was winding up the story of the Pig Faces and the attack on the inn. Angorstino watched him tensely.

"By the time I got downstairs, it was all over. I wanted to crack some skulls, but they were dead or gone. Afterward, we came across two wagons on the road, the drivers butchered."

"And the footprints in Belyrie. They weren't from these Pig Faces?"

"No, no. Way too big for them."

Angorstino looked as grave as one of my lawyers talking my appeal. "So it's true," he said half to himself.

Helmish was licking his sticky fingers. "What's true?"

Angorstino didn't answer for a minute. Then he said suddenly, "I have to return to Gowyith. Perhaps you could go with me?"

"I'd hold you back. That stable horse pulling my cart's seen better days, and . . ."

''We'll go in my drague. We'll be there in half a day with a change of horses at Dubre.''

Helmish pulled at an ear. ''I'm responsible for that cart and animal and if . . .''

''I'll see they're returned,'' Angorstino said impatiently.

Helmish beamed. ''Big and I would be happy to go with you. Dragues go like the wind, they say.''

''Leave now if you're smart,'' I barked. ''Tomorrow might might be too late.''

Helmish smiled proudly, like a teacher showing off his prize pupil. ''It's as if he followed what we said and now he's giving his opinion.''

''It's not a trick he's trained to do?''

Helmish shook his head. ''Not by me. He doesn't always bark when you'd expect, but when he does, you'd be surprised if he didn't. If you know what I mean.''

''I hope to find out.''

The servants closed the doors. I went to an open window and stood on hind legs to look out. Dim lights began to appear in the windows below. Blue smoke from chimneys hung over roofs. Beyond, the dark forest pressed in.

I thought about the first settlers from Europe. If they knew how thick was the forest that came right up to the shore, how immense the plains a thousand miles beyond, how high the mountains that came next, not to mention the bloodthirsty savages (Felicity calls them ''indigenous peoples'') lurking, they would have climbed back on the boats. It took an entire day swinging an axe to fell a single tree. One down, countless millions to go.

It wasn't like me to waste time on that sort of thinking. Who cares what the Pilgrims thought? They did their donkey work and got off stage. Way to go, Pilgrims.

I was trying to work out what season it was. In New York you're never in doubt. If no other way, you can tell by how many layers of clothes the bums have on. It got warm during the day here but cooled off at night. Does that mean it's fall, or am I in the northern latitudes?

Helmish was talking about his lenses and Angorstino listened with interest, or pretended to.

"When the glass is polished just right, you can set a lantern behind it and the light goes a much greater distance," he said.

"What is the use of that?" Angorstino asked after he thought a minute. A man after my own heart. What's the bottom line? A good businessman always asks.

"That's for others to decide."

That was like the malarky about "pure science" you hear where I'm from. The government falls for it every time. Supercolliders. How many billions went down that rat hole?

"This glass," asked Angorstino, "how do you get it?"

"It comes when I need it."

"But how?"

Helmish shrugged. "I was curious at first. I'm not a rich man and I wanted to thank who it was. I could never catch him, however. It's just something that happens. I couldn't do my work without it."

I was hungry, as usual. Not seeing any sign of being fed anytime soon, I decided to go down to the town and see what I could scrounge. I jumped from the window to the wall and then down to the ground. People in Spyngle were eating the evening meal, bickering about the portions.

"That's more'n I got."

"No, it ain't."

"Liar."

"You're the liar."

A heap of refuse stood outside every home. When it got tall enough, I guessed it got dragged off somewhere. I nosed around the tailings without finding anything but bones and rotten vegetables. In front of one home sat a shaggy old yellow dog with rheumy eyes and a gray muzzle.

He stood and we smelled each other. Then he sat down again. He gave the impression he had seen it all. At his time of life, a strange dog didn't hold much interest, no matter how big. He didn't ask where I came from or where I was going. He sampled the light wind.

"Something bad's coming," he said matter-of-factly.

I didn't say anything. A rat ran across the dirt road, pausing to take a vindictive look over its shoulder at us. "They're real excited," the old dog said. "Chattering among themselves like nothing I've ever seen. And bold. It's like they're losing their fear."

"I'd get out of town tonight if I were you," I said.

He turned his old eyes to me. "Why?"

"You're right, something bad's coming."

"You smell it too? No, not a smell but a feeling, like before the loud, white fire comes from the sky."

He was right. There was something in the air. Nothing you could put a finger on.

"I don't smell it, I know it," I said.

"What do you know?"

"Pig-faced monsters. Gutters. Trolls. Mogwert. They're all on the way."

"Why would such things come here?"

"They're after me."

He looked away. "Oh."

"I admit it sounds crazy."

He gave out a long skeptical sigh.

"I've been running from them for weeks. Might be longer. I've kinda lost track of time."

"And why they after you?"

"They want me to help them. A snake told me."

He didn't say anything, but I could tell he didn't believe a word.

"You said yourself something bad's coming," I pointed out.

"Yup."

"So?"

"So get out of town, you mean?"

"Right."

"I couldn't do that."

"Why not?"

"These Two Legs have had me long as I can remember. Fed me, gave me water when I thirsted. Petted me, played with me when I still played. I've seen their young'uns grow up and seen new ones take their place. I started protecting them when I was old enough and been doing it ever since. Yelling at strangers who came too close, be them other Two Legs or our kind. Biting when yells weren't enough. I don't suppose my Two Legs would've made it without me."

He wasn't bragging, just stating the truth as he saw it. "Whatever's coming, they'll have to kill me before they hurt them."

Felicity has five Pekinese. Nasty little things with runny eyes that she wipes. She ties ribbons on them and talks in baby talk. "Poopsie-oopsy! What's my little baby-boo barking at?"

Me. They've got it in for me. Barking is not all. I've been nipped more times than I can count. I reach for something near her and they leap at me with bug-eyed fury. Their bites don't break the skin but they're painful as hell.

"Poopsie-oopsy is in such a bad mood!" Felicity says when this happens. She puckers her lips and gives them air kisses. I've wondered if she does it to annoy me.

"The next time one bites, I'll throw the son of a bitch in the river," I've told her. I can't tell them apart, so I'd have to throw the whole pack over the side. It would be found out, of course. There isn't a wealthy home in the country that doesn't have a servant itching to peddle dirt to *Hard Copy* or one of those shows.

"Did you hear that, Poopsie-oopsy? He only shouts when he's very, very cross. You must learn better manners, my darling. We'll begin today, and I'll also teach you how to sit up. You must earn your keep."

I wasn't around dogs when I was a kid and never saw any point in owning one when I grew up. I had to admit the loyalty of the old yellow dog was impressive.

"There anything to eat around here?" I asked.

''There's just enough for us.'' He turned and walked inside with dignity.

He was right. I couldn't find enough to feed a gnat, so I went back to the Curiam house. The last rays of the sun were caught by clouds that turned rosy as I got there. The guards recognized me and opened the gate. They said the usual things about how big I was.

Helmish and Angorstino were still talking, the remains of dinner on a table by the fireplace. When they saw me, Angorstino called to a servant. He returned with a wooden bowl full of table scraps. I wolfed them down.

''A dog that size needs a lot of food,'' Helmish said.

I could have eaten a second bowl, but that was all I got. I licked my chops and lay alongside the fire.

''I believe there must be a connection between this dog and all that has happened,'' Angorstino said, his eye on me.

''The question is, what?'' Helmish asked.

Nobody wanted the answer more than I. The three of us stared at the fire as if it could be found there. Then Angorstino stood and said he was going to his room to write a report.

Everyone, animals and Two Legs alike, speaks English. That seems strange. Why not French or German or Zulu, not to mention fox, badger, snake and all the separate languages animals talk?

But maybe it's not English. Maybe I was thrown into this world speaking the native language. It comes so easy I assume it's English. Something else to puzzle over when I had the time.

''Still no word from the missing Border Rangers, Big,'' Helmish told me. ''They're worried about it in Gowyith. Angorstino is afraid they'll never be seen again.''

They were beginning to catch on finally.

Helmish smoked his pipe in silence. ''Well,'' he said slowly, ''they'll know what to do in Gowyith.'' His confidence in Gowyith was impressive. Helmish made the place sound like Athens or Rome in the golden age. He stretched and went to bed, leaving me alone by the fire.

I heard a scuttling sound. In a dark corner the light from the fire flickered in a pair of red eyes. It scared the hell out of me and I jumped up. "Don't be afraid," a squeaky voice said. The eyes moved out of the darkness and I saw it was a rat. It was an ugly-looking thing with what looked like two feet of naked pink tail. It crept closer.

"Who are you?" I looked around to see if he had any friends.

"I'm alone. My name is Ato. I'm a servant of Zalzathar."

"Who's that?"

"A very powerful wizard. He desires to be your friend."

The name rang a bell. The fairies had mentioned him. The bad wizard.

"Yeah? What's in it for me?"

"Whatever you want."

"You mean he can send me back where I came from?"

"Easily."

"What do I have to do?"

"Zalzathar will explain." He was starting out as shifty as the snake.

"Why can't you?"

"Only he can."

"Where is he?"

"Waiting in the woods."

"Why doesn't he come here? Why do I have to go to him?"

"He mustn't be seen. You must go to him."

Did they think I was stupid? They grab me and the whole game's over. I'm in their hands with zero bargaining power. And their PR stinks. First a snake and now a rat. But I decided to play along to see what I could find out.

"Tell me something about Zalzathar."

"What would you like to know?"

"Describe him, for starters."

"I've never seen him."

"Never seen him? How long have you worked for him?"

"Forever."

"Forever? What's that mean?"

"Always. As long as I can remember."

"That's not forever, pal. You were probably apprenticed to him or something when you were a little rat."

"Yes."

"If you've never seen him, how do you get orders?"

"He comes in a dream. He comes to all of us that way."

"You mean the other rats?"

"Yes, and his other helpers."

"He works for Mogwert, right?"

The rat hesitated. "They are friends, yes."

"How come Mogwert's going to war with the Two Legs?"

"Zalzathar can say."

"I bet he can. What kind of magic powers has he got?"

"They are many and powerful."

"As powerful as Helither?"

Ato shrank back. "Helither? You know of him?"

"I've heard the name." I was lucky I bumped into those fairies.

"Their powers are different."

"Go back to the boss and tell him I'll meet him someplace out in the open. We both come alone. If he can put me back where I belong, we'll do a deal. If not, I go with Helither."

I heard a woman scream far off in the town, a single scream that cut the night like a knife.

"They are here," Ato said gloatingly. "Now, we'll have our revenge."

"Revenge? For what?"

"You're a dog, you can't know what it's like to be one of us. Despised, hunted down, poisoned, cats set on us and, yes, dogs. The Two Legs hate us and so we hate them. But we'll feast on them this night. There won't be any left alive to drive us back to the darkness of our holes."

He turned, ran up the wall to the sill and was gone. There

were more screams and yells from the town. I stood on hind legs to look out the window. One fire, two, then four and then many. They got big in a hurry. A puff of breeze brought the smell of smoke. The guards were talking below, trying to make out what was happening.

Helmish rushed into the room, tucking in his shirt.

"What is it, Big?" He looked. "The Bright Giver above." More fires blossomed. "Those fiends will find they've bitten off more than they can chew. The people of Spyngle may be layabouts, but they're famous for their love of battle."

Angorstino came in buckling on a sword. "There's trouble in the town. Fires burn."

"Don't think that sword will help you if they've got Gutters with them," I said.

They looked at me.

"He's telling us something," Helmish said worriedly.

"I'm telling you not to go down there," I said.

"Stay with the dog," Angorstino said. "With the Censurom away, my place is at the head of the household guard." He left and a minute later, Helmish and I watched at the window as he trotted in front of a double file of helmeted men carrying swords, spears and shields. Chanting as they went, they were impressive. But the Gutters would make short work of them.

"I'm not going to stick around to see what happens," I told Helmish. He had a stricken look. He knew I was saying something important.

"If only I could understand you," he said.

I went to the front door and barked. I looked back at him.

"You want outside." He rushed to the door and threw it open.

"Get that cart and horse and let's beat it." I headed through the open gate to the stable. Helmish ran to get his valise, then hustled after me.

"But we'll have the use of a drague tomorrow. It'll get us to Gowyith twice as fast," he said.

"We stick around and there won't be a tomorrow."

I trotted to the horse's stall and looked back at Helmish. He got the picture.

"Noise!" the horse said. "Fire!"

He was so jittery Helmish had trouble harnessing him again. When we trotted out the gate of the Curiam house it looked like the whole town was on fire. I realized there'd be no Gutters down there because of the light from the fires. The sound of battle carried to us.

"Maybe we should help," Helmish said.

"What do you mean we, kemo sabe?" I kept moving.

We entered the forest. The light from the fires made shadows leap on the pines. I wondered when I had last slept through a night. I used to take it for granted.

"Hurry," the horse muttered to himself. "Bad things. Hurting things." We left Spyngle behind.

At dawn the forest didn't awake with its usual chatter. Instead it had a kind of uneasy quiet. I couldn't smell or hear any sign of trouble, so I left Helmish and looked for breakfast. A quarter mile into the trees I ran across a large tortoise moving with what was flank speed for her.

She withdrew into her shell when she saw me.

"Be away, Wolf," she said. "You won't make a meal of me." A deep, rusty voice.

"You'd be too much trouble," I said. I wasn't kidding. She had to weigh two hundred pounds. Nosing her over would be no picnic. Then how to get her out of her shell? I didn't have time.

She was silent.

"Where're you going in such a hurry?" I asked.

"Away."

"Why?"

"Mogwert come."

"What's that mean to you?"

"I remember. I was young then."

''What happened?''

''Mogwert kill everything. Not just killing, torturing. Mogwert like suffering. Without suffering, Mogwert grow weak. Many of my kind were cooked on fires. They died screaming in their shells. Old ones like me and young ones. For Mogwert's pleasure. Mogwert loves pain even more than killing. Death stops pain. Mogwert want it to go on and on.''

''You figure you'll be safe farther into the Fair Lands?''

The tortoise stuck her head and legs out and started to lumber forward. She still had her suspicions about me, but feared what was to come more. ''No. Mogwert have grown strong. Safer only for a time.''

I watched her go. Nobody knows better than I how wrong public perception can be. The number the media does on me is a good example. Instead of thanks for helping make the economy more competitive, what do they say? That I'm a shark, a predator, an asset-stripper, all the rest of that abuse. I'm ''controversial.'' One paper did a story about the increase in suicides among former employees downsized after my takeovers. Can you believe that? As if I could be held responsible for such personal decisions. Nobody wants to take responsibility for their actions, that's the problem. So I know what it's like to be misrepresented. Nobody knows better, unless it's Donald Trump or that poor bastard Milken. Look what they said about Howard Hughes when he was dead and couldn't sue for libel.

Even so, I was getting sort of uncomfortable with the idea of dealing with Mogwert. I had yet to come across anybody with a good word to say for them. But to be fair, I hadn't heard their side of the story. And the bottom line remained, I had to get back. Sooner or later my luck was going to run out. This place was more dangerous than the streets of New York.

I found a pair of toads copulating and polished them off

as fast as you would a Big Mac. Helmish hailed me with the usual relief when I got back.

"There you are." He stepped from the cart and stretched. "All this travel has made me stiff." He fished into his valise and found his cheese. His diet had to be constipating as hell. Felicity is very diet-conscious. As I cut up my porterhouse and fork it down, she'll nibble at lettuce sprinkled with nonfat dressing. "I like a woman with a little more meat on her bones," I joshed once when I found her studying herself critically in the mirror.

"I could care less." She turned for another angle in the mirror. She's not alone. All the women in her set look like rails. They play tennis, swim and do aerobics. Then make a meal out of lettuce leaves.

"Angorstino says a few in Gowyith worry that Mogwert will come again, according to the old prophecy," Helmish said in his to-himself voice. "But they are laughed at. He says we've become so fat and prosperous we've forgotten the Great War. Or we think it was won instead of ending when both sides were exhausted. Pity we didn't get a ride in his drague. I've heard they go like the wind. But perhaps he'll catch up before long."

But he didn't. We plodded down the empty road through the morning and afternoon without seeing anybody. I kept a watch for black birds but saw none. That didn't mean Mogwert didn't have other creatures spying on us. Helmish began to fret as the day wore on.

"You'd think he'd have caught up by now." He stood in the cart to look back at the road that disappeared into the trees.

The forest came to life by noon, but there was a half-hearted quality about it, as if the creatures had to go about the business of life but their minds were elsewhere. I came across a small wren sharpening its beak on a tree limb. It looked at me with bright eyes.

"On your way to Gowyith?" it asked.

"Yes." I must have sounded suspicious.

"Don't worry, I'm a free bird, not a slave like the following birds."

"The black ones, you mean?"

"I see you've been followed."

"For days."

"There are none to be seen today except at Spyngle."

"You've been there?"

"I saw from far off. The town of the Two Legs is gone, burned. Those still alive ran off into the trees. There are many, many strange creatures feasting on bodies and pawing through the wreckage."

"What do they look like?"

"Like pigs, except they stand like Two Legs."

"How many would you say? Just give me a ballpark figure."

"Ball park?"

"A guess. How many you think there were."

The wren cocked its head. "See that bush?"

It had thousands of red berries. I thought of Angorstino trotting down toward the town at the head of the household guard. No wonder he hadn't showed.

"Some were already leaving Spyngle when I flew past," the wren said.

"Where were they headed?"

"This direction."

I returned to where Helmish sat in the cart munching his cheese. I nipped at the heels of the nodding horse and it sprang into a startled gallop, throwing Helmish back into the cab.

"Big?" he cried. "What's got into you?"

"Dog so bad to me," the horse whinnied, eyes rolling. His hooves thudded in the soft dirt.

"There's more trouble on the way," I barked.

Helmish caught my fear and made free with the whip. At twilight we paused on a height and looked down at the lights of Gowyith. Behind us my ears picked up the sound of running. Many feet running.

[9]

I leaped up and bit the horse on the ass. "Yow!" he yelled. As Helmith held on for dear life, he took off with flattened ears for the lights of Gowyith. The cart rocked back and forth as if it was going to overturn.

The Pig Faces came boiling down the road, difficult to see in the shadows, squealing and shoving to get to the front. The road was too small to hold them all, and those pushed aside swarmed through the trees and undergrowth on either side. Their hot pig stink reached me. They stopped at the tree line as if on command and milled furiously.

I loped after the cart. There was a customslike building ahead with an arch for traffic. The cart shot through, grazing the side. Guards ran after it. I dodged past their legs as they yelled at Helmish to stop. One threw a spear at me but it missed wide. The cart had a wheel wobbling as it bounced toward a huge gate just closing in the high wall. Foot traffic jumped out of the way and rearing horses threw riders. The cart rattled across a bridge and through the gate.

By the time I got to the gate, the cart was mowing through a bazaar where sellers were just folding up their goods. Yells and curses blistered the air. The street was jammed with angry people shaking fists, so I fell behind. People were so mad that I moved among them without attracting notice. Broken melons and baskets were underfoot. Chickens bound by their feet flapped wings on the ground and toppled urns gurgled out wine.

"Did you see him—drunk on queeg, I bet."

"He was showing off with no hands on the reins."

"A simpleton from the country, by his looks. They shouldn't be let through the gate until they learn how to act in a city."

I followed the angry crowd until the street emptied out into a square with a statue. The cart had stopped and people were telling each other the driver was under arrest.

"The Quincy have him. He's saying monsters were chasing him," one man said.

Helmish, his face flushed and angry as he tried to explain, was being hauled off by four men in military-style tunics with truncheons dangling from wide belts. Cops, by the look of them.

I knew a man, Charlie McGowen, who was an investment banker. He was looking into some business opportunities in Latin America when his driver ran down some Indian kid and killed him. Charlie was thrown into jail with the driver and was there ten days before bribes got him sprung. I guess he got a good buggering from everybody and his brother while he was there, because Charlie came out a changed man. Before that happened, he had helped me line up the financing when I took over the Radnec Companies—hard disk drives, workstations and other computer stuff. I sold it to the Koreans, who took it offshore. Anyhow, my point is you don't want to get involved with police in foreign countries. Laws are different and everybody's corrupt, from the judge on the bench to the jailer who shoves the slops through the cell door at meal time.

Who knows how much worse they are here? As I waited for the crowd to thin so I could follow Helmish, my eye fell on the statue. It stopped me short. It showed a Two Legs, as even I have fallen into the habit of saying, standing with a sword over a fallen Gutter. It was a good likeness, a quality they don't admire back home. It's the government again. If it didn't underwrite weirdos with strange ideas about art, they'd have to get jobs or starve to death. The marketplace sure as hell wouldn't pay for their junk.

I looked at the statue. The three-fingered claws, the snapping-turtle beak, the shell-like skin—all that was missing were the glowing eyes. How did the hero kill it with just a sword?

Helmish was taken to a building without windows that had a stout door studded with nails. A snarling bear was painted on it. I waited for hours, but the only people who came and went were cops. I followed two when they came out and headed up the narrow alley. The buildings in Gowyith are small and whitewashed with arched doors and windows. The cops stopped at a cafe in the alley lighted by torches and sat at a table. They ordered dinner from a waiter in billowing trousers and a vest. One cop had yellow hair and the other red.

"Put some meat in the soup this time," Red said with a laugh to the waiter. "You working until cock's crow?" he asked Yellow Hair.

"No. Bobro comes at the watchman's fourth cry. If I'm lucky, that is. Sometimes he goes on sleeping and I have to pound on his door."

They talked shop for a while as I sat near them. Red noticed me.

"Mogwert stay gone, look at the size of that animal."

"Biggest I've ever seen."

They traded quips on this subject until the waiter returned with steaming bowls. They scooped with wooden spoons, talking as they ate.

"Belyrie—you ever been there?" Yellow said.

"No. Farm town, right?"

"Yes. Pretty enough. You'd want to live there when you're old."

"Old," Red laughed. "You don't live long enough to get old in Quincy."

"It beats being in the Border Rangers. They still haven't heard."

"I hear they're going to send a patrol to look for them."

"They'll find them lazing alongside a lake, thumbs up their behinds."

"They've got a fortune in field pay by now. It's a shame to be so greedy."

"They'll have a good story, trust me. Animals acting queer, something like that. They had to investigate. How many patrols have come back saying that to get their pockets filled?"

"Never this long," said Red with a shake of his head.

"That old coot who smashed up the market is one for the Taslot, isn't he? Odd for someone from Belyrie to get into trouble. They're quiet people."

"Trouble in his head is my guess. Monsters chasing him—that's a new one to explain galloping a horse inside the gates."

"What'll they think up next?"

"Here he comes now," said Red Hair.

Helmish walked up the alley, his face still fiery. He wore a large pendant on a chain around his neck. He saw me and came over. "Branded as a criminal by this, Big," he blustered. He fingered the pendant. "Do you believe it?"

The two cops grinned when they saw Helmish talk to me.

"If I remove this or try to leave Gowyith, I'll be thrown into one of their stinking cells until the Curiam gets around to considering my case."

We walked, Helmish muttering to himself. "Smelling my breath . . . Is there madness in my family? . . . Did I steal the horse and cart? . . . Insult after insult."

It was nearly dark and Helmish said he was hungry. We entered a crowded cafe where musicians plucked stringed instruments and two women sang in high voices. They sounded Arabic.

A frowning man in an apron approached. "Even if you weren't wearing that," he said to Helmish, pointing to the pendant, "you couldn't come in here with that." Meaning me. "Please leave. Your kind eats around the corner and down some."

"It appears I was wrong about Gowyith," Helmish said in a loud voice. "I thought a man of intelligence could expect to meet others of his kind. Mogwert have awakened from their long sleep and plotted war. When I try to tell those blockheads of the Quincy, all I get are questions about a trifling accident." The people stopped eating and drinking to stare.

"Mogwert?" asked a thin man who had eyebrows that met. "Did you say Mogwert?"

"I did, sir."

Everybody burst into laughter, the same as at the inn. Helmish walked out, his back stiff, and I followed.

"Fools," he muttered. We turned down a darker alley. It was filled with small shops closed for the night. The alley was so narrow the awnings nearly touched in the middle. At long intervals, torches in sconces burned but didn't make much headway against the darkness. "He said there was a place to eat," Helmish grumbled. "I suppose he was lying."

"You looking for something to eat, darling?" It was a woman's voice. She sat in a second-story balcony that looked down on us.

"Eh?" Helmish said, not seeing her.

"Up here, sweetness."

Helmish looked up.

"I said, are you looking for something to eat? A place to stay?"

"Why, yes."

"I'll be right down."

A minute later we heard a lock turn and a bar lifted. The door opened. In the light of her candle, I spotted her right away as a hooker. If the plunging neckline of her blouse didn't tell you, her painted face did.

"C'mon in, sweetness," she said. She took his measure

with one up-and-down look that I bet came within a couple faloons of nailing his net worth.

''Very kind of you,'' Helmish said. ''The dog is mine. I hope you don't mind if he comes in. A very intelligent animal. We've come all the way from Belyrie. Oh. Pardon me, ladies. I didn't see you in the darkness.'' He bowed.

There were six women sitting on cushions, not one of them a lady. A couple said hello and the others laughed behind hands. He couldn't hear them but I could.

''A dirt-digger from the countryside,'' one whispered.

''He'll smell worse than the dog,'' another replied.

''Belyrie?'' a third asked Helmish coquettishly. ''Now where would that be?''

''To the east of here four days at a reasonable pace,'' he answered. ''You keep it awfully dark in here.''

''Candles are money,'' said the woman who had answered the door. The madam, I guessed, She'd turn a trick herself when things got busy.

''Do I smell something cooking?'' Helmish said, rubbing his hands.

''Rabbit pie. A pistier for that.''

''Very acceptable if the portion is large.''

''I'll put it on the table. Pick one of them and she'll go upstairs and warm the bed, unless you want her to sit with you while you eat. It's extra if she eats. Same with queeg.''

Helmish didn't understand. ''Extra?''

''You don't have to. They ate before dark. The kind of work we do, you don't want a full stomach. Customers complain if the girls are windy.''

''Oh. Well, it would be up to the young lady.'' Helmish stopped. ''Warm the bed?''

''It's nicer than getting into a cold one.''

''I warm a stone at the fire when it's cold. It makes a bed cozy enough.''

''A stone is nice.'' A coarse laugh and a wink. ''A girl is better.''

Helmish thought about this. ''Come along, Big,'' he said

with dignity. "This is no place for us." We walked back into the alley.

"I've heard of such places," Helmish said. "I never thought I'd find myself in one."

I was disappointed. There was one woman I found kind of attractive. I use a high-class escort service in Manhattan so discreet it has Kennedys as customers. It supplies the women who ride home with me sometimes. I get paperwork done before and after sex. Felicity doesn't suspect a thing. Other than wanting me to take precautions against sexually transmitted disease (as I do), would she care?

Something bothered me as we walked. I'm a dog but I had felt a yen for the hooker. No problem in my old form, but what about my present one? There had to be taboos about sex between people and animals here, and normally I'd agree. But where does that leave me under the present circumstances? And suppose I came across a bitch in heat?

Would it be wrong?

I felt myself sinking into depression. It seems like I've been on the run forever. But it's weak to let moods set the agenda, so I fought it off. Still, to look at it objectively, time is passing and it is like I'm on a treadmill. We get to Gowyith and Helmish is arrested. Will there be a trial? What if he was convicted and got thrown into the slammer? I had hoped he would get me in touch with Helither so I could see if a deal was possible. What good to me was he with that criminal's brand hanging from his neck?

It was clear from how Helmish acted in the whorehouse that this place had a moral code that frowned on random screwing, and probably other things too. So that meant they thought about right and wrong. I guess I could have figured that out from his talk about the Bright Giver. Or maybe not. You go back in history and you find religions with gods who demanded that virgins be flung from cliffs or fed to the flames. But the fact that there was a whorehouse told me not everybody did what they're supposed to.

We came across a small inn where a yellow light burned in the window. Helmish went inside and came out after a minute and snapped fingers at me. "They've got room for us, Big. It's not fancy but it seems clean."

We went inside, and a humpbacked woman with a lantern led us to the rear of the building and a small room with a bed and a bearskin on the floor. I flopped on the skin while Helmish ate the dinner the woman brought. He sat at a table against the wall where a candle sputtered. He tossed me the rind from a sausage that smelled like it had started to go bad.

Helmish wasn't smelling all that good himself. He took a whiff of an armpit and yelled for water. He peeled off his shirt when she brought a bowl and pitcher with warm water. He washed with some sticky soap and called to the woman when he was finished.

"Please have this washed by morning," he said, modestly hiding behind the door as he passed his shirt to her.

"Extra for that," she said.

"Just make sure it's clean. I hope to have an appointment tomorrow with the Curiam."

She laughed scornfully. "The Curiam don't meet with criminals until their time comes. I heard about you today. Farmers don't know city ways."

"I'm not a farmer."

"No?" she sneered.

"I make new things."

"Old is good enough."

Helmish closed the door and sat on the bed. "It appears there are as many ignorant people in Gowyith as the countryside." He pondered this a moment. "But the Curiam will be different." But he didn't sound as sure as before.

He crawled under the quilt and began snoring. Hours passed. Long after I heard a distant watchman call out the deepest part of night, the door opened silently.

I stood on the bearskin, a low growl in my throat. A tall

man in a black robe with a cowl held a small purple light in one hand.

"Mr. Ingersol," he said.

Nobody had spoken my name in weeks. "That's me."

"I'm sorry it's taken so long."

I looked at Helmish.

"It's all right. He can't hear us. I am Zalzathar."

His lips weren't visible behind a long, thick beard that split into a V when it reached his chest, but I knew they weren't moving. He was communicating mind to mind. Telepathy—that's the word.

"What am I doing here?" I got right to the point.

He sighed. "A mistake. We wanted someone else. There was interference."

"I'm here because of some fucking mistake?"

"I understand your anger."

"Put me back where I belong."

"That might be possible. Later."

"What's 'possible' mean? And what do you mean by later?"

"You were told about the Final Victory."

"Yeah, a snake told me."

"The Final Victory approaches."

"What's that got to do with me?"

He took a moment to choose his words. "It's a long story. It goes back many epochs before we knew how to measure time."

"Can you cut to the chase? I can get the background later."

"Perhaps you'll do after all," he said thoughtfully.

"What do you mean?"

"It could be you have the qualities we need."

"What are those?"

"You just showed one. An ability to see the point of the matter. You saw my story would take too long before its meaning became plain."

"That doesn't take a genius."

"You think rapidly, the way the Two Legs do."

"You've got two legs yourself, I notice. How come you're on Mogwert's side?"

"Long ago I made a decision." Was there a shade of regret in his voice?

"To go with Mogwert?"

He gave a slow nod. "They would prevail in the great struggle. Or so it seemed."

"What's the great struggle about?"

"It's between the principles we each stand for. The Two Legs appeared doomed to defeat when I made my choice."

"And?"

"And they weren't. Our numbers were overwhelming, our warriors fierce and strong, our weapons superior. Time was on our side. We had every advantage, or so it seemed."

"So what happened?" Helmish turned on his back, gave a couple of choking gasps like an engine turning over on a cold day, then began snoring like thunder.

"We were outthought."

"They're smarter than you?"

He thought again. "Not smarter. It's the way they think. We plan long and carefully. Every creature knows his place and duty. Every detail is thought out so nothing is left to chance."

"How did you blow it?"

"An adjustment they made at the last minute. A small feint by a body of Two Legs gave consternation to our commanders. It was on our left flank and was so convincing it got our full attention. Orders were issued that wiped out the attackers. While we were distracted, the real counter-attack fell upon us from the other direction. Thus was victory turned into defeat. This has happened many times. We always prepare ourselves for the old feint, not the new one."

"What's this got to do with me? And why am I a dog, for crissake?"

"Allow me to complete my thought." He didn't like to

be interrupted. I could already see what the problem was. These guys were too rigid, like our corporate dinosaurs and their bureaucratic committee-style way of doing business. If you can't think on the run, the competition takes your pants off every time. Linear thinking is out and fuzzy logic is in.

"They cancel our advantages or somehow shift the balance in their favor. They win by the narrowest of margins at the last minute. We've been so close so many times."

"You still haven't told me why you picked me and why I am a dog."

"It's Helither's fault, an example of what I'm talking about. We know of your time and dimension. Yours is a companion world, one of an uncountable host. I wanted to borrow an advisor from it. But I wanted Bernard Soderberg."

I stared at him. Bernie Soderberg, the communications mogul. TV, cable, movies, print. The guy is a terror, maybe the world's greatest businessman. Normally I'd feel flattered to be mentioned in the same breath. He's got ice water in his veins, Bernie does. He would have his mother peddle her ass on the street if that is what it took to close a deal. He's got presidents and prime ministers in his pocket. They're small change to him. Bernie's an original, the first truly global entrepreneur, the modern man without a country. If they want to start a war in some parts of the world, they have to get a green light from Bernie first. He weighs the pros and cons and makes the decision.

The Americas, Europe, Asia: he's got fingers in pies wherever you look. And broads? You can't name a silver-screen beauty Bernie hasn't balled. Kiss a Hollywood career good-bye if you aren't willing to crawl between the sheets with Bernie Soderberg. Rumor is he doesn't care whether you're man or woman if he takes a shine to you. And you've got to want to make it bad because Bernie's an ugly little gnome. He looks like a throwback to the early hominids. No more than an inch over five feet, and that's with elevator shoes. A perpetual five o'clock shadow like Nixon, and he combs five or six strands of glued-together hair from one side of his head to the other. Coke-bottle glasses, bad breath and body odor that won't quit round out the picture.

He's pathetic-looking, but you would never feel sorry for Bernie. He's a steamroller. Smart people throw in the cards when they come up against him. Bernie does anything to win. If he wants your wife, he finds a way to get her. If you don't play ball, he chops you into little pieces. He's not satisfied with just winning. He destroys whoever crosses him. It's supposed to be an example to others, but Bernie also gets pleasure out of it. In all humility, I'm a piker compared to Bernie.

The Pope himself mentioned Bernie once in a speech about "the rapacious, evil exploitation of our fellow man." It got a lot of play in the financial press. We joked that Bernie would find a way to get even. That's how powerful he is.

I'm tough. I play hardball. Sometimes I might sail too close to the edge, as seen by the indictment. If it happens, it happens, but I don't go out of my way to hurt people as Bernie does. And I'm loyal to the good old U.S. of A. even though it's got a lot of things wrong with it. Too much government red tape, etc. In short, I may have my faults but I don't think of myself as "evil."

"As I was conjuring to bring Mr. Soderberg here, Helither interfered," Zalzathar said. "My concentration strayed for the briefest instant. My aim was deflected."

"You got me instead?"

"It could have been anyone from a secondary tier of candidates."

"So how do you get somebody from there to here?"

He looked puzzled by the question. "Magic, of course."

"Why the dog bit?"

"It's a convenient form."

"Convenient for who?"

"If you had been in Two Legs form, you wouldn't have survived the journey to here."

"What's happening to the real me back where I belong?"

"You're in a deep sleep."

So I was right, I'm in some fucking hospital. "What about Felicity?"

"I don't know that person."

"She's my wife."

He shrugged. "I see very little. The sorcery is very draining."

"I'll bet she's trying to have me committed so she can steal me blind."

Zalzathar saw the opening. "It would be in your interest to help us so you can return."

"Why should I help you? I was doing just fine until you screwed up my life."

"You want to go back, don't you?"

"The sooner the better."

"When the Final Victory is won, I'll return you to your world."

"How do I know that?"

"We'll have no further use for you."

"That being the case, why not throw me to one of your monsters?"

"Our gratitude would be great."

Helmith gave a gulping snore and sat upright in bed.

"Big? Is that you?"

Zalzathar had vanished by the time his fumbling got the candle lit. "I was dreaming. I thought you were talking to a dark wizard."

"I was until you butted in."

"One of these days I'm going to understand you. By the Bright Giver, I will."

Holding the candle up to light his way, he went down the narrow corridor. I could hear him peeing outside. He came back and piled into bed. Zalzathar didn't return.

[10]

The next morning was fine, though it was clear now that fall was well advanced. It was warm in the sun, but Helmish pulled his cloak closer as we walked in the shadows of the buildings.

"The biggest city that ever was," he boasted as we strolled. You would have thought he owned property and would consider offers.

Take the most primitive area of Albania and you might find a place like Gowyith. We threaded our way through narrow, twisting alleys where jabbering crowds swarmed. It looked like most of the town's business was done there, judging from all the haggling. We watched the sale of a piece of colored cloth the size of a napkin take a half-hour before it finally changed hands. The two men with sleeves pushed up bargained as if it was the Hope diamond. They took turns breaking off talks and stalking off, then reluctantly allowing themselves to be talked into coming back.

"You don't want to buy anything from a Varduki," Helmish said, watching them. "You'll walk away without your shadow."

The people seem to walk faster and talk quicker than elsewhere in the Fair Lands. It's like the difference between New Yorkers and the rest of the country. You go to the Coast and it's like everybody is in slow motion.

The buildings are pale and have blue tile roofs. The tiles must not be attached too well because every now and then one slides off and shatters on the cobblestones. I bet a lot of people got beaned. I didn't see any building taller than three stories. The upper windows are like slits, as if the builders thought people would be scared to look down from such terrible heights. Every few hundreds yards you go through a gate in a wall. It looks like the city grew in stages, a forty-foot wall thrown up each time. They were nervous about being attacked, I guessed. Not one example of graffiti. That comes with a higher level of civilization.

While I was padding around Gowyith, it occurred to me a smart thing would be to pick a choice location and open up a pizza place. The ovens here are crude but they would get the job done. It would be easy to train people to make pizza. Food is pretty boring here and pizza would blow minds. After the first was a success, you open another. Line up vendors and spread franchises into the countryside. A good businessman is first and foremost an idea man.

The more I thought about it, the less I liked being lumped in with Bernie Soderberg. A great businessman—no argument there. But that's not all there is to life. I still haven't been able to remember what I got indicted for. Probably some technical violation of securities law one of my shyster lawyers said was legal. Maybe a few people lost bucks, but hey. Caveat emptor. It's nowhere near totally destroying somebody for the fun of it.

But I admit I had a reputation.

''You'd do anything for money,'' Felicity told me once.

''So would you,'' I shot back. ''Look who you married.''

She liked the timely bon mot, as I've said, so she laughed. We both did. I heard her repeating it on the telephone a couple times. But as I think of it now, I don't think it puts either of us in a good light. Flying the skull and crossbones on my yacht wasn't such a terrific idea either. It gave an impression hard to shake.

Felicity and I met when I was trying to climb in society. If you are in the right circles and drop the right name, access to capital is easier and on better terms. It's not what you know, etc. A loan at a quarter-point below the going rate when big money is involved makes all the difference in the world. I hired a social secretary, a middle-aged woman named Gay Stone who was born with a silver spoon. But she married for looks and personality, and that individual made some bad investments and began drinking, so she had to go to work to keep the kids in private school.

She knew everybody and got me invited to parties, openings and so forth. I make a good impression if there's something in it for me, so the dinner invitations came next. People knew I was loaded and there are always divorcees floating around looking for their next meal ticket. So it wasn't all that hard to get launched. Once I knew my way around, I fired Gay.

I got introduced to Felicity at a benefit for charity. She left England under a cloud when her husband died in that fox hunting accident. The tabloids had jumped on the story. "She Snogs As He Dies," one headline said. The upper crust doesn't care about infidelity or scandal. Money is all it takes seriously, so Felicity didn't have any trouble moving back into the best circles on this side of the pond. "We had agreed to separate," I heard her say.

"You're Gay's friend, aren't you?" she asked when we met at the buffet table. It was an afternoon party in Belmont, and a shower had driven everyone into the mauve tents. She was gorgeous in a pale green silk dress that exactly matched her eyes. I've since learned a lot about women's fashions from paying bills. I'd guess it was in the five-thousand-dollar range.

"Yes, I am." I gave her the Bogey Ingersol killer smile. I had ten grand in those choppers. Caps and ultrawhitened.

"How much are you paying her?"

"I beg your pardon?"

"How much are you paying her to weasel your way into our crowd?"

Still smiling, I sneaked a look around because she was

pretty loud. Part might have been the champagne, but she also has a hearing loss in her left ear she doesn't want people to know about.

"Don't worry, everybody knows. Come on, how much? Heavens above, he's blushing." As my smile faded, hers got bigger. Felicity has naturally perfect teeth and full lips that come from injecting cow cells or whatever it is. Pale skin, as I've said. She makes the current Miss Universe look like she scrubs toilets.

"A living wage," I joked.

"Not from what I hear. People say you're cheap. Is that true?"

"Next thing, you'll ask if I'm still beating my wife," I said with a weak laugh. "And I'm not even married."

Pretty lame, I admit, but she haw-hawed. I said a few other funny things, which was not like me. As I say, humor is overrated. But you know how it is said first impressions are all-important? Maybe Felicity got it into her head that I was a card who belonged at the Algonquin, wisecracking with the other wits. She might have married me anyway, but maybe she would have looked around first for somebody more to her liking. She had talked to friends about a scouting trip to Texas.

With a total of six marriages behind us, we weren't dewy-eyed innocents. So we didn't bother going through the usual courtship stuff. Instead, we were joined by a justice of the peace in Vermont three weeks later. Felicity and the party of friends she brought thought the whole thing was a scream and giggled through the ceremony. "Such a hoot, darling," one said to Felicity. "So *recherché*."

I took Solly Weisner, who runs the country's third biggest mutual fund. The expression on his face told me he pitied me when Felicity's friends had to lean on each other from laughing so hard. I know he was thinking this would never happen to a Jew. He got a kernel of rice in his left eye from a handful someone sidearmed at us as we came down the steps. I drove him to an emergency room while the others went on to New York and the gala reception at the Pierre. He was blinded in that eye and had to give up his job at the mutual fund because the work put too much strain on the one that was left. Our friendship was never the same. People said it was an omen for the marriage.

Felicity and her lawyer were hard as nails when it came to the prenuptial agreement, and I gave away more than I should have. But I was satisfied by the deal. I got plenty of gilt-edged contacts out of the connection. Just to mention one that paid off, I met a mousy little guy through a friend of hers who slipped me a tip about Sutton Industries being ripe for takeover. I cleared fifteen million out of that one when they paid me to leave them alone.

Nothing I owned was good enough by Felicity's standards, from my underwear to the car I drove. She went with me on shopping trips in the Bentley I bought to replace the Cadillac she wouldn't ride in. "Are you serious?" she said. "Nobody drives American." That's when I bought the Rolls. I also got her a Mercedes, a Ferrari, and a Land Rover.

She gave away most of my pin-striped suits, and I blossomed out into pale silk suits that after ten minutes looked like I'd slept in them. My wing tips got replaced by pumps like stilettos. "You go through some big change in your life?" asked Bart Nielson, a guy I went to college with, when I bumped into him in San Francisco. I could tell he thought I had come out of the closet and was living in the Castro.

My place wasn't fancy enough either, so I bought a new one in the same building where Kissinger and his wife live. Felicity met them in the foyer and they became fast friends. He got her an honorary appointment at the United Nations that cost me a fortune in entertainment expenses. But Henry never had the time of day for me. I heard he thought I was just another dull money man with nothing else on the ball. Felicity probably told him that.

Toward midday, Helmish said, ''Come along. We'll be at the Curiam when the doors open.'' The Curiam was in a low building in a square. A big crowd of people already milled around in front.

''Farmers wanting relief from the last tax increase,'' Helmish explained, ''merchants needing permission to sell within the walls, husbands or wives wanting to be free, feuding neighbors. The Curiam deals with every sort of question.''

In Belyrie, nobody paid any attention when he walked around talking to himself. But in Gowyith, he got lots of looks. Between the two of us, we must have been quite a show, the village idiot and his shaggy dog. While we waited, I thought about the Curiam. It was like a cross between court and legislature. Helmish had to go before it for reckless driving, but it had also sent Angorstino out into the countryside to check the rumors about trouble brewing.

We spent three hours in line around before we got to the door. An officious-looking clerk, the kind you see in motor vehicle offices, sat on a high stool. A thick ledger rested on something like a lectern. He wrote importantly in it with a pen he dipped into an ink pot.

''State your name, where you live, and the nature of your business,'' he said without looking up.

''Helmish is my name, from Belyrie. I wish to speak to the Curiam about Mogwert.''

The buzzing crowd fell silent. The clerk lifted his eyes from the ledger.

''Mogwert,'' he began, then noticed the pendant around Helmish's neck. ''Oh, no. You can't see the Curiam before the time appointed for your questioning.''

''I got this for a minor accident. It happened because I was hurrying here to warn of Mogwert.''

''He blames Mogwert for his rampaging through the gate and running down half the bazaar,'' someone yelled. Laughter. The clerk scowled.

''I repeat, you can't see the Curiam before the time appointed.''

''I'm not making myself clear,'' Helmish said, reddening.

''I hope that I am,'' the clerk replied.

''There's trouble in the country. Three nights ago, the Inn of the Hare was attacked by demons with pig faces. Two nights ago, the town of Spyngle was set afire. My own village of Belyrie was visited by a monster who left great footprints. One of your own couriers is missing. Angorstino is his name.''

''Mogwert vanished long ago,'' the clerk droned. ''Return on the time appointed for questioning. Next.''

Flushing an angrier red, Helmish was starting to say something when a stringy old man with a limping goat pushed past him.

''Paid good money and just look. Gone lame inside of a week. I demand justice of the Curiam.''

''Wait a minute,'' Helmish said. ''I'm not finished.''

At a look from the clerk, a cop sauntered over, hitching up the studded belt his truncheon hung from. ''Better move on,'' he said.

''I will not. Not until I speak my . . .''

The cop had him by the elbow before Helmish could finish. He was led to the edge of the crowd. ''I could run you in for disturbing the calm,'' he said. ''What with your other trouble, it would mean lockup for sure.''

''Doesn't anyone care that Mogwert are on the move?'' Helmish cried. ''Burning towns, slaughtering and who knows what else?''

''I'm sure the Curiam will listen to what you have to say,'' the cop said in a soothing voice. It was clear he believed he was dealing with a madman of the harmless variety.

He strolled off and Helmish looked at me. ''We ride through danger at risk of our lives to warn these fools and nobody will listen.''

A thin man with shrewd eyes under dark brows and a nose like a bent scimitar sidled up. ''I heard what you said back there.'' He had a cooked-onions smell, mingled with the B.O. and foot odor bouquet everybody seems to have in the Fair Lands.

''In Belyrie we believe a man gets a fair hearing in Gowyith, if nowhere else,'' Helmish said. ''When I go back, I'll say better believe the cock's crow brings the sun.''

''A lot of things people hear about Gowyith, good and ill, aren't so,'' the thin man said. He had the furtive look of a ticket scalper. His eyes moved from Helmish to the crowd and back again. ''I'd like to hear more about what you were saying. I might be able to help.''

''Easily done,'' began Helmish. ''I'm from Belryie and one morning a week ago . . .''

The man made a shushing sound. ''No, not here.''

''Why not?'' Helmish asked with a puzzled look.

''There are listening ears.'' He looked over his shoulder.

''Good. The more, the better. You people need to wake up and listen.''

More shushes and looks around. ''I can help, but you have to trust me. There are strangers in Gowyith.''

''What do you mean?''

''Meet me at the bridge when the sun has moved this far.'' He spread thumb and forefinger apart.

''What bridge?''

''Near where bread is baked.'' With another look around, he melted into the crowd.

Helmish watched him go. ''What do you make of that, Big?''

It looked like bad Hitchcock to me. I wondered if this was the time to ditch Helmish. Maybe he was too much of a rosy-faced rube to do me any good. I needed an insider, somebody who knew somebody. Access is the name of the game, no matter where it is. If I were in my human form, it would be easy. I'm good at chatting strangers up, finding the lay of the land and so forth. But mute and captive in this dog's body, that was out. If this stranger looked like he could do me some good, I'd ditch Helmish without a second thought.

We hung out in the square, sitting in the shade of a tree. Helmish gave a running commentary on the passing crowd. "A Mordak from the north; colorful dressers. She's from Kronster; they're tall and fair. They're Rumstellers, a wild people who still wear stinking hides. He's a herder from the high plains, by the look of him." The crowd in front of the Curiam thinned as the petitioners were allowed inside, one by one. I guess they left from another door because we didn't see them after they went inside.

He squinted up at the sun. "Time to go see what that fellow wants, Big." He heaved himself to his feet and we left the square. He found his way through the maze of alleys by asking directions. After a time, I caught the smell of baking bread from a distance and led the way.

Helmish marveled. "You act like you know where I'm going, and I'd bet all Belyrie against a blind ass that you do."

We got to the wooden bridge near the bakery but the man wasn't there. "I don't keep people waiting and I expect the same from others," Helmish grumbled. We sat. He got more annoyed as time passed. We waited an hour before he gave up.

"This is a part of Gowyith I've never seen," Helmish said, making the best of it. "We might as well have a look around." As we sauntered, he went back to his commentary on people in the crowd. "A Veton from the south; they're a brawling, drunken people. A Seleri, they're known for their spicy food. A Tronten, gloomy, thick-headed people." I stopped paying attention. Then my nose picked up the scent of the thin man with the bent nose. He had passed this way. His scent was starting to fade, but I could still make it out.

"Smell a rabbit, Big?" Helmish chuckled. I ignored him, my nose to the cobblestones. The smell changed.

There was an overlay of fear now. You can smell it if you're a dog. I guess the glands pump it out along with adrenaline. The scent made a sharp turn down a dark alley no wider than a man's shoulders. I made out the smell of two other men overlaid on that of the man who was supposed to meet us.

"Where you going, Big?" Helmish called behind me. "Who knows where this alley goes? It might be to someone's back door." I heard his reluctant steps behind me. I came upon a pool of drying blood and sniffed it. It was our man's. His body had exhaled one last strong smell of fear before he died. It had been dragged off.

"What's that, Big?"

"They've killed him," I said.

"Looks like blood. Probably a goat killed for cooking. With so many laws in Gowyith, you'd think there'd be one against slaughtering animals in the streets. Come along. We've wasted enough of the day."

All I wanted was to get to Helither, supposedly the good guy, and find out if he could get me back where I belonged. Now there was a murder mystery. Who was onion-man and why was he killed? Who cared? Not me. I had enough trouble.

But as I thought about it, I got a bad feeling. Were the killers agents of Mogwert who had murdered onion-man because he was seen talking to Helmish? If Mogwert had a fifth column in Gowyith, the capital of the Fair Lands, it didn't look too good for the Two Legs. These people must have been asleep at the switch for years. Say what you will about Dutch Reagan, we were always ready to slug it out with the Russkies and they knew it. People don't give him enough credit for that, especially the left.

Felicity and I were invited to the White House for dinner a couple times. Not because we were big pals with the Reagans, but because I bought a table at a $10,000-a-plate fund-raiser for the Republican Party. We got our pictures taken with the first couple. I wished Felicity looked at me the way Nancy gazed at Dutch.

"I can't stand her," Felicity said as we waited on the South Portico for the limo to pick us afterward.

"What's wrong with her?" I asked.

She gave me one of her you-don't-have-a-clue looks.

Helmish was in a part of Gowyith he knew and didn't have to ask the way. He turned into a small shop. The smell told me this was where the grit was sold for polishing glass.

"Helmish," said a portly old man behind a counter made from a plank resting on two barrels. "It's been a long time since we were favored with a sight of you."

"How are you, Damish?"

"Stiff in the joints, but tolerably well, thank you. I can see the Bright Giver has been kind to you as well." His eye fell on me. "Near as big as you, Helmish."

"Smart, too. Smartest animal I've ever seen or heard of."

"That so? How's your glasswork coming?"

"Very well."

The old man had a leather apron on. He scratched his bald pate and smiled. "Still can't figure out why you'd want to send light across a room."

"Not only across a room, across the whole of Belyrie if I can make it right."

The merchant nodded. "That would be something." But he didn't sound like he really believed it.

Helmish gave his order. The old man said he would put it on the next wagon going to Belyrie.

"I hope it gets through," Helmish said.

"Why wouldn't it?"

"The dog and I saw two overturned on the road and their drivers butchered," Helmish said casually. " 'Course, I don't suppose that qualifies as news in a place as big as Gowyith."

"What! When?"

"Few days back."

''We haven't heard anything about this.'' The shopkeeper's mouth hung open.

''Must be nobody can get to Gowyith with word of it, the woods being so full of pig-faced marauders. They attacked Spyngle and set it afire.''

The merchant's look of astonishment was replaced by a slow smile. ''Oh, one of your jokes, Helmish.''

''Joke?'' Helmish said hotly. ''I wish it were.''

The merchant didn't know what to believe now. ''If what you say is true, the Curiam should know.''

''I can't see them.''

''Why?''

''Because of this ridiculous thing around my neck.''

Damish leaned forward to peer. ''Helmish,'' he said, ''what crime have you committed?''

''None. A horse stampeded through the gate with me in a cart.''

''Was that you? They said you were drunk on queeg.''

''They were wrong, whoever said it.''

''They said the driver was laughing and lashing at people with his whip.''

''Complete nonsense. The horse ran away with me and I couldn't halt the beast.''

Damish pondered, ''I believe you,'' he said at last. ''I know you to be honest. And what you say about Spyngle and the freighters—that's true too?''

''As true as I'm standing here.''

The door to the shop opened and a big man with a face like a bad road came in. His was one of the smells that had pursued onion-man. I lowered my head and moved toward him with stalking steps.

''Big,'' Helmish said commandingly. ''Come here!''

I leaped with a snarl and sank my teeth into the stranger's thigh and shook it. He screamed and tried to pull me off. Helmish shouted something I couldn't hear and grabbed me by the scruff. I released the man and he ran limping from the shop.

''That dog's dangerous,'' Damish said with a shaking voice. ''The Quincy puts them to death when they turn vicious.''

Helmish looked at me. ''He had his reasons for doing that. I don't know what they are, but I'm sure they're good ones.''

Damish removed his apron. ''It's Mogwert, isn't it? Mogwert have come down from their mountain lair again.''

''Now you're talking,'' I barked.

''I believe so, and so does Big.''

''The dog?''

''Yes. You heard him talk just now.''

''You can talk to the dog?'' Damish was wary.

''Of course not. But he tries to talk to me.''

''Come with me,'' Damish said, locking the front door and dropping the bar. ''We'll talk to the Skithye. He'll be in the Bright Giver's house.''

He led us to a back door. I looked around the alley it opened to. It was empty. ''This way,'' Damish said.

The Bright Giver's house was a church or temple, whatever. It had Moorish lines and pale blue tiles on a bulging cupola that also gave it a Russian look. A pale man in a robe and shaven head who looked like one of those Hare Krishna fruitcakes admitted us. It was dim inside. An altar of some kind and rows of benches. The smell of incense and sweet oils. Candles burned and I heard chanting somewhere. We waited in a small room where tapers surrounded a sunburst made from what looked like gold. I wondered if these were sun worshipers. Not in the L.A. sense, but people who thought everything came from the sun. I took an anthropology of religion course at Stanford, but I had a guy go to class, write the papers and take the tests for me, so I didn't retain much.

After a while, the man in the robe led us farther inside the building. An older priest waited. He saw me and frowned.

''Animals are not allowed in the House of the Bright

Giver,'' he said. He frowned at the younger priest.

``I'm sorry,'' he said. ``I didn't see.''

``How could you not? Take him back outside.''

``Go with him, Big,'' Helmish said.

I would have liked to see the Skithye. Maybe he could have helped me. I guessed he was someone like a bishop or archbishop. But there didn't appear to be any choice, so I followed the young priest back outside. He shut the door and left me on my own.

There was a middle-aged man with tousled gray hair and a friendly face working in the garden, digging with a spade. He saw me, wiped his forehead with a handkerchief and walked over. He sat on a bench with a sigh.

``Good morning, Mr. Ingersol,'' he said.

We looked at each other. He seemed like the simple gardener type, a salt-of-the-earther. Sleeves rolled up, sunburned face, crinkly blue eyes. I used to have four or five guys who looked like him take care of my grounds on Long Island. Mexicans came in and were cheaper, so I fired them.

``How'd you know my name?'' I finally asked.

``I'm Helither. You've been looking for me.''

I was stunned. I don't know what I expected. Somebody majestic, I guess. He had mud on his boots and dirt under his nails. There must have been doubt written all over my face. He wiped a sleeve across his sweating forehead and smiled.

``You thought I'd look like Zalzathar. Robes, long beard, staring eyes. I don't go for that hocus-pocus. Never saw the point. I suppose you're wondering what you're doing here and how you're going to get back?''

At last I was going to get some straight talk. But Helither didn't seem to be in any hurry. He sat down on the ground cross-legged, laced his fingers behind his head and looked up into the sky. I willed myself to stay calm. This wasn't easy the way my heart was hammering away.

``You're upset, and no wonder. Yanked out of your world into this one, who could blame you?''

"The first thing I know is I'm running through the woods, a dog."

"Why you?"

"Yes, why me? What'd I do to deserve this?"

"Zalzathar must have told you when he talked to you."

How did he know I talked to the wizard? As I asked myself, I realized he communicated with telepathy, like Zalzathar. But where Zalzathar was brooding and heavy, Helither was breezy, as if I had some minor problem easily fixed.

"He said you spoiled his aim," I said.

"He hoped to get a fellow who would have been a very difficult adversary. I don't recall the name."

"Soderberg. Bernie Soderberg. He's a big man where I come from."

"Soderberg, that's it. He would have given me all the trouble I could handle and then some. Might have tipped the scales their way."

"Whose way, Mogwert?"

"Yes, Mogwert and their master."

"The Dark One?"

"Splendid. You've heard of him."

"Like the Devil, a metaphor for evil?" Felicity's writers were always saying something was a metaphor for something else.

"Not sort of like. The Devil exactly. He just goes by a different name here."

"I don't believe in that business. The Devil and all that."

"No? I suppose you don't believe in God either? We call him the Bright Giver in our world. You must've heard Him spoken of?"

"I'm an atheist."

He laughed. "Are you? Splendid. No need to waste any more time talking."

He grinned and turned his eyes back toward the sky. It didn't seem like he was going to say any more.

"I think I'm entitled to an explanation," I said stiffly.

''This is just a dream, Mr. Ingersol. Dreams have no meaning and need no explanation.'' He sounded drowsy. The bustle of Gowyith seemed to fade. ''What do you believe in, Mr. Ingersol?''

I thought a minute. ''The bottom line.''

''The bottom line?''

''Bottom line meaning you want assets greater than liabilities.''

''You mean to say you're a practical man.''

''You got it.''

''What you see is what you get?''

I was starting to feel uneasy. I had gotten the impression I was key to the Final Victory. Helither acted as if he could take or leave me.

''You don't believe this is actually happening?''

''I'm not saying that.''

''What's your practical explanation then?''

''I'm stumped. I thought maybe I was in some kind of accident and was in a hospital.''

''Dreaming this?''

''Well, yes.''

He shrugged. ''So, dream on. I've got to get back to my digging.'' He got up and walked away.

I followed. ''Wait a minute. I'm open to other explanations.''

Helither dug for awhile. The earth looked good, rich and loamy.

''There's only one other possibility,'' he said finally, giving me a direct look. ''That is Zalzathar meant to transport Mr. Soderberg to this world and this time and got you instead because I intervened.''

''Okay, I accept that for the sake of argument. How do I get back? That's what I want to know.''

''The same way you got here. Zalzathar could return you. Or I suppose I could in a pinch. It takes a lot of time. He doesn't have anything to do but fool around with magic. I have better things to do. People are born and die, just to name two jobs I've got. I learned what he was up to at the last minute." He leaned on the shovel with a worried look. "I don't know if that means I'm losing power or Zalzathar is gaining it."

"You or him, I don't care who sends me back as long as I get there."

"Did Zalzathar say how you could help him?"

"You guys think too fast for them."

"After all this time they've learned their fatal flaw." Helither looked grim. "Mogwert is very regimented. Nobody is trusted, so no one is given authority, only orders. Every decision must be passed to the top for approval. They are very slow to react as a result. You would advise them, I take it."

"I guess so."

He changed the subject. "You've come a long way."

"Tell me about it."

"Why didn't you go directly to Mogwert?"

"To be frank, nobody's got a good word for them except snakes and rats."

"They've earned their hatred a hundred times over. Ten thousand times."

"Okay, you're the good guys and they're the bad guys. But why should I get into the middle of your fight?"

"Did you see anything unusual on your journey?"

"Anything unusual? Like Trolls, Uulebeets, Gutters, Eaters, Pig Faces and talking birds and animals?" I couldn't keep the sarcasm from my voice.

"Gutters?" He asked me what they were and I described them. "You've got a statue of one in the square."

"You saw one?"

"It would've got me if I hadn't gone through solid rock."

"Then you used the protection I gave you."

"What do you mean?"

"It was good for one time. You have no protection now. It's used up."

''You got me passed through the rock?''

''It was my spell, yes. I wasn't sure you'd need it but I wanted it available in case it was.''

''There was a tunnel.''

''It led you to safety.'' He brushed the details off as unimportant. ''Just the one Gutter?''

''I saw one another time. It killed a big cat with tusks.''

''Two then, although it could have been the same one twice. He straightened from the shovel and put his arms across his chest. ''War must be close. The evil Narcros, to use their proper name, don't live long.''

''It's already started, if you ask me. Those Border Rangers everybody thinks are sitting on their tails won't be coming coming back. Spyngle's burned down and the woods are full of Pig Faces.''

He gave me a sharp look. ''What do you know of these things?''

''You people are amazing. You don't even know what's happening in your own backyard. Spyngle, that dump a couple days from here? It was attacked by Pig Faces and set afire. A bird told me the survivors ran off into the woods. I talked to a captain in the Border Rangers before he died. I had his dispatches but rats stole them. The Pig Faces chased me and the old guy I'm traveling with right to the edge of the trees where you look down and see the gates of Gowyith.''

''But there's been no report of any of this. None. The Curiam would have acted.'' Then, more slowly. ''My own sight has been veiled by a greater power.'' He was shaken as he went back to digging. He stopped and said, ''Fair Lands has been betrayed.''

''Somebody here must have suspected something.'' I told him about Angorstino.

''Where is he now?''

''Dead is my guess.''

More digging and thinking. When he didn't say anything for a long time I said, ''What's this all about?''

"What do you mean?"

"This war. You and Mogwert."

"The endless conflict between good and evil, Mr. Ingersol. That's what it is all about."

"Can you be a little more specific?"

He leaned on the shovel. "Surely, you've noticed in your world that there's good and evil?"

"Depends on your point of view, I suppose."

"You either see it or you don't. There is war, an evil. There is peace, a good. There is anger, there is kindness. There is sickness, there is health. There is selfishness, there is charity. Sweetness and bitterness. The conflict between good and evil is seen everywhere in the smallest things. There is the kind word and the harsh word. The helping hand and the blow."

"I see your point." I didn't want to queer things by arguing.

"I'm not sure you do. Goodness and evil are forever in conflict. The Bright Giver—God, as your world knows Him—and the Dark One are locked in battle. Their wars are waged in all the worlds; yours, mine and all the others, unseen and unimagined."

"How many worlds are we talking about?"

"They're like the grains of sand on the beach, each the scene of a vast testing between goodness and evil, the Bright Giver and the Dark One."

"Nobody ever wins?"

"Both do. Sometimes the Bright Giver is triumphant, sometimes the Dark One. It is an equal struggle. When the Bright Giver wins, there is peace and plenty, an inkling of the Paradise to come. When the Dark One prevails, a living hell is created where the strong prey on the weak and misery and suffering are all anyone knows. There are countless numbers of worlds where the struggles have already been decided. Our world will be one or the other, as will yours."

I was a schoolboy when I became an atheist. I used to pray for things that never happened. A friendship with another boy, a father who gave a shit, roast beef instead of boiled fish again for dinner. Sometimes I got what I wanted, but I decided it was just a matter of chance.

"They say God's omnipotent," I said. "How come He doesn't just kick ass?"

Helither shrugged. "Sometimes I wonder if the struggle is a way of making time pass. The Dark One is wonderously complex and subtle, capable of infinite surprise; a worthy foe. He knows the Bright Giver will abide by the rules of the game He himself created."

"God's also supposed to know everything. How can he be surprised?"

"Perhaps he suspended that power to give the contest greater zest. Who knows? God is unknowable, as even an atheist must have heard."

I heard Helmish's voice and glanced toward the church. When I looked back, Helither had vanished. An elderly bearded man in white robes carrying a staff hurried to keep up as Helmish walked quickly toward me.

"Come along, Big," Helmish called. He was excited. "We're in luck. The Skithye is personally taking me to an audience with the Curiam.

I wondered how Helither got away so fast. He didn't even leave a smell behind. If the shovel didn't still stand in the dirt, I might have thought I dreamed him up. I fell in with Helmish and the Skithye as they hustled toward the Curiam.

"It's shocking, shocking," the Skithye kept repeating. Then he'd say, "It must be a mistake, may it please the Bright Giver."

We approached the Curiam by a different side. When the guards at the door saw us approaching, they stood back. "Make way for the Skithye," one yelled.

"They're with me," he said. The guards let Helmith and me pass through in the wake of his billowing robe.

People bowed before the Skithye as he bowled down the corridors. "Your Gracious Honor," they murmured.

He led us into a large chamber where it looked like the last of the petitioners was making his case.

"And so I ask the lords of the Curiam to hear my plea," He was saying. He stopped when the Skithye walked in and hurried to where a dozen bearded men sat on one side of a long carved table. He whispered into the ear of a man in the middle. The others wore tan robes but his was blue.

He looked startled as the Skithye whispered. "Clear the room," he called out. "Clear the room."

Guards hustled the petitioner out. "My lords of the Curiam, a minute more of your time. I've nearly finished." The door slammed behind him.

"That man wears the pendant of an accused," a lord in a tan robe protested.

"I ask for a special dispensation, Lord Veriter," the Skithye said.

"The rules are well known. No one may address us in advance of his time for questioning. This man is accused of a serious offense."

Lord Veriter looked shaken. "I ask that we suspend that rule." There were murmurings but no one else objected.

The Skithye stamped his staff on the floor. "Fair Lands is threatened by Mogwert. We have no time to waste."

Mouths dropped open and some of the lords jumped to their feet. Everyone began shouting.

"How do you know?"

"No. Their defeat was final. They've long been dead."

"Not since before the time of our father's fathers and their fathers before them . . ."

"It's a lie."

When the hubbub died down, Lord Veriter said, "Sit down, my fellow members of the Curiam. You may speak, Skithye." The members of the Curiam watched with scared looks as he collected his thoughts.

"Thank you, Lord Veriter. This gentleman is from Belyrie," he said. "Some of you know it perhaps, a pleasant place. A short time ago the dog you see—note its huge size—showed up in the village. Since then, many strange and terrifying events have occurred. Vast footprints were discovered in the village. An inn was attacked by creatures with pig faces."

You could have heard a pin drop. The crowd noises came in from outside.

"The following night, Spyngle was attacked and burned."

"Spyngle?" one of the lords cried. "Why weren't we told?"

"How do you know?" another shouted.

"This man witnessed these events," the Skithye replied.

"Proof? Where's the proof?" This from the lord who said the rules kept Helmish from speaking. He had a red beard and close-set eyes.

Lord Veriter said, "Lord Dracie has a point. Where is the proof of these astounding claims?"

"Easy enough to find out," Helmish said in a small voice. "Send somebody to Spyngle."

"Have there been no travelers who have returned on that road since the supposed events occurred?" asked a small lord with a round face and golden ringlets. "Ask at the inns."

The Skithye dropped his head. "This explains the mystery of the Border Rangers. The patrol must have been destroyed by Mogwert."

One of the lords cried out, "No!" The man next to him put an arm around him as he began crying.

The Curiam began questioning Helmish, drawing the story out of him. It took an hour. At first their questions were aggressive, looking for flaws in his story that would expose it as false. "You claim," they said. "Didn't you say before . . ." But Helmish couldn't be shaken. He flushed a couple of times but didn't lose his temper. At the end, the questions trailed off and the members of the Curiam were pale and silent.

"Our thanks to you," Lord Veriter said to the Skithye,

"and to this citizen of Belyrie. We must speak among ourselves now."

The Skithye bowed and he and Helmish withdrew. I followed at their heels like a graduate of obedience school. If these people were elected, they were in for a hot time when the voters found out. I wondered if they were as disliked as politicians where I came from. If so, they better put more guards around the building for when the mob came demanding answers.

"You'll stay with me," the Skithye said to Helmish. He looked at me. "And the dog."

"I would be honored," Helmish said gravely. "Big is honored as well."

The Skithye gave him a funny look.

"A dog is a dog. His size matters not."

"Size alone doesn't make this dog different," Helmish said, patting me on the head. "He understands."

The Skithye dropped the subject. "The Curiam is upset. There will be consequences."

"They have a lot to answer for. They haven't kept a watch . . ." Helmish stopped dead in the street. "Belyrie," he said. There was a stricken look on his face. "What about Belyrie?"

The Skithye put a hand on his shoulder. "If Spyngle is gone, surely Belyrie must be as well."

I hadn't given it a second thought, nor it seemed had Helmish. Mogwert's monsters must have steamrolled through Belyrie. That quiet, orderly place with its quiet, orderly people were history. The stinking Pig Faces would have slaughtered everyone, man, woman and child. Too bad. They seemed like nice people, if a little on the dull side.

The Skithye took his elbow and slowly led Helmish. It looked like somebody had hit him with a baseball bat. He stumbled along, eyes staring. His body sagged, as if boneless. People in the street fell silent when they saw the tragedy in his face. We got back to the house of the Bright

Giver and they went inside. The door was firmly closed in my face. I lay in the shade of a tree.

I felt sorry for Helmish. He had lost everything, like me. At least he still had his human form. His world, too, even if it was threatened. But I was in no position to pity anybody else. I needed every drop of sympathy I had for myself.

I found myself thinking of Barnes Drake, one of the founding partners of my company. He retired after a massive heart attack that nearly finished him off. He went off his rocker in retirement, divorcing his wife (tits out to here) and moving to Guatemala, where he fed the hungry and handed out Bibles. I went down to see him once, hoping to buy out the ten percent share he retained in the company. He was making more money than when he was a full partner, thanks to me.

I got a car and driver and traveled up into the muggy volcanic mountains outside of Managua—scared stiff guerrillas would kidnap me for ransom—to where Drake lived. It was a miserable village in the jungle. Drake used to be fastidious, but now he was skinny and unshaven and his hair was long. He was shirtless and wore short pants and sandles. His bifocals hung crooked on his face and were held together with tape.

"You look like John the Baptist," I joked when he opened the door of the ratty hut where he lived.

He showed no surprise. We had been partners, but not what you would call friends. He was a Yalie who went to Harvard law, as males in his line had done for generations. A great-grandfather had been a Presbyterian minister famed in New England for his sermons. That's probably where Drake's late-in-life religious mania came from.

"You've put on a lot of weight." That was the first thing he said. "Look at you. Your face is red and you're sweating like you've been doing honest work for a change. That pith helmet and safari jacket look ridiculous, whatever they told you at Abercrombie and Fitch.'' He had never been one to mince words.

He invited me in and offered a cup of water. I held the cup to my face, pretending to sip. No telling where it came from. Some foul well or polluted creek was my guess.

We sat and he waited for me to speak as Indians looked in through the open windows.

I cleared my throat and looked around. ''Pretty nice set-up you've got here. The simple life—there's a lot to be said for it.''

''What do you want?'' he said. ''You didn't come all the way here to say words you don't mean about how I live.''

''Blunt as ever,'' I said, forcing an insincere laugh.

''I don't waste words, if that's what you mean.''

''You never did.''

''Now less than ever. There's no time.''

I guessed what was coming next. I'd heard his heart attack was his favorite topic of conversation.

''My heart attack taught me that.''

''Yeah?'' Some of the Indians were pretty skinny. I wondered if I was breathing in tuberculosis germs or worse.

''I saw the white light at the end of the tunnel.''

I let him rattle on about that, not wanting to get on his bad side by rushing him. He had seen his mother and father and a lot of long-dead friends on the other side of the tunnel. ''I was happier than I' ever been.'' With the happiness came the realization he had lived his life all wrong. Not a week goes by that one of the supermarket tabloids doesn't print similar twaddle.

He was resuscitated by a 911 crew buying doughnuts across the road from the golf course. He had been stricken as he waited to tee off. When he recovered, he got the divorce, sold everything and went to Guatemala to spread the Gospel.

When he finished talking, I made him my offer. Ten million dollars. ''It would be like a hundred million down here.''

He smiled the way he did when he caught someone blowing smoke. "I think not."

"It's a fair offer," I protested.

"More than fair."

"So why not?"

"Shall I be honest?"

I wanted to say that would be a change from what I remembered, but I still hoped to sweet-talk him into accepting. "Please do."

"Your money is ill-gained. I take some of the curse off it by spending it on the poor abused Indians. You don't know how pitiful their lives are."

And I didn't care. "Ill-gained?" I said. "You didn't complain when you were still pulling your share of the load."

He ignored the dig. "That was before the heart attack."

I didn't want him to start on that again. "Make it fifteen million."

He shook his head. "Make it any number you want. You're a smart man, Bogey. You've made a lot of money and you're going to make a lot more. I'm happy with my small share."

He was right about that. I was working on the Dole Petroleum deal at the time, a takeover that netted us seventy-seven million dollars. That gave Drake seven point seven million to buy beans and rice for his starving friends. We didn't part on very good terms when I left. A couple years later, the guerrillas stood him against a wall and mowed him down. His estate still collects ten percent.

I heard a noise behind me. It was Helither, whittling on a stick.

"Where'd you come from?" I asked.

"Oh," he said vaguely. "I come and go. What did the Curiam decide?"

"My guess is that they're in deep shit."

He whittled awhile. "Mogwert were silent for so long we let down our guard. Even me. But that doesn't explain everything. There is a traitor or traitors in high places in the Fair Lands.''

''You're going to have to pull a rabbit out of the hat.''

''It's not that easy.''

His whittling was kind of hypnotic after a while. My eyelids got heavy.

''Have you decided?'' he asked. There was an edge to his voice that made me alert.

''Decided what?''

''Whose side you're on.''

''I told you, I'm not on anybody's side. I'm neutral.''

''Neutrality is not a choice.'' My heart sank when I saw how he looked at me. Stern and hard-eyed. ''In war you pick a side.''

''Look, all I want is to get back to where I came from.''

''Whether you like it or not, you're involved. You know enough by now to make your choice. Make it.''

''Does this mean you're not going to send me back?''

''After the war.''

''Wars take time. I've got things to do.''

''What is more important than the Fair Lands?'' He asked in a voice strung as tight as piano wire. ''If Mogwert wins, the Fair Lands are finished. The people and animals, even the birds in the sky, will be slaughtered or enslaved to become the playthings of Mogwert. What compares to that?''

I couldn't think of an answer, which is not like me at all. I can usually come up with something, even to loaded question, like his. *Forbes* magazine called me ''fast-talking'' and ''never at a loss for words.''

''What can I do?'' I said weakly. ''You guys don't need me. You think faster than Mogwert. They may outnumber you, but they're like dumb oxes. You said so yourself. You'll outsmart them, like before.''

He shook his head sadly. ''They are too strong this time. Far too strong. I've been to the four corners of the Fair Lands. Already, they've destroyed many towns and villages. Others will fall before the Curiam can marshal its armies. The people, the ones who survive, are fleeing to Gowyith. They'd all be dead if Mogwert's monsters didn't stop to rape, torture and plunder. Farms are burned with the harvest in the fields. Orchards are chopped down, livestock have their tongues torn out for sport. The poor things wander until they die of thirst."

He turned his head to listen to the sound of trumpets. Bells began to toll at the same time. "The alarm is being sounded. Too late, too late."

"Look, I know it doesn't mean much," I said, "but for what it's worth, I hope you guys win."

"You're right, Mr. Ingersol. It's not worth much. Actions, not words, are needed. You must help us."

"How?"

"You must join Mogwert."

"Are you crazy?"

"Look at it from—what's the term you use?—the bottom line. If you want back where you belong, you must join them. I won't have the time it takes to return you before the attack falls on Gowyith. There is too much to be done. Such powers as I have will be taxed to the limit. And if the Fair Lands fall, I won't be able to help afterward."

"So you don't mind if I cut a deal with them?"

"Oh, yes, Mr. Ingersol." His eyes flashed. "I do mind."

"Then what do you mean I should join Mogwert?"

"Join them but work for us."

"You mean as a double agent?" I didn't want any part of that. "No way."

"You have to convince Mogwert you are supremely selfish. That you would sacrifice all of the Fair Lands and every single one of its people and creatures to return to your world, regardless of the misery and suffering you leave behind. Anything short of that and Mogwert will suspect you. It won't go very easy for you if they have the slightest doubt of your sincerity."

"Supposing I do what you say. What then?"

"Steer them wrong. Tell us of their intentions."

"As easy as that," I sneered.

"You're our only hope, Mr. Ingersol."

The priests came out of the house of the Bright Giver to find out what all the hullabaloo was. When I looked back, Helither had done his vanishing act. If he had stuck around, I was going to buy time by saying I needed to think, the same as I did with Zalzathar.

A man rode up on a horse and shouted at the priests. Two rushed inside and a minute later the bells starting tolling. From around Gowyith other bells kept adding to the chorus. People were running back and forth in the narrow alleys. Mothers snatched up little kids and took them indoors. It looked like those newsreels of London during the blitz.

I saw Helither was right. He would be too busy working on the defense of the Fair Lands to do me any good. That left Zalzathar, who looked like he was going to come out on top anyhow. The question was how and where to find him.

I was pondering this when I saw the crooked old man, Heffernan Sterngeld, hurrying with his crab-like walk as he leaned on his crooked stick. Another of Mogwert's eyes and ears in Gowyith. He disappeared into the crowd. A couple of ravens flapped lazily overhead, taking things in from up there.

I needed to get out of Gowyith before they shut the gates.

[11]

The streets were in chaos. People rushed in every direction, shouting and screaming. Men buckled on swords as they hurried or ran with long pikes bobbing. Alley merchants frantically packed up their junk so it wasn't trampled. All the while the bells rang. Nobody paid attention as I trotted toward a gate in the older part of Gowyith. I passed through and headed toward the tree line beyond a cornfield. The stalks sounded as if they were whispering behind hands about the uproar. Maybe they were. Nothing surprised me anymore.

I didn't want to run into Pig Faces, so I tested the air as I approached the trees. No trace of their nauseating stink. I moved into the coolness of the forest and kept traveling until I couldn't hear the bells of Gowyith anymore. I wiggled my way through a tight tunnel made in low-lying bushes by little creatures until I found a place big enough to lie down. If anything approached, I'd hear. I circled three times to drive away snakes and lay down.

Maybe I wouldn't have to go all the way to their mountain lair to get in touch with Mogwert. If I found Zalzathar, I could ask him to pass word that I had signed up and to call off the dogs. But where was the bearded wizard in black? I mulled the problem before sinking into sleep.

I dreamed of Felicity as usual. It was about the time I surprised her after hearing her tell someone on the telephone that I was dull and predictable. I'd rather be called cruel or vicious, wouldn't you? At least that's interesting.

What dull implies is a kind of stupidity. I was mad for a couple of days, then I bought the yacht. I picked the right moment to announce we would sail around the world. It was as we prepared to go to a dinner for People of the American Way, an organization I detest. I cleared my throat to get Felicity's attention, then dramatically threw open the doors to the drawing room, bowing deeply. Tanned crewmen in white tropical uniforms stood at attention.

Felicity was as dumbfounded, as I'd hoped. When she recovered, she dazzled them with a smile. "Hello, fellas," she said with a comic wave of her hand. Boring was I? Predictable?

Then she said, "How long does it take to go around the world?"

"Four months," I answered. The boat has computers, a communications room and a satellite dish. I would be as in touch with the markets as I was sitting in my office.

"Four months," she repeated, thinking aloud. "I wonder if Donna Siegel could get away. She has the orphans' benefit this year. The Merrydales, of course. Sissy and Alicia." These were her closest chums, members of the wedding party. "Weldon, of course. He has a new book out." He used to be a member of the Students for a Democratic Society and now was on the faculty at Berkeley. Whenever the media wants abuse heaped on capitalism, they call up Weldon. We despise one another.

"I hoped it would be just you and me," I said.

She turned startled green eyes to me. "Just you and me?" It was the funniest thing she'd ever heard. She threw her head back and laughed. The crewmen looked at each other uneasily. I shut the door.

"What are you laughing at?"

"What would we say to each other for four months?"

"What do other couples talk about?"

"Ideas, I would hope. Things they have in common. Books. Food. Friends. All you talk about is business. I'd go mad."

"If I'm as dull as that, why stay married to me?"

"Your money, darling. You know that."

I knew it well enough, but who wants to hear it said aloud? We didn't take the trip around the world, but I was stuck with the yacht anyhow. I got some write-offs, but my accountants were always sour about it. They could have come up with a thousand better ways to shield income. That old saying about how a boat is a hole in the water that money is poured into is true. And, as I say, that skull-and-crossbones flag didn't do me any good imagewise, funny though it seemed at the time.

The forest suddenly grew quiet and I woke up. I heard the caw of a raven overhead, a sound I had come to dread. A minute later, I heard a large body of creatures trampling through the underbrush, coming my way. My nose picked up Pig Face stink.

I lay still, barely breathing. They were so cocky they didn't bother trying to be quiet. By the sound of it, two dozen or more were headed in the direction of Gowyith. They went past where I had wiggled through the bushes and then were gone. I waited a long time before crawling out into the stink they left hanging in the air. I backtracked over blades of grass tromped down and just starting to pop up again. Every now and then I came across some small creature they had ripped apart, a chipmunk, a weasel, a lynx. No reason for it that I could see.

I traveled through the afternoon in the general direction of Spyngle. Twice more I heard parties of Pig Faces. I spied one from a wooded knoll as it tramped across a meadow. Each Pig Face carried a rucksack and a nasty-looking axe slung over a shoulder. Ravens flew in wide circles; aerial reconnaissance, I suppose. From time to time, a Pig Face dashed from the ranks and returned with something live. The others crowded around, squealing with delight, as it was pulled apart.

Toward twilight, a grouse fleeing from a civet cat flew right into my jaws. No kidding. If I'd moved my head an inch in either direction I might not have caught it.

"That's mine," the cat hissed.

"Dream on," I said. It made a nice dinner. The cat watched me, hoping for leftovers. I didn't leave any.

"I hope Mogwert get you," she said spitefully.

"Same to you."

When it began to get dark, I looked for a place to hide in case Gutters were around. I found it where one tree had toppled onto another, creating a cave at the bottom of their trunks. It had held a lot of guests over the years, judging from the smells. A bear, a panther, wolves, coyotes, badgers. I curled up for the night, but hardly slept at all. The moonlit forest was tense and listening. I got the feeling fell spirits were abroad. Once I heard something big crashing through the woods a long way off. I moved as far back into the cave as I could.

[12]

I took my time the following day, sneaking through the woods and taking a long time to check things out when I crossed open ground. In the late afternoon I came across a small white house with green shutters in a glade filled with wildflowers. Sitting on the bank of a stream, it had a steeply pitched roof and a small porch. It could have been designed by whoever makes the big dollhouse for F. A. O. Schwartz, the one that costs five thousand dollars. It was so deep in the woods I would never have found it if I hadn't been trying to avoid Mogwert's monsters.

I waited for a long time to make sure nobody was around because I had to pass the house to reach the trees on the other side. When I was satisfied the coast was clear, I loped into the open. I would have gone right past the house except a fish splashed in the stream. You never know about your next meal here, as I have said, so I stopped to see if this presented culinary possibilities. I was looking at the shadows of fish moving in the clear running stream when I heard a lovely voice.

"Hello, doggie," it called sweetly. If you made crystal into sound, that's what her voice would be like.

I turned to look. A beautiful young woman stood on the porch. She wore a summery outfit that showed off her good legs. Black hair, white skin, lips like rubies.

"Come here, doggie," she said.

I hesitated.

"I won't hurt you," she said with a laugh.

I trotted to the steps of the porch. As gorgeous as she was at a distance, she was even more so up close. She had dark laughing eyes.

"My name is Sigh-ya (I'm giving it phonetically). What's yours?"

I didn't say anything.

"Would you like water? Something to eat?" She clapped her hands. "Your tail is wagging. I think you would."

There's no point playing dumb if you've got equipment that gives you away.

"Now, you wait there and I'll be right back." She went inside and came to the door a minute later with a big crusty roast beef on a platter. It hadn't even been carved yet.

"This is for you." She motioned me inside with a smile and laid the beef on the floor. I started gulping it down as I stood, but it was so good I sat down to enjoy it. Well done, the way I like it. That comes from my boarding school days, I guess. They boiled the vegetables limp and cooked the meat gray. The chichi restaurants Felicity favors take such pride in their fresh vegetables you half expect waiters to serve them with gardening gloves. A waiter thought it was great once when I found a worm on my salad. He said this showed how fresh the greens were. I just about tore him a new asshole before he took it back to the kitchen.

"That's better," Sigh-ya said when I settled down with the roast. "You don't have to eat in such a hurry." She sat in a chair and crossed her ankles. What a knockout. She could be a model at one of the top New York agencies.

She looked troubled. "Have you noticed anything strange, doggie? The woodland creatures seem afraid. They usually come out at this time but I haven't seen any today. It's as if they're hiding."

Isolated as she was, she didn't know Mogwert had gone to war but sensed something was wrong. I looked around. The place was cheerful and tidy. Flowered curtains with matching cushions on hand-carved furniture. Candles on the mantel of the small fireplace, a spinning wheel next to a harp. A polished floor that smelled of beeswax, a throw rug with a pretty hand-woven pattern. A nice set up.

Sigh-ya went to the harp, pulled up a stool and began to play. I've snoozed through more concerts than I care to think about, but her music was different. I licked my chops and listened. It was light and graceful and made you think of a breeze that fluttered the leaves and made little ripples on a lake. Sigh-ya glanced at me at times to see if I enjoyed her playing. Shadows grew long outside as she went from one piece to another. She sang in a clear voice. Not words, just a smooth ribbon of song.

Full-bellied, I got drowsy as I listened. Felicity elbows me awake at the opera or concert hall. "You're snoring," she whispers angrily. I awaken to see people around us staring indignantly.

Her music seemed to darken as the sun went down, and her voice took on a strident edge. My head was on my paws by then, eyes closed. I tried to rouse myself but couldn't. The music got atonal and dissonant, like something written by a professor of music. Sigh-ya's voice suddenly broke under the strain and sounded old and cracked. She stopped and then the silence was broken by her laughter, a hee-hawing cackle.

I managed to pry my eyes open. It was as if I was drugged. Sigh-ya sat at the stool naked, looking at me, bony and scabbed legs spread wide to show a lank pubic bush. She was a skinny old hag with stringy white hair and a long sharp nose that nearly touched her cleft chin. As she laughed with open mouth, I saw the blackened stumps of a few teeth. A carload of toothpaste wouldn't make a dent on the toxic-dump breath that reached me. It mixed with a fecal smell from her other end.

I should have known. A witch.

She cavorted around the house, hopping from one flat foot to another. Her breasts were like long tubes that hung to her belly. They flopped in time to the dance she was doing. She was celebrating.

"It's been a long time since anyone was fool enough to accept Sigh-ya's hospitality," she screeched. "Hee hee hee."

The house itself had changed. Instead of the cheerful place it had been, it was filthy and dark and hung with cobwebs. Maggots moved in the flesh of a decayed body of a small animal that lay on the floor. The roast I'd been eating. I retched.

"You're big. You'll get me through winter easy."

I tried to get up but couldn't. It felt like the time I had my knee scoped and the anesthetic was just starting to take me under. I couldn't move but that didn't mean I didn't feel panic. It sounded like she planned to eat me.

I wasn't left in doubt very long. The witch picked up a dirty cleaver and tested the edge with her finger. "Your head will make a nice soup with your brains reserved as a relish on the side. It's been years since I made that dish."

She put the cleaver down. "But first you'll give me a pleasuring." The lewd look on her face made it clear what she had in mind. She advanced, the light from a flickering black candle making shadows dance on her wasted body. Then she shrank back, fear on her face.

"Release him from your spell." Zalzathar stood at the door. "I have use for this creature."

"No," she quavered. "He's mine. It's been a long time."

"Very well," the wizard said impatiently. He snapped his fingers and the heaviness left me instantly. I jumped to my feet.

Sigh-ya wept. "I'm just a poor old woman alone with winter on the way."

Zalzathar looked at me. "Shall we go?"

I was out the door like a shot. The moonlit glade was filled with Pig Faces, hundreds of them. Their hot stink poisoned the air. They watched me in silence. The flowers were gone. They had also been an illusion. It was a swamp. As the Pig Faces moved, their feet made sucking noises in the mud.

Zalzathar was at my side. ''You're lucky. What she does before she kills isn't pretty.''

''I don't want to know about it.'' I heard more Pig Faces in the trees. I was trapped. ''She's a witch, right?''

''That's the name used in your world.''

''They don't exist in my world.''

''If you say so.''

''You mean they do?''

''Of course. And a good many other things you think don't exist.''

Felicity has friends who come to her feminist weekends to pound empowerment drums who say they are witches, but I never took them seriously. I don't think they are who the wizard meant.

''How'd you find me?'' I asked.

''I was drawn to your suffering. Pure luck.'' He hesitated. ''Or so it seemed.'' He thought a minute, then shook his head. ''No, it's not possible. Luck alone saved you, Mr. Ingersol.''

''I've been looking for you.''

''Yes?''

''I want to sign up.''

''You've been in Gowyith and saw their weakness?''

''That's what made up my mind. I go with the winners.''

''Some in Mogwert wonder now whether we need you at all.''

''You don't have a lock. Those people aren't cream puffs.''

''That's what I tell Mogwert. We need every advantage. We've never been this powerful or they so unready. But we've been confident in the past only to be denied.'' He thought a minute. ''You saw Helither?''

''He's really sweating it.''

An icy smile. ''We go back a long way, he and I. We're equals in a way.''

"You're both wizards, you mean?"

"Helither isn't."

"What is he?"

"An angel."

"You're kidding."

Felicity has walked me in grim treks through every museum in Europe. All the religious paintings showed angels with big wings and halos. As I said, Helither looked like a gardener.

"I'm a wizard. Big difference."

"But you both do magic, right?"

"He calls his miracles. My power comes from the Dark One. His authority is from the Bright Giver. You could call us surrogates."

"What is Mogwert, then?"

"Companion powers. The counterpart of the Curiam, if you will." He smiled thinly. "Think of them as a necessary evil."

"So am I hired or what?"

"You're hired, Mr. Ingersol."

"You'll put me back in my world when it's all over, right?"

"You have my word."

That probably was worth exactly nothing, but now that I was in his clutches I wasn't in the best bargaining position.

As if he followed my thoughts, Zalzathar said, "When the Final Victory is gained, there'll be no further need for you."

"Let me ask you again, what's to keep you from whacking me?"

"We have what you would call a bad press, but we reward our friends for services done. It's possible to rule by fear." He glanced out at the Pig Faces. "It's the only way with this lot. But for creatures more evolved, the carrot must also be offered. It creates enthusiasm for the cause. This is sometimes preferable to blind obedience."

''The cause?''

''The Final Victory.''

''Does it ever come? Helither said the Bright Giver and the Dark One are forever slugging it out in more worlds than can be counted.''

He shrugged. ''The question doesn't interest me. Let Helither waste time on such matters. The Final Victory in the here and now is the only one that counts.''

''No use worrying over what you can't do anything about.''

''You're a sensible man, Mr. Ingersol.''

''I'm practical.''

''The bottom line.'' He smiled.

''You got it.''

I looked at the little house. The nice paint job was gone and it looked derelect in the moonlight. Sigh-ya peered from the window, backlit by a candle.

''She on your side?'' I asked.

''Witches have many good qualities, but they're too independent. Mogwert need obedience.'' He looked at me. ''Except from you and me. Our job is to outthink the enemy.''

''You've got a lot on the ball, Zalzathar. You're as smart as Helither.'' It's hard for me to brownnose. I'm used to it being the other way around. But it looked like I'd better get used to it.

He shook his head. ''I've been with Mogwert too long. Their habit of thinking rubs off over the years. The many years. I've become like them, one foot put after the other. It's hard to know when to change direction, hard to react to surprise. Nothing stands before us if met head-on. We crush opposition into the dirt. But Two Legs dodge and feint and confuse us with trickery.''

''You can disappear, can't you? Why not go to Gowyith and listen to what they've got up their sleeve without them seeing you?''

"Helither, of course. Just as he cannot pass unseen by me."

"He's stronger?"

"We're equal in strength." He had a faraway look. "Many have been the battles Helither and I have fought."

He was remembering them, I guess, because he didn't say anything for a while. The Pig Faces shuffled impatiently, their feet making sucking sounds in the mud. This roused Zalzathar from his reverie. He lifted a finger and a sizzling bolt of something, electricity or lightning, shot out. A Pig Face danced like a puppet at the end of strings, then collapsed into the mud. The smell of burning flesh reached my nose. The others moaned and fell silent.

Zalzathar said, "You have to kill one now and then to keep the fear of the Dark One in them."

"Makes sense to me," I said. I was shaken but tried not to show it. One second he's deep in thought and the next he murders without even a change of expression. It was only a porker blasted to hog heaven, but even so.

"He'll do to feed Sigh-ya over winter," Zalzathar said with a thin smile. "But she'll need all her powers to make him edible."

He led us off through the dark forest, not saying where we were headed. What a strange sight we made. A tall wizard in black followed by a dog and an army of pig-faced creatures with tusks and horns.

[13]

Toward dawn Zalzathar gave the signal for the Pig Faces to make camp. They dropped down on their haunches and leaned against their axes, grunting to one another. I was bone tired and about to curl up when Zalzathar signaled me to join him at the tall tree where he sat.

"We'll rest here during the day," he said. Apart from the Pig Faces, the spooked forest was silent. Usually, it would be starting to wake up as the nocturnal critters retired. It was like a shift change.

"Great," I said. I put a lot of enthusiasm into it. I figured I'd better try to make up for my foot-dragging before.

"You're a businessman in the other world?"

"Right."

"Like Mr. Bernard Soderberg?"

"Not as big as him. Nobody is."

"But big?"

"You could say so."

"I wanted Mr. Soderberg."

"You told me already. Helither bumped your arm at the last minute, so to speak."

"So to speak," Zalzathar said sourly. He pulled unhappily at his beard. "Years did I spend learning how to pierce the membrane between our worlds." He shook his head. "The lore I mastered. It's how I made the long bitter time pass since our last defeat."

"How did you decide on Bernie?"

"In consultation with the dark spirits in your world."

"They gave you my name?" I didn't like the sound of that.

He ignored my question. "I was too ambitious. I wanted the man in your world most influenced by the Dark One. My desire was too narrowly focused. It was therefore easy for Helither to frustrate my intention."

It looked like the talk that Bernie had mob connections was true, same with the rumors of drug trading and contract murders. You heard a lot of talk about Bernie, but I always thought it was just mud thrown by people he had ruined. I get enough of that in my own life to take it with a grain of salt.

"You," Zalzathar said with something like disgust, "were barely eligible. Your prominence was brief but enough for the dark spirits to be misled."

"I was indicted and tried for something. I can't remember the details." I had a memory of cameraman scrambling for position as I came down the courthouse steps with my lawyers. I gave the jackals a thumbs-up, showing confidence I didn't feel with the attorneys already talking appeal. Did the dark spirits get their information from the papers? Did they read Liz Smith?

"It was mere fraud," Zalzathar said with contempt. "But people spoke of you with an intensity that exaggerated your value. The misunderstanding came from that."

It was clear he thought I was small potatoes. I felt big-time relief. Bad enough to find out there were "dark spirits" back home, but worse to know they had me in their sights.

"What kind of deal was it?" I asked.

"You were chairman of a foundation that benefited crippled children."

That was one of Felicity's charities. She had an annual ball where Lester Lanin played. "What about it?"

"You 'borrowed' from it to help corner the market on a commodity."

There's borrowing and there's stealing. It all comes down to intent, doesn't it? But whatever it was, look at the mess it got me into. Given what I've been through, I'll gladly go to the slammer, forget the appeal. I wondered what the commodity was. Control a market and you dictate price. But there's a lot of risk. I must have had insider dope for sure.

"You're not what I wanted at all," Zalzathar said spitefully. I didn't say anything. I should apologize? Who's the victim here? Without another word, he wrapped himself in his robes for sleep.

We rested through the day. With Zalzathar sleeping, discipline among the Pig Faces got slack. They fought and screwed with vigor and returned to camp with little creatures to tear apart. Now and then one gave me a red-eyed look of hatred, but they didn't bother me.

The sun had gone down and the moon was rising when Zalzathar awakened and began greeting strange shapes that moved out of the woods. Some walked on two legs and had horns and tails and others had human heads on snake bodies and slithered through the long grass. There were monsters and goblins, fiends and furies. I recognized the trolls from the time on the bridge with Quick. The Pig Faces watched in terrified silence and I didn't blame them. Every last one could give you bad dreams for life.

Zalzathar spoke to each as it arrived and then made some kind of speech when they were all gathered in front of him. I wasn't close enough to make out what he said, but it looked like a pep talk. After about an hour, they broke up and melted back into the trees. The Pig Faces seemed to let out a collective sigh when the last was gone. Then they were pumped up. With all those demons on their side, the Two Legs had a snowball's chance in hell. Zalzathar called to me. "You saw our friends?" he asked.

"Impressive," I enthused.

"There are more on the way."

"Fabulous. The more the merrier."

He studied me sourly. "Merriness means happiness. We

are not happy, except when there is what others call sadness or suffering.''

''That's what I meant. When this goes down, there'll be a world of misery.'' He had a tetchy side.

''A world of misery,'' he repeated, liking the sound. ''Helither doesn't have allies such as this.'' Helither was on his mind a lot.

''What's he got on his side—fairy godmothers?'' I guffawed.

He was scornful. ''They exist only in children's stories.''

There was a shock. Finally, something that was just imaginary.

''He hasn't needed help,'' Zalzathar admitted. It was clearly a sore point. ''This time it will be different.''

Zalzathar said the same thing a dozen different ways in the following days, as if he had to keep pumping himself up. We continued our sweep through the forest, doubling back until we reached what was left of Spyngle. As we neared it, we kept coming across the bodies of Two Legs who had run from the sack of the town but were overtaken and slaughtered. Flies so horribly bloated they could hardly move lifted in slow buzzing clouds as we passed. There were hundreds of dead, thousands. Men, women and children. Sometimes you saw from how they were laid out that the fathers and mothers had put the kids behind them to make a last stand. It was heartbreaking to look at. But the Pig Faces were ecstatic. They pointed and danced and gave imitations of death throes. They fell to their knees and begged or rolled over and pretended they were being battered by mortal blows. It was hard to keep a smile plastered on my face.

Spyngle already looked like it had been destroyed for a hundred years. It was torn to pieces the way they tore living creatures apart. When we got there, thousands of Pig Faces waited and more could be seen journeying in torchlit columns toward the town. Each carried a haversack of travel rations. Lowing cattle with rolling eyes were goaded into big stockades made from thornbushes. They were rustled from the farms and ranches of the Fair Lands, I guessed, to feed the army.

Zalzathar set up shop in what was left of the vandalized Curiam house. Couriers came and went all day, as did ravens that flapped in from every point of the compass. "They have abandoned the countryside and retreated to Gowyith," Zalzathar told me. "I feared they would attack before my army was fully gathered. Instead, they're preparing for a long siege."

"They're playing into your hands?" I asked on a hunch.

"Exactly." He walked around, unable to hide his excitement. The guards caught his mood and squealed and stamped axe handles on the floor. "They don't know about the Narcros," Zalzathar said. "Their walls won't protect them."

"Narcros?" I asked, playing dumb.

"A creature from the Dark One. We've had them before at our side, but never in such numbers. With you, they are key to victory."

"I think I might have run across a couple of them on my way to Gowyith. Big ugly guys with beaks and claws?"

"You are lucky to be alive," Zalzathar said. "They are perfect killers." He looked at me sharply. "How did you escape them?"

"They didn't see me." It wouldn't be smart to let him know Helither gave me that escape hatch.

"You were lucky," he said again.

"They'll make the difference for sure," I said. Showing this phony enthusiasm didn't come easy to me.

"One weakness only do Narcros have."

"What's that?"

Zalzathar looked at me but didn't answer.

"You don't want me to know?" I shrugged like I could care less. "But if I'm an advisor, doesn't it makes sense to put me in the picture?"

Zalzathar considered this for a minute. "Light," he said. "They can't bear light."

"A pretty big minus, isn't it?"

"Some nights are long and moonless. Long enough to give us the Final Victory. Once the walls of Gowyith are breached, the battle is won. Order and discipline will collapse when Narcros are among them. Their army will become a mob. Each soldier will think only of his family. Helither will call vainly to them to fight."

I visualized the Pig Faces rampaging through the narrow, twisting streets of Gowyith. There'd be no stopping them. The Gutters, as I called them, would be frosting on the cake.

"How sweet it is," I said.

"The day the Final Victory is ours, you'll be returned to your world."

"It can't be too soon to suit me. When's the big push?"

"The moon is new. When it is no longer in the night sky, we attack. Meanwhile, our army grows stronger each night that passes."

"Where are you getting all these guys?"

"Every corner of Mogwert's domain."

"Very impressive."

Zalzathar was tense. "In the past, we've held back enough warriors to protect the high dark place in case of defeat. But this time all will be committed to the battle. If we fail, victory will be Helither's for the taking. We'll be too weak."

"One last roll of the dice," I said. "And the dice are loaded in our favor."

Zalzathar didn't reply. "Mogwert come soon," he said at last.

He gave a signal that said scram. I trotted off into the woods to get away from the awful smell of the Pig Faces. The more they massed, the worse the stink. I kept a sharp eye peeled because I didn't want to run into any of Zalzathar's demon friends. Get far enough from Spyngle and the forest lost its hush and the normal noctural business went on. I came to a rushing stream where my nose told me bears were fishing earlier. They had tossed more salmon ashore than even they could eat, and I dined famously. I was licking my chops when I heard a buzzing near my ear. At first, I thought it was a mosquito and paid no attention. Then a tiny female fairy landed on my muzzle.

I jumped. "You scared me."

"Helither sent me."

I looked around to see if anybody was watching. She used her tiny wings to balance as I turned my head right and left.

"Why aren't you singing and dancing?" I asked, still rattled. "You might not have too much time left for it."

"Helither asked our help."

Talk about scraping the bottom of the barrel. Fairies were cute and all that, but they could be swatted dead the same as flies. What good would they be when the Gutters blew through the walls?

"Have you decided?" she asked in her tinkly voice.

"Decided what?"

"Whose side you're on."

"Same one as always; mine."

"Helither says the battle is lost without your help."

"I'm just one guy. That's crazy talk."

"Helither says."

"So? Does that make it law? What's he want from me?"

"Do you know when Mogwert will attack?"

"When there's no moon," I blurted. "They've got plenty of these Gutters I told Helither about. But they're scared of light. That's their only weakness. I'll give Zalzathar bum steers when I can." Her head was so tiny I wondered if she could remember what I said. I asked her to repeat it back and she did, word for word.

"When I've got something to tell Helither, I'll sneak out into the woods. Okay?"

"Yes." She rose in the air and sped off, a tiny pinpoint of light. I watched until I couldn't see her anymore.

Unbelievable logic dictates one decision and I go the opposite. I couldn't even call it a hunch as justification. I'm tight with the odds-on favorite but throw in with the underdog. It didn't make sense. I wondered if Helither had cast some kind of long-distance spell on me. How else to explain it?

But on further thought, maybe this wasn't so dumb. I had kept my options open with Helither, and Zalzathar didn't know I was double-crossing him. But there was no doubt I was on the razor's edge. One slip and it was all over.

Even more Pig Faces had arrived at the ruined city. As far as the eye could see they covered the ground. They sat, stood, slept, fought, copulated dog-style. Their grunts and squeals made a constant roar, like the sound of surf. One approached me. He had a dirty ribbon on one arm that I guessed was a badge of rank. He grunted and made a sign to follow. He led me to the ruins of the Curiam house. Pig Face warriors sitting in the dirt gave me the evil eye as I passed.

Zalzathar sat at a table where a candle burned. There was a large hand-drawn map before him, elaborate and detailed. "It will be useful when we break into Gowyith." It showed every street and alley and the various rings of walls and their gates. "We won't mill around while the enemy recovers from the shock of seeing his walls breached by the Narcros. Our soldiers will know exactly where to go."

"Where did you get that?" I asked admiringly. A map that detailed had to come from someone official. Helither was right. Gowyith had been betrayed by a big shot. My heart started to hammer. If Helither let on he was getting information from Mogwert's camp, word would get back to Zalzathar. It wouldn't take long to add two and two. I stood on my hind legs, put my front paws on the table and pretended to study the map. "Where did it come from?"

I could tell Zalzathar debated whether to tell me.

"If you've got a source inside Gowyith, which is what this map says, it'll help me dope out strategy."

"Yes," he said reluctantly.

"High or low?"

More thought. It was like pulling teeth.

"High."

"That's great," I said with enthusiasm. "Who is it?"

"I won't say."

"You're the boss." I bent my muzzle closer to the map as if studying detail. "It's a mistake to keep me in the dark, though. The more I know, the more I can do for you."

Zalzathar shifted uneasily. I didn't look at him. He knew rigidness was what hexed them in the past. One slogging foot after another.

"Mogwert must be asked."

"Whatever you say, pal."

I was far from feeling as breezy as I sounded. I'd be leaking Mogwert's war plans to Helither and the traitor would leak back how the Two Legs meant to parry them. Even if Helither didn't spill the beans about me to the traitor directly—I assumed worst-case scenario and someone on the Curiam—Zalzathar sooner or later would think the stalemate was suspicious.

There was another problem. I didn't know the first thing about war except what I saw in *Patton*. I'd have to wing it. "These walls," I said, putting a paw on the map. "How thick?"

"Two strides."

"Call it six feet." I acted like it meant something to me. "How tall?"

"Six standing on shoulders."

"Something over thirty feet," I mused. "How many foot soldiers do we have?"

"You mean the Kwansorie?"

"The guys who look like pigs."

He opened and closed his hands ten times. "That many Talons."

"How many in a Talon?"

"Two clans."

We went back and forth this way until I estimated Mogwert had an army of twenty-five thousand, plus monsters and demons. I turned back to the map. Gowyith was a pretty big city. But if you kept moving closer to the core and the original walls, it got fairly small. Figure a population of fifty thousand, half of it women and children.

"It's pretty obvious," I said, still looking at the map.

I felt Zalzathar's eye on me. "Explain."

"You want to wear them out. Hit-and-run raids. Death from a thousand cuts."

I could tell he liked the thousand cuts idea. It sounded like more pain, and that was what they were in business for. But he wasn't totally convinced. "One overpowering attack to victory. That's our way."

"Doesn't work. You said so yourself." I dropped back down on all fours. "They have the advantage of interior lines of communication." What did that mean? It just popped into my head.

Zalzathar was impressed. "Interior lines," he repeated slowly.

I winged it. "They move their people to meet the point of attack faster than you can bring reinforcements. The defense has the advantage."

"Point of attack," he said.

Use jargon and people think you know what you're talking about. Doctors, lawyers, businessmen, football coaches, they all use it. The poor schmuck hearing insider lingo doesn't want to admit he doesn't get it. Zalzathar didn't want to admit it.

"You wear them out," I explained with a touch of impatience. "You get them rushing back and forth from one attack to another. They all look alike after a while. When they're on the ropes, you deliver the knockout punch."

"Knockout punch," Zalzathar muttered. "On the ropes."

I've had people try to dazzle me with jargon. Advertising people are the worst. "Cut the crap," I say. "Give me the straight dope in plain English." It doesn't sound nearly as great when they do.

Zalzathar stared at the map, straining to break free from his old way of thinking. It wasn't easy. The steamroller approach was all he knew. He paced the room, hands behind his back.

"Death from a thousand cuts," he said at last. "It's as they would do."

"I'm not guaranteeing a win," I said, already thinking ahead. "Nobody can guarantee that. You take your best shot and if that doesn't work, you think up something else. Know what I mean?"

"No." He looked at me. The Two Legs were lucky these people had such thick heads. No wonder they lulled themselves into thinking they had nothing to worry about.

I decided to throw out a cliché, the next best thing to jargon. "If at first you don't succeed, try again."

Zalzathar worked this around in his mind for a while. "We believe that," he said finally.

"But don't keep trying the same thing. Mix it up. Do something different."

"I must think about this," he said abruptly. "Mogwert come tomorrow." I think his brain was on overload and he didn't want me to see it. He waved a hand to dismiss me.

I trotted outside. The guards shot me the usual dirty looks. The sky was starting to look gray in the east. The Pig Faces were getting ready for their day's snooze. I headed west to get out of camp and away from their foulness. Breakfast was a couple of frogs sounding off in some reeds alongside a small lake. By the time I curled up in long grass, the sun was over the horizon.

It was toward noon when I heard the sound of somebody moving with stealth through the trees. I quietly got to my feet. After a minute, a Two Legs crept out of the trees. He carried a sword in one hand and had a shield strapped to his back. He wore chest armor and a kind of skirt. He had leather moccasins that hardly made a sound in the grass. If I wasn't a dog, I wouldn't have heard him.

He crossed the little meadow by the lake and disappeared into the trees on the far side. I shadowed him as he moved toward Spyngle. I guessed he was a scout reconnoitering. He moved slower as he approached the ruined city. Then he had the bad luck to nearly step on two Pig Faces asleep in high grass. They sprang up with squeals. The Two Legs lopped off the first one's head with a sweep of his sword and squared off against the other, who had picked up his axe. They parried back and forth, the Pig Face showing great agility in dodging the sword thrusts. The Two Legs caught the blows of his axe on the shield. It was an even match. Then the Pig Face swung his axe and it glanced off the shield, the flat side hitting the Two Legs on the head. He went down.

The Pig Face lifted his axe with a triumphant squeal. My silent leap at the small of his back knocked him down and sent the axe flying. I ripped his throat out quicker than it takes to tell it. I turned to the dazed Two Legs sitting on the ground. He looked at me with fear, thinking he was next.

I wagged my tail to tell him not to worry. After a minute, relief replaced fear on his face and he got up. His fingers went to the goose egg the axe had left, and he shook his head to get rid of the cobwebs.

"I've seen you before," he said. "In Gowyith."

"I'm a friend," I said. He didn't understand, of course. I moved off into the trees toward Spyngle and stopped and looked back.

"You want me to follow?" he asked. I wagged my tail some more.

He got the idea and we moved through the trees. After a mile or so, I heard a party of Pig Faces approaching. I sank to my belly and heard him drop to the ground. After a few minutes, sixty passed to the north. When it was safe, we continued toward Spyngle. I led him up a forested hill that had a view of the city.

''Bright Giver above,'' he whispered when he looked down at the ruins where Pig Faces sprawled in sleep everywhere you looked. It was like an ant heap. ''It's all gone.''

He began counting Pig Faces, making little knots on a rawhide cord. It took a long time. He was pale when he finished. ''And there are many more I can't see from here,'' he said to himself. He looked at me. I wished I could tell him there were twenty-five thousand of the bastards, but I'd have to figure some other way to get the information to Helither.

''Thank you,'' he whispered. He turned to go. I followed him back to where I had first seen him to make sure he got away safely. He turned when he reached the trees and waved. Then he was gone.

[14]

Late afternoon next day brought fleecy clouds in a blue sky. I was looking at them from a wooded ridge and wondering as usual what I'd be able to scare up to eat when I saw several large flying objects. I was high enough so they were level with me as they flapped past over the valley. They were Uulebeets. One I sank deep into a bed of ferns and spied through a barrel of greenery. When I first saw one I thought never see anything as scary. That was before the first Gutter.

All the horrors were gathering. I reluctantly started toward Spyngle myself. As twilight approached, the forest was silent and cowed. The creatures knew evil was abroad. The huge throng of Pig Faces at Spyngle was nervous and restless. Seeing the formation of Uulebeets fly in terrified them but made them surer than ever of victory. If you can be elated and scared at the same time, they were. Spyngle wasn't much before they got there, but what they turned it into was a crime. It was pulled apart like one of the animals they caught. You had to watch your step because Pig Faces shit whenever and wherever they feel like it. They parted sullenly as I made my way through the horde toward the Curiam house.

Even Zalzathar's usual morose calm had an edge to it. He stood on a balcony watching the arrival of night. He turned as I trotted in. "Mogwert come."

I looked in the direction he did but all I saw was the darkening forest. ''Later tonight,'' he said.

''Coming down from the mountains must be like a vacation,'' I said brightly, trying to make conversation. Zalzathar turned away. Time crawled by on broken knees. The Pig Faces lit campfires and ate their swill, fighting over it with loud squeals. I bet they could be heard for miles.

Toward midnight Zalzathar and I heard music far off, slow and dirgelike. Drums and pipes of some sort. They signaled the approach of Mogwert. The Pig Faces fell silent. Mogwert advanced from the direction of their mountain lair, accompanied by the monsters and demons Zalzathar had given the pep talk to. Big fanged brutes with horns and tails and heavy brows, imps who spun and somersaulted madly, wet-looking swamp creatures who left sticky trails in the moonlight. Pale incubi and succubi, banshees, ghouls, vampires, fiends, furies and harpies.

''Only the approach of the Final Victory could call all them forth from their dark places,'' Zalzathar said proudly. ''Never before have so many gathered.''

Bad as they were, Mogwert were far worse. They were disembodied, looking like fog flowing across the ground. Even at a distance I felt their bone-chilling malevolence. The Pig Faces parted to make room, their breath steaming in the sudden temperature plunge. Huge bats flew overhead. On second thought, I wouldn't say it was music. It was moaning without hope to a rhythm like a failing heart thudding its last beats, *thunk thunk*.

It took every last bit of courage I had to keep from bolting into the forest and not stopping until I was miles away sucking clean air into my lungs. But if I ran, they'd probably send the Gutters after me. And if they didn't, what did the future hold? Assuming I got back safely, I could die with the others when Gowyith fell. Or I could live a lonely fugitive's life until the birds picked my bones clean. That would probably be when they pulled the plug on the life-support system in my world.

The parade stopped and Mogwert flowed up the broken steps of the Curiam house in a silence so deep it felt like the whole world listened in fear. Zalzathar stood at the top of the stairs in welcome.

The feeling Mogwert brought can't be imagined. It was far worse than dread. It was like mixing anxiety, fear, unbearable stress, terrible loneliness and every other negative thing and then throwing hopelessness into the hopper. I threw my head back and howled.

"Yes," Zalzathar said, pleased. "Now you understand."

I broke it off, aware that I was being studied by Mogwert. I felt a kind of hive intelligence as old as time and as wicked as anything the mind can grasp. A sudden insight told me they knew every black secret since time began.

"He is not who you said," Mogwert said in a whisper that sounded like the scrape of dry leaves pushed by wind.

Zalzathar bowed his head. "He is another," he admitted.

"He's not one of us."

"Yet he has potential." There was a plea in the wizard's voice.

"Potential." Mogwert was scornful.

"He is practical. He is ruled by the bottom line."

"What is that?"

"He decides things by what is good for him."

Mogwert were silent. Every ear in the camp strained to hear.

Zalzathar broke the silence. "He'll do anything to return to his world."

"He would betray his own kind?"

"I want to get back where I belong," I blurted. "I'll do anything."

"He's already been useful," Zalzathar said with a look to silence my yapping. "He told of a strategy of death by a thousand cuts. I've decided it is how we'll attack Gowyith."

"Explain."

"We conceal our intentions by many small attacks. The enemy becomes exhausted and confused before our decisive blow is struck. Final Victory is then ours."

The Pig Faces broke into squeals and drummed spears on the grounds. Zalzathar stuck out his hand and killed three with his fiery bolts before they shut up. The smell of burning flesh filled the air.

"A thousand cuts." Mogwert seemed as intrigued by the possibility of slow death as Zalzathar had been.

"Maybe it works, maybe it doesn't," I pointed out. "If not, we cook something else up."

I felt a freezing hostility from the fog. "If he would betray the enemy, why not us?"

I had to admit it was a good question. Why believe anything I said? I wouldn't in their shoes.

"He wants to return to his world," Zalzathar argued. I had a feeling he had gone out on a limb and was forced to defend me. "This is how we have his loyalty."

"I'll do anything to get back," I whined.

"Helither could return him," Mogwert said.

"He doesn't have time," I said.

"You have spoken to Helither?"

That was a mistake. I felt Mogwert's suspicion sharpen. There was nothing to do but babble on. "Yes. I went to Gowyith. You guys are going to tear them up. It'll be a piece of cake. A walk-over. A blow-out."

"Helither refused you?"

"Not exactly. He said he didn't have time because he had to get ready for the war. You caught him with his pants down. He's busier than a one-legged man in an ass-kicking contest, take my word for it. But he said he'd send me back afterward."

"*Afterward*?" You couldn't pack more menace into one word if you tried.

"After the war." I was starting to pant. "He hopes Two Legs can pull it out, but they don't have a prayer." Another mistake. I was sorry I used that word as soon as it came out. I blundered on. ''Spend a few hours in Gowyith and it's pretty clear. That's why I came back to you guys. I go with the winner. It's like Vince Lombardi said . . .''

Zalzathar cut me off. ''Helither wanted him. That shows his value.''

''We don't need this creature. Kill him.''

Zalzathar wouldn't have to kill me because I had stopped breathing.

''I spent a long time to bring him here,'' Zalzathar said doggedly. ''I learned long-forgotten conjuring skills and created spells never before cast. I spent all the time since our last defeat on this. I penetrated the membrane separating the worlds, a feat never before achieved. I should have your praise. Instead, I have your doubt.''

''You wanted another from that world,'' Mogwert reminded him.

''This one has the qualities needed.''

''There is no proof.''

''Just as there is none that the forces we have gathered, great as they are, will be enough. The walls of Gowyith are stout, the Two Legs courageous.''

''We are more powerful than any army in all the wars that have been fought. The Dark One has been generous.''

''We've been strong in the past.''

''Never this strong.''

''Helither and the Two Legs are clever.''

Mogwert were silent. Maybe they were thinking of all the times they had been outsmarted with victory nearly in the bag. If so, they were also remembering exile in the barren mountains while the Two Legs lived it up in the Fair Lands.

''Another defeat couldn't be tolerated,'' Mogwert whispered. ''We would never regain authority over the wicked spirits. They would go their own way and Helither would destroy them, one by one.'' I felt Mogwert's fear. ''The Dark One is not forgiving.''

''It is as you say,'' Zalzathar said, bowing his head. ''That is why we must use every weapon, including this one.''

Everyone waited to see what happened. I had the feeling all apart from Zalzathar wanted me dead. The Pig Faces wanted to tear me apart to satisfy their curiosity about what made me tick. You don't know lonely until you're in a situation like that.

''He must be tested,'' Mogwert said suddenly.

Zalzathar asked the question that was in my mind. ''Tested?''

''Send him to the Great Balwar. If he returns, we will use him.''

Zalzathar acted as if he hadn't heard right. ''The Great Balwar?''

''Yes.''

''No one has returned from there. Ever.'' The wizard's voice was pained.

''If this one can be of any use against the Two Legs, he will find a way to come back.''

''I ask Mogwert to reconsider,'' Zalzathar said. He was bitter.

''Our decision is final.'' The cold fog withdrew, flowing back down the steps and floating over the ground toward the trees where I could see a clump of Gutters gathered. Two dozen of them, maybe more.

Zalzathar had a hard time holding in his anger. He muttered to himself, biting off the words. Then he turned to me. ''You see how hard it is to deal with them.''

''What's the Great Balwar?''

''A place far from here.'' It was clear he didn't want to say more.

''It doesn't sound too nice.''

''What do you know of it?'' he sneered.

''Nothing. But if Mogwert are sending me there to prove something, it can't be all that great.''

Zalzathar softened. ''It is a terrible place. It is said that the Dark One and his Foe took material form long ago to test their powers in physical battle.''

``And?''

``They fought many days and nights until the Dark One begged for a recess and escaped. He realized he could not prevail in direct struggle. He would need to find another way to win. The place where they fought is the Great Balwar. The ground is still torn up from their mighty contest. Many strange things are there.''

``Stranger than here?'' It wasn't possible.

``No one returns from the Great Balwar,'' Zalzathar said bleakly. I wanted to ask more questions, but he wrapped his dark cape around him and clammed up.

I was napping toward dawn when Zalzathar appeared before me. ``It's time to go,'' he said harshly.

``To the Great Balwar?'' I asked faintly.

``A Uulebeet will carry you.''

I would have run for it, but he had a gang of Pig Faces with him. Nothing would have pleased them more than hacking me to pieces. We walked out of the Curiam house to where a Uulebeet stood in a clearing of Pig Faces. Zalzathar ululated to it. It turned and lumbered off, and for a minute I thought I had been given a reprieve. But it was gathering speed for takeoff.

The Uulebeet got airborne and flew off slowly. ``Try not to move,'' Zalzathar said. ``Its strength is great but it is clumsy.''

He stepped back as the creature winged toward me. Terror froze me. I couldn't have moved if I had wanted to. The Uulebeet got bigger as it neared, its mass blacking out the stars. I closed my eyes and suddenly I was snatched up by the scruff of the neck. I swayed sickeningly back and forth in its clutches as the wind rushed in my face.

When I opened my eyes, the forest was far below and we were flying east. I was scared it would drop me and that would be that. But I almost wished it would. Each flap of wings took me toward some new horror nobody had ever returned from. If I somehow did, would I be too late to be a factor in the war? Helither would think I had gone back on my promise and was helping Mogwert, or at least was sitting it out on the sidelines. And after disastrous losses, Mogwert would wake up to the stupidity of the thousand-cuts strategy. They might still have enough left to sledgehammer Gowyith into submission, but they would want revenge for my bad advice.

After a few hours, the dark forest gave way suddenly to tortured volcanic rock. The Uulebeet began a steep descent and the faster rush of air blew me beneath him so our bodies were parallel. The creature began to make a strange sound, and it occurred to me it was whimpering. If it was afraid of what was below, whatever it was had to be really god-awful.

The ground rushed closer and I could see the Uulebeet was aiming for a small open spot in the jumble of jagged rocks. I thought he would land to unload me, but instead he dropped me like a sack. I landed running but I was going so fast I tumbled ass over appetite three or four times and the breath was knocked out of me. As I struggled to breathe, I heard a high scream from above. I looked up. The Uulebeet was frantically flapping its wings but was flying backward, deeper into the Great Balwar. It disappeared in the night sky, its screams growing fainter.

Backward. How could that be? It defied the laws of nature. But what here didn't? I decided to lay low until daybreak and hope for some sudden flash of inspiration about what to do.

An hour or two passed, and faint gray appeared in the west. I have a good sense of direction, but I must have gotten turned around on the flight from Spyngle. The light got stronger and I began to make out detail. The rocks were black and glassy and treacherous underfoot. I moved as quietly as I could, hoping to sneak out of there without anything seeing me. I was worried about the Uulebeet going backward. Who or what could pull that off?

Should I go in the direction I thought was west or toward where the sun had risen? I pondered this as I moved through the rocks. The smell of water came to me and I realized I was thirsty. My nose led me to a still pond that reflected the sky. It smelled okay, so I drank. The weirdest thing: The more I drank, the drier I got.

"Stop drinking." The voice came from behind me.

I spun and was looking at one of those half-human, half-horse creatures from mythology. She was pale and beautiful and naked from the waist up. The horse part of her was white as milk. She had brown hair twined in long braids and a kind face. Green eyes like Felicity.

"The more you drink, the thirstier you'll be," she said. A light voice, kind and gentle.

She was right. Now that I'd stopped drinking, my thirst seemed to abate a little.

"How can water make you thirsty?" I asked.

"How can a creature fly backward?"

"A riddle?"

"Nothing is what it seems in this strange place."

She shifted and stamped a foot. I could see the back part of her was black as coal.

"Who are you?" I asked. I wondered if I could outleg her if it came to that.

"I'm Kyrus."

"Have you been here long?"

"A long time. You are from beyond?"

"Yes. Beyond beyond, you might say."

"A riddle?"

"The truth, unfortunately."

She glanced around the dismal surroundings. "It is hard to leave here. Many have tried but none have succeeded."

"I have to get back. There's going to be war."

She was sad. "There always is."

"The battle to come might put an end to it for good."

Kyrus shook her head sadly. "The war has gone on nearly forever."

''Everything has to end sometime.''

''It's nice to think so.'' Her hindquarters twitched and she looked alarmed. ''We have to talk more quietly. He might wake up.''

''Who?''

She motioned with her head for me to look. ''Be very still. He's a light sleeper.''

I was horrified. Her other end was a man with a body as hairy as an ape. He was slumped in sleep, head hung to one side. He was heavily bearded and had thick eyebrows that met in the middle. Where Kyrus was clean and neat, he was dirty and unkempt. He made a blubbering sound as he slept.

''What's that?'' I whispered.

''Boog-Weir. He is evil.''

They were joined in the middle, each having two legs.

''How did this happen?'' I asked.

She looked at me sadly but didn't answer.

''How can you move?'' I asked.

''When he sleeps, his legs follow where I choose to go.'' A sad smile. ''But when it is my turn to sleep, my legs do as he commands.'' Her smile faded. ''What terrible sights I have awakened to. I hate him.''

''How long does he sleep?''

''Half the time.''

''The time you're awake?''

''Yes.''

I didn't want to be anywhere near him when he woke up. ''How much longer will he be out?''

''I don't know. I start to feel sleepy when he begins to awaken.''

''Can you help me get out of this place?''

''I can try.''

''First thing I need to know is what direction is east.''

She pointed.

''But the sun rose in the other direction.''

She shrugged.

''How far to the forest?''

''Travel is slow through the rocks. A day.''

''Can you show the way?''

She nodded and moved with a light mincing step toward an opening in the black rocks. Boog-Weir's thick torso and huge head swayed back and forth. The volcanic rock was sharp and jagged, and I would have had a hard time finding a path on my own. Kyrus picked her way delicately, turning from time to time to make sure I followed.

Noon came and went, and I was beginning to hope we'd reach the forest before Boog-Weir came to when I saw Kyrus yawn.

I trotted alongside. ''Stay awake,'' I begged.

She looked sleepy, as if she couldn't keep her eyes open. ''I'm trying.''

''Maybe if I talked to you.''

''Yes,'' she breathed. ''Talk to me.''

''So do you like it here?'' I said brightly. It was dumb but I couldn't think of anything better.

Kyrus shook her head tiredly. ''Nobody could, except Boog-Weir.''

She walked slower and her head began to droop.

''Don't go to sleep!'' I yelled. We were moving through a small canyon of dark glassy rock. Kyrus stopped and the black half of her, Boog-Weir, suddenly reared. ''Where have you taken me, Kyrus, you whore-bitch?'' His voice was as loud as the air horn on a truck that wants your lane.

His astonished eye fell on me. ''Who are you?''

''Ingersol's my name.''

He studied me suspiciously. ''What are you doing here?''

I couldn't think of a good lie. ''I got dumped by a Uulebeet.'' Maybe name-dropping would help. ''He was ordered to bring me here by the great wizard Zalzathar.''

''Uulebeet? Zalzathar? Wizard? What is a wizard?''

''You don't know about them?''

''No,'' he bellowed. My ears rang.

"Mogwert and Two Legs? Helither? The Final Victory? You don't know about those?"

"What are these things?" He stamped a foot threateningly.

"Take it easy. I didn't know myself until a while ago. I'm new in the neighborhood."

"Where are you from?"

"Like I told Kyrus, I'm from beyond the beyond."

"What is beyond?" he thundered.

"The other side of these black rocks."

"And what is beyond that?"

"Another world. My world. It's not a bit like this one."

He was silent, trying to make sense out of what I said. It looked like he had a short fuse because he didn't waste much time on it.

"You don't belong here."

"You're absolutely right. I'm trying to get back where I belong."

"Then why go in this direction?" He acted as if he'd caught me in a lie.

"It's the way back to the forest, isn't it?"

"Kyrus told you that?"

"Yes."

"And you believed her?"

"Why shouldn't I?"

"Because she never tells the truth."

"Kyrus?"

"She's evil."

"Evil?"

"The way out is that way." He pointed his head in the direction we had come.

He looked sad. "My appearance is against me, I know that. We're judged differently. Because Kyrus is beautiful and I'm hideous, it is assumed she is good and I'm evil. But the truth is opposite."

I'm thinking to myself, "What a crock," when he continued.

''I remember when I first saw myself. Or rather my reflection. I bent to drink and saw what you see, a being hairy and repulsive. I believed the water was enchanted. I knew how her cruelty gave the lie to Kyrus's gentle beauty. I knew I was good and she was evil. I thought the reflection had reversed my true nature. Proof would come when Kyrus drank. She would be so hideous. If I could remain awake just long enough to see her wickedness unmasked, I would know for sure.''

''So what happened?''

''I always weakened from my endless struggle with her and was overcome with fatigue. I never saw her drink. But it made no difference. I came to know from the luckless creatures who wandered into this terrible place that the water wasn't enchanted.'' He ran dirty fingers through matted hair. ''They ran from me but not Kyrus. That was their fatal mistake.''

''Fatal?''

''When I slept, Kyrus hunted them down and slew them. She enjoys killing. She remained by their torn bodies until I awakened from exhausted sleep. When I opened my eyes, her crime was spread before me. I raged at her, but she slept like a baby.'' He turned his head to look back at her. ''Kyrus, you cursed monster! How I hate you!''

It seemed a cry from the heart, full of rage and frustration and bitterness. Boog-Weir stood silent and brooding, forgetting about me.

''How long has this been going on?''

He roused himself. ''How long?''

''When I asked Kyrus, she said nearly forever.''

''I would have said forever. The days and nights come and go beyond count. The lights in the night sky which speak of the brilliant realm beyond wheel through the darkness. The hot time of the year becomes the cold and the cold becomes the hot. But Kyrus and I stay imprisoned in this hard place, jailers to one another.''

''What's to stop you from leaving?''

"Kyrus. Every step I make toward freedom when awake is undone by Kyrus when I sleep. I hate Kyrus." He returned to brooding, running fingers through his hair.

He had a good con, I had to admit. But choosing between the two, beautiful Kyrus in gentle sleep, braids modestly covering her perfect breasts, and butt-ugly Boog-Weir was a no-brainer.

"You really don't know about Mogwert and the Two Legs?" I asked.

"I know nothing except Kyrus and me. Nothing else can interest me until our struggle is ended. I rack my brains for ways to prevail, but my determination is matched by her cunning."

He was suddenly suspicious. "You lull me with talk."

"Sorry. I just want to get out of here."

"I've told you. It's that direction. You can be at the forest by darkness. There's no one," he added bitterly, "to bring *you* back while you sleep."

He saw my hesitation. "You don't believe me. You think Kyrus told the truth and I lied."

"I didn't say that."

He had an inspiration. "You know by now things aren't what they seem here."

He had me there. "Yes."

"Then it follows that Kyrus is not what she seems, any more than I am. Go. Go quickly if you value your life."

I was frozen by indecision. Every instinct said believe Kyrus. She told the truth and this ugly bastard lied. But Boog-Weir was right. Things were cockeyed in the Great Balwar. The backward-flying Uulebeet and the water that made me thirsty were evidence. Maybe he was telling the truth and Kyrus was the liar. If that was the case, I was heading opposite to where I wanted to go.

"Make up your own mind," Boog-Weir said indifferently. "I can wait no longer." He turned and trotted in the direction we had come.

His not caring what I did (or at least not seeming to)

made up my mind. I decided I'd been hoodwinked by Kyrus. "Wait up," I yelled. "I'm going with you."

He kept trotting, the sleeping Kyrus swaying back and forth like a pendulum. The hours passed, and finally Boog-Weir's pace slowed to a walk.

"Tired," he said when I drew abreast. "She'll awaken soon. You better run for it." He struggled to keep his eyes open. "Hurry. I can't . . ."

Kyrus reared as Boog-Weir had in awakening. She uttered a little cry. "You're still here?"

As soon as I saw the fear on her pure face I was ashamed of believing Boog-Weir. She understood without me saying a word.

"Don't feel bad," Kyrus said. "He is very clever. He is not happy unless he persuades his victims that I am the evil one. Then he kills them."

"I could kick myself."

Kyrus thought this was very funny and laughed. "There," she said, "I haven't done that for a very long time."

I frisked and wagged my tail.

"You are very large for a dog."

"I'm really human. I don't suppose you know what they are."

She shook her head. I told her my story as we traveled back in the direction I'd come with Boog-Weir.

[15]

When I finished telling Kyrus how I got into this jam, we walked in silence.

"Do good and evil contend in your world as well?" she asked at last. That was all anybody ever talked about. It sure got old.

"Sure," I said, "we've got crime and wars and all that stuff. We just don't dwell on it."

She turned to me with surprise. "What could be more important?"

"Lots of things. Business, for example. I happen to be fairly important in that line where I come from. Fun. Good food. Fine cars. Lots of things. The price of tea in China. You name it. Whatever your bag is where I come from, you're too busy to worry about good and evil. Who's got the time, if nothing else. In this place it's black and white, one or the other. Your nose is rubbed in it. For them or against them. Friend or foe. Where I come from you have gray areas."

"Gray areas?"

"Neither good nor bad. Or a little of both."

She was shocked. "That must be very hard. Not knowing."

"At least you don't have to worry about one side wiping out the other and taking you with them. We have what we call compromise. Believe me, it works."

"Compromise?"

"Give and take. You scratch my back, I scratch yours.

One hand washes the other. To get along, you go along.''

''There can be no compromise with Boog-Weir. I would rather die than accept the smallest part of his pollution.''

Boog-Weir hadn't seemed all that bad to me, to tell the truth. Maybe he was just misunderstood. With a good mediator, it was possible these two could bury the hatchet. But I didn't say this to Kyrus. Anger had put roses in her cheeks. She'd be damned good-looking without the horse part and Boog-Weir riding caboose.

''Well, whatever,'' I said. Nothing I said would change how she thought. She looked at the sun overhead. ''There's not enough time before he wakes. He'll do you harm this time.''

Kyrus turned her gentle eyes to me. ''You must leave. I'll return the way we've come. If I start now, maybe I can get far enough so he won't overtake you before you reach the boundary.''

''You're not going to leave me alone?''

''I must if you are to live. Just continue in this direction. Tell Helither and the Two Legs I hope their struggle is victorious. Hurry.'' Kyrus turned and cantered off, her Wagnerian braids flying. Boog-Weir rocked up and down, arms folded and head sunk in sleep.

When she was gone, my misgivings returned. Was this really the right direction? Then I had an idea. Instead of choosing between what they said, I'd go a third direction. I wouldn't know if it was south or north, but at least I'd be moving. I set off at a trot. But it wasn't easy finding a way through the black rock. It was like a maze for testing lab rats. Sometimes I had to retrace my steps when I came to a dead end. The time I lost made me nervous. I was surprised I wasn't hungry, but then I remembered the water that made me thirsty. Maybe not eating kept your belly full. Eat a bite and you'd be starving. As he had pointed out, that backward logic made Boog-Weir my friend and Kyrus the enemy.

But I was tired of the whole business. The problem in

this world was people didn't have enough to think about so they got fixated on one thing. No wonder they were fanatical. A healthy dose of mass media would get their minds on other things. Oprah, Geraldo, Ricki. Their freak shows didn't rival the one here, but at least they would be a change of pace. I wondered how Ted Turner or Rupert Murdoch would assess market potential here. Coming in on the ground floor, you could sell everything from hardware to programming. I've met both. Brilliant guys in different ways, but both know how to turn a buck. I was thinking about this when I came around a glassy rock, and there was Felicity.

She was sitting on a rounded boulder. She wore one of her couture cocktail party dresses, a ten-thousand-dollar number, as I recalled. The pattern was licensed from the Picasso estate and was one of a kind. I could tell she was steaming by the way her arms were crossed as she gazed off into the distance, tapping a foot.

''Felicity!'' I cried. I couldn't help myself. I was so overjoyed I bounded around in frolic. She watched coldly as I stood on hind legs and pawed the air.

''It's me,'' I said, wagging my tail and wiggling toward her.

A talking dog naturally came as a surprise. ''Who?'' she asked.

''Your husband.''

Her face went blank. A pause as she studied me. ''Why are you wearing that costume? You look ridiculous.''

''It's no costume. I got turned into a dog.''

''Oh, brother,'' she said in disgust and looked away.

''What are you doing here?'' I asked.

She didn't answer.

''Felicity?''

''Having a dream,'' she said irritably. ''I must have dropped off. I'm asleep and I'm dreaming. What a bore.''

''That's what I thought for a long time. I thought I was dreaming too.''

"You're lying in a hospital bed in Our Lady of Charity Hospital. That's what you're doing."

"What happened?"

"The doctors can't figure it out."

"Did I fall down and hit my head?"

"No." Her foot tapped faster and she sighed.

"Well?"

"Well what?"

"What happened?"

"They found you with your head on your desk. They thought you were napping. People are so scared of you they didn't try to wake you up until it was time to go home."

"The doctors can't do anything?"

"You respond to nothing," she said wearily. "You just lie there in a deep coma. You're a vegetable."

"I suppose you're going to ask for a conservatorship?"

She shot me a quick look that told me I was right.

"I can't say I blame you."

She relaxed a little. "You could be like that for years, the doctors say. Become an old man in that bed. I want to get on with my life. I'm still young."

"Don't count me out. I hope to get back somehow."

Felicity looked around. "I've been trying to figure out what this dream means from a Jungian standpoint. These dark rocks. What do they mean? And you in the dog costume. What's the significance of that?"

"I told you, it's no costume. This is me."

She looked at me more closely. "It does seem real." She reached out a hand and stroked my head.

"That makes the dream even more complex," she mused. "I wonder if Freudian theory explains it better."

"That's all crap. I'm here because a wizard put me under a spell."

Felicity laughed.

"I'm not kidding. I wish I was. You wouldn't believe all that's happened to me. I've been through hell."

"A wizard," she repeated, a smile on her face.

''Zalzathar's his name. He wanted somebody else but he got stuck with me. He wants me to help him win a war. Good and evil are fighting it out.''

''What side are you on?''

''I haven't decided yet.''

''That figures.''

''What's that supposed to mean?''

''If you don't know, I can't explain it.''

''It's not as easy as you think. There's a lot of things to consider. You may think you're dreaming, but I've been living this nightmare trying to find a way back.''

''I guess that's what it is,'' Felicity said.

''What is?''

''This dream. It's a nightmare. These black rocks. You as a dog.''

''That's nothing. You'd faint dead away if you saw some of the things I've seen. Right now I'm trying to get away from something that's half human and half horse. One end is female and the other is male.''

''Right,'' she said in a bored voice.

''The Bright Giver and the Dark One—God and Satan, we call them—had a big fight here. That why this place looks so strange. Kyrus and Boog-Weir were left behind somehow.''

''You don't believe in God,'' she reminded me. ''Who are those other people?''

''The half-human, half-horse creature. Kyrus is the white half and Boog-Weir is the black half.''

''Definitely Jungian archetypes,'' Felicity said. ''Dream figures representing something.''

''Good and evil,'' I said.

''No, that's too easy. You don't know anything about psychology, although therapy might have made you half-way human. No, it's something more complex.''

That was the irritating thing about Felicity. She made up her mind and that was it. Talk until Sunday and you wouldn't budge her.

"They told me that themselves," I replied. "You know something about their world that they don't?" I didn't keep the sarcasm out of my voice.

"I've decided to go to Buenos Aires," she said.

"When?" She was always veering from one subject to another. It was her way of keeping me off balance.

"Next week. You won't notice the difference."

"What do you mean, I won't notice the difference?"

"In the hospital. The care is very good. The nurses talk to you a little every day to see if you're coming out of it."

"How long will you be gone?"

"Two or three months. By then, the scandal will have died down."

"What scandal?"

"Your conviction," she snapped. "What do you think? Some people think you're faking your coma to keep from going to prison. It's humiliating."

"I'm guessing it was some technical violation. A lawyer must have told me . . ."

"Technical violation?" Felicity's eyes blazed. "You called it 'borrowing,' but the government had another name for it and the jury agreed. I haven't been able to go out for the shame. I can't stand the phony sympathy from those jealous women who hate me. Their syrupy words and false smiles are nauseating."

She got up and began walking back and forth, and I realized again what a knockout she was. Long legs and the grace of a runway model. "I wish this dream would end," she said. Then she was gone.

Flat disappeared. Just like that.

My sad howl echoed through the black canyons. It was heartless to tantalize me with Felicity. Who was that cruel? Zalzathar? Helither? Kyrus? Boog-Weir? Or maybe it was some other power that existed independently here in the Great Balwar. Whoever or whatever it was, I was in the dumps.

I curled up with my tail around me and slept a long time.

Escaping, I guess. It was late afternoon when I woke. What was the deal with Felicity? Was that really a dream she was having or was it my hallucination? I jumped to my feet, alarmed by how much time had passed. I pressed forward in the direction I'd been going. North or south, I didn't know. If I kept going long enough, I was bound to reach the end of this jumble of black rock. It couldn't last forever.

Toward dark, I heard the clatter of hooves from behind and it scared hell out of me. I broke into a run, dodging through the rocks like a broken-field runner. I fell a couple of times, and I knew I was in danger of serious injury. Some of the rocks had edges so sharp you could shave on them. I had to find a place to hole up fast.

''Dog!'' It was Boog-Weir's voice calling, loud as a thunderclap. ''Don't run. I can help you. I am good. She is bad.''

Screw it. I wasn't going to trust anybody. I found a narrow tunnel between two big smooth rocks and squeezed through. The tunnel began to rise and finally led to a small level area. I crept out and looked down over the edge.

Boog-Weir was just coming into sight, galloping easily, arms behind him like somebody showing off with a look-no-hands stunt. I saw flashes of Kyrus's whiteness behind.

''Dog!'' he called again. He galloped past and I saw he had an axe hidden behind him. The help he had in mind would separate my head from my body. It was nice to have that situation clarified. How could I have been so stupid to doubt Kyrus? As they passed, she rocked back and forth in sleep, her arms at her side and her fine pale breasts bouncing.

I waited until long after the hoofbeats faded to nothing before sliding back down the tunnel and continuing. The longer I traveled that night, the stronger and fresher I felt. The paradox didn't surprise me. I wondered again if anything ever would from now on.

Daybreak came, the sun rising in the east or west, whatever it was. I didn't care anymore. I was going to keep loping in this direction until I got somewhere. The scenery didn't change. Mile after mile of glassy obsidian. The Indigenous People, as Felicity calls them, used to make arrowheads from it.

I haven't mentioned the conferences Felicity has at our Long Island estate. Not the women's weekends where I had to take a powder so the lesbians weren't offended, but the others. There were endangered species conferences attended by vegetarians in sandals and walking shorts. There were toxic waste congresses that drew scientists and their wives and noisy kids. There were conferences on metaphysics and linguistics where people agreed everything was unknowable, despite language or maybe because of it. I wondered why I let them eat my food and drink my liquor if that was true. What was the point of wasting further breath on the subject? Speaking of liquor, when the Indians (as I call them) came for their annual powwow, we locked up the firewater.

Sooner or later during the conference, there would be a workshop on how "Euro-Americans" stole the land. The real radicals said everything should be handed back. They were silent on whether we should all board boats and go back to wherever our ancestors came from. This group wore buckskin and feathers and stayed in teepees squaws put up on the lawn. Judging from the complaints of the women as they struggled with the poles, they didn't favor going all the way back to the old ways. The moderates were happy to spend the night in our guest rooms. Their position was that they'd settle for billions in indemnification. Baloney, I told myself from the rear of the room. The strong take from the weak. It's natural law. You see it around the water hole and when an advanced race meets a primitive one. You see it every day of the week in the business world, and you would see more if it weren't for government meddling in the marketplace. Felicity warned me against expressing this or any other opinion.

"I don't want the dynamics of the conference spoiled," she said. "We're making real progress." She never explained what the progress was toward. ''Understanding,'' I suppose.

One year some of the red men drove into town and returned with a pickup bed full of firewater. A neighbor sent a member of his domestic staff over to find out what all the whooping and hollering was about. He was stripped naked and bound to a stake. Squaws capered around, pinching and prodding and making fun of his private parts. I settled out of court.

I heard Boog-Weir's huge voice calling to me from far off. Then there was silence. I guessed Kyrus had taken over. I knew she wouldn't come looking for me, so I was on my own.

It looked as if she and her Siamese twin were the only two living creatures in the Great Balwar. I didn't even see an insect. I traveled all that day, through the night and all the next day, not feeling the slightest fatigue or hunger. But toward afternoon of the second day, I began feeling a little peaked. Then tired and thirsty. It seemed each step I took increased hunger, thirst and weariness.

I dropped down to my belly to rest. My tongue felt huge in my mouth and I was too tired to think. Then it hit me through the mental fog that I must be on the border of the Great Balwar and the normal laws were coming back into play. Physical activity tires you, no water makes you thirsty, no food makes you hungry and weak—those laws. That had to be it. I had run on batteries so long there was no juice left.

Should I keep going and become so weak that I perished, or turn back? I wouldn't be hungry, thirsty or tired anymore but I'd be marooned in the Great Balwar. That must be why no one ever came back. Boog-Weir had all the time in the world to hunt down whoever wandered in and lop off his head. Those were the terrible sights Kyrus awakened to.

I crawled thirty or forty yards back into the Great Balwar and felt strength begin to return and hunger and thirst ease. I could think more clearly. To test my theory, I trotted back toward the boundary again and the same symptoms flooded back. I retreated again.

I sat to think about my quandry. By the time I crossed the border separating the Great Balwar from what lay beyond, I'd be so weak I probably couldn't do more than crawl. I wouldn't be able to catch anything to eat or find water to quench my thirst. I'd be history.

I wondered what was happening between the Two Legs and Mogwert. I couldn't be sure how much time had passed, but it may have been enough for the attack on Gowyith to begin. Night came on. It was utterly silent and the cold stars shone down. Around what I guessed was midnight, I heard Boog-Weir's voice echo in the black canyons many miles off. A couple hours later, I heard it again, closer but still miles away. In my revived condition, I was sure I could stay ahead of him. With no need to ever eat, drink or rest, I would be able to play cat and mouse with him indefinitely.

When loneliness became too much, I could steal in and talk to Kyrus. We discuss about good and evil.

I decided to make a break for it when it got light. Get as far across the line as I could and see what happened. If I died, I died. It would be better than dodging around these black rocks for the rest of the time that remained to me. I would have howled, except it would have led Boog-Weir straight to me.

Instead, I whimpered. What would the financial press say when I was toes up? "Death of a Corporate Raider," the headlines would announce with satisfaction. The liberal *New York Times*, always in favor of strengthening regulatory agencies and handcuffing business, would remind its readers about my troubles before the fatal coma. The crew on my yacht would fly the skull-and-crossbones flag at half mast. Would anyone shed a tear? Would Felicity? Morbid thoughts fill your head when you think it's your last night.

Just before dawn, when birds would be stirring if there were any, I heard Boog-Weir's voice again. "Dog!" his voice blared. "I can help." He was a half-mile away, if that. I wondered if he was being guided by some malign power. He had zeroed in pretty accurately.

But it didn't make any difference now. He couldn't go beyond the invisible line separating his world from what lay beyond. Maybe he would stand and watch me slowly expire beyond the boundary. Then stick around so Kyrus would see my body and weep.

I heard the drumming of hooves and figured I'd better start making tracks, even though dawn hadn't quite broken. It would be quicker to let Boog-Weir whack my head off, but I didn't want to give him the satisfaction. I ran as fast as I could for the boundary, hoping momentum would carry me a few yards farther when my legs gave out.

I went from strong to weak as a puppy. I willed myself to keep moving even when everything in me said stop and lie down. I slowed to a walk, then tottered forward on rubbery legs. As the sun rose, I was dying. I heard Boog-Weir's laughter boom behind me.

My legs gave way and I collapsed, dirt forcing its way up my nose when I landed. Sneezing feebly, I saw a questing ant wave its feelers an inch away. He and his pals would be feasting on me soon, nipping my flesh off with their tiny pincers.

I didn't care. I felt detached, like a spectator at my own funeral. Time passed, I don't know how much. A shadow flitted over me. The first of the vultures, I supposed. The ants and flies would have competition. I heard wind through pinions and the sound of a bird landing.

I had just strength enough to open an eye. It was a pelican waddling toward me. I thought this was strange, but what wasn't? I closed the eye. Something hard was pushed between my teeth. Then water flooded my mouth. My swollen tongue seemed to soak it up like a dry sponge. I swallowed and felt it trickling through my parched innards. It was sweeter than anything else I had ever tasted. I opened the eye again. The pelican bent again and put the tip of his bill to my mouth. More water gushed into my mouth. When my thirst was quenched, the pelican coughed up a small fish from his pouch. I slowly ate it. A few minutes later I could stand.

"Dog!" Boog-Weir boomed from the other side. "I can help."

[16]

The tree line was a mile off and I walked toward it slowly. Very slowly. Boog-Weir gave up yelling and watched. I just concentrated on making it to the woods. It seemed to take as long as to get a zoning permit if you don't grease palms.

But at last I tottered into the shadows of the trees. I stumbled through the undergrowth and bumped into a huge bear standing in silence. I recognized him as the one who had tried to jump me before. I sat down to await death.

''Been waitin' for you, dog,'' he said at last. He was so close I saw the network of old scars on his muzzle and a knot over his left eye. One ear was half crumpled. His breath would knock you flat.

I didn't bother answering. I hoped bears didn't play with victims before killing them as cats do.

''This be for you, frien','' he said. He moved to show a freshly killed buck. Then he turned and moved ponderously into the undergrowth. I heard him crashing through it for a long time as he put distance between us.

First a pelican and then a bear. Why his change of heart? I feasted on the deer all that day and the next. Nothing like red meat to get you back on your feet. In between I slept like I was dead. By morning of the third day, I was feeling pretty frisky and began to look around.

The forest was full of game—deer, elk, moose. Squirrels chattered in the trees, beavers in ponds slapped tails when they saw me lurking on the shore. I scented a muskrat, gave a porcupine a wide berth and likewise a skunk. A wild boar with fierce tusks shook his head threateningly and swore at me before leading his family into the brush. It was good to see pigs on all fours where they belonged. A wolverine snarled at me and a bobcat hissed over a shrew it had killed.

"Try to take this and die," the bobcat said. They're great bluffers.

"My belly is full," I answered. But he kept suspicious yellow eyes on me as I passed, ready for a trick.

After a while I noticed all the animals except beavers and the burrowing animals who stay put were drifting in the same direction. It wasn't a panicky rush, but there was no mistake that a migration was going on. Judging from their absence, birds must have already passed through. It didn't take a genius to figure out the creatures were fleeing trouble behind them. A doe with two fawns stiffened in fear when she saw me. The little ones darted behind her and peeped out with big eyes.

"Don't worry," I said. "I won't hurt you or them."

"May the Bright Giver bless you," she quavered.

"What are you running from?" I asked.

"Mogwert. Mogwert and many awful creatures never seen in the forest." She shuddered and looked behind her.

"How far?"

"We've been on the run a week." She looked at her fawns. "I can't travel fast. They're slow and they get tired. Nearly all the others are ahead of us."

"If you were alone, how long to get back?"

Her eyes bulged with horror. "I would never go back."

"A couple days?"

"I suppose." She looked at me. "Why do you want to know?"

"I'm going there."

"No!" she cried. "There are pigs who walk on two legs and worse."

"It's a long story," I said and left. I didn't want to waste more time. I was worried about what had happened while

I was in the Great Balwar. If either side won without me, what incentive was there to send me back home? I could appeal to Helither's good side if he wound up on top. But given the odds against him, it was like hoping to win the lottery to buy next week's groceries.

I trotted along at a pace that ate up the ground, sorry I'd spent so much time recuperating. The doe was right. She and her fawns were at the tail end of the migration. The only animals I saw after them were sick or gimpy. An elderly raccoon worn out by the trek and ready to give up the ghost called feebly to me.

"Go back if you want to see another spring."

I didn't answer. I moved through deserted corridors of tall trees. The golden afternoon sun slanted through them prettily. It would be a nice place if you had a picnic hamper and a blanket to throw down so you didn't pick up a tick. Felicity avoids the outdoors because of them. She has a horror of a tick burrowing into that perfect alabaster body of hers.

That meeting with her in the Great Balwar made me realize why I put up with everything. The humiliations, her coldness and scorn, my home turned into a conference center to promote causes I don't care about, or even oppose. The venomous writers, the goddess crowd and its lesbian faction gunning motorcycles and causing the neighbors to complain, all of it.

I was crazy about her. She was the only person in my life I didn't dominate. Was the secret of her power that she didn't give a damn what I thought? I was just background noise to her. When she did tune in, my talk about Wall Street bored her. She needed a lot of money to promote her various causes, including reviving drawing-room conversation. But how that money was made held no more interest to her than how plumbing carries shit from the home to the sea.

When you're used to people toeing the line, indifference is like seasoning. Or like color in a black-and-white world.

Success came easy to me. Work hard, develop good habits, snag a little bit of luck in the beginning, and it falls in your lap. There's no great mystery, despite all the books and motivational tapes that promise to reveal the "secret." Outwitting dull boards of directors had stopped being a challenge long ago. I could do it in my sleep.

But Felicity was always beyond reach. I could never connect with her. When we made love, I felt as if she had a clock on me and waited to say, "Time's up." She fulfilled the letter of our contract, but no more.

Some weeks I had to make appointments to see her. If I wasn't on her calendar, we had no more contact than strangers stopping in the same hotel. Our oddness as a couple was clear to everyone. She was a bright star in society and I was barely visible in the aura of her brilliance. Old-timers were reminded of Jackie and Onassis. But I didn't mind their smiles and the trophy-wife talk so long as she stayed Felicity Ingersol.

I never lost hope that one day she would return my feelings. If you work hard enough for something, it comes to you. If I believed in anything other than the bottom line, it was that. There wasn't any question of her leaving as long as I gave her what she wanted (although I was dragging my feet over the private jet). But I needed more. I needed her to love me too. I didn't expect grand passion. I knew that was unrealistic. I'd settle for comfortable affection, an easiness between us. Her head laid on my shoulder, her hand on my arm, the same bright smile she gave others. My opinion asked for now and then. Little things.

Seeing her in her dream or my hallucination, whatever the case was, made my love for her even stronger. I whined as I padded along. If I ever got back, I'd do whatever it took to melt the ice. I'd retire from business. Take up modern painting. Save a tropical rain forest if I had to buy it. Drum in the woods on male-bonding weekends to get in touch with my inner self. Get Rolfed, work with crystals. Whatever it took.

I crossed valleys and hills, the forest getting taller and darker. Making your way through woods that thick is no easy thing. For every step forward, you take two to the side. It would be almost impenetrable for a human. This was first-growth stuff that would bring a fortune if you came in and clear-cut. The Japanese pay top dollar for first growth.

I came to an obstruction. Thinking it was rock, I slowly made my way along it looking for a way past. Then it dawned on me that the rock was suspiciously smooth. It was stone piled on stone in regular blocks. The trees were so thick I couldn't see how tall it was, but it was too high for a wall. I must have traveled a mile before I came to a small opening. There had been a door there at one time, but it had rotted away. Stone steps led up a narrow tunnel. I tested the air. All I could smell was cold stone and mildew.

I went up the steps in complete blackness and silence. If a pin dropped, it would sound like Saturday night at the bowling alley. I climbed stairs for a long time; then the tunnel came to a door. Protected from the elements, it was still whole. I nosed it open. A broad stone corridor was before me, dimly lit by sunlight coming through tall rectangular slits in the wall. This was a castle of immense size. As primitive as life was here, it must have taken armies of stonemasons hundreds of years to build. I hesitated, wondering which way to go, right or left. The corridor curved slightly, so after about a hundred yards I couldn't see where it led in either direction.

I picked right because those are my politics. I trotted along, toenails clicking on the flagstones. After a few minutes I reached an intersecting corridor, as vast and gray as the one I was in. I turned right again and continued. It had rooms at intervals with closed doors I couldn't open. It is a serious handicap when you've only got paws to work with. You see how valuable the opposable thumb is. This corridor was straight. Far off I saw where it joined another. Who needed this much space? It was like an airport.

I came to that corridor and turned right again. More

rooms with closed doors. I reminded myself that to get back to the tunnel I just had to turn around and then keep turning left. After a long while, this corridor led to a broad stairway down into darkness below. I didn't find that inviting, so I continued along the corridor. Whenever I met one that intersected, I turned right again. After a long time, I caught a familiar scent. It was me. I was back at the tunnel that led to the forest. This time around I would turn left when I came to an intersecting corridor.

More of the same. Hallways of vast length with closed doors and another stairway leading down. I took the stairs this time. I couldn't see a thing but had the sense I was descending into a huge chamber. I came to the bottom step and a stone floor. It must have been hell keeping this place warm when people lived here. I followed a draft and it led me into what I sensed was another huge room. The draft was from a fireplace a football team could stand in. Big rooms. Big fireplaces. That appeared to be all I was going to find out without light.

I followed my nose back to the staircase and climbed the steps. Interesting as the place was, I wasn't a tourist. I had to get back to Gowyith as fast as my legs would take me. At the top of the stairs I turned right and wound my way back through the corridors to the tunnel.

The door was shut. Mine was the only scent that lingered on the stone floor. There wasn't any breeze, so the door couldn't have blown shut. I listened intently. Total silence. The light coming through the slits from outside was beginning to fade, and the corridor darkened. Panic rose. I struck off down a corridor again. I reached narrow stairs leading up after several hundred yards. I labored up steps until I emerged onto a turret. I stood on hind legs and looked down on a vast empty courtyard. High as the wall was, trees outside had grown close and tall enough so you could step onto their limbs. The builders must originally have had space cleared to prevent an enemy from doing just that. This meant those trees had grown from seeds. A long time had passed. Maybe a century.

The sun was setting fast and it was getting cooler. All there was in every direction was thick forest. Empty forest, as I knew. I thought of the door that had closed. It would be better to spend the night on the turret. It was easier to keep an eye on the opening that led below than to also guard against something sneaking up from behind. I hoped there would be enough light come morning to find a way out. I lay down and wrapped my tail around me.

I awoke to light flickering on the stone around me. I stood to look over the saw-toothed turret wall. Far off toward Gowyith, a huge light show was going on. Alternate bursts of white and purple color lit the sky, and a deep but faint rumble came from there. If I were back home, I'd know what it was. Some rock group featuring skinny drug users with tattoos and long hair. They would have sound equipment that pumped out more decibels than World War II. As I watched, the purple flashes got brighter and more frequent. Then both the light and the sound stopped suddenly. When they didn't start again, I lay back down to sleep.

More time passed, and I woke up again, this time to the sound of partying. It scared me that my sleep had been so deep I hadn't heard the revelers arrive. I cautiously looked over the turret. The courtyard was ablaze with torchlight and filled with Two Legs dressed in party gear. Women with low-cut dresses hurried from carriages, escorted by men wearing fancy dress. Servants led the arriving horses and carriages off somewhere. There was laughter and talking. Everybody was having a fine old time. Gowyith fights for its life, but these people were having a ball. Literally. Music came up the stairs from below.

This was my chance to beat it. In the confusion of the arrivals, no one would notice a dog in the shadows. I crept down the stairs to the corridor. Peering around the corner, I saw it had been transformed as I slept. Candles burned in sconces on walls hung with rich tapestries. Their patterns and colors were repeated in carpets that muffled footsteps. The rugs and hangings took the chill off the stone. The corridor was filled with happy people hurrying in both directions. The women in gorgeous ball gowns were rosy from excitement. Their hair was piled on their heads, and jewels glittered on white bosoms. Some of the men had decorations that blazed on sashes. Now and then a man in a military tunic walked with his hand on a lady's elbow. Nobody paid the slightest attention to me, so I padded out into the crowd. As I wondered how all this had been done without my hearing a sound, snatches of conversation came to me.

"The Princess Gundori was very kind to acknowledge me. Last year she . . ."

"Did you see how Hujolding looked at her? Not since the planting season has he . . ."

"Of course, it's in her interest to maintain a certain innocence . . ."

I came to a door and looked in. It was full of handsome furniture, and wood burned in a fireplace. A beautifully dressed couple stood holding fluted wine glasses. There were bearskins on the floor and paintings on the wall. A table where candles burned was filled with food, as if they expected guests. I took in the scene with a glance and moved on, not wanting to attract attention. Each door along the hall was open. The rooms were spacious with high ceilings. There was no way you could justify that wasted space in an economic sense. Some had people in them, others didn't. I guessed the doors were open so you could admire the richness of their possessions. Try leaving your door open back home. Burglars would clean you out so fast it would make your head swim.

As I moved cautiously down the corridor, careful not to trip anyone, the music grew louder. I could pick out some of the instruments. Violins, flutes and horns, maybe a bagpipe in there somewhere. I reached the big staircase and looked down.

The room was as immense as I'd sensed. Hundreds of candles burned, maybe thousands. It looked like a whole cord of dry wood snapping and crackling in the massive fireplace. Couples stood at a fair distance from it because of the heat thrown out. There had to be a couple hundred men and women in the room, every one of them talking. The roar from them would have drowned out the music if it wasn't so loud.

Nobody paid me any notice. It was as if I didn't exist. That was all right with me. I wanted to get down those stairs, pick my way through the crowd, get outside and find a gate open so I could make for Gowyith. That light show might mean the final battle had started, and I still had a long way to go.

I reached the bottom of the stairs and then began to work my way through the throng. I had to watch it because people were too busy talking and waving their arms to pay attention to where they stepped. I was uneasy now. I don't know about you, but if I was at a party and a huge dog suddenly appeared, I would notice it. Point, make a comment. But these people were totally engrossed with one another, nearly shouting to make themselves heard.

I was nearly to the tall double doors that had been opening to admit couples when I noticed a man staring at me. He was strongly built, average height, balding. He stood with his hands behind his back, looking around pleasantly and bowing. The smile left his face and he headed toward me. I kept one eye on him and the other on the doors. When they opened, I'd bolt for it. If I had to knock a few people off their pins, so be it.

But they stayed closed and he reached my side.

''Who are you?'' he asked.

''That's a strange question,'' I answered. I wanted to buy time until the doors opened.

''Strange?''

"I'm a dog, aren't I? How many dogs do you know that talk?"

He waved a hand in dismissal. "Of course you're not a dog. You're under a spell."

"How did you know that?"

"I'm asking the questions. Who are you?"

"Ingersol's the name."

"I don't care what you're called. Who are you and where are you from? You're not from here."

"You know that?"

He glared. "I can make you talk."

I decided I'd better give him a straight answer. "You're right. I'm not from here. I'm from a place called Earth. I was brought here by Zalzathar."

Understanding flooded his face, and he seemed to relax a little. "Zalzathar. So that's it."

"You know him?"

"Of course. There aren't that many of us."

If he was friends with Zalzathar and a fellow wizard, maybe he could spirit me back to Spyngle. As if he read my mind, he said, "We're not friendly. He's forever asking me to join him in that stupid war." His glance took in the crowd and he smiled proudly. "His enemies are not necessarily mine."

"So you're for the Two Legs?" Maybe he could put me in Gowyith with a simple wave of a wand.

"I have no interest in them."

He saw my puzzlement. "I'm for myself, a party of one. Let others go their way and I'll go mine."

My sentiments exactly. "I couldn't agree more."

His look said he didn't care what I thought. He was already starting to lose interest in me. He returned a wave from someone across the room.

"How do I get out of here?" I asked.

"Why would you want to leave?"

"I have to get to Gowyith or Spyngle. Whichever is easier for you."

''What for?'' His smile was cold.

''There's going to be a fight for the Final Victory.''

''Another one?'' he said with weary disgust.

''They say this is really it this time.''

''Who says that?''

''Zalzathar.''

''He's been saying that longer than you can imagine. He's obsessed. It is what comes of associating with Mogwert. They take pleasure only from pain. They care nothing''—a sweep of his arm took in the room—''for beauty.''

The crowd eddied around us. The women fanned themselves and the men bowed to each other.

''It's quite a party,'' I said. ''But don't they care about the danger Gowyith is in?''

He seemed to find the idea funny. ''No more than I.''

The orchestra in the next room struck up again. People clapped and laughed. It sounded like a polka.

''So you don't care who comes out on top?'' I asked.

''We have our own world here. Now you're part of it.''

''What do you mean?'' I quavered. I had enough experience by now to know whatever he meant wasn't good.

''You're one of us now. You'll live in the stables with the other animals.''

He made a little movement with his hand and looked surprised. He made the movement again.

''You have a very strong protector,'' he said.

''I do?'' I looked around.

''He's not here.''

''What's he doing for me?''

''His magic prevents me from doing what I want.''

''What's that?''

''To kill you. To make you one of them.'' His look took in the room.

It took a second for it to sink in. ''They're all dead?''

He didn't answer. His silence was sinister.

''They look pretty lively,'' I said faintly.

''You doubt me?''

''They just look so alive.''

''They are to me.'' His eyes returned to me. ''Where is this place you're from? Earth?''

''That's what we call it. It's on the other side of what Zalzathar calls the membrane.''

''Membrane?''

''It separates our worlds.''

He thought for a moment. ''He brought you from there? Very impressive. Zalzathar grows in knowledge and power.'' He looked a little worried.

''I want to get back where I belong,'' I said. ''Zalzathar said he'd help me when the Final Victory is in the bag. Maybe that protector you mentioned is him.''

He made the little movement of his hand again. ''No. It is not a wizard's spell. It is something different.''

It had to be Helither. Something told me not to mention him. ''What are you called?''

''Brofelio.''

''Nice place you've got here. It's yours, right?''

''Everything is mine. Except you. They are all my creations. They come alive every night to celebrate my triumph.''

''Triumph?''

''Their creation.''

They were illusions. Some clever bit of fakery.

''You party every night?''

''Every night. After the ball, I select a guest to sup with. They are enchanting, every one. Each with his or her own story and way of telling it. Their own personalities. Their own smiles and frowns, unique to them. Each individual is different. Some more interesting than others, of course. But even the least of them gives me entertainment through a meal.''

''It would be years before you finished having supper with them all.''

He nodded. ''Years. That's what you call time? Yes, as many as there are, I've supped with each many times. Their celebration of my work has gone on a long time. Very long.''

He was a smug bastard, no doubt about that. But what he pulled off every night was still impressive. Stuff went on all around you. It was better than one of those virtual reality parlors you see in malls.

''Everybody here was human once?'' I asked.

''Human?''

''They're called Two Legs here.''

''Long ago they were, yes. I collected them, choosing them for their beauty.''

He had good taste. They were all lookers, even the men.

''Some lived in towns, others the countryside. Their lives would have been pitifully short.''

''If you hadn't killed them?''

He gave me a sharp look. ''They would be long forgotten now. Those who loved them are long since dust. Yet these live on—in a manner of speaking—each night. They will continue to do so until I weary of them.''

''Facinating,'' I said. Spock's hackneyed line on *Star Trek*, but I couldn't come up with anything better.

His was a look of vindication. ''There are those, Zalzathar among them, who call my accomplishment a waste of time. They say it is madness, masturbation.''

''They're just jealous,'' I said fawningly. If Zalzathar thought he was a nutcase, that was good enough for me. Zalzathar was no paragon of sanity himself.

There was a big stir in the crowd. Cries of amazement and applause. Four sweating servants carried in a huge roasted boar on a platter. Its skin was brown and crisp and gleamed with fat. The place suddenly smelled like a hofbrau.

''The feast begins soon,'' Brofelio said. I salivated and licked my chops. The crowd began to move toward the room where the music was.

''It's time to select my guest for supper,'' Brofelio said, looking around. Just then the doors opened for some late arrivals and I shot past legs and was outside before they closed. I was in the courtyard, where cold stars and a quarter moon stared down from the inky sky.

If I had the time, it would be interesting to hang around to watch Brofelio party. Sort of be a naturalist. I suppose after his intimate supper, whoever was lucky enough to get picked that night got pulled into bed for a romp. That probably was what Zalzathar and his fellow wizards meant by masturbation. I wondered how many wizards this place had. I hoped I didn't come across any more. Two was plenty.

There were knots of servants standing around outside gossiping and smoking pipes, domestics and people who handled the horses and carriages. It would be one thing to be in Brofelio's dream or whatever it was if you were inside. You had nice clothes and were about to sit down to a feast. It would be something else to have to fetch and carry and do the rest of the dirty work night after night. But I had no time to waste on sympathy for the riffraff.

Like their betters inside, they paid no attention to me. They kept chattering among themselves. I loped across the courtyard toward the wall, hoping to find a way back into the forest. The castle was like a city. As many people as there were at the feast, many more were outside. I stood on hind legs and looked in windows as they sat down to humble meals lit by candle stubs. They wore coarser clothing, animal skins for the men and homespun for the women. Toothless old folks sat in corners by the fire, spooning soup from bowls. Brofelio sure was a stickler for detail. This was like some huge movie set with countless scenes going on. I could see why he felt he didn't get enough respect.

I stood and stuck my nose in one window where a table was filled with men and women raising flagons. Receiving their toasts was a portly man in peasant dress at the head of the table. His balding head was shiny and reflected the candlelight. He turned to me at the window and smiled. *It was Brofelio*. No way could he have changed clothes and got across the courtyard that fast. I dropped back down to the ground and ran as fast as my legs would take me. Ahead were paddocks and a stable. I passed through the stable with stalls on either side and emerged to more paddocks. A huge black stallion was furiously mounting a mare. As he humped away, he turned to look at me. There was no mistaking that look. Brofelio.

I kept running and reached the wall. I ran along it until I came across to a passageway lighted by a torch. I shot down it until it reached an intersecting corridor. This was small and narrow, unlike the ones in the castle. Torches burned every few yards, giving feeble light. I was looking for one of the tunnels that led outside. After running maybe a half-mile I found one. I also found a figure in black helmet and armor standing in the middle of the passageway. A sword was in his hand. In his other was a shield that had Brofelio's profile. I skidded to a stop. We looked at each other in silence.

"No one leaves here," he said finally. It was Brofelio's voice.

"Look," I panted. "I've had a great time. Really. But I've got places to go, people to see."

He made a few practice swings. The blade swished wickedly. I remembered what he'd said before.

"You can't hurt me. Something's protecting me."

"Nothing will protect you from this blade."

Was he bluffing? There was only one way to find out. I started walking toward him. He dropped the shield, gripped the sword with both hands and spread his legs. I kept coming. Did I have a choice?

When I got close enough, I would head-feint in one direction and go the other. He'd be faked out and I would shoot down the tunnel to the outside.

My move was all-pro, but it didn't fool him for a second. I saw the sword slicing down at an angle that would take my head off. Then there was a flash of light and a loud clang and Brofelio shrieked in pain. I didn't wait to find out what happened. I galloped down the unlit tunnel until I came to a rotted door. It gave way when I stood on hind legs and pushed. A huge windstorm was blowing outside.

[17]

The last time I'd seen a storm like this was when Quick the fox and I were traveling together. The wind shrieked through the trees, which tossed so much it looked like they were trying to pull up roots and join the general migration. I wondered if this blow was connected to the far-off light show I had seen from the castle.

Instinct said to find shelter and ride it out. But I didn't want to hang around. Who was to say Brofelio wouldn't come looking for me? A wizard who could create his own world wasn't somebody you wanted to give a second chance. I guessed Helither's powers had kept me alive in the castle. I owed him for saving my bacon again.

I pushed on, ears laid back. There were so many tree limbs snapping off it reminded me of corn popping in a movie theater lobby. Bushes and long grass whipped back and forth. I yelped every time I got slashed in the face. If I were back in the U.S.A., this wind would have a name and TV reporters in trench coats would give live updates.

Felicity was big on throwing parties to benefit the poor bastards who lost homes in natural disasters. You can get rich people to donate money if you give them dinner, booze, and live music for dancing. This was all on me, of course. It meant I ended up kicking in twice because I also had to write a check. It had to be bigger than anyone else's.

"We have to be an example," Felicity said.

"Why?" I asked.

This was never worthy of an answer. If I hadn't always been looking for write-offs, I would have put my foot down.

After an hour, it sounded like the wind was picking up even more. I decided getting clobbered by a falling tree was a bigger danger than becoming a member of Brofelio's repertory company. I found a giant of a tree that looked like it could weather whatever the wind dished out and crawled in among roots that looked like mighty tendons growing out of the earth. I sweated out the rest of the night there. The wind began subsiding toward dawn and by the time the sun came up, it was calm.

There was a eerie hush as I moved through the trees. The forest got less thick as I traveled. I guessed that Brofelio was responsible for the choking growth around his castle. It was his way of keeping people from stumbling onto the place accidentally. Leave it to me.

In the late afternoon as I lapped water at the edge of some reeds on a river bank, I heard the splash of paddles in the water. I dropped to the ground and belly-crawled into the reeds. After a minute, a canoe came in sight. Three Two Legs paddled like crazy and their boat flew through the water. It was like the ones made of bark you see in anthropology museums. After a minute, I saw why they were going so fast. They were being chased by three war canoes, each paddled by six Pig Faces.

The boat with the Two Legs shot past where I lay hidden. They were bare-chested and their torsos were daubed with dried mud beginning to run from their sweating. Camouflage, I guessed. They darted looks over their shoulders. They disappeared around a bend in the river and then the Pig Faces swept past, swarming through the water. They dug into the river with steady, confident strokes.

I stayed hidden until I saw that nobody else followed. Six to one were odds Pig Faces liked. I wished the Two Legs well, but I didn't think much of their chances of avoiding being ripped open to see what made them tick. I had to get to where the action was, and the sooner the better. The first thing was to get across the river.

A grayish-blue torrent, it was fifty yards wide with more reeds on the far side. By the time I got there, the current would have carried me quite a way. In the meantime, I'd be exposed, a sitting duck. What if alligators were waiting for their next meal?

As usual, I had a sad shortage of options. I took a couple deep breaths and plunged in. The river was so cold I yelped. It was like runoff straight from a glacier. I dog-paddled for the other side as the current swept me along like a cork. When I rounded the bend, I saw the canoes far ahead. I reached the reeds a half-mile downriver and hauled out, winded and water pouring from me. I gave myself a sodden shake and looked around. The forest was as still on this side. I came to a small pond a mile or so inland. I was shocked at my reflection. I was nearly as ratty-looking as Quick had been. Older, too. Still in a dog's prime, but for how much longer? I knew dogs aged faster than humans, but this was ridiculous. Everything I had gone through had taken its toll, that was clear. There was even gray in my muzzle.

Swell. Add a speeded-up aging process to everything else. I wouldn't be able to feed myself much longer. I'd be reduced to chewing roots and bark. I glumly headed in the direction of Gowyith and Spyngle. I kept going long past the time I would normally stop for the night. Toward eight or nine, I came across a patch of mushrooms and ate until I was full. Only afterward did it occur to me they might be poisonous or hallucinogenic. I wouldn't want to hallucinate in my hallucination, would I?

As I told myself to guard against negative thoughts, there was a sudden flash of white lightning on the horizon, and a short time later came the rumble of thunder. Then there was an answering flash of purple lightning and more thunder. This went back and forth like the night before. Again, the purple lightning got more frequent and brighter.

After the light show stopped, I found a place to sleep until dawn. The following day, my nose led me to a carcass some predator had tucked away in a thicket to eat later. It had never returned, either because it joined the migration or was killed by Pig Faces. I began to see their scouting parties later in the day. As usual, they didn't bother hiding their presence. They tramped noisily, grunting and squealing as I spied from cover. Their smell hung around like a beer fart long after they were gone.

Even with those interruptions, I made good progress. As twilight came on, I judged I was somewhere near Gowyith or Spyngle. I came to a rutted dirt road and instinct told me it led from one to the other. Decision time. Who do I go with, Zalzathar or Helither? It didn't take a rocket scientist to figure out where the smart money would be. I started toward Spyngle but stopped. Zalzathar and Mogwert had no idea when I would get back, or if I ever would. No one came back from the Great Balwar, after all. Who would know if I sneaked a look at Gowyith?

Obviously I wanted the Two Legs to win. Who wouldn't? But when Slippery Rock plays Notre Dame, you have to be realistic. Tough, but so is life.

I padded along the deserted road. Sitting on a rock under a tree was Helither. Unless my eyes tricked me, he just appeared out of thin air. He was whittling a stick. Still looked like somebody's gardener.

"It's a long time you've been journeying," he called.

I walked over and lay down. "I've come all the way from the Great Balwar. You know about that place?"

"One hears stories. A place of doubt and confusion."

"The Mogwert ordered me taken there. You wouldn't send your worst enemy to it, take my word. It's hell. There's something there half human and half horse. A woman in front and a man in the back. She's okay but he's a real shithead."

He shook his head. "Hell—that's what you call Eha-

Kred? No. No matter how vile the Great Balwar is, it's not EhaKred. I see that you needed my protection.''

''How can you tell?''

''It's not hard.''

''You know a wizard named Brofelio?''

He nodded. ''He pursues evil in his own way.''

''He's a weirdo who lives in a castle with a bunch of, I guess, spirits. They party every night. He swung a sword at me. I thought I was a goner.''

He nodded and gave me a look. ''And a bear and a pelican helped you?''

''Thanks to you?''

Helither nodded again.

''I guess I owe you big time.''

His nod acknowledged the debt. ''You left unexpectedly.''

''I wanted to check things out and get back to you.'' I tried to sound offhand.

''We've been busy organizing the defense of Gowyith since you left. Mogwert and their army attacked.'' I saw now he was drawn and hollow-eyed from fatigue. You don't think of an angel as needing rest. But then, you don't think of them as looking like gardeners either.

''Are you guys holding your own?'' I asked.

''Barely. If they hadn't made a serious error, Gowyith would have fallen already. They're far stronger than anyone could have expected.''

''What's the error?''

''Instead of a single powerful blow that would have carried all before it, they have made many small attacks at great cost to themselves. We've beat them back so far, may the Bright Giver be praised.''

''You can thank me for that. I told them how to win was death by a thousand cuts.'' I explained how I had conned Zalzathar and Mogwert.

It was clear Helither thought my debt was paid. ''The Bright Giver will bless you for that.'' He said it so tenderly I felt a twinge of shame. Then I steeled myself. If you let sentiment intrude on decision-making, bad choices result. Helither was shaking his head in wonder. "Do you see the marvelous and subtle ways he works?"

He looked like a teacher expecting an answer from his prize pupil.

"Beats me," I said.

"After epochs of study guided by the Dark One himself, Zalzathar gains a mastery of wizardry never imagined possible. Through a spell, the veil that separates our worlds is pierced. His aim is to find a mind clever and diabolical enough to guide them to Final Victory. Instead, he gets someone who will give him a final taste of bitter defeat."

Helither looked up. "Thank you, Bright Giver."

Of all the billions of people on Earth, the Bright Giver had reached into an office in midtown Manhattan and found me at my desk. Why not some military guy who knew tactics and strategy? There must be millions to pick from. A plebe at West Point would know more, plus he'd have the advantage of youth. Or pick some spiritual person who would be one hundred percent behind the program no matter what the odds.

I could see Zalzathar fouling up. He was a wizard, just a magician on a bigger scale. But wasn't the Bright Giver all-powerful and perfect? Why pick me, somebody who might opt to go with the opposition and plan to make up for it with heavy-duty penance some later date? Maybe this whole business was like slot machines. If he lost here, the Bright Giver just pushed on to the next world and stuck a quarter in for another play. No wonder there are cynics.

"I remember you said you upset Zalzathar's aim at the last minute," I said.

"Well do I recall," Helither answered. He breathed deeply as if trying to collect himself. "I was sleeping high on a mountain in Ibisken, far from here in the Raiers mountains to the south. I go there for its silence. The Bright Giver's voice came to me to warn of the spell Zalzathar was casting at that very moment." Helither was beatific.

"What happened next?"

"My mind found Zalzathar in the foul place where Mogwert dwell. He was in deep concentration, almost at the end of his conjuring. He became aware of my scrutiny. He tried to ignore me but his mind strayed the tiniest flicker."

Soderberg's office is four or five blocks from mine, also on the thirty-fifth floor. I suppose anybody in that area with a place on the thirty-fifth floor could have been the victim. I look from my window into the law offices of Stern and Killiam. Seventy-five lawyers, each right down Mogwert's alley. None would have the slightest hesitation throwing in with monsters and fiends. Their kind of crowd. Even if I ended up going with Mogwert in the end, Helither was lucky my number came up. At least they got a little more time before the curtain came down.

"Did you know I'd be coming down this road?" I asked.

"No, but I hoped I'd find you." Something in his manner made me think he had feared I'd been going back and forth.

"Gowyith is but two hours away," he said. "Come, we'll stroll together."

We headed down the road. "We will see the enemy in an hour," Helither said. "The city is encircled but there is a secret way. I'll show you."

"How long have I been gone? Time gets away from you in the Great Balwar."

"A long time," he said vaguely, his mind elsewhere. "Lately," he said after a worried pause, "these small attacks so costly to the enemy have come less often. It is as if they've become dissatisfied with this tactic. But it is not like Mogwert to change what they do. Whether from pride or stubbornness, they never depart from what has been set in motion."

"I told them it might not work. I said we—I mean they—might have to come up with something different."

Helither wasn't listening. "Still, it has given us time for messages to go to Ferwaay and Neve Afrather. They are raising armies. If we can hold out until they get here, Mogwert and their evil host will be defeated.''

My ears pricked. ''How long will that take?'' This was the first inkling that Helither and the Two Legs might end up winners.

''This sun must rise and set this many times.''

I counted as he opened and closed his fist. Twenty days. ''That's not so bad.''

''The siege has been long. We're near the end of our strength. Unlike Mogwert, we were not prepared for war. Our people are tired and food is short.'' He sounded like a doctor who monitored vital signs and didn't like what he saw. The flicker of hope went out like a candle in a draft.

Panic gripped me. ''When you say I was in the Great Balwar a long time, what do you mean? Show with your hand.''

I had been gone three months. It had seemed just a few days. Time was screwed up there more than I thought. What was happening to the real me back in the hospital bed? If they didn't trim my hair and nails, I probably looked like Howard Hughes at the end.

Maybe to save money I had been transferred from the hospital to some nursing home where flies buzzed and they didn't change the sheets unless they felt like it. Nobody would care that I'd been to the White House for dinner with Dutch and Nancy. I would be just another piece of meat. You read about those horrors. The owners laugh off the fines when they get written up by inspectors wanting a bigger bribe. My philosophy is if you're going to grease a palm, give people more than they expect. Make a big deal about it. Praise the guy so he feels good about himself. A lot of people are guilty about accepting bribes. If you're stingy, guilt gets mixed in with resentment and the next thing you know you have trouble. If you get into payoffs, be generous. Ingersol's Law No. 17.

My paws hurt. I stopped to look at them. The pads were

cracked from hard travel. "Look at that," I said. "They're bleeding."

Helither squatted to look. "Let me see." His hands were soft and gentle. They passed over my paws, one by one. When he stood, they were as velvety smooth as puppy paws.

"How'd you do that?" I asked in amazement. Take healing powers like that into the major markets and you would need a hundred 800 numbers to handle the business.

"It's nothing," he said.

"No, I'm serious. That's like a miracle."

"Miracles are far different."

"Yeah, well, you know what I mean. And while we're on the subject, it seems to me that with your powers you could beat Mogwert and Zalzathar with one hand tied behind your back." Maybe he was holding something back for the last minute.

"My powers are not great enough," he said grimly.

"Zalzathar is outgunning you?"

"His powers are vastly enhanced. They are far greater than any wizard has ever known."

"But you've got the Bright Giver on your side. That's got to count for something."

He smiled tiredly. "The Bright Giver is a great one for delegating. This war is mine to win or lose."

"But what if the Dark One is giving Zalzathar help on the sly? That wouldn't be fair."

"Come, Mr. Ingersol, you disappoint me. Fair? The Dark One, mighty as he is and vaulting as his ambition, is no different in fundamental nature than I. We are both angels. He is Fallen and will never again see the face of the Bright Giver. That is his terrible punishment for rebellion. I will see that face one day. That is my reward. Apart from that, we are similar. We contend as equals."

It sounded good in theory, but I wondered if Helither was kidding himself. Back home you heard about the Devil, even if you didn't believe in him. Other than Gabriel, who blows the horn when the game's over, who can name another angel? They are just faces in the crowd, bit players. The Devil, in contrast, is a marquee name. That he rebelled showed he had a pretty good opinion of his abilities. Helither going up against that kind of stud? A nice guy, but you had to think no way does he pull it off. The oddsmakers would take it off the boards. I didn't say this, however.

We continued along the road. ''We'd best move into the trees,'' Helither said. ''It won't be long now.'' We climbed a wooded hill that overlooked the road and then moved in the direction of Gowyith again. Through the trees I saw Pig Faces below standing around a pile of rocks dumped on the road to block it.

''Every road to Gowyith is in their hands,'' Helither whispered.

We continued until he stopped at a bush with brilliant red berries. ''Crawl under this and you'll find a small tunnel. Follow it until you reach Gowyith. There we will meet again.''

I looked where he pointed, and when I looked back Helither was gone. I wormed my way under the limbs of the bush, and found a hole. I squeezed through it into the darkness. It smelled musty and the roots felt like they were giving me noogies on every side as I squirmed through the tunnel.

[18]

The other end of the tunnel was a hole in dense shrubbery by a building in an alley where pottery was made. I stuck my nose out cautiously. The alley was empty except for a scrawny yellow tomcat. I said hello.

"Hello, yourself," he returned sourly. He sank down until his belly touched the cobblestones the way cats do when they expect trouble. He laid his ears back.

"I'm not going to bother you."

"I guess you won't. I know dogs. All yapping noise. A claw across your nose will send you yelping back to the bitch who dropped you in a ditch." Have I said cats have a big chip on their shoulder?

"I've been away. How are things?"

"Why come back, you fool? There's naught here but too many mouths and not enough food."

"I've got business."

"Putting your nose where it doesn't belong? Digging a hole. Barking at the moon?" This was said with a scornful laugh.

"There's not enough food?"

"I used to be fat and purring. Look at me now. Food the Two Legs used to throw away, they now eat and leave not a scrap. This alley was full of tasty things before. Scare away the rats and you ate your fill. Now there's nothing to eat, nor any rats."

"Why not?"

"They left the day before the bad ones tried to get into Gowyith."

"You mean Mogwert?"

"Don't say that name," the tom hissed, afraid he had said too much. "Someone might be listening." After glancing around, his eyes returned to me. "You won't hear me say one word against Mogwert. They have never done me any harm and I don't pay attention to the chatter of ignorant voices." He said this in a voice meant to reach any listening ears. That is a cat for you. They are your friend as long as you can do something for them. Otherwise, adios.

I left him and trotted to the end of the alley. It opened onto the square where the Curiam met. It was empty except for a few people wrapped in cloaks against a chill wind. I wondered how much longer before winter descended.

The wind brought a familiar smell of pipe tobacco and queeg. Helmish had passed here not long before. Nose to the ground, I tracked him across the square and down three narrow alleys. Before, they had been crowded. But I came across only three or four hurrying people. They flattened themselves against buildings as I passed.

Helmish's scent led to a closed door up a step from the cobblestoned alley. I scratched and it opened. "By the Bright Giver above," Helmish cried, "it's Big." He dropped to his knees and hugged me. My tail wagged like crazy and I broke free to scamper about. I spun in circles and barked. My dog side was fond of the old guy.

"Come in, come in," he said, getting to his feet. "I thought you was gone for good, killed by those fiends." I followed him inside to a big drafty place full of shadows. Everywhere I looked there was glass, those lenses he was forever polishing. It occurred to me for the first time that his obsession might mean he was crazy. Great.

Helmish gave me a worried look. "It looks like you had some hard travel."

"To put it mildly."

"Oh, Big, I wish I could understand you."

"Feed me."

"Barking at me. What's he want?" The light bulb went on. "I bet you're hungry."

"You got that right."

He shuffled off. His clothes hung on him. He had lost weight and that round belly of his was gone. So were the rosy cheeks. He returned with a small knuckle of beef. "I've been saving this in hopes you'd be back. Another day or so and I would have eaten it myself. Food's short. Females and young ones are suffering. Everybody stays indoors to save strength except those who fight on the walls." He watched me gnaw.

"Lots of things changed since you've been gone, none for the better. Mogwert and their foul legions attacked Gowyith. There's been hard fighting every day since. We've pulled back inside the last wall. They've tried to break through the North Gate, the West Gate, South and East gates. Queenzel's Gate, Jabikee Gate—they had a try at all of them. But we've kept them out. Every man able to hold a weapon's been called to arms. Some are so old and pitiful they're in the way more than any help. The younger women have been fighting too. Heaving rocks down on the Pig Faces. Never heard of fighting women before." He loaded a pipe and tried to light it with an ember from the fireplace. He smiled ruefully. "Well, not outside the home. Plenty will give you all the fight you want there."

He pulled sadly on the uncooperative pipe. There isn't a good restaurant on either coast now that permits pipes or cigars. I like a good Havana after dinner, or did. The last few times I've lit up, people acted like I was a war criminal. I would have stared them down except for Felicity. "Oh, put it out," she said. "Nobody likes that stink."

"You're the first woman I've known who doesn't like the smell of a good cigar."

"Don't be stupid. The others were just afraid to say so."

Helmish got it going at last. "Gowyith is surrounded, completely cut off. No food getting in and water's short.

There's wells inside the wall, but not enough. The Curiam had all the food gathered and they dole it out. Same with water. Every week we get less. People have started to die, the old and the sick. Spirits were high in the beginning, but now they're low. The followers of the Corn God parade every day and say we should give up the Bright Giver. They call Him a false god. There's been riots the Quincy was hard put to break up. They say armies are on the way, but some claim that's just talk to keep us going.''

He looked around absently. ''I've stayed busy. I've made more progress since I've been here than in five years at Belyrie.'' The mention of his old home made him sad. ''I was happy there, Big. I didn't know how happy. I think of the people. They weren't full of themselves like they are here. They were simple but good. I wouldn't give ten Gowyiths for one Belyrie.''

I polished off the bone. ''That didn't take you long,'' he said. ''Sorry I don't have more.'' He fiddled with one of his lenses. It was the size of a Border Ranger shield. ''Want to see how this works, Big? Watch this.''

He carried the lens to the brightly burning fireplace. ''Watch that far wall.''

The lens collected the light from the fire and focused it to a small dim circle on the wall. He had spent years on this? It was pitiful.

''You like it?'' He grinned ear to ear.

I yawned and curled up near the fire. He went back to polishing glass. I half listened as he talked to himself.

''I've been trying not to think what'll happen if Mogwert and their evil horde break through. It would be the end of us, of course. Then the devils would spread to the rest of the Fair Lands. The Final Victory people been talking about for ages would be theirs. People call out to the Bright Giver for help. There's prayer meetings every night. But nothing happens. The folks who follow the Corn God aren't the only ones who say we've been forsaken. Some whisper that we ought to throw ourselves on the mercy of Mogwert and throw open the gates. Just a few at this point, but I wouldn't be surprised if more didn't come around as the hardship gets worse. What we need is Torc, who led us to victory ages past when it seemed the dark forces would overwhelm us. What mighty legends are sung about him."

A knock came at the door. "Wonder who that is," Helmish muttered. He went to the door and opened it. Helither stood in the wind. Awed, Helmish stepped back and Helither entered.

"You honor my house," Helmish stuttered. "Big, on your feet. We have a guest."

Helither sat on a stool and rubbed his face wearily. "Did you have any trouble?" he asked.

"I just followed my nose," I answered.

"You understand what Big says?" Helmish said with astonishment.

"He's not a dog. He's from another world. In that world he looks like us."

"I knew it! I knew he was trying to talk. No dog's that smart." He beamed happily. "Another world! Who would have thought?" He turned to Helither. "How is it you can understand him?"

"We'll talk of that another time."

"This is the hero of Gowyith," Helmish said to me. "Helither with his singing sword always stands at the head of our warriors when Mogwert's fiends storm a gate. Hundreds of Pig Faces has he killed single-handedly. Without him, we would have fallen long ago. Legends will be sung of him as they are of Torc."

"That supposes someone will be left to write legends," Helither said tiredly. He made an effort to shake off his exhaustion. "Gowyith is full of heroes, each of whom deserves a legend."

He looked around the warehouse. "You've been busy with your glass, Helmish. What success has crowned your efforts?"

"I was just showing Big." He did his trick focusing light from the fireplace on the far wall.

Helither looked a little less grim. "Your work may yet turn the tide."

Helmish and I were puzzled. "What do you mean?" I asked.

"Mogwert's strength is at its greatest when the night is moonless. They draw power from darkness as we do from sunlight. Helmish's discovery can pierce the dark with light."

Understanding dawned. "You're the one who has given me glass all this time," Helmish said. "Always at my door every morning."

"I foresaw you would devise a weapon of defense."

"But . . . how . . ."

"He's an angel," I said. "Can't you see that?"

"What's he saying?" Helmish asked.

"Never mind," Helither replied. He looked at me. "Come walk with me. We'll inspect the defenses of Gowyith."

"I don't know anything about defenses."

"I want the people of Gowyith to see you at my side. Already talk sweeps the city that a terrible ally of Mogwert walks about boldly. It's you they are talking about. Rumor is a terrible thing, especially when seen as omen."

"You don't know how bad rumor is until you're in the tabloids," I said.

"Do you mind if I come?" Helmish asked humbly.

"You're welcome," Helither said. We waited while Helmish threw on his cloak. Outside the wind was keener.

"There's winter in that wind," Helither said worriedly. "Will they get here in time?"

"You speak of the armies said to be coming?" Helmish asked. "Some claim it's just talk."

"They're not on their way yet, but soon will be. They will lift the siege, provided winter snow doesn't delay them until too late."

"What we need is for Torc to come back," Helmish said.

"Nothing against you, but he came straight from the side of the Bright Giver to lead us to victory. None could stand before his mighty glance."

"I've heard the legends," Helither said dryly. "Even he might find this a difficult test."

"No," Helmish said proudly. "Not Torc."

"Any chance of getting in touch with him?" I asked. "Let him know we could use a hand?"

Helither bent to whisper to me. "I am Torc. I wasn't invincible under that name, whatever the poets say, and I'm still not. Nor did I come straight from the side of Bright Giver. Do these 'tabloids' embellish the truth?"

"No, they embellish lies."

"They are an instrument of the Dark One?"

"No doubt in my mind."

We came to a sentry guarding steps that climbed to the top of the wall that girdled innermost Gowyith. He leaned against his spear, looking like he was ready to fall down.

"Vigilance, Ranger," Helither said gently.

The ranger jerked awake. "My eyelids got heavy for a second," he said, reddening.

"We're all tired." Helither put a hand on his shoulder, and it revived him.

"I'm all right now," he said, standing straight.

We passed him and climbed the stone steps to the top of the wall. Damned if Helither didn't make me walk every step of it. It must have been five miles. Helmish fell by the wayside after a couple of miles and said he would meet us at the Curiam. Thick knots of Pig Faces could be seen beyond the wall its entire length. They pounded axes against shields and squealed as if it was the Pig Bowl and they were six touchdowns ahead. Some bent over and showed Gowyith their knobby purple buttocks.

"There are about twenty-five thousand," I told Helither as we paused to watch a party of Pig Faces threaten an attack. They swarmed pell mell, stopping just as soldiers on the wall began to raise bows and arrows. Then they retreated, capering and hooting.

Helither's sigh was was heavy. "Too many. Too many," he said to himself. "There were only a quarter that many when the Torc of song and legend turned defeat into victory. How well I remember my despair when I saw their numbers. And now there are four times as many."

"Do angels get down in the dumps?" In paintings they are usually serene or exalting over something. They have wings, too. The wings are metaphors for something, as Felicity's writer friends would say.

"Of course. What a foolish question."

We paced in silence for a distance. "What happens if the city falls?"

"A great slaughter of innocents would follow."

"The Bright Giver would allow that?"

Helither didn't reply.

"He would allow evil to win," I pressed. "That's what you're saying?"

"I don't understand any more than you. Perhaps defeat on occasion gives victory a greater savor." He shook his head. "No, there must be a better reason. No one can comprehend the mind of the Bright Giver. Whatever the outcome, we must submit in humility to his design in the assurance that good ultimately prevails over bad."

"Ultimately is a long time. What about all the people you call innocents, the little kids and so on, who get it in the neck if Mogwert bust through?"

Another shake of his head. "They will be welcomed into the loving arms of the Bright Giver."

We walked in silence for a while. "What about you?" I asked.

"My fate would be to witness their suffering and thereafter to dwell in this world until the end of all worlds. Every day I would look upon cruelty perfected, evil refined. The Dark One would tempt me." Helither sounded afraid.

"But you're an angel."

"We aren't beyond temptation. Our natures include much of what you are. Many of us have been seduced and fallen."

He squared his shoulders. "Already the Dark One's influence grows. I fear defeat when I should have trust in victory." He smiled. "It will come with your help."

My ears shot up in alarm. "What do you mean?"

"You have already done much. Your counsel to Mogwert gave us time to organize our defense and send for help to distant Ferwaay and Neve Afrathar."

That was true. I had suckered Zalzathar. Candy from a baby. But I wondered if he would have fallen for the death-by-a-thousand-cuts routine if he hadn't put all that time and effort into importing cunning from my world.

"In all honesty, that could have been a fluke."

"You are too modest."

"Nobody ever said that about me before." That was true. People today rip off anything, even credit for something somebody else did. You have got to be like a full-time barker, always telling the world how great you are. Otherwise you get lost in the shuffle. Felicity's friends who hire writers to dream up witticisms for her salon understand this perfectly well. Look at Rush Limbaugh. I know him, a great guy. He knows how the game is played.

"Nor called you good?" Helither asked with a gentle smile.

"That either." Also true. They slapped a lot of adjectives on me—ruthless, arrogant, mean, tricky and so forth—but good wasn't one of them. It might be the more advanced society gets, the less it worries about good and bad. When it is still developing, maybe differences are so sharp you can't help but notice. Or maybe people have more time to sit around and think about them. There is no TV or theater or even books, so thinking is the only way to kill time. Life is tough in primitive societies. Up at dawn to plow and hard, slogging labor until sunset. But there must have been slack time for the old-timers to do their thinking. Not just about good and evil, but about the stars and the rest of nature. Pretty soon, they wondered what does it all mean? Socrates and that crowd had slaves to do the work while they pulled their chins and had long thoughts. When you've got to answer to shareholders, however, time spent on matters that don't impact the bottom line is time wasted. You've got to keep humping to stay ahead of the crowd.

I followed Helither down the stairs from the wall. If the people of Gowyith were afraid before that I was from the other side, now they treated me like a hero. The Rangers called and patted me as I passed. "Wait till the Pig Faces see him," one said. "That'll make them squeal." I have to admit I hot-dogged a little, prancing and chasing my tail a couple times.

Down below in the city, Helither began knocking on doors. When they opened, he went inside as I tagged along. He was trying to build morale, I guess. He was full of smiles and encouraging words. Women and children were inside, all the men being on the walls. Helither seemed to know everybody's names. Little kids toddled to me and hugged my neck and pulled my ears. It was mealtime and people were eating what looked like old bread soaked in water.

"Has he come to save us?" a sick-looking woman asked. "Never has a dog so big been seen in the Fair Lands." Even though indoors, she wore a heavy cloak and muffler and a scarf on her head. Everyone was dressed that way. The littlest kids looked as wide as they were tall from all the clothes. I could see why. The place was cold enough to hang meat. The windows were closed to keep in what little heat came from a small fire. Tiny candles threw out the only light.

"There is little firewood in Gowyith," Helither explained, as if he read my mind.

"What will happen when the Bright Giver hides his face and his frozen tears fall?" asked the woman who had commented on my size. "Without firewood, we will all go to the place where no one returns.'' I thought she meant the Great Balwar, but then I realized she meant death.

''The enemy will be defeated before winter,'' Helither said. He put on a cheery manner, as if everything was under control. ''Every fireplace will have plenty of wood and throw out good heat.''

Firewood came up often as we went door to door. The light of hope shined in wan, pinched faces as he spoke and put his arm around shoulders. Helither would be great on the motivational circuit. With those crinkly smiling eyes and down-home manner, he could also do major business as a televangelist.

Televangelists—good or evil? Or a mixture of both? They get people thinking about God. Then one gets discovered in a motel room with a prostitute. She goes on TV to say how kinky he was—liked to be whipped or something. People end up saying to hell with religion.

I hated to give up atheism. I was used to calling the shots. It's as if somebody takes control of your corporation in a hostile takeover. One day you are the boss and what you say goes, unless you've been dumb enough to let the unions in. The next day, somebody else is in your chair giving the orders.

But what choice did I have in this situation? I wondered what kind of God I was dealing with. The wrathful God of the Old Testament always putting people to the test? Or the loving God of the New Testament who forgave? All the trials I've gone through say the first. I recalled from the chapel we had to attend in boarding school that Jehovah was always making people prove their faith. They weren't easy trials, either. As many flunked as passed.

If God, or the Bright Giver, is all-knowing and all-seeing, Helither screwing up Zalzathar's aim at the last second was part of the divine plan. Unless the plan is subject to imponderables, such as free will. Maybe like a home builder, God puts down the foundation but leaves the finish work to others. Maybe He's too busy or too bored or just hopes to be pleasantly surprised by how it turns out. But is God capable of being surprised? Doesn't He see the sparrow's fall or whatever it is that shows how detail-oriented He is?

These aren't idle questions when your neck is on the block. Do I stay here or try to get back to the real world and undo some of the harm I did? It wasn't actually all that bad, I have to say in my own defense. Shaking up a complacent company and getting rid of deadwood helps it survive, which means continued employment and profits in the long run. You wouldn't believe how badly run a lot of American companies are. But maybe in some cases I was too keen on maximizing profits. Some people got thrown onto the street who shouldn't have. When you manage a takeover, you fire people and cut wages and benefits as a matter of sound business practice. But if God is the ultimate CEO, labor units (as I thought of them for accounting purposes) become people and the arithmetic changes. Return on equity is not all you have to worry about. Performance will be evaluated on other grounds.

Which would please God more, going back to make amends or staying here to help Helither and the Two Legs? It seemed to me going back was the correct answer. I didn't belong in this world. It made sense that it should work out its fate with the original cast. After all, it was Zalzathar who upset the natural order by reaching from one world to another for Bernie Soderberg and got me instead. Going back would merely return conditions to what they were before, except that I had wised up.

But to be honest, I have to admit my reasoning was influenced by the fact I didn't want to be around when all the fiends and Pig Faces came over the wall.

After Helither finished his pep talks and we headed toward the square where the Curiam was, I saw a familiar figure scuttle down an alley, crablike. It was the crooked old man with the crooked old stick, Heffernan Sterngeld. When we reached the alley, he had disappeared. Seeing him reminded me of the map of Gowyith that Zalzathar had.

"You were right about a traitor. Zalzathar has a map of the city. It shows everything. And I just spotted one of his spies."

"The crooked man?"

"How did you know?"

"He has private conversations with Lord Darcy. His efforts to appear inconspicuous made his comings and goings all the more noticable."

I remembered Lord Darcy, the red-bearded member of the Curiam who hadn't wanted Helmish to speak. "I guess it wasn't tough to figure that one out."

"Darcy communicates with Zalzathar by means of large black birds who do the bidding of the crooked man. Or he thinks he does."

"He's wrong?"

"My winged friends stop them. There's one now."

I looked up. A raven was snooping overhead, flapping in an unhurried way. It didn't sense the falcon diving from above, talons outstretched. There was a collision and a squawk from the raven. The falcon flapped off with it in his claws. Three black feathers wafted in slow circles toward the ground.

"You didn't tell anybody on the Curiam I came up with the thousand-cuts idea?"

"No one knows but you and I."

"That's good. Look, I'm struggling with my conscience."

Helither smiled. "That's what you're supposed to do with a conscience."

"I'm serious. Maybe you can help me."

He stopped and looked at me.

"I'm thinking my place is back where I belong. Things are slow now, sort of the calm before the storm. I was wondering if you could take time and do the spell or whatever it is that'll send me back?"

The angel's face fell. "I was counting on your help."

"What more can I do? The only thing that's going to

save Gowyith is the arrival of those armies. Right?''

Helither gave me a long, sad look. ''You want to go back now?''

I looked away in shame. ''Well, yeah. I did a few things that weren't exactly kosher and I should try to straighten them out. You know, wipe the slate clean.''

His hand was on my head. ''I understand. Tonight.'' His voice was kind and understanding. He walked toward the Curiam house where Helmish sat under a tree. I padded after him, head hanging.

[19]

Helmish stood. ''I don't need to ask if those fiends still prance outside the walls showing their backsides.''

''They're still there,'' Helither said briskly. I guess I was the only one he let see how he really felt. If he looked downcast for even a minute, it might start a panic. The guards stepped aside respectfully and we entered the building.

The Curiam broke off talking about food rations to cheer Helither. They crowded around, shaking his hand and pounding his back. ''No one knew such a hero lived within the walls of Gowyith,'' one said to another.

''None can even remember seeing him,'' the second replied. ''Yet he was here all the time.''

Lord Viviar moved through the members of the Curiam to grasp Helither by the hand. ''When this is over, Gowyith will show its gratitude. A statue in the square and other honors.''

''There's no need for that,'' Helither said. ''I take it you've been talking about food.''

''We must cut rations by another quarter,'' Lord Viviar said grimly. Like everybody else I'd seen, the members of the Curiam had lost weight. Their faces were haggard and there was desperation in their eyes. ''Many more will start to die.''

''Even worse,'' said another lord, ''our fighting men will be weakened. When Mogwert begins their final attack, I worry that we won't be able to swing our swords for want of strength. The Pig Faces are well fed from stock plundered from our farms and the harvest laid up for winter. Their axes will whistle.''

Lord Darcy spoke casually. ''There is talk one hears of sending ambassadors to Mogwert to see if there are grounds for . . .''

He was interrupted by shouts of ''No!'' and ''Never!'' and ''Better to die first!''

Lord Viviar held up his hand. ''Let him speak.''

Lord Darcy continued. ''I don't necessarily agree with this talk, but it is understandable after all that the people have suffered.''

''What would be gained by treating with Mogwert?'' Lord Viviar asked. ''They would see it as weakness.''

''They know all they need about our weakness by now.''

''I agree. There are spies and traitors within the walls of Gowyith,'' Helither said.

Lord Darcy shot him a look, but Helither was inspecting his hands as if debating whether a manicure was needed.

''I see the giant dog has returned,'' Lord Viviar said, hope in his face. ''This is a good sign?''

I felt Helither's eyes on me. ''No,'' he said. ''He will be gone before this day is over.''

''It wouldn't hurt to at least see if there are the smallest grounds to open discussions,'' Lord Darcy persisted.

''What would we talk about?'' Lord Viviar answered icily. ''How wide to open the gates? We know Mogwert's intentions. Death for the fortunate and slavery for the rest. The women and children would be butchered first and only the strongest men allowed to live.''

''We can't be sure,'' Lord Darcy said doggedly. ''No one has spoken to Mogwert. None has a family member so ancient they can recall if *their* oldest ancestor ever saw Mogwert, much less spoke with them.''

''For good reason,'' Lord Viviar replied. ''Mogwert is the creature of the Dark One. There can be no compromise.

They are opposed to us in the smallest particular. What we see as good, they see as evil. What we see as evil, they see as good. How can there be agreement between sides so opposite?''

''Perhaps there can't,'' Lord Darcy answered. He twirled a lock of red hair. ''What you say may well be true. This could be swiftly learned in a meeting with Mogwert.''

They debated back and forth; Lord Viviar was angry and scornful and Lord Darcy smooth and persistent. The rest of the Curiam seemed behind Lord Viviar, but I sensed in their beaten-down manner the beginnings of a willingness to consider Lord Darcy's proposal.

I half dozed, chin on paws. I wondered if the low spirits I had were from bad conscience. In the other world I would sometimes kick myself for a bum decision that cost money, but that is not what people call conscience. Maybe what I felt was canine loyalty because I had bonded with these people.

I turned that over in my mind as Lord Viviar and Lord Darcy continued to argue. If it was canine loyalty, forget it. I could care less what the dog part of me thought. I'd soon be rid of that anyhow.

Lord Viviar asked for a vote on whether Mogwert should be approached under a flag of truce.

''Rather than be hasty,'' Lord Darcy said good-naturedly, ''I think the Curiam should think it over. Take a day or two. Perhaps some who believe the Bright Giver commands us never to deal with Mogwert may decide that it would be all right if we set that belief aside just once, in light of the situation.''

''If a commandment can be set aside,'' Helither said softly, ''it is no longer a commandment.'' My ears were the only ones sharp enough to hear him.

''We should settle the question now,'' Lord Viviar said stoutly. They went back at forth about whether to vote on having a vote. If you watch CSPAN, you know how interesting that was. Instead of panning back and showing an empty chamber while some windbag talked as if a packed house hung on every word, a camera would show me stretched out releasing silent dog farts. The meat on that knuckle Helmish gave me had probably gone bad.

"Someone should take that creature outside before he soils the floor," a Curiam member said.

Nobody did, though, and pretty soon they voted in favor of a vote on whether to have a vote. That passed easily, and Lord Darcy narrowly won the next one to think for a couple days about whether to talk to Mogwert. The meeting broke up and I followed Helither and Lord Viviar outside. Helmish tagged along, talking to himself under his breath. You would have thought he'd have broken the habit after all this time in Gowyith.

"So the mighty Curiam is no different than the rest of us, quarrelsome and uncertain what to do," he muttered.

Lord Viviar looked upset but Helither was careful to keep his face blank as we moved through the few onlookers in the square. We threaded our way through mostly empty alleys until we came to a parade of people led by a fierce-eyed man who carried a pike that had a likeness of the Corn God on top.

"Come back to the true god, the Corn God," he shouted hoarsely. "It's because you left him for the false Bright Giver that Gowyith is encircled by enemies. Come back to the old god, the Corn God." A few doors opened and people clapped and yelled encouragement, but most stayed closed.

"The Corn God," Helmish said with disgust. "Why not bow down before the Pea God and the Bean God while they're at it?"

"As if there wasn't enough to worry about," Lord Viviar sighed, "this religious fervor sets citizen against citizen when we must be united against the common enemy."

"Worse are the people seized at night by demonic possession, despite my vigilance.'' Helither said to me telepathically. ''At first two or three, now a dozen or more a night. They lie frozen in terror with staring eyes and locked jaws until I reach their side. At times, I am too late. They die from fear of the demons who possess them.''

We came to Lord Viviar's home. He might be chairman or whatever the title was of the Curiam, but it didn't look like he lived any better. The inside was just as humble as the homes Helither popped into for his pep talks. A table, four chairs, a cold fireplace, a lumpy bed behind a curtain. There were a sword and a shield leaning against the wall in a corner. What did you get for being Numero Uno in the Fair Lands? Just the honor? The President of the United States gets paid peanuts (what is it, 200K?) but the perks have got to be worth $100 million a year.

We climbed stone stairs and went out on a balcony that overlooked the alley. The opposite buildings blocked the wind and it was almost warm in the sunlight. They sat on cushions, Lord Viviar with a defeated look.

''Gowyith has changed. In times past, no one would have dared suggest approaching Mogwert. Anyone who did would have been sent away and never allowed to return.''

''Don't be too hard on them,'' Helither said.

''The people are with you,'' Helmish said stoutly.

''Are they?'' Lord Viviar asked.

''There are complainers, of course. But they're only a few. In Belyrie, we would know how to handle them. We'd duck them in the pond.''

Lord Viviar smiled grimly. ''Water is too scarce in Gowyith.'' He paced with hands behind his back. ''We've expected word by now from the distant provinces, but there is only silence. Perhaps our messengers didn't get through.''

''The armies have been raised,'' said Helither. His eyes were closed. ''They will set forth soon.''

''How do you know that?'' Lord Viviar said sharply.

''I know.'' You would think this would make Helither

look happier. Help on the way got my tail wagging. I could leave without being tormented by my bad conscience, if that was what it was.

"Bright Giver above, thank you," Helmish breathed.

Lord Viviar studied the angel in silence. "If this is true," he said at last, "perhaps we can hold out until they get here."

"Mogwert and his foul host will attack before that," Helither said in a flat voice. "If they got here, they would find Gowyith destroyed. But they wouldn't get here. Mogwert would meet them en route and overwhelm them."

I looked at Helmish. The wind had gone out of his sail too.

"What terrible words you speak," Lord Viviar said. He was pale.

Helither nodded grimly. "The only question is what form their final attack will take and where the blow will fall."

"If we knew where, we could concentrate our defenses. We would at least have a hope of turning it back," Lord Viviar said.

"How can you know unless someone listens as Mogwert concocts their evil plans?" Helmish asked.

"Can't the birds tell you? Or the fairies?" I asked.

Lord Viviar was startled by my barks. "He can talk," Helmish explained. "Helither understands him."

Lord Viviar's keen look went from me to Helither and back again. "How can a dog talk, even one as strange as this?"

"A spell," Helither said. Lord Viviar nodded to me with sympathy. No need to explain that in this place. In the silence, the wind made a lowing sound.

"No one could even get close to Mogwert," Helither said.

"What should we do?" Lord Viviar asked. We looked at the angel for an answer.

"I don't know," he finally confessed. He changed the subject. "Lord Darcy is a traitor."

Lord Viviar stared in astonishment.

''He has had secret dealings with Mogwert. He hopes quarrels within the Curiam will weaken unity.''

''I have my differences with Darcy,'' Lord Viviar said slowly. ''But this.''

''Even good men can be led astray,'' Helither said. ''The snares of the Dark One are subtle. It's even possible Darcy's intentions are good. But he misjudges Mogwert. Even if it seemed they showed good will, it would be only falseness and treachery.''

''I'll have the Quincy put Darcy where he can do no harm,'' Lord Viviar said.

''Would that be wise?'' Helmish said. He blushed. ''The Curiam's doings are far above the head of a simple countryman like me, but wouldn't the other honorable lords think you did that to silence Lord Darcy? It might give him support he wouldn't have otherwise.''

Helither smiled. ''You're not so simple.'' To Lord Viviar, he said, ''He has a sound point.''

Lord Viviar admitted it. ''What should we do, then?''

''Nothing. Let him conspire. His messengers are intercepted before they leave Gowyith. Perhaps his plotting may yet turn out to be useful in some way we can't now see.''

Only my ears heard it, the nearly silent sound of wind through pinions. I looked up and the others followed my gaze. A large bird approached rapidly. Within seconds I saw it was an eagle. It spread its great wings to brake and landed on the balcony, folding them. It hopped to where Helither stood and turned its head to fix him with a fierce eye. There was a moment of silent communion.

''A powerful storm builds,'' Helither said.

''Winter,'' Lord Viviar shrugged.

''No. It is the wrong direction for winter. Great clouds form over the Dark Mountains.''

''Mogwert can make storms. I saw it,'' I yapped.

It was Helither's turn to be astonished. ''When?''

"When I was coming from the Boundary between our worlds. It was a blizzard. I had the feeling it was trying to turn me back to the Dark Mountains."

The angel couldn't hide his shock. "If they can make weather, it means the Dark One himself lends assistance." He looked at me. "You should have told me."

"It slipped my mind," I whined.

Helmish and Lord Viviar looked at the angel uneasily.

"A storm surely is not that serious," Lord Viviar said.

"Normally, you would be right. But a storm summoned by the Dark One will not help us, of that you may be very sure." Helither smacked a fist into one palm. "But what is its purpose?" He thought a moment. "It must be to conceal the enemy's movements."

"How long before the storm comes?" Helmish asked.

"Two days. No more than three."

I was relieved. I'd be out of here. Helither stood to go. "There is much to do," he said. He was gone almost before the rest of us could move.

I barely caught him before he was down the stairs and out the door. I trotted at his side in the alley.

"I must know Mogwert's plans," he said to himself.

He was so deep in thought as he hurried along I almost didn't want to butt in. "So when will you send me back? No hurry, as far as I'm concerned. An hour or so won't make all that much difference."

He stopped in the alley to look at me. "But don't you see? This changes everything."

"Don't I see what?" My heart sank.

"Zalzathar I could fool. He's only a wizard, however powerful. But the Dark One I cannot. He would become aware of my spell. It would be broken and you would be intercepted."

"You mean I have to stay?"

"What do you suppose would happen if you were returned to Mogwert, your betrayal known?"

I didn't want to think about that. I was in another of those emotional free falls from penthouse to outhouse. No way I would ever get used to them.

"I'm sorry," Helither said. His hand was on my head. Strangely, it made me feel better. A kind of warmth flooded through me. "It seems your fate and Gowyith's are strangely intertwined. Perhaps it was meant to be after all. As subtle as is the Dark One's thinking, the Bright Giver can follow its twists and turns." His hand lifted and the cold in the pit of my stomach came back.

"I thought you said he doesn't care how the game turns out."

"He cares. But he values our freedom to choose, perhaps as much as the outcome. It is his gift to us."

Some gift. It's fine for him; he gets his curiosity satisfied. But not so great for somebody who chooses good but ends up on the losing side, a martyr. If might makes right, it's smart to go with might. Better to ride in a Rolls than walk in bare feet, as we say on Wall Street.

"If good always won, the choice would be easy," Helither said.

So what, I thought. Why not just make a perfect world without the Devil and his snares? We could live our lives like saints, doing one good deed after another, knowing we would collect our reward when we died. We would be welcomed at the pearly gates with a smile, a handshake and a "Well done." What would be wrong with that? Or would the lack of suspense be too dull for the Bright Giver?

Personally, I could do without freedom of choice, given the downside when you pick wrong. You could fall into a rut and go on making wrong choices and pay for it when the show is over. As for divine forgiveness, there has to be a line somewhere. Hitler, for example, or Stalin. They killed millions. Suppose they said they were sorry and *really* meant it. Do they get forgiven? How about serial murderers or child killers? You see my point? At a certain point, doesn't an act become so horrible that forgiveness is out of the question? Or is that putting limits on the Bright Giver, who by definition has none?

As another option, the Bright Giver could fix the game so people still made choices, not knowing how they would turn out, but arrange matters so that the Dark One doesn't end up on top. That way innocent people don't suffer. I pointed this out to Helither.

"That's mere logic," he smiled.

"What's wrong with logic?"

"Logic is how people fool themselves into thinking they understand the mystery. Logically, there was no reason for the Bright Giver to create anything. He was full and complete and perfect."

By this time we had reached a small tree-filled knoll where there weren't any buildings. A sort of park, I guess. Develop this site and you could sell the view. The knoll was empty except for Helither and me. He sat on a rock, took out a knife and began whittling.

"The mind of the Bright Giver cannot be understood," he said. "If it could, tragedy could perhaps be explained. The death of children, the suffering of the old after lives of virtue and usefulness. Hatred, betrayal, cruelty and selfishness, their purpose would all become clear."

I didn't say anything. This was too big for me to tackle.

He continued to whittle. I got the feeling he waited for me to say something. The more shavings that built up around his feet, the stronger the feeling.

"You want me to try to find out what Zalzathar and Mogwert plan," I finally burst out.

"It's our only hope," he answered evenly.

"If I show up now, they're going to wonder where I've been all this time."

"As you said, nobody ever returned from the Great Balwar."

"Suppose somebody saw me here? You had me parade around the whole place at your side."

"It was necessary to quiet panic. I admit there's a risk."

I was cornered like a rat. Helither was right; my fate and Gowyith's were tied together in a knot. If it went down the toilet, so did I. If I didn't somehow manage to sneak out in the confusion when the Pig Faces broke through, I would end up with a circle of them hacking at me with axes. And if I did slip away, I would be a solitary wanderer here for the rest of what wretched life remained to me. But if Gowyith survived, I might yet get back where I belonged before I died of neglect in whatever fleabag nursing home Felicity had me in.

"I'll send Desina with you."

"Who's that?"

"A fairy. She's small enough to hide somewhere on your body. You can use her as a courier. If you find out their plans but can't get away, she will return to Gowyith with your message."

"You make it sound easy."

"It's not easy." He tossed away the stick he was whittling. "Only simple."

Helither did his disappearing act and I was alone on the knoll. Maybe he didn't want to seem to put pressure on me. I'd have to remember to thank him for his thoughtfulness.

With nearly everyone inside conserving strength except the Corn God mob bellowing in the city's eastern quarter, Gowyith looked as if it had already fallen and waited for time to wipe away all trace that it had existed.

If the Devil was personally helping quarterback the show on the other side, it seemed to me Mogwert had it sewed up. I padded through the empty alleys back to Lord Viviar's place and scratched on the door. Helmish welcomed me and I lay by a puny fire in the fireplace.

"From another world," Lord Viviar marveled. "What times these are. If it weren't for the evil host at the gates, I would scarcely be able to think of anything else."

"I don't understand why Helither said Big would leave without helping Gowyith," Helmish said with a worried look. ''Clearly, he was sent to be with us in our time of need, even as Torc was long ago.''

Lord Viviar was skeptical. ''What can a dog do, even one like this? What interests me more is why Helither left so quickly and with such a troubled face. I fear the bird brought bad news.''

''Big knows. If only we could understand him.'' The two looked at me, as if they hoped stares could grant speech. I closed my eyes and dozed. One of the few nice things about being a dog is you can do that and nobody calls you rude.

Rudeness is one of Felicity's most frequent complaints about me. She hates when my beeper goes off or I talk on the cellular phone. ''Other men don't work every waking hour.'' She makes it sound like a vice.

''Your friends all inherited their dough,'' I reply. ''I have to work for mine.''

She says I keep busy because of a shallow mind. ''Webley Industries is up four points,'' I answered once after I hung up from a call. ''You call that shallow? It means someone is acquiring position.'' That phone call enabled me to get on the bandwagon and make ten million bucks when the stock kept going up. When I pointed that out later, Felicity shrugged. She couldn't have shown less interest if I'd told her I cleared twenty dollars selling a load of gravel from the quarry.

When darkness fell, Helmish was telling Lord Viviar about his glass, but he didn't seem too interested. I scratched at the door as if I needed to lift a leg outside. When Helmish opened it, I headed for one of the gates. ''Where are you going, Big?'' he called after me. I didn't look back.

A guard stood at the barred door in the gate. His grip tightened on his spear as I approached.

''That's all right, Ranger,'' a voice said at my side. It was Helither. ''He's leaving Gowyith.''

''How did you know?'' I asked sourly. His hand was on my head as the ranger unbarred the door.

"I guessed." He uncupped his other hand and showed me a tiny fairy with wings. "This is Desina. Carry her with you. She's small enough to hide in your ear if need be. She'll be your messenger."

Desina's face was so tiny I could hardly make out her features. She peeped a greeting and I gave a grudging answer.

"It sounds like you don't expect me to come back," I said.

Helither gave me a frank look. "It's not likely you will return."

I expected him to say I'd be back before I knew it. Honesty isn't always the best policy when you're asking somebody to risk their life. Sweeten the medicine so it goes down easier. I swallowed hard. "You figure they'll waste me?"

"Waste?"

"Kill me," I burst out. "Put me in the ground. Whack me. Send me to the Happy Hunting Grounds."

"Not necessarily. If they believe your story, they'll want you close when the battle for Final Victory begins."

Not necessarily. If they believe your story.

The ranger had lifted the thick bar to the door and we looked out into the gathering gloom. I edged through the door, Desina hanging on to my ruff. Helither followed for a few steps.

"You will find the Pig Faces you must pass through are sleeping," he said.

"Thanks a million," I said acidly.

"I'm truly sorry you had to be dragged into this," Helither said. He was sincere, but so what? It didn't make me feel any better.

"Acts of virtue are sometimes unavoidable."

"I'd call it being between a rock and a hard place," I said.

I didn't see any point in further talk, so I slunk away. Helither was right. A hundred yards beyond the wall I passed a clump of smelly Pig Faces. They lay on the ground snoring, mouths open and their unspeakable breath fouling the air. Desina was no heavier than a mite, so I soon forgot she was along for the ride.

When I entered the woods, I saw they had a tired, kicked-around look, like a campground at the end of summer. Tree trunks were scarred by tusks and oozed sap and foliage was trampled down or uprooted for the fun of it. Pig Faces were as hard on scenery as on cities. No living things remained but them. They didn't bother hiding their whereabouts, so they were easy to avoid. I smelled a fermented mash being stewed at several points in the forest. The Pig Faces were getting ready for the final push by cooking up Dutch courage.

I didn't bother rehearsing what I'd say when I reached Zalzathar. I have found in appearances before hostile boards of directors that it is better to go in cold. You can't predict the questions that come from left field as they show off for each other, so there is no point memorizing answers.

As I ducked through the trees, ears pricked and nerves strung tight as fiddle strings, it occurred to me that what I was doing could be called heroic if you didn't know the particulars. I was risking my life against insane odds to save a city I could not care less about. It made me wonder how many so-called acts of heroism hailed in history books came under similar circumstances. Some poor sap gets a choice between certain death and near-certain death. He chooses No. 2 and gets lucky, so he is celebrated when all he did was clutch at straws. Push me and I'll admit there might sometimes be real heroes. Anything is possible. But in general, I bet they are just people who got backed into a corner.

"Hello, friend."

I nearly jumped out of my skin. It was a voice so deep it sounded like it came from a sepulchre. There was no warning. No sound, no smell in the air. A man in a cape with a high collar leaned against a tree, nearly invisible. Only his pale face gave him away, a blob hanging in the darkness like a small moon.

''Who are you?'' I blurted.

''Meneloper. And you?''

''Ingersol's the name,'' I said in a voice that shook.

''I haven't seen you before.''

''I can say the same about you.''

''We've been told to watch for strange things. It's said the angel Helither has deep cunning. It is strange to find a dog alone in the forest. Dogs cleave closely to Two Legs.''

''I'm not a dog. Check with Zalzathar. He'll green-light me.''

''Green light?''

''He'll say I'm okay.''

''Okay? What do these words mean?''

''Look, you can trust me, all right? Where can I find Zalzathar?''

He was suspicious. His stiff cloak rustled as he moved. I wondered if he was bracing to jump me. I tried to think of something to say.

''Where I'm from, your kind is called vampire,'' I babbled. Felicity is a big fan of Anne Rice. I've looked at the book jackets in the john when there wasn't anything else within reach. Women will read anything. Yet here one was in the flesh.

''Vampire?''

''You drink blood, right?''

''Yes.''

''Never die?''

He didn't answer.

''What do they call you here?''

''We are Czoltine. When you say where you are from, what do you mean?''

''Another world.''

''Another world?'' He thought this over. ''And in this world there are my kind, Czoltine?''

''Vampires. We call you vampires.''

''We thought we were alone.''

''Everybody does. It turns out there are more worlds than

it's possible to imagine. So where do I find Zalzathar? I need to talk to him. Trust me, I'm advising him on how to run the war."

"Then why don't you know where he is?"

"I've been in the Great Balwar on a test."

"No one returns from the Great Balwar."

"Well, I did. I'm back and raring to go."

Suddenly, the creature was at my side and I was lifted into the air by superhuman strength. We rushed through the dark forest with stunning speed and in utter silence. The wind in my face was so great that tears blinded me. How it could move that fast and not run smack into something was unbelievable. When I smelled the terrible reek of Pig Faces, I knew we were arriving at the main camp. We shot into a clearing thick with them and the vampire lifted into the air so we rushed past just inches above their astonished heads. A wave of grunts and squeals followed us. We stopped at a translucent tent lighted from within by a purple light. The Pig Faces guarding the entrance fell back at the sight of the vampire.

"Tell Zalzathar I come with a strange creature I found in the woods near Gowyith." He wasn't even breathing hard.

There was no need to tell him. Zalzathar swept the folds of the tent aside and glared with folded arms.

"*Ingersol!*" he said with astonishment. His arms fell to his sides. The vampire released his grip and withdrew into the shadows.

"I'm back," I said with false heartiness. "Greetings from the Great Balwar. A lousy place to visit and you sure wouldn't want to live there." In human form, I'd be starting to sweat through my clothes.

There was a long, suspicious silence as he continued to glare. "Come in," he commanded, standing back to let me pass. The purple light came from a triangular object on a pedestal. The ground was covered by rugs with magical symbols and writing. Pillows were scattered here and there.

Zalzathar had been studying his map of Gowyith.

He stared at me. If it weren't for the adrenaline pumping, I would have passed out.

"No one has ever returned from the Great Balwar," he said.

"I can see why. It's even weirder than this place. Everything's backward there."

He nodded. "Yes, that is the legend."

"There's a creature part man and part woman and the rest horse. When one sleeps, the other runs the show. Then that one goes to sleep and the shoe is on the other foot."

"That too is said."

"They represent good and evil, right? Always fighting."

Another nod.

"It took me a while, but I busted out when Boog-Weir—that's the guy—wasn't looking. I nearly died, though. You're using up all your strength but don't know it. So when you want to leave, you're weak as a baby."

"Yes," Zalzathar said reluctantly, "this too."

"You could say I lucked out."

There was nothing to do but believe me. Nobody could make that story up.

He wanted details and I gave them, skipping the part about Helither's help and my visit to Gowyith. I told him about Brofelio.

"He's got it made. Parties all the time."

The look on Zalzathar's face wasn't pleasant. "When the Fair Lands fall, Brofelio and others like him who didn't answer the call will be sorry."

This was my opening. "So how's the war going? You must be mopping up by now."

"Death by a thousand cuts didn't work," Zalzathar said accusingly.

"No? Well, you remember I warned it might not."

"One warrior in five has died in futile attacks."

Twenty percent attrition. I passed it off as what a seasoned general would expect. I told him you can't make an omelet without breaking eggs. I had to explain what an omelet is. "What about the other side?" I asked.

"We have friends behind their walls but their messages do not reach us."

"So they might be hurting bad for all you know?"

Zalzathar thought. He had been focusing on his own losses. "What you say may be true," he admitted.

"One big push and they could cave in."

"Mogwert is through waiting. They ordered me to go back to the old way of war." That would be the steamroller approach.

"Armchair generals," I said sympathetically. "Nothing's easier than Monday morning quarterbacking." I had to explain that too.

Zalzathar didn't answer. I could tell he was still sorry he hadn't snared Bernie Soderberg. The Fair Lands would have been conquered by now and Bernie would be back in New York. If the Dark One was as grateful as the wizard said, he'd be bigger than ever. There would be no stopping him.

"That character who brought me here nearly scared the pee out of me," I said casually. "Your monsters must be paying off in a big way."

Zalzathar made a gesture of dismissal. "They are agents of terror only. The Two Legs fear them. But they are little good in actual war."

There was a tickling in my left ear and I nearly sat down and scratched with my hind leg until I realized it was Desina climbing over the fine hairs. There was a stir outside and a guard pulled back the folds of the tent.

"The War Council approaches," he said.

"They come to plan the final attack," Zalzathar told me.

"Want me to hang around? I might be able to help."

He didn't say yes or no. I had a feeling resentment over my lousy advice struggled with surprise over my return out of the blue. Mixed with that probably was gratitude for the sympathy I showed about the heat from Mogwert. Zalzathar wasn't cut out for command. He was the middle-management type, better at following orders than giving them. I've seen a lot of his type.

A grizzled row of Pig Faces came in. They wore dirty, ragged Two Leg uniforms with dark bloodstains. I supposed they had been ripped from fallen soldiers. They stiffened, and the hair on their shoulders and back bristled when they saw me.

"Where did he come from?" the oldest and grayest squealed.

Zalzathar paused impressively. "He has come from the Great Balwar."

That blew them away. They squealed and gave me looks that mixed hate and respect. Zalzathar held a hand up like a headliner quieting a crowd in Vegas. "No one has ever returned from the Great Balwar."

In my human form, I would have clasped hands overhead like a champ. Instead I just gave a cool look around, as if there was nothing to it.

"He comes to help us win the Final Victory," Zalzathar said dramatically.

Pandemonium. The Pig Faces hopped and squealed and pounded one another on the back. One masturbated quickly and another shit on the rug. Before, Zalzathar might have shot out a bolt of fire and fried one to shut them up. But he let them whoop and holler. There hadn't been much to cheer about lately.

"The Dark One be praised," the grizzled old-timer cried. "Victory will be ours. We'll enter Gowyith and release their mysteries."

He meant everybody would be ripped apart.

"We're going to kick butt," I barked, as if I could hardly wait for the fighting to start.

When they quieted down, Zalzathar gave me a significant look before addressing the War Council. "The first stage of our campaign is over."

"Many of us have died," the old Pig Face groused. "Too many." He looked around for agreement and the others grunted. It occurred to me they came in for a showdown with Zalzathar and the wizard had picked up on it. My arrival was sheer luck.

"It had to be," Zalzathar said smoothly. "Now the enemy is confused."

"They're on the ropes," I chipped in. "They're ready to fall."

"No more small attacks," Zalzathar continued. "The thousand cuts have been inflicted. Now we make plans for our last mighty blow."

More celebration, then it was down to business. The Pig Faces bent around the map and grunted among themselves about where along the city's wall to aim the final attack.

"It doesn't look to me like you have a choice," I said in a thoughtful voice. Everybody got quiet and looked at me.

"What do you mean?" Zalzathar demanded. "The wall is long."

"Yeah, but you want to put them in a position where they'll be jammed up on the other side and can't match your numbers." I rose on my hind legs and put a paw on the map where the wall turned at an angle and stretched south. "Like there."

Any fool could see that if the Pig Faces broke through the wall at that point, they would have to funnel down narrow alleys for nearly a mile before they reached a square and could fan out so their numbers became decisive. The Two Legs could stand on roofs and shoot arrows and pitch spears and rocks every step of the way.

"Nothing could stand before you. You would push the enemy back through the alleys to here," I said, my paw on the square. "By then, the rout will be on and Gowyith yours." I dropped down on all fours as if the case was so airtight there was no point in further talk.

"No need for thanks," I said grandly. "We're more advanced where I'm from. It lets me see the big picture."

Zalzathar and the Pig Faces stared at the map in silence.

They were used to hashing things over for hours. That anthill approach with everybody putting in their two bits guarantees lousy decisions. No wonder they always blew it.

"This is too quick," one grunted. "War plans need long discussion."

"Not when the way to win is as obvious as the tusks on your face and the horns on your head," I replied.

He reached one paw up to touch a yellow tusk while the other felt a horn. The others watched. Yes, I saw them slowly think, those are certainly obvious.

"Let me know if you need anything else," I told Zalzathar. "I'll be outside."

My breezy confidence bowled them over. Einstein giving a freshman physics lecture wouldn't seem so sure of himself. They whispered to themselves as I trotted out. After an hour or so, Zalzathar came out.

"We will attack the wall where you said two nights from now."

"Attaboy."

"You are certain this will work?" I got the feeling he was scared but didn't want it to show. Mogwert must have really had him on the griddle. Everything was riding on the battle for Gowyith. The bad guys weren't going to hold anything back. Zalzathar would be the first to get it if the war was lost.

"I'm so sure I want to talk about it afterward," I answered cockily.

"Afterward?"

"Sending me back where I belong."

This reminded him I was still under his thumb, and some of his confidence came back. "You will be returned when the Final Victory is ours."

"That doesn't mean I have to stick around while you finish off the rest of the Fair Lands after Gowyith falls, right?"

Zalzathar pretended to give this thought. He knew the rest of the Fair Lands was a cakewalk once Gowyith fell.

"No," he said magnanimously. "I will see you are returned when the city is captured."

I thought it was a good idea to fake doggy happiness. I yapped and spun, then did my walk on hind legs, pawing the air. Zalzathar turned away sourly. Happy wasn't his thing.

I calmed down. "Where's Mogwert?"

"They wait two days from here. They won't be seen until Gowyith is ours."

It wasn't hard to figure that out. If Zalzathar's attack flopped, Mogwert didn't want defeat rubbing off on them. They'd wait until the win was in the bag before showing up to take the credit. Throwing somebody to the wolves when things go wrong and taking the bows when they work out is actually good management strategy. I've done it myself more than a few times.

"What about Helither?" I asked. "He's a tough nut."

He gave me a suspicious look. "Helither will be taken care of when the time comes."

It sounded as if he had an ace up his sleeve, but I didn't think it was a good idea to press him now. Maybe I could worm it out of him later.

I told Zalzathar I was going upwind of the camp so I could breathe.

"I don't see how you stand the smell of these guys."

"You will be at my side in the attack," he said.

"Sure thing. I guess we'll be on a hill telling people what to do." Generals always sit well back from the shot and shell so they can think clearly and eat off china.

"No," he said grimly. "I'll be at the head of the army, as Helither always is."

Zalzathar at the head of the Pig Faces would be a big fat target in those narrow alleys. If I was trotting alongside, so would I.

"I don't know if that's such a smart idea," I said weakly.

"It is Mogwert's order. But you needn't worry, my powers have been greatly augmented." I remembered then how much stronger the purple lightning had been when I watched from Brofelio's castle.

He turned back into the tent and I headed out of camp. The Pig Faces gave way with their usual surly reluctance, lifting lips in silent snarls. They would rip me apart in seconds to look for my "mystery" if I wasn't under Zalzathar's protection. It took me a half-hour to put their stink behind. I kept traveling until I reached a small pond surrounded by bullrushes.

"You can come out now," I said to Desina. I couldn't stop my ear from twitching from the tickle as she climbed hand over hand through the fine hairs. She crawled over my head until she stood on my muzzle. I had to shut one eye so I wasn't looking cross-eyed.

"You heard everything?" I asked.

"Yes. The attack comes in two nights."

"It'll be right where that garden is with the well. Where the wall changes direction."

"Helither will know."

"Go back to Gowyith and let them know."

She sprang from my muzzle and flitted out over the lake, a tiny spark of light over the dark water. As I watched, I was thinking things were beginning to go my way at last. Zalzathar and his hordes would run into an ambush when they attacked Gowyith. The Two Legs would cut them to pieces as they squeezed through the alleys. All I had to do was think up some excuse to keep from accompanying the wizard into that death trap. Maybe I could come down with some bug I'd picked up from the Great Balwar.

Desina wasn't fifty yards from me when a frog leaped from a water lily and swallowed her whole.

[20]

The *kerplop* of the frog landing in the water with the poor fairy in his jaws was like a starter's gun for me. I ran as fast as my four legs would take me in the opposite direction. It wasn't as fast as it used to be. As I dodged through the trees, I felt thick and sluggish. It was clear my legs had lost the youthful spring they had at the beginning of this nightmare. If I was a ballplayer, the coaches would look at each other and shake their heads. Bogey's over the hill, they'd say.

I probably ran three-quarters of a mile before I stopped, wheezing like an old bellows. There was only silence. Not even a bug burrowed in dry leaves, a sound you can almost always hear. I lay under fanlike ferns and tried to rein in my racing thoughts. Was that frog an agent of the Dark One? If so, the game was over.

Then, as I got my breath back, I told myself not to panic. Maybe Desina making a meal for an alert amphibian could be explained as just bad luck. This was the wilds, after all. Everybody is always shopping for the next meal. The frog could have mistaken her for a firefly flitting across the water. It was her own fault she didn't fly higher.

When I broke the problem down, it was clear this was the assumption I had to go on. If the outcome was a done deal and the Dark One was just having his jollies, it was time to lie down, wrap my tail around my nose and wait for the end. I wasn't ready for that yet. But what now? I couldn't get back to Gowyith before dawn to warn of the coming attack. If I tried to sneak through the gate in daylight, I'd be spotted for sure. The word would get back to Zalzathar and the first thing he would do would be scrap my plan of attack. He and the Pig Faces would decide on another and it would be sayonara for Gowyith. A small push with Gutters leading the way and the defenses would cave in like a house of cards.

As my pounding heart returned to normal, I found myself wondering how Felicity was doing in Rio. She'd look great in one of those string bikinis they call "butt floss." She wasn't above maddening the male populace by wearing it in public. I felt a stab of desire. Maybe she was already checking out husband material. As I cowered under this fern, maybe she strolled some golden beach with a likely prospect, a paunchy industrialist or financier. Come to think of it, though, she didn't have to marry for money anymore. So maybe it was one of those bronzed young men with too much hair, a towel boy whose muscles had caught her eye.

Everybody would understand if she divorced me, a convicted criminal and human vegetable on life support. "He just lies there, poor man," she'd tell people. "He'd want it this way." Anyone who knew me would know that was a lie, but I couldn't think of anybody who would go to the trouble of pointing it out. And what difference would it make if someone did?

I must have been whimpering because an old oaken voice that sounded as if it came from a deep barrel said, "Why are you sad?"

I yelped and sprang to my feet in terror. I couldn't see anything in the darkness. "Who said that?" I cried.

"Me." The voice came from a tree stump ten feet away. I crept closer, hackles up. But instead of a stump, it was a Woodman like the one Helmish and I had seen on the road. He didn't seem as far long in the transition to treedom, however. His beard was less mosslike and there weren't roots growing out of his feet.

"Why are you sad?" he asked again.

"I'm in a jam."

"Jam?" he asked, puzzled.

"Trouble. I'm in trouble," I snapped.

"Oh." A pause. "Trouble should be avoided." He said this as if it was wisdom fit to be engraved on stone.

"What kind of trouble?" he rumbled after a moment.

"Where have you been keeping yourself?" I said sarcastically.

"Here. I'm testing this bit of ground."

"Testing it for what?"

"To decide if I should put roots down."

"What's to decide?" I sneered. "You either like it or not."

"Ho. Ho. Ho." His laughter was slow, like a record played at the wrong speed. "I've only been here five years."

"Five years! How long does it take to make up your mind?"

"It's not something decided in a hurry. I'll live in a place hundreds of years until the Bright Giver calls me and I fall. There are many things to decide. Will I get enough sun? My brother and sister trees around me . . ." He slowly looked around. "Are they good neighbors? Some aren't. They'll put out limbs and steal the light. Others lean against you to make you grow crooked."

I lost interest. Maybe a botanist would care. I started to leave when he said, "You didn't say. Why are you sad? Maybe I could help."

"I'll give you a clue," I said with impatience. "Mogwert."

"Many years ago, Mogwert came down from their mountain lair. It was a hard time. I was a young dwarf then, full of green spirits."

"They're back again, worse than ever."

A long, astonished silence. "Flee," he said, his hollow voice urgent. "We must flee."

"Forget it. There's no place to flee to."

"So long as Gowyith stands, we are safe."

I had gotten bad news so long it was a pleasure to dish it out for a change. "Give up that pipe dream."

"What do you mean?"

"Gowyith will fall in the next couple days."

Horror slowly rose up from his woody depths. "No!"

"The handwriting's on the wall."

"Handwriting? On a wall?"

"It's an expression."

"The Fair Lands will die! Mogwert never stops killing. When they are finished, only a desert will remain."

"That sounds about right."

"What will *you* do? Where will you go?"

I didn't reply. I would go back to Zalzathar's camp. I would accompany him into Gowyith and hope he would send me home when the city fell, as he promised. Without the city knowing where the attack would come, walking at his side would be fairly risk-free. Once the Gutters clawed through the wall, the few surprised defenders on the other side would be overwhelmed.

"There is nothing to be done?" the Woodman asked with despair.

"There is one thing," I admitted.

"Say it."

"I know when Mogwert will attack and where."

"The Two Legs must know. Tell them!"

I guess he thought I was too dim to figure that out. "The city is surrounded. Even if I got through, I'd be recognized and Mogwert would change plans."

He slowly considered this. "Send someone with a message."

"Look around. Notice anything?"

The Woodman turned, his torso creaking. "The forest is silent. Where are all the nocturnal creatures? The green-eyed panther and the silent owl, all the hunters and the hunted?''

''They did the smart thing and scrammed. No one's left but you and me.''

He slowly turned to look in the other direction. ''I've been deep in my own thoughts. I didn't notice.''

''It's time to wake up and smell the coffee.''

''Coffee?''

''Never mind. It's been nice but I got to go.''

''Wait! We can help.''

I looked around but didn't see another of his kind. ''Who's we?''

''My brothers and sisters. They will remember Mogwert from when they were seedlings and saplings.''

''What can they do?'' I scoffed.

''Call to our kind inside the city.''

The image of an oak or an elm answering a telephone absurdly came to mind. ''What good would that do?''

''There was one who understood us in Gowyith.''

''Yeah?'' I said without interest. ''How long ago?'' He would be dead and turned to dust by now.

''When Mogwert last threatened.''

A blinding flash of inspiration. ''Wait a minute,'' I said. ''What was his name?''

''Torc.''

''He's still there. He goes by another name now.''

''Then he will hear our call.''

I felt a sudden lift. Maybe things could get back on track. ''How long does it take to get a message through?''

''A day. Perhaps longer.''

''We don't have much time. A day's cutting it thin. It can't be any longer.''

''It won't be,'' the Woodman said grimly. He asked where the attack would be and I explained. He walked slowly to the nearest tree and leaned against it. I was expecting something dramatic like the pound of tom-toms, but that's all he did. I watched awhile to see if anything else happened. When nothing did, I left. I wanted to be back to Spyngle before dawn to show Zalzathar I was raring to go.

[21]

I moved through the mob of Pig Faces at the filthy encampment when I got back, watching where I stepped. They were oddly still and tense and paid no attention to me for a change. In the distance, Zalzathar stood on a platform with a dozen Pig Faces. They were chained and their heads hung.

Zalzathar was speaking in a clear, powerful voice. "I said none were to taste of the potion before the time, yet these disobeyed." He half turned, lifted a finger, and a sizzling bolt of lightning leaped from it and blew a leg off the Pig Face on the end of the line. Great gouts of blood pumped out, splattering the platform floor. The Pig Face clutched the one next to him to keep from falling and looked down at where his leg had been. He didn't believe his eyes. Zalzathar went down the line, zapping limbs off every one of them. An arm here, a leg there. The prisoners surged back and forth in their chains and squealed hysterically. Splat, splat, the blood pumped out onto the platform in rhythm with their racing hearts.

"My orders must be obeyed as you would obey Mogwert and the Dark One himself," Zalzathar was saying. He had started at the beginning of the line again and blew another limb off each captive. The look on his face reminded me of Hal Applebaum, a commodities trader I used to know. Applebaum ate five or six times during the business day. Trading is high pressure. You can make or lose a fortune in minutes. Eating was his way of dealing with the pressure.

He ate full sit-down meals with crystal and silver, served in his office on linen tablecloths. Waiters wheeled the food on steam tables from restaurants. Applebaum was immensely fat, as you might expect. Anticipation made him vibrate like a tuning fork as he was served. The greedy look on his face was like Zalzathar's expression as he watched the suffering of the Pig Faces.

It took maybe fifteen minutes before he finally gave each the coup de grace, blasting their heads off. By then the platform was full of gore and blackened arms and legs jutting up at different angles. The hem of his black cape had a bloody border. The sickening smell of scorched flesh hung over the crowd. He left the platform without looking back and went inside the Curiam house. I found him there a few minutes later. His lethal fingers were steepled as he meditated. A fury who called herself Tisiphone smirked at me from a dark corner. She was as hard-faced as a Vegas hooker at the end of a bad night. Clap would be the nicest thing you could expect from her.

''A spot of trouble?'' I asked Zalzathar jauntily. I didn't want him to think I had turned a hair at what I'd seen. In my business, I learned to ignore the unpleasant. Hal Applebaum wasn't a tidy eater, for example. He was in such a hurry to finish and get back to the ticker, food flew everywhere. The smock he wore so his clothes didn't get dirty was covered when he was finished. I always pretended I saw nothing unusual about these pig-outs and stayed on his good side. People who got grossed out didn't get the benefit of Hal's deep wisdom about the markets. He was very sensitive for a big fat slob. I mention this to show how it is possible to steel yourself not to notice stuff.

''They drank of the dark potion,'' Zalzathar said, turning to look at me.

''Is that what they've been cooking up the last couple of nights?''

''It won't be fully ready until twilight the night of the attack. Not a precious drop must be wasted.''

"It must be powerful stuff."

"Those who drink it fight with ferocity."

It sounded like angel dust, a big problem in the cities back home. The minorities get high on it and don't feel a thing. Cops pound heads with nightsticks or blast away with stun guns and they don't feel it. I hoped they were brewing up something similar in Gowyith so there would be a level playing field.

"I can hardly wait for the show to start," I said eagerly.

"The dark potion is not for you," Zalzathar said. "It clouds the mind."

"You're right. I want to stay sharp."

"You'll be at my side." He didn't want me forgetting it. "We will move our army into place when it is dark again." He looked to the east, where a hint of gray said day was on the way. "There will be no moon tomorrow night. All are here who answered my call. I will deal with those who didn't another time." I wonder who beside Brofelio flaked out. He was about to say more when he cocked his head. "What is that?"

It was a low-pitched humming, so faint it barely registered. "Beats me," I said.

He listened and his face darkened. "It is thondreakus," he said. "The cry of the forest."

"What does it mean?"

"It is very rare. Wizards who lived long lives before me never once heard it. Only Aixis in the time of Kirietin spoke of thondreakus."

I played innocent. "Wow, no kidding." The Woodman must have worked faster than he thought possible. I hoped the message got through ungarbled.

Zalzathar gave me a sharp look, and I was afraid I was overplaying the wide-eyed innocent bit. But his attention returned to the humming. You didn't so much hear it as feel it in your feet. Maybe the trees communicated by their root systems.

"Why now?" he asked uneasily. "Why just before the last battle bestows Final Victory?"

"Maybe they're spreading the good news," I suggested.

"What good news?"

"About how you're going to clean their clocks in Gowyith."

"Speak plainly or hold your tongue."

"I mean defeat the Two Legs. Maybe they're already celebrating."

"They would have nothing to celebrate. They will be shaken from their deep thoughts to feel pain they've never known before."

"Trees feel pain?"

"All living things do according to their capacity. Some sooner than others, some more than others." It was clear he liked the last best.

We went back to listening. The faint hum dropped below the hearing level. "It is finished," Zalzathar said at last. "What did it mean?"

Zalzathar wrapped himself in his cloak and appeared to sleep, although he might have been conjuring up some devilish spell. I took that as my signal to depart. The fury twined a lock of her hair with a finger and gave me a come-hither look.

Some of the Pig Faces stood around grunting to one another, probably rehashing the executions. The rest readied themselves for sleep, lying down and pulling hoods over their ugly faces. They drop where they stand when they are ready for sleep. It doesn't matter what's below—offal, slops, mud or dung. It's the same as clean sheets to them. Filthy brutes doesn't begin to describe them.

I went into the forest until the air was clean enough to breathe and found a little cave just big enough to squeeze into. How long would the battle last? Days? A week or more? I had the feeling it wouldn't be long, whichever way it went. I started to worry whether enough Pig Faces would be killed as they funneled through the narrow alleys in

Gowyith to make a difference. They could take thousands of casualties and keep on coming, especially if they were berserk from the dark potion.

But I learned a long time ago that that kind of worry is counterproductive. Once events are set in motion, sit back and ride them out. Pacing the floor and wringing your hands do no good. Any highly successful person will tell you that. Of course, this was different. I wasn't waiting to see if the market went up or down or what a hostile board of directors decided. Those were nothing compared to what was riding on this.

To take my mind off it, I wondered what kind of shape I'd find my business affairs in if I got back. I have stock options that come due every day of the week. What had happened with them? Unless one of the members of my board stepped forward as managing partner, Ben Shapiro was running the show. He was chief financial officer, a smart enough guy but cautious. When opportunity knocked, Ben weighed pros and cons until the cows came home. He wouldn't lose you a pile unless the bottom fell out, but he wouldn't win you one either. Steady-as-she-goes Shapiro is what I called him. If the market had taken a dive and there were margin calls, this would spell trouble for yours truly. Shapiro would slowly mull what to do as the house fell down around his ears. There was no sign of a downturn on the horizon when I was there, but plenty can happen in a short time. The overthrow of the government in some wog country where oil is produced can throw the market into a panic. There are any number of broken men who used to be big shots on Wall Street who got caught short one day. They have plenty of time on their hands now, and they'll explain chapter and verse what went wrong if you care to listen. While I was thinking of these guys who had gone down the toilet, I fell into a dog doze.

When night fell the Pig Face horde left the ruins of Spyngle for Gowyith. Zalzathar strode at their head with his wizard's staff, and I trotted at his heels. The road was far too small to hold the evil army and creatures crashed through the undergrowth on both sides. Pig Faces like to trample down the foliage as they go, giving them the look of flamenco dancers stamping out a beat. But Zalzathar's pace was too fast for that fun this time.

I tried to make conversation, but the wizard didn't answer. He wanted to get to Gowyith as fast as possible. ''At long last, Helither,'' I heard him mutter at one point. ''It's your turn to know the bitter taste of defeat.''

[22]

I wondered what the guys at the Bankers Club would think if they saw Bogey Ingersol lead the forces of darkness into battle. Those hypocrites were the first to call for my resignation when the scandal broke. The rest of the clubs I belonged to jumped on the bandwagon until a library card was all I had left. I'll admit I had been no more popular at the Bankers Club than anywhere else. It had lots of members I had outfoxed at one point or another, and they nursed grudges. If I didn't have anything else on for lunch, I would drop by to grin and wave just for the looks on their faces. They wouldn't be the least bit surprised to see me with this crowd.

The line of march showed the pecking order. Zalzathar carrying his wizard's staff and the globe that put out a purple light was first. The Pig Faces on the War Council followed me. Then came the Gutters and monsters of various sorts. The tumbling imps and the moronic trolls brought up the rear of that group. Following them was the mass of the army of Pig Faces. They made a hellish noise, rapping axes on shields and squealing. They drowned out the dirge played by the ensemble that had piped Mogwert into camp and now escorted us to Gowyith. Now and then an arrow shot out of the darkness from Two Legs scouts falling back before us. They landed home with *thwacks* and Pig Faces squealed like you know what. Others capered around the victim, delighted by this unexpected bonus of pain. But these arrows were just pinpricks, and the army rolled on like a juggernaut. A couple times Gutters were let loose with a wave of Zalzathar's arm. They lunged into the trees like retrievers and returned with scouts flailing in their jaws, bloody but still alive. The wizard made a signal and the Gutters ate the poor bastards as the Pig Faces squealed and pogo-hopped.

We crossed the meadow with the inn where Helmish and I stayed the night it was attacked. It was rubble, of course. The evil host kept filtering out of the woods, filling the starlit meadow with sinister shadows. We forded the stream that bordered the inn. I wondered how many miles the water had to travel before it got rid of the filth washed from the Pig Faces.

I seriously thought of cutting and running, hiding until the battle was over. With Zalzathar committed to attacking Gowyith at the spot where the defenders waited in ambush, I had done all I could. He was more likely at this point to assume I disappeared because I was yellow rather than because I was a turncoat. I was scared of being getting speared or shot by an arrow when we poured through the alleys. But if I ran, Zalzathar would just send a Gutter to retrieve me. And taking a powder would jeopardize what small chance I had of getting sent back as reward. He didn't need an excuse to break his word, but it wasn't smart to give him one either.

As we got closer to Gowyith, rats began joining us. Then snakes slithering through the grass hooked up with the march. If there was anything that didn't make your skin crawl that was not headed toward Gowyith, I don't know what it was. After a while, the Pig Faces fell silent. I welcomed this at first, but then that mournful dirge repeated over and over got under my skin. It was like a combination of moan and death rattle set to atonal music.

In the wee hours we started to encounter the Pig Faces who held Gowyith under siege. This reunion brought on a great hullabaloo of squealing and grunting. An hour later we reached the plain where pale Gowyith lay spread before us. It was near dawn and the musicians stopped with that sound like a struggling heart giving up, *ka-thump, ka-thump*. Zalzathar ordered the Gutters gathered and a huge black tent was raised over them. They were completely enclosed so not the faintest light could get in. I wondered how they breathed. I guessed they went into reptile hibernation. The Pig Faces pitched camp and dished out their morning swill from filthy, encrusted pots carried on two-wheeled carts. They slobbered over it, making sucking and smacking sounds. When no one was looking, I killed a snake and ate it. One less worry for Gowyith. It tasted a little like chicken.

The tall wizard called me to his side. He looked at the city that brightened as the light grew stronger. Drums beat and bells rang as the city awakened. Men appeared on the walls, looking and pointing to where we settled into camp.

"Fair Gowyith," Zalzathar said to himself. "How I've longed for this moment. An army at my back and you before me, the prize to be plucked."

He turned to me, his eyes gilttering so weirdly I wondered if he was on something. "Long did I sit in the cold stone mountains, thinking of the enemy, fat and happy on this pleasant plain. While I fed on grubs and dry bark, they had only to reach out a hand for luscious fruits. They were snug behind their walls when winter's sharp teeth pursued us into our innermost caverns. The snow lay deep on the ground and we huddled in our winter capes long after spring had come to them. But I knew this moment would come. Hardship made us stronger as ease softened them. We kept the warrior's edge while they became farmers and herdsmen. Our discipline became stronger as freedom made them slack. We sharpened axes while they prated of philosophy and art and other nonsense. We stayed so hidden they believed we had vanished from the face of the Dark One's domain."

He was silent, and I thought I was supposed to say something. "Reminds me of Sparta and Athens," I said. "They were Greek cities and . . ."

"Cease your stupid prattle," he snapped. This was his big moment and he didn't want anybody butting in. I bet he had practiced it in private. "Even the great Torc, now called Helither, allowed his vigilance to lapse. He became so intent on stopping Two Legs from killing each other, he forgot the greater danger. Perhaps he, too, dared to hope we were gone for good. Fool, if he did!" Zalzathar smiled to himself. He was smart not to smile too often.

"He has known of the deadly peril that faces the Fair Lands only since he interrupted my conjuring. But his awakening was too late. Our numbers are many times greater than the last war, thanks to the Dark One, may his black heart be praised. While we killed female infants except for those needed for breeding, they allowed them to live. Half of Gowyith is now female. The price they will pay for this sentimentality will be high. We will keep only those of use to us. All others will be put to the sword when they have made every last trace of Gowyith disappear. They will flogged until not one stone stands on another. All will be scattered. Lonely will be the wind that blows over what was the pride of the Two Legs."

They say no one is as fanatic as a convert, and here was proof. Zalzathar went over to Mogwert's side thinking history was with them and became as evil as them when it didn't pan out and he had to freeze his ass off year after year in the mountains. Maybe there was once a spark of decency in him, but it had long since died out. I thought of the debate at the Curiam about trying to reason with this crew. Funny how people fool themselves. Anybody sent to parlay would go back in little pieces. Zalzathar turned and stalked off.

The morning wore on and I lay in the sun snapping at flies. Instead of sleeping as usual, the Pig Faces got tanked up on the dark potion. They ground their teeth, gripped axes and shot murderous looks at Gowyith. Others fought among themselves. The monitors who kept order in the ranks couldn't stop the lethal quarrels from breaking out among them. The losers were torn apart, of course. The smell of blood hung heavy. Toward mid-afternoon, some Pig Faces began making rushes at the walls of Gowyith. Dozens were left kicking on the ground when Two Legs archers sent flights of arrows down into them. Zalzathar strode back and forth, furious over the breakdown in discipline. He pointed his finger and zapped the craziest, cowing the others into returning to the lines. But he no sooner put out one fire than another pack of Pig Faces elsewhere broke loose and took off with psychotic squeals to throw themselves against the wall.

I didn't like the looks I got while Zalzathar was busy keeping order, so I decided to put some distance between me and the Pig Faces. It was like waving a red flag in front of a bull. As soon as they saw me slinking away, thirty or forty peeled off and chased me, waving axes and yelling for my blood. I ran for my life. That ju-ju juice gave them amazing endurance. Normally, a Pig Face gives up when the chase is too long. But these just kept coming, no matter how wide the gap. A mile into the forest, I was starting to run out of gas while they were strong as ever. When they saw me slow, they squealed in triumph. The ground rose and then dropped. Instead of continuing straight, I cut right on the far side and went to ground beneath a stump. They kept going straight when they topped the rise. The dark potion must have shaved off IQ points they could ill afford to lose, because they didn't notice I was no longer in sight.

I lay spent and blowing beneath the stump, listening to their clamor fade and wondering if I was going to have a heart attack. I was losing canine fitness by the day, no doubt about it. How much longer could I pull it off when I had to run for my life? High overhead a raven flew, pursuing the Pig Faces who had chased me. When it was gone, I took stock of my surroundings. I was near the road to Spyngle and somewhere close was the tunnel Helither showed me. I searched for the bush with berries until I found it and wiggled down the hole past the roots. My skipping out would be explained by the need to flee or be killed. I didn't envy those Pig Faces when they got back to camp. Zalzathar would make them grease spots for running off his military advisor. I was actually starting to feel pretty good as I squirmed through the tunnel toward Gowyith. When I passed below the Pig Face lines, I heard the muffled sound of them whooping and hollering. It was nearly nightfall when I came out of the hidden tunnel exit in the alley. It was freezing cold and I smelled snow in the air, the storm Zalzathar had whipped up. The alley was empty and there was no scent of anyone nearby. The men would be concealed by now on the roofs along the route the evil host would come, and I guessed the women and children were stashed as far as possible from the coming battle. An expectant hush lay over Gowyith. Helither would be too busy fine-tuning defenses to notice I was back. The smart thing to do was find some place to hole up to sit out the fighting. When it looked like there was a winner, I'd show myself. I would yap noisily and make a show of worrying some wounded warrior on the losing side who was too far gone to fight back. Maybe I'd limp and hold up a paw piteously. Helither or Zalzathar, whoever came out on top, would assume I'd been in the thick of it.

I came to a home left in such a hurry the door was ajar and pushed it open. It was an empty furnished room with cold ashes in the fireplace. Somebody's parlor, I judged. I nosed the door nearly closed and looked for a place to snooze until it was time to make my dramatic entrance. I followed my nose into an adjoining room. Sitting on a chair with shiny cowboy boots up on a table where a candle burned was a man in a blindingly white jumpsuit with a huge silver buckle and cape with silver spangles. He started to strum a guitar. I recognized "Love Me Tender."

"How ya doin' man?" he said casually as he looked up. It was his voice, his soft southern accent. His thick glossy hair combed in a pompadour. His blue eyes that made female hearts flutter. His sideburns and his thick, sensual lips that seemed to sneer. It was Elvis the Pelvis. The King.

"It's been a while since I played this. The fingerin' is kind of tricky."

He sat with his head bent over, picking out the song. I was never an Elvis fan. Still, it was a shame he checked out like he did. A heart attack sitting on the can as he strained to expel a hard stool. Not much dignity in that. The tabloids hadn't let him alone, even in death.

He went from "Love Me Tender" to "Heartbreak Hotel." When he was finished, he laid down the guitar. "Playing the gitbox was never my real strength," he apologized. "Lots was better. Ol' Carl Perkins, for one. You should've seen that country boy play."

" 'Blue Suede Shoes,' " I said.

"Yeah, he did it first. Did it good, too. Better'n me." He laughed. "Whatever you do, don't step on my blue suede shoes. They don't write 'em like that anymore, do they? Ain't a thing to eat around here. I done looked. I believe I could kill for a french-fried peanut butter and banana sandwich." I remembered that was Presley's favorite late-night snack. What a double whammy, pumping cholesterol into clogged arteries and also causing constipation, the combination that finally proved fatal. It was a wonder he lasted as long as he did.

"Are you really Elvis?" I asked.

"Are you really a dog?"

"No."

"Same here." He got up and went to peer out a window. "Startin' to snow." He sang a snatch of "White Christmas."

"Who are you, then?"

"Anyone I wanna be. I thought you'd be innerested in Elvis, seein's where you came from. Everybody's lookin' for him, right?"

"That's just media hype."

"Hype?"

"Lies. Baloney. Crapola, B.S. to sell papers. There might

be some fat old waitress slinging hash somewhere who believes Elvis is alive, but that's it.''

He sighed. ''You bein' square with me, boy?'' He looked at me closely. ''Yeah, I reckon you are. Well, shoot. You'd be surprised how hard it is to get good information. People'd rather lie than tell the truth, I swear.''

''What's your story?'' I asked. ''How'd you end up here?''

''Got a lot of stories. Which one you want to hear?''

''Take your pick.''

''How'd I do with Elvis? Do I look like him?''

''It's perfect.''

''All *riiight*.'' He pumped a fist. Then he began to pace the room. The older Elvis, he filled out that white jumpsuit and then some. It had about ten different zippers. I wondered how he managed to squeeze into it.

''They fixin' to have their war out there?'' he asked.

''Later on tonight.''

''Who you bettin' on?''

''I figure it's a toss of the coin.''

''You're kiddin'. Zalzathar's gonna win easy.''

He did the Chubby Checker twist.

''How do you know?''

''Just guessin'. He's got him a mighty big army. I'm impressed.''

I decided against mentioning the ambush.

''I just got back from travelin','' Elvis said. ''Been away on business. Almost didn't get back in time.''

''I'm butting in here,'' I said. ''I'll find another place to stay.''

''No, man. There's plenty of room. Stick around.''

He sat down again and put his boots up. ''So tell me about yourself. How'd you get to be a dog?''

''Not by choice.'' I was getting leery. He was another wizard, obviously. But why wasn't he with Zalzathar? ''I got kidnapped from my world and brought here. I'm a human.''

''Yeah, I knew that straight off. Who snatched you, Zalzathar?''

"Yes."

"That boy's been doin' his homework." He laughed.

I glanced away and when I looked back, Adolf Hitler sat where Elvis had been. I yelped in surprise. The hair brushed to one side, the little moustache smudge under his nose, the crippled arm held close. He wore the black uniform of the SS, the one with the skulls on the choke collar. His boots were polished to a mirror shine.

"Who are you?" I asked.

"*Ich bin der Geist der stets verneint.*"

"I don't speak German."

"No? A useful language, very cultivated. Deeper than English, more profound. Germans make the best philosophers. Something in their nature."

I didn't answer.

"How do I look? Did I get Hitler right?" He marched up and down, limping slightly.

"Very realistic," I faltered.

"A better general than he gets credit for. Too excitable, that was his problem. He flew off the handle, though that rug-biting business was just a propaganda lie. Yet for all his flaws, it took the rest of your combined world to beat him. A fine fellow. I nearly pulled it off with him."

You hardly ever hear a good word said for Hitler outside the locker rooms of some really exclusive golf clubs I've been in. "Pulled it off?"

"Not that I've given up. I'll be back for another crack. Conditions are ripe. Famine, new plagues, wars with new weapons. Some parts of your world sinking back into tribalism and barbarism." He rubbed his hands. "Very encouraging. It won't be long now."

I felt my hackles rise. Literally.

"My name in this place is the Dark One. Rather nice, don't you think? Just the right note of forboding." He stood with hands on hips, studying my reaction. "You're silent. Cat got your tongue? Stunned, I suppose. Most are when they meet me. Like the boogey man, I'm not supposed to exist."

"You're the Devil?" I asked in a tiny voice.

"Lucifer, Beelzebub, Satan, Mephisto, Apollyon, Old Nick, Father of Lies. Plenty of names to choose from where you come from. I answer to them all. Call me anything you like, except late to supper. Hee hee. Who might you be?"

"William B. Ingersol."

"What's the B for?"

"Bogart."

"Chain-smoking member of the famed Hollywood rat pack. What do you do where you come from, Mr. Ingersol?"

"You don't know?"

"Don't confuse me with the Other. I know a lot, but hardly all things. I'm just as glad. Can you imagine trying to keep track?"

"I'm in finance."

"Oh?" A cigar appeared in his hand. He raised it to his lips and drew on it, leaning his head back to blow smoke. The tight collar pinched, making red marks on his Hitler neck. "What kind of finance? Usury, I hope."

"Corporate." My throat was dry.

"Don't be afraid. I'm not a bad sort. If I take a shine to someone, I know how to treat them."

Suddenly he was Marilyn Monroe in the skintight dress she was sewed into when she sang happy birthday to John F. Kennedy. "I know how to give them a really good time," she said in her sex-kitten voice. She moved toward me slinkily, those famous hips rotating with slow sensuality. "Ever done it doggie style?"

Then he was a statesman from the Twenties. Gray suit and vest, high wing collar, pince nez, hair parted in the middle, look of stern New England probity. Calvin Coolidge. "Just kidding," he said in a high nasal voice. "I don't have time for that right now. Hey, we're going to have a hot time in the old town tonight, aren't we, kiddo?" When I didn't answer, his eyeglasses flashed in the candlelight and he asked again. "Aren't we?"

"What do you mean?" I said, cowering.

"Oh, you know. Final battle for Final Victory. I sometimes watch if I'm not busy."

"Y-yes." I was shaking. Beneath this brilliant mimicry, I sensed malevolence deeper than the ocean. It made everything I had seen so far seem like child's play.

"Splendid. What's your role? You're suspiciously alone. A coward in hiding?"

"I . . ." It was true. It hit me like one of those revelations that ruin people's lives. They drop everything to go off and bandage sores in Bangladesh slums or someplace even worse. Nobody likes to think of himself as a coward. You find ways to rationalize. The time wasn't right, or other factors kept you from bravery. But Lucifer saw the truth. He saw I was gutless.

Silent Cal clapped his hands. "Wonderful. I like cowards, especially the kind you can't turn your back on. My kind of people." There was a china cup and saucer in his hands. He sipped. "Oolong from sultry Sumatra, where coolies are flogged under the pitiless sun by cruel colonial masters. Or were. Does that still go on? I've been out of touch."

"I don't know."

"Don't keep up with events, eh? Too busy making a buck. I like that too." He smiled a wintry New England smile. "So put me in the picture. How's Zalzathar doing?"

"You don't know?"

"No. I just flew in and, boy, are my arms tired." He did a rickety soft shoe. "This body certainly wasn't made for dancing," he said. He sat where Elvis had strummed the guitar. "Who's the local angel?"

"Helither."

"Helither, eh?" He thought. "Can't place the face. One of the back-benchers, I suppose." He was a quite ordinary-looking man now, the kind you look at and immediately forget. Brown hair beginning to thin, a sports outfit from Wal-Mart, shoes from the same place, glasses from Lens-Crafters. The anonymous serial killer type.

"Want to be my new best friend?"

"Sure," I answered miserably.

"Tell me how it's going."

"Your people are outside the walls. They attack to-night."

He squealed and hugged himself. "Oh, goody. It reminds me of the Somme. There was a sight! What slaughter. What about what's-his-name's people?"

"They're waiting to defend the walls."

"Yes?" He looked at me brightly. "Go on."

"Your people have a big numerical advantage."

"Big enough?"

It suddenly occurred to me that this wasn't an act. He really didn't know.

"Plenty," I said.

He pumped a fist again. "Yessss."

"You probably know how it's going to turn out without having to ask." I said, trying to sound casual.

"Oh, but you're wrong. He knows." He mouthed G-O-D. "Talk about unfair advantages. Still, I hold my own. It certainly wasn't what I feared when all this began. I mean, He had all the cards. All-knowing, all-powerful—you name it. The dude was all-everything. I just had my cleverness." He laughed gaily. "But it's been enough. Right now, I'm batting .538." He saw the question on my face. "I'm winning a little more than half of these 'Final Victories.' " He looked at me. "Don't you want to know why?"

"Yes," I said.

"I don't know myself." He mouthed G-O-D again. ". . . is kind of hard to figure out. Confidentially, that's how I made that first BIG mistake. I thought He had bitten off too much and needed a partner. My aim with the revolt was altruistic. I knew He would never willingly lay down any of the burden, but might if presented with a fait accompli." He peered at me closely. "You believe that?"

"I sure do," I replied fawningly.

"Then you're a fool. I was trying to muscle in, and He spotted it right off the bat. He wasn't born yesterday. In fact, He *invented* yesterday. Same with today and tomorrow. He invented everything. He invented you and He invented me. "I sometimes wonder if He's ever sorry about me." The serial killer adjusted his glasses thoughtfully. "No, of course not. He doesn't feel regret because He never makes a mistake. A logical fallacy. I'll do my Plato for you, if you like. Socrates gets more praise, but Plato was twice the man."

"So how come He's behind?" I blurted.

"What?"

"You're batting .538, you said."

"Oh," he said impatiently. "I wonder how much we matter in His scheme of things. He's got a lot of balls in the air and creates more all the time. New universes parallel to the ones He's already made, new dimensions, etc. These worlds are just about the least of what is on His plate."

A spiteful look crossed his face. "I didn't want much. I could have run this sideshow for Him. A paltry crumb from His table. I would have done it on the square, as per any instructions. So much goodness, so much evil. The one rewarded and the other punished according to whatever formula I was given. But no, He had to have it all. He forced me to revolt. He made me do it." He slammed his fist on the table. He sat in brooding silence, reliving the old quarrel. The minutes dragged by.

"Where are you going?" he shouted.

"I . . . I thought you wanted to be alone." I cringed, tail between my legs.

The Devil looked at me shrewdly. "I hope you're lying. I like liars."

"No, honest."

"I hate honesty."

"All right, I was lying."

He laughed. ''Good. Now I don't know what to believe. That's the way. Mistrust—where would we be without it?''

I started a servile creep toward the door again. One paw softly put in front of another. I didn't dare look back. Was he watching, or had he sunk back into his bitter reverie?

[23]

Once outside, I ran through the silent city toward where the Pig Faces would attack. That is where I'd find Helither. My heart was in my throat. You would think you would get used to blind panic the way you do anything if it happens enough. My paws slipped on the icy cobblestones and I skidded around corners. I didn't know what Helither could do about it, but he had to know the Devil was inside Gowyith. The final nail in the city's coffin. Snow fell heavily and the air was cold and dense. Smells hang like pictures on a wall in air like that. I followed my nose.

I ran through alley after empty alley. There was no direct way to the point at the wall where Zalzathar's attack would come any minute. My mind raced as I followed a zigzag route toward the wall. Why did the Devil allow me to get away? At first I believed he let me sneak away to another place to hide. But wasn't that too obvious? He was renowned for his cunning, after all. Maybe I did exactly what he wanted. You would think he could find Helither on his own, but maybe not. Maybe he had to use me to find the angel. I slammed on the brakes. No, that was stupid. The Prince of Darkness had to be capable of at least that. Still, the way he pumped me about how things were going hinted at surprising limits. What should I do? I was suddenly seized by terrible indecision. This wasn't like Bogey Ingersol, famed for a steel-trap mind. Seconds ticked past as I wrestled with my quandary, and suddenly it was too much.

I threw my head back and howled. *Oooooooo.* Gowyith threw back the echo. Before, the howl would have set dogs yammering. But they had long since disappeared into the pot. Man's best friend provided one last favor, a meal.

A soft light moved in the alley toward me, the descending snow creating an aura. "What is it, my friend?" It was Helither in a pale cloak with hood. He wasn't carrying a light. Instead, it seemed to radiate from his person. He put a calming hand on my head, and my shaking stopped.

"The Devil's in Gowyith," I said. "Back there."

"Where?" he asked. Then his voice got steely. "Oh, yes. I see him now."

I turned. A deeper darkness approached from behind in the alley.

"Stand behind me," Helither ordered. He didn't have to say it twice.

The Devil called mockingly. "You must be Helither."

"Yes, Azimbrel-Zafieri."

The darkness came closer. "So formal. I don't believe we've met."

"No, but you're well known to me."

"Such disapproval, my, my." He stepped into Helither's light. He was the Devil of folklore, horned, hooved and caped. He even carried a pitchfork. A yellow eye winked at me to say this was for my benefit. He wanted his wit appreciated.

"I suppose we should feel honored," Helither said. If he was nervous, he didn't show it. "Hatred, ignorance, selfishness and the other ways your existence declares itself, these we have felt. But never a personal visit before."

"Sarcasm does not suit you, my friend. Earnestness is more your line. Our dog friend here says another final battle looms."

"There is only one final battle."

The Devil's smile was patronizing. "Only one? I've seen hundreds, make it thousands. Oh, but I forget. You've been stuck in this sorry little backwater so long you probably think it's important."

"It is."

"Chalk up another brownie point. You must have quite a lot behind your name in the divine log by now."

"You will not prevail here, Azimbrel-Zafieri." This in a quiet voice.

"I can't tell you how many times I have heard that from the likes of you," the Devil said. He looked at me. "That I didn't know his name shows he's nothing. I didn't bother calling his sort to the banner of my revolt. These worms don't interest me. Or perhaps you thought all angels were equal?"

"I never thought about it," I answered.

He slapped his forehead. "But of course. Your world is long past that kind of ignorant superstition. Science is in the saddle, explaining all. No terpsichore on the heads of pins for you. You're even mucking around with DNA molecules now, if I'm not mistaken. You want to find that aggregation that forms the individual." A mocking smile. "The soul, so to speak."

"The government's spending billions," I admitted.

"Government," he twinkled. "One of my finer accomplishments."

"Don't listen to him," Helither said easily. "Everything he says is a lie."

"Not everything," the Devil corrected with good humor. "If one always lied, who would listen? No, sprinkle in the truth from time to time for the sake of confusion."

He drove his pitchfork into the snow and looked at me. "Cold, don't you think?" He chafed his hands, then smiled. "Actually, I don't feel it. Hot as hades or, paradoxically, cold as hell, it's all the same to me." He looked at Helither, who had shed his cloak and stood in a shining robe.

"Ever hear from the Big Shot? Or does He still maintain that enigmatic silence? That was always a bone of contention. It was always up to me to figure out what He was thinking. He could have said the word and my rebellion would have ended just like that.'' Blue sparks flew when he snapped his fingers. ''But no, He was always off somewhere creating his universes, one after another, worlds without end. Such fatiguing industry.''

''What is between me and my Master is none of your business,'' Helither said.

''Oh, you think so?'' The Devil did a little dance that ended with a spin that sent snow flying from under cloven feet. ''Everything is my business. It's the franchise G-O-D gave me. I poke and pry where I want. I know if you are good or bad, so be good for goodness sake.''

He turned to me. ''Santa Claus—a stroke of genius, if I do say so. A jubilee of commerce held in honor of a pagan figure worshiped in the dark northern forests. What modern embellishments there have been to that original. Rudolph, the red-nosed reindeer! Hee hee. The cash register bells drown out the church bells.''

''Cash registers don't have bells anymore,'' I said inanely. ''They're tied to computers that track inventory.''

''Really? Well, you get the idea,'' he said to Helither. He glanced around. ''This place is a real dump.''

''I don't agree,'' Helither answered steadily. He never took his eyes off the Devil.

''Don't you ever wish for greater scope, a larger stage? Be honest. A bigger arena for your talents?''

''No.''

''You don't waste words, do you?''

''Not on you.''

''Worried about my famous snares and delusions? Where's your self-confidence? What do you know about me, by the way? Not much, is my guess. There was a lot of rumor circulated when I got the heave-ho, hardly any of it true. I ordinarily don't mind gossip, but I must say I was pictured in the wrong light. We might have more in common than you think.'' He laughed. ''Everybody's got a little bit of the devil in them. Right, Mr. Ingersol?''

''Nobody's perfect,'' I answered, stealing a look at Helither. I didn't know whether I should talk or clam up.

''My point exactly. Yet we're supposed to act as if we are, to name another grievance. Are you perfect, Helither?''

''Only the Bright Giver is perfect.''

''Is that what he's called here? Nice, very nice.'' He chuckled. ''That makes me the Dark Taker, I suppose.''

''You are Azimbrel-Zafieri.''

''I don't like that name,'' the Devil snapped. ''Don't call me that.''

''He gave it to you. You are who you are.''

Lucifer collected himself. ''You haven't said if you've heard lately from the Big Guy. My guess is no.''

Helither said nothing.

''Come on,'' the Devil coaxed. ''It's just between you, me and our friend here. We won't tell. Any great voice enter your mind lately, squeezing out all other thought?''

Helither considered his answer. ''No.''

The Devil pounced. ''And you won't. We muddle through, trying to guess what He wants. Make a mistake and you get it in the neck. Take me, for example. I thought that He would approve of someone who showed initiative, grabbed the bull by the horns. Couldn't be more wrong, as it turned out. He wants us to toe the line, play the game by His rules. Is that fair?''

''What could be more fair?''

''Answering a question with a question is my game. What do you really think? Come on, be honest.''

''I think it's perfectly fair.''

''Don't you just hate a brownnose?'' he asked me. ''I mean, really?''

I didn't answer.

The Devil leaned against the pitchfork. ''I get the credit or blame, depending on how you look at it, for evil,'' he told Helither. ''But who is ultimately responsible? Being perfect, your Master could have made perfect worlds instead of what we have. We don't have to look far for an example. Say the horde beyond the wall yonder bursts through and slaughters everyone after a spot of torture for their amusement. Their deeds will get laid at my doorstep and the survivors will curse my name. But who acquiesces in those crimes? He who could halt them if He but chose, is the answer. I'm no less an agent of His power than you. Didn't He create me? Take our friend, the dog. In his world there is genocide over the shapes of noses and even how the inhabitants chose to worship your so-called Bright Giver. Unimaginable cruelty is an everyday thing as nations collapse into chaos and anarchy. On a more personal level, good people sicken and suffer years before death mercifully releases them. Or they die in ridiculous accidents that mock any idea there is anyone serious in charge."

"Your influence must be great," Helither said.

"I admit I'm very big there. Look at Hollywood. But my point is, who lets me corrupt, degrade and befoul? Fathers rape their own children, mothers spend the grocery money on drugs and the little tykes go hungry. Murder, pillage and rapine. They can't build prisons fast enough to hold them all."

"But there are good people?" Helither asked me.

"More of them than bad, I'd say," I answered.

"There's your answer," Helither told the Devil.

Lucifer sneered. "You make me tired." He cupped hand to pointed ear with an exaggerated sweep of his arm, like a hammy actor harkening to a sound offstage. "What distant sound of battle joined reaches my listening ear?"

From across the city, great blows struck the wall. "Run and give what help you can," Helither told me quietly.

"You certainly have the wool pulled over his eyes," the Devil told me admiringly. He laid a finger alongside his nose.

Helither looked at me questioningly.

"I found him looking for a place to hide," Lucifer laughed. "He meant to lay low until the fighting's over. A man after my own heart."

I hung my head. "It's true." Shame scalded me.

The whisper of falling snow was the only sound in the alley.

"I was wrong," I said. "I'm sorry. Can you forgive me?"

Helither's gentle smile seemed to bathe me in warmth. "Oh, yes. That's easy."

"He'll forgive you anything," the Devil said smoothly, arms folded. "The prodigal son is always welcomed with open arms. Perhaps you know the story. But his forgiveness isn't worth spit when Gowyith falls. The bottom line, as you put it with such clarity, is to get back where you belong. I see a certain redhead in a bikini who lies beneath a beach umbrella. My, what justice she does to that skimpy garment. It's little bigger than an eye patch. Such fine breasts bared to the gaze of passersby staring with naked desire. Is there no law against public indecency in that tropical paradise? And who approaches with cooling beverages shaded by tiny paper umbrellas? Ah, a lithe youth with masses of dark curly hair, himself in a bikini that barely encloses a coiled male organ that puts yours to shame. The man's a stallion. He smiles. She smiles. But now the future vision fades."

"I thought you said you can't see the future," I said.

"He can't," Helither said.

"One is entitled to surmise from the facts in evidence," Lucifer said. He winked a yellow eye at me. "As our friends the lawyers would say."

"I'll do what I can to help," I told Helither.

The Devil's wink at me was conspiratorial. "I suppose I must resign myself to the fact I failed to make a sale." He gave a stagy sigh. "Well, you can't win them all. Woe is me."

"To the wall, Bogey," Helither said quietly.

Lucifer's brow darkened. "Wait just a minute," he said, moving toward me. "If you hope to get back where you belong . . ."

"Run!" Helither cried.

I turned and ran in the direction of the mighty hammering. I paused at the corner to look back. The Devil and Helither wrestled in the falling snow. I ran as fast as I could.

Relief flooded through me. I had done the right thing, hang the consequences. I had done right before, lots of times. You can't help it in life, the law of averages being what it is. But doing right was never the reason to make a choice, just a by-product. Usually, there was some PR factor involved. But this was different. I had come to a fork in the road and put myself on the side of angels. I didn't care if I spent the rest of my days rotting in a nursing home until the plug was pulled.

I picked up the smell of Two Legs, lots of them. They had recently passed this way. Then, as clear as a diamond in mud, I caught Helmish's scent. It led me down a side alley to where a ladder stood against a wall. I climbed it with great difficulty. Lassie makes it look easy on TV, but believe me it's no picnic. The buildings of Gowyith were built one against another, so you could step from one flat roof to the next. The flickering light of small torches shielded by cloaks stretched toward the wall where the Gutters clawed with hysterical ferocity. Every man of Gowyith waited silently for the Pig Faces to pour down the alley below.

My nose led me to where Helmish stood. "Keep the lens dry," he was whispering. The light from the torch held by a Ranger showed a lens laid flat on the roof, protected by men who held a blanket over it like an awning. Also shielded were straw and dry kindling. I pushed my muzzle into Helmish's hand.

"Big!" he whispered hoarsely. He dropped to his knees to hug me. "I knew you'd come back."

My tail and rear wagged furiously and I licked his face.

Our reunion was short. There was a loud rumbling like an avalanche from the wall. "They've broken through," Helmish said, scrambling to his feet. "Get ready now," he called in a low voice. "Do just what I've shown you." There was a godawful sound of squealing where the wall was breached. "Here they come," Helmish muttered. "The evil host approaches." He looked skyward into the falling snow. "Be with us, Bright Giver."

We went to the building's edge and peeped over. My ears picked up the thud of Gutters bounding with huge kangaroo hops toward us. A growl came from me.

"Light the straw," Helmish ordered. The torch was plunged into the straw and it flamed up. "Lift the lens," Helmish said. Two rangers raised it to the edge. The cloak was pulled away and the lens focused the light from the fast-burning fire on the alley below.

Trapped in that shaft of light and another one from the other side of the alley were three Gutters. More were coming fast behind them. Other lenses hoisted into place shined weak spotlights down into the alley. They reminded me of lights dimmed by a brownout. But the Gutters skidded to a stop, furrowing the snow and holding up claws up against the faint illuminations. It was as if they were caught in the blaze of a noon sun. They uttered cries between moans and shrieks, but these were drowned out by the din of the Pig Faces behind them. Their blood lust blinded them to the stopped Gutters. Then their front rank saw the danger and tried to stop, but the weight of bodies pressing from behind pushed them ahead.

The Gutters turned to flee back down the alley, away from the light that seemed to sear them. They ran into the Pig Faces and then the alley looked like a rugby scrimmage, porkers flying in every direction. That was the signal for the men of Gowyith to rain down arrows, spears and heavy stones from the rooftops. Within seconds, the crush in the alley was so dense the squealing Pig Faces couldn't even raise their arms to protect themselves. The Gutters bounded over their heads back toward the hole knocked in the wall, flattening warriors each time they landed. The pandemonium was indescribable. The Pig Faces were shrieking in terror, their stink rising from them like a vile cloud, and the men of Gowyith were yelling as they slaughtered their ancient enemy. The weight of the Pig Faces pushing through the wall was no longer able to move the mass ahead, and the army was at a standstill in total gridlock, unable to move forward or back. I almost felt sorry for the poor bastards. They died as they stood.

But where was Zalzathar? He was nowhere to be seen even though Mogwert had commanded him to lead the army into the final battle. With Helither wrestling the Devil, he could still turn things around with bolts from those lethal fingers. I ran across roofs until I was far enough from the din of fighting to hear better. There it was. At another part of the wall, a half-mile from the breach, there was more pounding. I ran back to where Helmish hurled rocks down on the Pig Faces. Battle had him stoked, and I couldn't get his attention. Finally, I grabbed him by the shirttail with my teeth and dragged him from the edge. I barked furiously.

"What's wrong, Big? What is it?"

He wanted to keep throwing rocks but reluctantly followed. I padded through the snow blanketing the rooftops until the noise of the massacre was far enough behind so even his ears could hear the pounding.

"The fiends are breaking in another place," he cried. He looked at me. "Go quickly. I'll follow as soon as I can."

He opened a trap door in the roof and I felt my way down steep stairs to the ground level. My nose guided me in the pitch black to a door standing ajar and I sped through the falling snow, which caught the light from the torches behind. It turned out the snow was a mistake. Zalzathar had whistled up the storm for an extra edge, hoping to further blind Gowyith's defenders to his movements on a night already pitch black. But that dim red reflection of torchlight from the rooftops on tumbling snowflakes spooked the Gutters where they had broken through the wall the second time. They fled in panic back through the hole. A Pig Face was just coming through when I got there. I launched my body and hit him in the chest, driving him backward into the crack. Instead of helping him up, the Pig Face behind, a big-tusked bastard I recognized from the War Council, stepped all over him to get at me with his axe. The writhing hog underfoot made him stumble and he paid for it with his life when I got him by the throat. Two shakes and a squeal and that was it.

I fought them one by one. That Pig Face who writhed furiously as he tried to get up was my biggest ally. Another Pig Face lurched through the opening off balance, allowing me to dispatch him before he could swing his wicked axe.

Time slowed, the way it does when it's life or death. I felt strangely removed, as if I was a spectator taking it in from a very good seat. I fought until my legs felt like kegs of nails. I must have sent a dozen of them to hog heaven when it seemed they were coming out of the wall faster. Suddenly, I faced two of them and a third stepped from the crack. Something hit me in the head and I staggered. At that moment, I heard the sound of running feet and yelling, Helmish's voice the loudest of all. In the leaping light of their torches, the Pig Faces were killed and it looked like the threat was over when tall-hooded Zalzathar stepped forth. I was still standing dazed to one side and he didn't see me.

"At last, Gowyith," he cried, "know your doom." He raised a hand to zap Helmish. I didn't think I would get there before the pointing finger killed the old lens polisher. But I did. My jaws closed over his bony wrist and the world disappeared in a blinding flash of purple light.

[24]

A fan in a white ceiling slowly turned overhead. I watched it stir the warm air for a long time. I had a metallic taste in my mouth, like the time I was a kid and got a shock from a power drill. I gave up making models after that. I began following the stock market instead.

I heard a noise to my left. At first, my head wouldn't turn. When I finally got it going, I saw a thin, gray-haired nurse. She sat in a chair with a cigarette hanging from the corner of her mouth, one eye squinting from the smoke. A newspaper was propped against a crossed leg and she was reading. On a table next to her was a tray with the remains of a meal. I wasn't a dog anymore. Relief swept through me. It was like when a sudden cloudburst floods a dry lake bed, filling every parched crack and fissure.

I was back.

I felt like shouting, like singing, like turning handsprings. The spirit was willing but the flesh wasn't. I lay there watching her ash get longer. It must have been a damned interesting article. Once she said, "Oh, my."

Odd the thoughts that went through my head. I didn't have to sit down to scratch an ear anymore. I could drink water from a glass instead of lapping. I could talk instead of bark and hope people figured out what I meant. I could order from a menu instead of having to hunt to eat.

My arms were on top of a white bedspread that stretched to the foot of a white iron bed. Tubes taped to them led to translucent bags hanging overhead. A white clock on a white nightstand measured the time with slow ticks. I turned my head to the other side. There was an open window where a white curtain moved gently. A tree beyond had leaves giddy in their young fluorescent greenness. Moving my head made the world spin, and I closed my eyes to stop it.

It was a long time before I could speak. ''What happened?'' I whispered. My vocal cords seemed rusted over.

The nurse jumped to her feet. ''*Eeeeeeee*!'' She ran from the room.

She came back a minute later with a powerful-looking woman who had red hair and a metal badge pinned to her bosom that said Nursing Supervisor. The first thing she said was, ''Who's been smoking in here?'' She glared at the nurse.

Then she came to the bed and stared accusingly. She had pale freckles and icy blue eyes. ''They said you'd never snap out of it.''

''Where am I?''

''Danforth, Florida.''

''Danforth?''

''They call us the Capital of Convalescence because we have more long-term care sanitaria per capita than anywhere else. Wages are cheaper. That's because the unions are kept out, I'm happy to say.'' She hesitated as if waiting to see if I sank back into the coma so she could speak to the nurse about smoking. When I didn't, she said impatiently, ''Well, how do you feel?''

''What happened? How long have I been here?''

She fussed with the covers. ''The way I heard, you laid your head down on your desk one day and never woke up. You've been here six months. I don't know how long you were unconscious before that.''

That was what Felicity had told me in the Great Balwar.

''Felicity?'' I asked.

''Who is that individual?''

"My wife."

"You have had no visitors. Not one. Rare, but it happens. People know we can be trusted with their loved ones. We pride ourselves on the small touches that mean so much, like fresh flowers every day." She looked around. "Where are the fresh flowers?"

"I—I don't know," the nurse answered.

You could see the Nursing Supervisor reopen the personnel file in her head and make a notation after the one about smoking. "Notify the doctor," she ordered. The nurse came back with a bald doctor in a white smock. He must have been at lunch because he was still chewing.

"Will wonders never cease," he said through a full mouth. He swallowed. "I'm Dr. Jessup." He felt my pulse. "How do you feel?"

"Weak."

"You've been in what we call a persistent vegetative state for more than nine months."

He asked if I wanted Felicity notified. "Your wife is in South America, I believe. We communicate through the Merchant Bank of New York."

Strangely, seeing Felicity wasn't high priority. She was a part of a life that seemed long ago. This one was new. The leaves seemed to dance in welcome. I turned back to the doctor. "How soon can I leave?"

Dr. Jessup shoved his glasses up onto his freckled head. "I can't say. We don't want you to conk out again. You're going to need physical therapy, a lot of it. Your muscle tone is lousy."

He was right. I was weak as a kitten. It was days before I could get out of bed, and I shuffled around behind an aluminum walker for a week before I could manage a few steps on my own.

A barber came to shave me the day I woke up. The chalky face in the mirror he held to me looked like a death camp survivor. Where was the person who used to stare back so commandingly from mirrors? Bogey Ingersol had confident baby blues that *Time* magazine called "laser-like." But those peeping from these eyes hollows looked bruised and uncertain. Gone was the Bogey Ingersol who churned through his days, creating a powerful wake that left others gasping like landed fish. Instead of the $125 haircuts I got from barbers who came from the Temple of Shorn, my hair looked like it had been cut with the blunt scissors they give school kids. It lay flat on my skull except where it stuck up, as if I was making some kind of punk rock statement about alienation.

"Take the mirror away," I quavered.

The barber felt sorry for me. He patted me on the shoulder in the awkward way of men. He put hot towels on my face. "You don't remember, I suppose. I've been coming to shave you every other day. You never said nothing or even opened your eyes like they do sometimes. You just lay there breathing."

His razor scraped my stubble as I peered up into his face. He had dark eyes and the kind of thin moustache that cads wore in the silent movies. "I used to tell you the ball scores in case they sunk in. They say sometimes people in comas hear things."

Specialists of various kinds came in the days that followed. They shined lights in my eyes and tested my reflexes with rubber mallets. A neurosurgeon from Miami sat by my bed one afternoon. His name was Dr. Rubin. He was small and elfin but had a symphony conductor's head of hair.

"I've talked to the boys in New York," he said. "There was no reason they could find why you went into a coma, so I guess there's no reason you can't come out of it. They're surprised, though."

"I had a strange dream."

"Strange dreams? I'm not surprised."

"Not dreams. One dream."

He laughed. "Oh, I very much doubt that."

"Why?"

"One dream for nine months? Impossible."

"I was a dog in a strange world."

"Really?" He looked at his watch. "I don't want to miss that shuttle."

"It was like I was in a fairy tale."

"I don't work that side of the street. You might find a psychiatrist to listen. Jaekel's not bad." He got up from his chair. "Your case will interest the medical journals. They like these offbeat cases with happy endings. I wouldn't be surprised if Oliver Sacks took an interest."

The bank sent someone to make sure I wasn't a ringer. He took my fingerprints and compared them with a set he brought with him. "You're you, all right," he said. He gave me papers that I signed with a shaky hand. I telephoned Adrian Vance, who was the vice president for administration of my corporation.

"Adrian," I said, "it's Bogey."

There was a long silence. "Bogey who?"

"Don't you recognize my voice?"

He hung up and I called back.

"Why'd you hang up?"

"Look, I don't know who you are, but this is in bad taste."

He hung up again.

It wasn't until the third call that Adrian believed me. "They said you'd be like that for good."

He started to brief me, sketching in what had happened while I lay dead to the world. But my mind wandered. After what I had been through, what difference did it make if Sandry Industries went up three and an eighth on active trading?

"They took your portraits down," Adrian was saying.

There were ten hung in the lobby and corridors at my company, one painted by the man who did the official portrait of Gerald Ford that is in the White House. They all showed W. B. Ingersol as a corporate titan glowering with far-sighted global vision. One had me standing in the prow of a rowboat like General Washington, a hand shading my eyes as I scanned the horizon. Vice presidents pulled the oars in their shirtsleeves, shining faces full of trust in the skipper.

"What did they do with them?"

"I . . . I think they're in storage." He waited for me to blow up, but I didn't care about the paintings either.

I read the newspaper as the days passed and watched television, but the world they reported seemed flat and dull. I wondered if one morning the old Bogey would rise from bed, ready to roll up sleeves and take on the world once more. But it didn't happen. He had vanished like Fair Lands.

What had happened there? Did Gowyith survive? The dark wizard could have still turned the tide after I got blasted back here, especially if he got help from the Devil.

Or was it just a dream after all?

One night as I dozed, I was awakened by slow footsteps in the corridor. I turned my head on my pillow as they approached. A figure filled the doorway, backlit so I couldn't make out who it was.

"Who's there?" I asked.

I switched on the lamp on the bedside table. Helither stood in the doorway in his gardener's outfit. He looked like he had gone twelve rounds for the title. His face was covered with old cuts and yellow bruises and his movements were stiff and painful. But his eyes twinkled and his chin lifted at an angle that said winner. He smiled through puffy lips and gave a thumbs-up. Then he turned and shuffled away.

At first, I thought it had been a dream. Then I changed my mind. Helither didn't want me to worry. The evil host had been defeated and Gowyith was saved.

When I was strong enough, I booked a compartment on Amtrak to New York. I sat by the window and watched the countryside pass. The wheels made a *yakkety-yak* sound on the rails as if commenting on all that talking I had done to CEOs, boards, investors, bankers and lawyers.

Outside a little town, I saw a brown dog from my compartment window. He trotted alertly, stopping to smell a garbage can, then stood on hind legs to nose off the lid. His tail wagged with hope. That could be me wondering what savory delicacy awaited discovery.

Most of my talking had been in jargon, a business shorthand only others like me understood. If someone changed the subject to the weather or weekend plans, I looked at my watch. *Yakkety-yak*, the rails said. *Yakkety-yak*. Other men had plowed the earth. Or they built roads or drove trucks or entered burning buildings to save lives. They worked at jobs that created useful products or valuable services. How many words had I spoken that had anything to do with real things? A number in a stock table rose or fell, and I won or lost money. However it might be dressed up with free-market philosophizing, that's what my life boiled down to.

Spring and summer were no different than autumn and fall, except sometimes a lackey held an umbrella over my head as I stepped importantly from my Rolls. What had I contributed? What had I made better? Lying in my bed nursed by strangers, I pondered questions I had never given a second thought to before. I had never held an infant, planted a flower or cooked an egg. I had never done a thousand ordinary things people take for granted as part of normal living. I had lived in a bubble of abstraction, as removed from reality as one of those kids with an immune disorder who lives in a space suit.

Henry Kissinger was stepping into a car when I reached our apartment building. He didn't return my wave. Maybe he didn't recognize me in my jeans and sweatshirt. He probably thought I was some apple-knocker in town to gawk at celebrities. But he wouldn't have waved at the old Bogey Ingersol in pinstripes and wing tips or the revamped version in silk suits and pointed Italian pumps either. I showed the doorman identification to get into the building. It was so long since I'd been in the news that my media fame had vanished.

"You better get a new driver's license," he told me. "That picture don't look like you."

I opened the apartment door and listened. It was silent and felt as if it had been so a long time. At the far end of a hall, a green wash of light from the park flooded in through windows. I looked around, struck by the lacquered beauty of the rooms. They were the creation of the moment's hottest decorators. I had barged though them before, making wake, too busy to pay attention. They were voids between the spaces where I slept and worked.

"Beauty is wasted on you," Felicity had said. "You could live in a four-by-four room with blank walls." I had taken that at the time as a compliment to my single-minded prowess as a businessman.

I was hungry but there was nothing in the refrigerator but a box of baking soda. Why baking soda? Was it perishable? I was studying the canned good in a cabinet when the telephone rang. I answered it.

"Mr. Ingersol?"

"Yes."

"It's Dr. Jessup. You have my deepest apology."

"For what?"

"You haven't seen it?"

"Seen what?"

"*The Tattletale*."

"What about it?" I could hear a woman crying in the background.

"I guess we get it before you people in New York. There's an article about you." I heard a paper rattle. "This is the headline: 'Nurse Uses Mental Powers to Wake Wall Street Crook From Coma.' " The woman cried harder. "She was paid a thousand dollars by a man who claimed he was a medical technician. It turned out he was one of those guttersnipe reporters with a Cockney accent. They made up the stuff about her having mental powers."

"Tell her don't worry," I said.

The old Bogey Ingersol would have thrown chairs. But

the media had lost its power to torture me. Let them say what they wanted. I telephoned Juan Viertel, who was handling the appeal work in my criminal case. "What did you say the name was?" he said suspiciously.

"Bogey Ingersol. I'm back. I wanted you to get it from me instead of *The Tattletale*."

"I don't read that rag." He breathed virtuously through his nose. I explained that I had come out of my coma. He said he was glad to hear it. My conviction was wending its way through the appeals process. "I'm optimistic." Then he coughed with embarrassment. He said another lawyer in the office was handling the divorce.

"What divorce?"

"I guess you haven't been told? Your wife has remarried in Rio. Spur of the moment, I gather."

"The towel boy, I suppose." The Devil had said he liked to sprinkle in the truth.

"I'm sorry, I don't know the particulars of the gentleman. I'll have Finkelstein call when he comes back. You'll want the trust she set up dissolved, of course. The prenuptial agreement becomes binding once more."

Afterward, I looked in my closet at the rows of suits, dozens of them. They would flap on me now like a scarecrow. Felicity's closet was twice as large. She had talked about hiring a wardrobe mistress. Her friends wondered how she got along without one. I wandered through the rest of the rooms, feeling almost disembodied. Who were the strangers who had lived in these cold surroundings? What would happen if I bumped into my former self coming around a corner? We wouldn't like each other, of course. He would look me up and down, his face darkening in wrath. Who was I and how did I get in here? Sizing up my weakened appearance and deciding I was no threat, he would step forward bullyingly.

"Won't answer, eh? Well, by God, I'll make you." The hand with the heavy pinky ring from Cartier grasping my collar, he would bawl for the servants. Someone would pay for this breakdown in security or he would know the reason why.

I let myself out of the apartment and took the elevator to the foyer. As I was leaving the building, a TV van with a corkscrew satellite dish coiled on top squealed to a stop. Lettering on the side read "The Real Scoop." The crew that got out, an anorexic female reporter with a raptor's fierce beak and two technicians, walked briskly walked to the entrance. I sauntered two blocks to a news kiosk and found a copy of *The Tattletale*. The story of my voodoo-inspired revival was on the cover. I read the first paragraph.

"Hardened Wall Street master criminal W. B. Ingersol, convicted of a scheme to swindle a crippled children's charity, has been brought from a deathlike coma by a nurse versed in ancient mental powers. 'I had to go to hell where his spirit dwelled, but I pulled it off,' Nurse Ingra Tsalter told *The Tattletale*." A crudely forged photograph showed me levitating a foot above my hospital bed as she looked on.

I strolled the streets. I had never given much thought to how rapidly people in Manhattan walked. Like the TV reporter from "The Real Scoop" and her crew, they had goals and deadlines. They had ground to seize. Quotas to fill. They jostled one another and cut in front. Their hectic pace said their business was so important there wasn't a minute to lose. They thrusted through the crowds, using elbows to gain a step here and there. Were they trying to get ahead of the game or just straining to stay in it? Maybe they heard steps behind them, the kind Satchel Paige warned about. They didn't dare look back to see what was gaining on them. They were in their own bubbles.

I didn't want to be in the rat race any longer. I lounged on a bench in Central Park and thought. I had helped save Fair Lands, and it seemed the favor had been returned.

It was a fine day with a playful breeze, not that the high

achievers noticed. Their eyes were set on the future. When they clawed their way to the top, they would at last be able to see—what?

Whether the race made you a rat or attracted that type in the first place seemed a question worth thinking about. The old Bogey wouldn't give it a second's thought. His lip would curl. What a waste of time! Things were the way they were, and that was that. Furthermore, they were meant to be. The evidence could be seen in his own success. If he had been a wog scratching out a living in some shitty third-world country, it would be a different story. A man would be justified asking questions about the point of life. But that was a preposterous thought. He was who he was. That was the bottom line.

Poor Bogey, I knew him now at last. Decades sitting in the lotus position under a shade tree wouldn't have given a clearer picture. How he had earned Felicity. How he would agree that he had. I had to smile.

A homeless person with a mutt at the end of a rope was encouraged by my smile to ask for spare change. I turned my pockets out. Silver rang on the pavement. I released my currency from the money clip, and bills skittered off in the breeze. I felt a weight ease. If I gave enough away, maybe I would become light enough to float. ''Take it,'' I laughed. ''Take it all.''